The Senator's Wife

Book One

JEN LYON

The Senator's Wife

First Print Edition

Copyright © 2024 Jen Lyon

ISBN: 979-8-9877320-0-7 (paperback)

All rights reserved. Thank you for buying an authorized edition of this book and supporting independent authors.

This is a work of fiction. Names, characters, places, and incidents either are the product of the author's imagination or are used fictitiously, and any resemblance to actual persons, living or dead, businesses, companies, events, or locales is entirely coincidental.

This book contains content that may be considered sensitive in nature to certain readers, including mature situations and adult themes.

Published by Doss About Publishing

Edited by Marni MacRae

Cover design by ThreeArtMedia

For Donna; my Catharine.

Chapter One

"You're the only person I know who can find themselves miserable on vacation, A."

Caleb dragged his toes through the hot sand, drawing a set of parallel lines in front of the rock he was sprawled on, before destroying the design with a sweep of his foot. He was fielding an imaginary soccer ball to Alex, a game that usually roused her from her stupors, but today she hardly noticed. Instead, she remained staring out over the beach in front of them, her knees drawn up to her chin, her mind far from the coarse sand shoreline of the little island wedged between the coast of Savannah and Hilton Head.

She forced herself to smile, a halfhearted lifting of the corners of her mouth, the action never reaching her eyes. Her gaze remained trained on the ocean in front of them.

"A." The blonde-haired boy—young man, really, Alex realized, as he'd turned twenty-eight the week before and was no longer qualified to be considered a boy, regardless that she always thought of him as one—probed again, seeking her attention. "Alex!"

His use of her name stirred her from her daydreams. He never called her Alex. It was always "A." Or "A-Bomb." Or "Grey"—her last name; some variation of playful pet words that could be strung together.

She flicked her eyes to him, brow lifted in question.

"Where were you?" Caleb inquired. She had barely spoken twenty words since they'd arrived the night before, which was quiet, even for her.

"Just thinking." She shrugged, drawing in a breath, savoring the warm humid air, allowing herself to return to the present. A wry smile touched her lips. "I'm a miserable travel companion, aren't I?"

"Pretty much." Returning her smile, he popped to his feet. "We're supposed to be here to relax. Have fun. I doubt that idea's ever crossed your mind." He kicked sand at her, teasing. "Come on! Let the game go for a little while. It'll be there when we get back. How about a swim?" He extended a tanned hand in her direction.

Caleb was her best friend. More than that. He was her confidant, her champion, her protector—her brother, in a way—brother of no relation. They'd met in an after-school therapy class vaguely disguised as a sports program, both enrolled before either had reached their teens. He'd been an overly energetic twelve-year-old who'd been shuffled back and forth from foster home to foster home, always finding himself back where he started in the South Carolina Union Way Home for Boys. Four times he'd been placed with families, but his enthusiastic spirit proved to be too much for any one household to tolerate indefinitely.

Alex had been assigned to the program after her parents were killed in a small plane crash while on vacation in Alaska. She had been a wispy, shy ten-year-old girl—the only child of the prosperous, eccentric architect, Alexander Grey, and his wife, Martha. Grey was renowned for his brilliant, original, and exorbitant designs for many of the Lutheran and Baptist churches all over the globe. The couple's death had been a heavy blow to the tight-knit Southern religious community.

After their death, Alex had been placed with her mother's brother and sister-in-law: her uncle, a respected pastor in Union County, and her aunt, a Sunday school teacher at the local Baptist church in Carlisle. But they were a childless couple—their eyes turned only to God—so Alex, a reserved, quiet child, found herself lost and alone in her ten-year-old year, becoming more withdrawn and empty than her uncle and aunt knew how to handle.

And so, the two despondent children had bonded in their after-school program, though they could not have been more different in nature. Wild and confident, Caleb had never met a stranger. He was outgoing and full of energy he didn't know how to expel. The "sports therapy," really no more than an afternoon babysitting group, gave Caleb the outlet he needed to harness his vigor, and it offered Alex a goal; something to work toward and practice, where her focus could be on improving and excelling, mastering activities she had never been exposed to.

Both were natural athletes, despite their differences. And both had found solace in each other.

Alex helped Caleb with his schoolwork. She prepped and encouraged him for tests, spent hours forcing him to memorize spelling, grammar, basic arithmetic, history lessons, and periodic tables. In turn, he pushed her to her athletic limits—treated her like one of the boys; taught her to pass, shoot, kick, dribble, swing, and throw.

She was the only family he had ever known, and he was the only person she found to rely on: the only person who did not look right through her, their thoughts cast to the next sermon, the next Scripture, the next lesson from God.

Now, so many years later, they were still inseparable. When Alex was courted for Clemson University's soccer team during her senior year, Caleb, who'd finished high school a year earlier, worked tirelessly at the Dairy Queen, Miller's Hardware and overnight custodial at the local bowling alley, saving every penny he earned so that he could afford to move to the small college town a hundred miles away to stay near Alex. Alex knew he would have come even if she'd accepted the offers at Stanford or UCLA. He'd have followed her anywhere.

But now they were here, on a beautiful, secluded island, just a few hundred miles from where they'd first met, their past long behind them.

They were celebrating Caleb's new job offer. A week earlier he had accepted a position with Markel Sports, a prestigious international athletic complex design company. It was a dream career that the boy who flunked out of first year geometry had never imagined possible. But with Alex's tutelage and perseverance in forcing him to care about his academics, Caleb had found himself on the honor roll in his senior year and garnered a scholarship substantial enough to pay for his education at the local junior college. He didn't care about a fancy university or bachelor's degree. He only wanted to stay close to Clemson, where Alex had been recruited on a full scholarship to play soccer, and where he came out with a technical degree in design from the JC—something that would pay the bills.

So the job offer from Markel was beyond his wildest expectations.

Alex never had the heart to tell him she had begged her uncle to call in a family favor to the human resource manager at the firm, who had been a good friend of her father's. There was no reason for him to know. He earned the education and skills on his own merit and the contact was all he needed to land the position. It would have happened one way or another—the Good-Old-Boy call only hurried the process along.

As for Alex—she'd signed with South Carolina Rage FC—a club who had won more championships than any other team in the National Women's Soccer League—straight out of college. Women's professional soccer was far from the prestigious, well-paid sport the men enjoyed, but it was a game she loved, and she was good at it. Despite the low pay, it was a dream come true for the girl who longed to make her living kicking a ball around a field, and every month she still managed to make ends meet, even if it took every dime she earned.

She'd been selected by Rage as a first round draft pick, a fact her aunt and uncle took great pride in, despite the reality they'd never once shown interest in her natural ability and athletic prowess on the field prior to the full ride she was awarded to the university. In high school, they had denied her the opportunity to attend the U-16 and U-17 National Team camps she was invited to, insisting her studies were more important than sports. Then, after the scholarship, soccer took on a new meaning to her makeshift guardians. The full collegiate ride had been worth over a hundred thousand dollars, leaving the money her parents left in an account for her college education suddenly available—unneeded—and it had slowly dwindled at the hands of the pastor and his wife.

But Alex didn't care about the money. She didn't care what her parents left behind and what her aunt and uncle helped themselves to "for the good of Alex." All she wanted was to excel on the field. Be the best there was. Earn her place alongside the names of legends who had been her heroes growing up.

And so, while it was sweet of Caleb to arrange the vacation, she couldn't help but wish she were back on the mainland with her squad, training for the upcoming mid-season games, working through set-piece drills and tactical formations that would hopefully push them into an advantageous position for the playoffs.

But it was only three days, she reminded herself. The teams were at leave during the International break and wouldn't resume training until the beginning of the week. She could at least try and enjoy the time off for rest and recuperation.

Dragging herself from her thoughts, she looked down at the tanned, outstretched fingers Caleb extended toward her. "A swim." She nodded, echoing his words. "I guess." She smiled, and without warning unfurled herself from the rock she'd been sunning on, landing squarely beside him in the sand, before taking off unceremoniously toward the water. "But only if you can keep up!"

Their laughter filled the still air as they raced to the water's edge, pushing and pulling each other aside to try and be the first to reach the ocean.

Alex won, though she knew Caleb slowed at the last minute to give her the advantage, but she didn't dwell on it as she ran into the chilly, froth lined sea, diving headfirst into the surf. She took off swimming hard, parallel to the shoreline, listening to his fast, even strokes behind her, and for a little while Alex forgot about everything but the water and her breathing and the great expanse of coastline before them, unaware that the short morning swim would alter the course of her life forever.

Chapter Two

Catharine walked down the treelined drive, her heels clutched in one hand to dampen the noise her feet made along the unpaved road. She slipped past the pool and gazebo where her husband—Senator Carlton Cleveland—was entertaining Congressman Chisholm and his wife. She couldn't remember the man's first name, Bill or Bob or Brad. She'd met him on plenty of occasions but usually spent most of the time avoiding his too-friendly hands and wandering eyes. This evening she was grateful his wife, dull and unimaginative as she was, accompanied him. Like a little lost pup, she was always at her husband's heels, ready to do his beck-and-call. Just like all the other mindless, doting wives who floated aimlessly about in the Southern political circle. Only to be seen. Never to be heard.

Catharine winced at the woman's simpering laugh, an echoed response to something the congressman said, and quickened her pace down the drive, unnoticed thanks to the sweeping branches of the majestic red maples covering the quarter mile trail to the beach. There were a few other couples sprawling about, all from the mainland, eager to listen to Senator Cleveland announce his plans for his upcoming campaign trail. At least they feigned eagerness as they listened to her husband boast about his plans; the reality was each only stayed quiet long enough to earn the right to talk about themselves, none actually listening to the other. They all had races and rallies and townhalls coming up for one political position or another, and as long as they weren't in direct competition, it was tit-for-tat. You scratch my back, I'll scratch yours.

She hated these parties. Last she saw Carlton he was half a bottle deep through an ancient label of scotch and showed no signs of slowing down. It would at least be an hour before he took note of her absence. Enough time to catch a breath of peace by the shore before her presence would be required at dinner.

Chapter Three

Half a mile down the shore Alex pulled up, her arms finally feeling the strain of a fast-paced swim against the tide. She loved swimming, it was one of the few things she remembered doing with her parents before they were gone, and the ease of it came naturally to her.

As a teenager, she swam every day after soccer camp at the public pool, lap after lap, improving her stamina and strength, both of which gave her a leg up on the soccer field. Even today, when swimming was no longer a part of her daily routine, she was able to out-swim Caleb by at least a hundred yards, trudging to shore more than a minute before he came within earshot.

"You're killing me, A." He was breathless, staggering over to her with exaggerated fatigue and throwing himself onto the sand where she waited. "You sure soccer was your calling?"

"You're out of shape." She smiled with a coy sweetness before rolling her hazel eyes in mock annoyance. "I thought the tide would come in before you ever got here."

Caleb rolled onto his side and perched on an elbow so his face was close to hers. He had an intent look that made her stomach muscles tighten and forced her to avert her eyes to the sand. She'd seen him look at her like that a few times over the last year or so. It wasn't the affectionate, brotherly look she'd known from him since they were kids, and it made her uneasy.

"Glad you waited for me." He spoke softly—too softly—reaching a palm out to her cheek. Alex turned away, carefully avoiding his outstretched hand, and pushed herself to a sitting position.

"Let's walk down to Bloody Point." The words blurted out in a forced carefreeness she didn't feel. She had a sudden urgency to be moving, putting distance between them, quelling the awkwardness that tried to sneak into the solidity of their friendship that had never been there before. "I heard you can see Turtle Island from there."

Caleb reluctantly shifted to his knees, the mask of his handsome face trying hard to hide his disappointment. "I need to grab my phone from the inn," he said, a little wistful, brushing the damp sand from his chest and shoulders. "There's a conference call I'm supposed to check into at four." He smiled, a touch forced, but without the hurt that had flashed across his face a moment earlier. "And after that I'm done for the weekend and you'll be forced to put up with me until Monday." He hopped to his feet. "Want to go on a run?"

Alex was always up for a run, especially on the beach. There was little she enjoyed more than sprinting along the wet sand, picking her way through the breaking waves as they washed up on the shore. But right now, the idea of a few minutes of privacy—time where she could just sit by herself, tending to her own thoughts and enjoying the solitude of the beautiful summer afternoon—was far more tempting than a run to the inn down the road where they'd booked two rooms for the weekend.

"I think I'll wait here." She gave him a reassuring smile. "Get your work done so it's out of the way."

Caleb was back to his easy, nonchalant self. "It's because you're lazy," he teased, flicking the top of her head with a fingertip before trotting backward through the sand. "An hour, hopefully less! Need anything?"

Alex waved him off with a shake of her head. "I'll be here! Good luck!" She knew conference calls and scheduled meetings and white-collar responsibility were all new to him. "You're going to need it!"

He made a face before turning on his heels and picking up his pace to jog down the beach.

When he was gone, Alex felt like she could finally breathe, drawing in a slow, energizing breath filled with sea air and sunshine. When had things gotten so complicated?

In the distance, clouds rolled her direction, their gray, cumbersome bodies brimming with moisture. She doubted they would reach the shore, likely spilling out the collected humidity miles off the coast, but she welcomed the slow progress they made in their journey across the sky, absorbing the harshest rays of the July South Carolina sunshine.

Even if the summer storm did make land, it wouldn't last long. And if it did, so be it—she loved a rainy day at the beach.

Chapter Four

There was a narrow wooden pier that jutted off the sand from the private waterfront that lay directly across the road from the Cleveland Manor. It was old and decrepit, much like the rest of the island, the wood rotting from years of neglect after exposure to the unforgiving elements of the Carolina coast. A simple Sunfish sailboat—a leisurely sailing dinghy—bobbed rhythmically in the surf, tethered at the end of the dock.

The deteriorating jetty was in sharp contrast to the glistening manor and its immaculately manicured grounds. The faded wood, splintered and salt worn, was one of the only visual reminders of the dilapidated state of the Cleveland property when Catharine first set foot on the sparsely populated island more than twenty years earlier.

At the time, her soon-to-be husband, Carlton, had boasted to her that the manor had been in his family well over a century—before the war, even— and was once the grandest estate on all the Carolina Islands; rich in history of wealthy, blue-blooded South Carolinians, at one point some of the most prominent landowners on the coast.

Catharine never really understood the pride her husband felt in his marred family history. Even today, in a country that moved in a progressive path toward equality and liberty for all its citizens, Carlton Cleveland reveled in stories of "the good old days," reminiscing about the era in which his family made their fortune in the slave trade, selling humans like live- stock, amassing their wealth on the strong backs of foreigners forced to this land.

Catharine had been a young woman—just twenty—when she'd wed the Carolina man. A marriage of convenience orchestrated long past the times when arranged marriages were the custom of the day. But Catharine had been given little choice. An ultimatum: move to the States and marry Cleveland, an up and coming American politician—fifteen years her senior

—who'd befriended her father during the course of a summer he spent in London, or find herself disowned from her family, cut off from their considerable fortune—cast out, penniless and without a name.

"You'll be no child of mine," her father had threatened that fall afternoon, so many years ago, when the world, as Catharine knew it, came crashing down. "The shame you've brought to this household..." Her mother sat at their formal dining room table, her eyes never leaving the cup of tea she cradled in front of her, the contents long gone cold. She'd winced every time her husband's hate-filled words punctuated the air. Catharine was her only child. Her pride and joy. But she was too terrified of the man to interject. So instead said nothing.

"You'll marry the American, redeem yourself and wash away the stain which you've brought on our family. There will never be mention of this madness again."

Catharine could still hear the sound of his hand slamming down on the table, feel the way the solid oak had shifted beneath the force, his anger permeating the room. Her mouth and cheeks burning red where he'd repeatedly struck her earlier in the morning. Scared, lost, and humiliated, she'd finally mumbled her consent. She would accept the arrangements with Mr. Cleveland and move to America to become the politician's wife.

But that was all long behind her now, a distant memory that sometimes drifted across her thoughts when she came down to the tottering old dock to sit by the sea.

Carlton had used the substantial sum of money her father had gifted them as a wedding present to completely renovate the manor and overrun grounds. The Cleveland finances had dwindled to near nothing when Catharine took the name as her own. Carlton never had the business sense his father did, and after the elder Cleveland died at the unexpected age of forty-five, his son had gambled, squandered and otherwise wasted away the small family fortune that had already been in drastic decline, beginning with the abolishment of the slave trade.

At the time of their marriage, all Cleveland had to offer was an old family name—one of the earliest recorded in the Carolinas—and a failing estate on the peculiar island of Daufuskie, along with a narrowly won race the previous year to become a state assemblyman. But it was far from

England, far from everything—*everyone*—Catharine loved, and that was enough for Colonel Brooks.

And as for Carlton—Catharine and her seemingly limitless family money were far more than he had ever bargained for.

Catharine listened to him brag to his friends that his English wife was the most stunning woman he'd ever encountered, crowing on about her classic beauty, her striking features, her golden hair and azure blue eyes—amongst other things he was sure not to mention directly in her company. He made her feel like he'd purchased the Venus de Milo in marble, instead of a wife.

From the beginning, he'd made it clear he didn't care if she loved him. Love had never been what he was looking for. What she brought to the table was far more invaluable—his marriage into the Brooks legacy elevated his status beyond his wildest expectations, opened doors he'd been certain would be closed forever. She was everything his political career needed—and more. The perfect union. For him.

And so, the first decision he'd made once their marriage was consummated was to use his new-found funds to rebuild his family estate.

Catharine had not objected. She hated the filthy, collapsing manor and its ruinous grounds. She'd come from a life of privilege and grandeur, accustomed to all the best the world had to offer. Bringing the estate back to its former glory was mere necessity, though Carlton never asked for her opinion. She could not have stopped him had she wanted to. At twenty years old, she was little more than a girl. Married to a stranger. In a country that wasn't her own.

The only thing she asked from her new husband was that the dock—the run down, nineteenth century jetty—was left untouched. She found herself drawn to the historic character of the relic and loved it as it was.

Carlton showed no interest and permitted her request. He rarely went to the ocean beyond ferrying to the mainland and had never set foot on the small quay that had been in his family for centuries. He disliked the sea, so it was one place Catharine could come to for sanctum. A place that was all her own. The one place she allowed herself to indulge in memories of the past—memories she couldn't quite let go.

As the only heir to the Brooks estate, Catharine's father had arranged for his daughter to take over the reins to the family business on his sixtieth birthday. It was always their agreement, something he had groomed her for from an early age, and in exchange for her acquiescence to the marriage overseas, it was an agreement he honored. He had never gone back on a business accord, not once in his life, and this was no exception. Despite all that transpired, Catharine was not surprised he maintained his word. She had always been treated as a business transaction, ever since she was a child, so it was no curiosity he would conduct their relationship as such when she became an adult.

The agreement was such: She was not to tarnish their family name and he would not meddle in the business affairs once he released the management of the corporation to her discretion. He would maintain fifty-one percent stock. The majority control. But he would become a silent shareholder, no longer maintaining an active position on the board and would take no part in the day-to-day operations of the company. Upon his death, the remainder of the stock would go to Catharine.

She'd spent nine years building their North American base, eventually assuming the position of CEO, a time period that saw her honored as one of the youngest female executives to run a billion-dollar enterprise.

On the eve of her father's sixtieth birthday, she flew to London and met her father in their corporate solicitor's high-rise office, where Colonel Benjamin Brooks signed over forty-nine percent of Brooks Corporation into his only child's name. They had not seen each other since the day she left to be wed, their only correspondence via phone and email. All news Catharine received from home had come through her mother.

"It's done," was all he'd said before the ink was even dry. "Honor it."

Catharine had reached to shake his hand, but he'd recoiled at her outstretched fingers, all the venom of the years still between them. It was only the decorum of his upbringing that at last overcame his revulsion, and he pressed a cold palm to hers.

Nine years and he still couldn't look her in the eye. Catharine felt the familiar dull ache creep into her chest she'd worked tirelessly to suppress over the years. She'd grown into a strong, independent, successful woman —she couldn't understand why she still felt wounded at his disapproval after all these years. Perhaps it was because she had done everything he asked of her, bowed to his every command. She had given up everything she loved to abide by his demands. Yet even now, he couldn't—no, *wouldn't* —love her. Nor show her the respect she desired—an acknowledgement of all she'd achieved. Any diminutive indication she held some value in his life.

Tripling the enterprise value, expanding in over a dozen previously interdicted countries, negotiating exportation with heads of state across the globe; marrying a man she never loved and leaving her entire life behind—it would never be enough. It would never buy his approval.

She walked away that day and never looked back. They had not spoken in the thirteen years that had passed and she doubted they ever would.

If she could do it all over again, she would forfeit the estate, the family business, the fortune, the Brooks name. She would have drummed up the courage to walk out of their London townhouse that day, twenty-two years earlier, and followed her heart. But she was neither strong nor courageous back then, and there was no sense in dwelling on a past that could not be changed.

From an outside perspective, she lived the ideal life. A prominent senator's wife, the CEO and owner of one of the largest shipping companies in the world, a pillar of southern society and a woman who otherwise led a glamorous, decadent lifestyle. She was nothing resembling the timid young girl who arrived in America more than two decades earlier. An influential, powerful woman—an opinionated and respected figure amongst the most distinguished social and business circles in the south. The epitome of the American dream. If only the American dream had been her dream.

Catharine dropped the heels she'd been carrying onto the dock and slipped into the cockpit of the Sunfish. As the clouds rolled in overhead, the water became increasingly choppy as she dropped the centerboard and ran the halyard, releasing the sail and shoving off into deeper water. She paid no mind to the shifting weather. She needed to get out on the sea, if only for a little while. She couldn't stand one more minute on Cleveland grounds with those pompous, fool-minded friends of her husband. She needed to clear her mind—to feel like she was free.

Chapter Five

A small boat cut swiftly through the waves a few hundred yards from where Alex sat cross legged on the beach, her gaze to the horizon. At first she paid it little attention. Daufuskie was a vacation destination, and though this side of the island was mostly vacant, except for the few great manors that made up Bloody Point, Alex figured a vacationer had opted to sail the eastern side of the shore to enjoy the peaceful solitude.

But as the boat sailed along, she became impressed by its navigation of rocky crags protruding from the shallow stretch of sea along the beach. It wasn't an area she would wish to sail in, she thought, watching the agile dinghy heel sharply before changing direction. Especially as the afternoon breeze picked up, blowing glittering white caps of water against the sand. The coastal weather was known for its rapid changes throughout the summer, but the solo sailor appeared unconcerned.

As Alex rose to stroll along the shore, she saw the striped red and white sail dip hard, heeling too far, and the colorful triangle was suddenly in the water. She watched a moment, waiting to see if the boat would right itself, but the sail only disappeared further into the sea until the black fish decal at its head was submerged completely.

It was a few long seconds before the figure appeared from beneath the surface, swimming to the side of the boat, attempting to right it in the water. As the wind increased, the waves grew in strength, rolling in to pummel the white sand, the sailor struggling with the building momentum.

An agonizing moment passed as the dinghy was submerged beneath the force of a breaking wave, before the sailor appeared to get a handle on the capsized vessel, drawing the hull upright as the striped sail emerged from beneath the surface, swinging toward the sky.

The loose sail cloth whipped in the wind, snapping against the mast in a chaotic flutter, before being struck once more by an unrelenting gust blowing in from the open water. Overpowered, the boat pitched with the redirection of momentum, and the sailor was violently flung from the dinghy, the body colliding against a quarry of rock protruding from the sand bar.

One. Two. Three. Alex subconsciously counted the seconds, waiting to see if the figure would reemerge, but with the rising swells it was lost from view as the empty boat slipped further out to sea.

Damn.

Before she could give the situation much thought, Alex snapped out of her daze and was on her feet, racing toward the shoreline. She crashed into the water at full speed, running as far as she could until it was deep enough to dive forward and pick up a free stroke against the powerful pull of the tide.

Chapter Six

Catharine had sailed in the static waters of the Doldrums to the violent gales of the Irminger Sea, and just about every condition in between. She'd been less than a summer out of nursery when her mother first taught her to sail on the River Thames, beginning the tradition of spending season after season snaking down the narrow passages of Oxfordshire or the exhilarating stretch of water traversing the London cityscape.

Emily Brooks was a lifetime member of the Thames Sailing Club, as her father and grandfather had been before her. Her great-grandfather had been a founding member of the elite water association in the late 1800s and Emily loved to tell Catharine that saltwater ran through their veins.

It wasn't something the Colonel approved of. He was opposed to women partaking in "men's sports" and frowned upon his wife's passion for the water. But after Catharine was born, Emily found an ounce of courage she'd previously subdued throughout her marriage to the domineering business tycoon, and to her husband's surprise, fought adamantly for the right to raise her daughter on the water—the same way she'd been raised. In time, Colonel Brooks gave in, feeling it wasn't worth the turmoil. Despite being neither a loving or affectionate man, he did wish his young wife to be content.

Thus were born long, leisurely days of sailing along the ever-changing tides of the Thames; from Catharine's earliest recollections of her childhood, her happiest memories with her mother, and then later, to her last days in England, before everything had gone wrong—her life had always revolved around the water.

It was these thoughts Catharine found herself lost in when the afternoon gale came up, battering the sport sail with a robust southerly wind that whipped the boom sharply to the port side, listing the Sunfish at a low angle.

Without concern, Catharine tacked the dinghy into the wind, coming about in a quick snap as the bow lifted out of the water to glide over a swell, narrowly missing one of the rocky crags revealed in low tide.

Catharine's hands slid deftly along the lines, comfortable from years of application and knowledge on vessels of every shape and size. Knowing she was bound to be missed soon at her husband's gathering, especially since the change in the weather would drive them inside, Catharine began the zigzag pattern back to the dock, savoring the ocean spray that covered her face and neck and arms, wrapping her in the scent of the sea. She would need to change and wash the salt from her skin before Carlton saw her. He detested the way she smelled when she'd been on the water, and today, with the Georgia congressman present, he would be overtly on edge.

Her *proletariat behavior,* Carlton referred to her sailing. It didn't fit his vision of perfection, the model politician's wife. She ought to be fawning over his career, catering to his every whim, jumping at his beck and call. It didn't matter that she was the very measure of modern-day social propriety —old money, high class: a woman raised in the elite circle of London's finest; exemplary at decorum, grace, and manner. That was not enough. It would never be enough. He wanted her without an opinion, her brain empty of any thoughts he did not put there. He wanted control over what she wore, how she looked, what she said. A mechanical, programmable robot designed only for his comfort and existence. And for the most part, Catharine was willing to acquiesce to his demands. His career was important to him—to his ego. She wanted him to succeed.

But for the charade she was most often willing to display, there were plenty of other things he constantly battered her about.

The fact that she still played a vital role in her company's day to day operations drove Carlton insane. He frequently reminded her that she employed a board of directors for a reason, that the company would run itself if she would let it. He never ventured outright to say it to her—even he was not that brazen—but he strongly felt women had no place in business. They were meant to be mothers, caretakers, homemakers. To serve their husbands and families. "Seen and not heard," he liked to guff to his friends when he thought she was out of earshot. He didn't dare say something so insolent to her face, but he loved to talk-the-talk over a bottle of scotch with his posse.

The irony was not put past her that it was her money that got him where he was, her fortune that paved his path to congress, and it would be her resources that he would fall back on when he eventually made his presidential bid for the White House (though Catharine kept silent hope it would never come to much fruition).

He seemed to forget—or at least ignore—that fact. She never held it over him and rarely questioned how or what he spent money on. It wasn't of great concern. Occasionally she would discreetly redirect his financial whims, always careful to make it seem like his idea. Everything had to be his idea, elsewise whatever the suggestion was, he would consider it a bad one.

But Carlton Cleveland was not the clever, masterminded individual he envisioned himself to be. He was educated but not intelligent, well-read but not well-learned, a conversationalist but not a philosopher. All of which were likely the reasons their marriage had survived so long. Catharine knew how to handle him, how to gently manipulate and sway his vast ego when it really mattered. She had never loved him, she had never even tried. From the first day they met, she knew their marriage would never be anything more than a facade—a situation suiting them both. Carlton could never have been a faithful man, no matter who he wed. He had not even had the wherewithal of character to remain faithful through their first year. But as long as he did not make a laughingstock of either of them, that his indiscretions remained discrete, and his political career nor her business were affected, Catharine didn't care. On the contrary, his wandering eye was a relief, a lightening of the burden of their marriage.

Another gust of wind came blazing across the water, this time from the east, catching the leeward side of the sail and slamming the boom in the opposite direction. The velocity of the violent shift caught Catharine off guard, unable to steady the teetering hull before it careened on its side, submerging the mainsail.

The Sunfish was made to capsize. It wasn't an unexpected event for sport dinghies and was often an easy correction. Climb the centerboard, lean over the hull to uncleat the mainsail, then use your bodyweight to flip the vessel back to an upright position. Catharine had done it countless times, even as a child.

But this time the choppiness of the water presented a hurdle, and Catharine, though a confident swimmer, found difficulty getting back to the boat.

Kicking against the current, her shin connected with something sharp—one of the barnacled crags hidden beneath the surface—and the blistering pain forced an involuntary gasp, resulting in a mouthful of salty water, before she managed to regain her senses and continue her swim for the boat.

By the time she reached the hull, it was all she could do to cling to the fiberglass, trying to catch her breath and clear her lungs of the sea. The situation was ridiculous. She was furious at herself for having not tacked sooner. For the stupidity of having gone out at all. Now it would be impossible to slip into the house unnoticed—soaked, her hair matted, and judging from the pain radiating up her shin, likely bleeding.

Carlton was going to have a meltdown.

With some difficulty, Catharine pulled herself up over the hull, and reached to the underwater side to uncleat the main. If she didn't set it free, the boat would flip over in the opposite direction when it was righted.

Her hands fumbled as the dinghy was jostled by the pounding surf. She dipped her head in the water to have a better reach and her fingers finally found their mark, unhooking the boom before pushing herself up to take in air.

She was taller than the average woman and naturally athletic, having been raised riding, sailing, playing polo and rowing, but even in calm water she required significant effort to flip the dinghy when it was submerged. Her slender weight worked against her when it came to hauling backward on the centerboard to resurface the sail.

Gripping the lip of the cockpit, she knelt on the fiberglass board and leaned back over the water, countering her weight to leverage the capsized hull. The boat listed, the red and white of the sail rippling through the water's surface, and Catharine felt a mounting sensation of relief as it pendulumed upright. As little as she cared to admit it, a touch of fear had sprouted, and fear was something she had never known on the water.

She brushed it aside, preparing to heave herself back into the dinghy to secure the mainsheet, but before she'd fully lifted out of the water, a flurrying draft caught the rising sail and slapped it back into the ocean, forcing the mast downward and flinging the lightweight boat violently upside down.

Catharine tried to push herself free, but the force of the shift flung her backward, suspended in the air, until she was cast down, her body crashing against the jagged rock ledge extruding from the ocean floor.

Chapter Seven

Alex wasn't sure she'd taken a single breath during her mad swim through the turbulent sea. If her muscles ached from the enormous strain, she couldn't feel it. Her adrenaline took over, piloting her through the rough swells, forcing her to swim faster than she'd ever swam before.

Only once did she pause, taking a second to arch her head out of the water, making certain she remained on target toward the boat drifting further and further off the coast.

"Hey!" She was hoarse and breathless when she came up near the dinghy. She didn't know what else to do. The waves were coming in high, pressing sets, making visibility nearly impossible. "Hey! Where are you!"

The boat was floating capsized a dozen yards away, teetering on the swells, its white belly a jarring contrast to the darkening sky.

There was no answer—Alex hadn't really expected one.

Her adrenaline fading, a feeling of helplessness crept up as she bobbed up and down in the ocean, scanning every direction for signs of life. She didn't have a plan of attack, hadn't had any plan at all, really, when she ran into the shore toward the dinghy. She just knew she needed to get there.

The coach of Rage, Marty Bale, had found occasion to chastise her for her temerity and lack of planning on the pitch. "You just go in—all heart and no head!" It was her fallback criticism for Alex in the locker room when a match didn't go their way. She never protested her swift-footed approach when her rashness led them to a win, Alex had noted early in her first season in the NWSL. Then, it seemed, "all heart" was exactly the right play at the time. "Grey demonstrates an intuitive, seemingly spontaneous connection to the game, with an instinctive touch that can only be felt from within," the Carolina Times after a huge victory against the Portland Warriors during the playoffs last season. Her teammates razzed her on the corny, overblown prose, but after scoring two late goals in the last fifteen to secure Rage's spot in the finals, they cut her some slack. Her full-throttle style had paid off.

Now, treading water a quarter mile from shore, working hard to keep her own head above the surface, the athlete conceded that maybe Marty was right. Maybe she did rush in too often without thinking. Maybe she was reckless. Maybe she should have gone for help instead of trying to take matters into her own hands.

In answer to her thoughts, just as desperation was about to set in, Alex saw a flash of color floating against an outcrop of rock, out of place amongst the kelp and foam of the sea.

"Hey!" It was the only word that came to mind as she swam toward the figure.

The body was inert, slapping rhythmically against the rough surface of the crag, a pale, slack face veiled beneath a wash of blonde hair. Digging her fingers into a cluster of barnacles, Alex wrapped an arm around the waist of the lifeless figure, propping the head out of the water.

She was surprised to find herself staring into the face of a woman, her expression a mask of serenity, despite the horror of the situation. There was a trickle of blood that slipped down the temple, disappearing into the sea-swept golden hair, but other than that, she looked as if she could have been sleeping.

For whatever reason, Alex had expected it to be a man. The discovery caught her off guard.

The woman's eyes were closed, her mouth lax and unmoving.

Come on. Alex felt a rising sense of dread. *Please don't be dead.*

She didn't know the procedure for CPR in the water—hell, she wasn't even sure how to check for a pulse. Only what she'd seen in movies. Her focus turned to the beach, flashing in and out of view with each rolling swell, and she prayed desperately for a sign of help. Enough time had passed—Caleb should be back by now. And yet she knew her sense of time was skewed. Indistinguishable between seconds, minutes, hours.

The shoreline was empty, the approaching storm having chased any beachgoers inside, and the reality was, there were no tourists this far down the island. Only a couple massive estates, where the elite lived behind high, gated walls.

A decision had to be made and made quickly. Alex was strong and fit and at the peak of her athletic prowess, but even she could not support them both in the escalating storm for long.

Surveying the area around them, she saw a wooden dock not too far to the west. It was about a hundred yards away, less distance than a soccer field, and the path appeared clear of obstruction from the rocks and reef that rose from the shallow sandbar.

"I'm going to get you to shore." She spoke out loud more for her own benefit than the woman's. For all she knew she was talking to a dead body. But she couldn't be sure, and she certainly wasn't going to abandon her, unconscious, in the sea.

She knew the basic rescue stroke from a freshman semester of water polo, but as she wrapped her arm around the slender ribcage and gathered the lifeless body to her chest, she found herself reluctant to let go of the safety of the rock. She'd never needed to put the skill to use before, and the pulling current was a long way off from the security of a heated high school pool. But there was no other choice.

Forcing herself to action, she drew her knees to her chest and shoved off hard, kicking with all her strength to propel them shoreward. With the woman's head cradled between her neck and shoulder, she found a steady, arduous rhythm and directed all of her energy toward the dock, fighting the pull of the tide with every stroke. The closer they drew to the shore, the harsher the waves broke, and despite Alex's best efforts, she found them both submerged on more than one occasion, struggling to stay afloat.

It may have been only minutes before they reached the dock, but it felt an eternity. When at last her fingers found purchase on the rotting planks she was shaking with exhaustion and it took her a few seconds to get a solid hold and maintain it. Finding her breath, she waited for the next swell to come in and took advantage of the rising water that crashed over the dock to propel the woman onto the safety of the landing. With the women's legs still dangling over the side, Alex heaved herself up by her elbows and crawled to her knees before grabbing the woman's blouse and dragging her entirely out of the water.

They'd made it. Somehow, by the grace of God or dumb, stubborn luck, they'd made it.

Now, however, came a moment of terror worse than the swim. Exhausted, she knelt down beside the woman and rolled her onto her side, shaking her more violently than she intended. But with the immediate danger of drowning over, the adrenaline was flooding out of her body and a new wave of fear took its place. She was terrified the woman was dead.

"Can you hear me?"

Around them, apathetic to their plight, the crashing waves sprayed over the dock, showering them both as the sky opened into a blinding downpour.

"Come on, please! Wake up." It was sheer stupidity, but the plea fell out regardless, muffled by the heavy drops of rain pelting down around them. In a last ditch effort, Alex brought her palm down hard against the woman's cheek, the smack echoing the rumble of thunder threatening in the distance.

Chapter Eight

The world was tilting, turning on its axis, dark and out of sorts. Catharine felt stuck in a dream from which she could not wake. In the distance there was a panicked voice stifled by the blackness. She opened her mouth, willing herself to speak, but no words emitted. From within the dream she found she couldn't breathe, couldn't form any sound at all.

A sudden, sharp pain against her cheek cast a white light across her vision, forcing her to cry out, a noise that immediately evolved into a horrid fit of coughing. Catharine gasped, struggling to push up onto an elbow, trying to find air. The burning sensation rising up from her stomach was overwhelming, searing through her chest, lighting her lungs on fire, before she found herself overwrought with an uncontrollable wave of nausea.

"You're okay?" It was a stranger's voice, layered with uncertainty—a question—and then, more reassuringly, "You're okay!" A hand was placed on her back and careful fingers lifted hair away from her face as she spit up saltwater and bile onto the dock, gagging, desperate to catch her breath.

"Breathe. Just breathe." A tentative hand patted her back, trying to sooth her through her sickness.

Despite her nausea, Catharine became aware of the vague sensation of the sky opening, a torrential downpour cascading down around them, the raindrops pelting the dock with enough force to mute the voice beside her.

"…to get you to shore…" the distorted words weaved in and out of the thunder, "…get help."

The rain spilled down her face, clearing the salt from her eyes, washing the bitter acidity from her lips. She blinked, trying to focus, to push away the threatening envelope of unconsciousness that lingered at the peripheral of her vision. She was surprised to find she was on her dock, weak and disoriented, a girl kneeling at her side.

Last she recalled she'd been on the Sunfish, trying to right the hull out of the water. An utter imbecile, she'd allowed an accidental gibe, permitting a capsize. She'd been careless with the shifting course of the westerly, and allowed the mainsheet out too far.

Congressman Chisholm and his wife were at her house.

Carlton would be livid.

"Who—what—" The words were met with another barrage of coughing. Another tide of burning.

As the coughing subsided, she raised her eyes to find the girl had risen to her feet, her expression rinsed with worry.

"I need to get you help." She had to yell over the rain, over the cacophony of the storm. "Can you stand?"

Catharine's head was pounding, a symphony of percussion crescendoing between her ears. She was struggling to find her bearings. To understand the question. Dazed, she reached up to touch her throbbing temple, and was puzzled to find blood on her fingers when she drew them away.

Could she stand?

She managed to lift herself onto her hands and knees. The world swayed, a spinning labyrinth on a carousel.

She refocused on the figure in front of her. The girl was young—but not as young as she'd first imagined. A young woman, more accurately. Dark hair pulled back in a ponytail, navy swim suit, white board shorts—she looked like she belonged on the set of a fashion shoot for a surfing magazine rather than standing in the rain on the battered dock, staring at Catharine, covered in bile, blood trailing down her cheek, beginning to drip off her chin.

Regardless the oddity of the situation, Catharine felt a sense of self-consciousness take hold.

She'd been knocked out of her senses.

Carlton was going to be fit to be tied. Never mind that she'd almost drowned. That would be irrelevant when it came to embarrassing her husband in front of the Georgia congressman and his wife.

Another wave broke over them, forceful enough that Catharine staggered on her knees. The young woman crouched back down beside her.

"I think I can carry you." She started to hook an arm around Catharine's waist. "We have to get you help."

Catharine couldn't reply, her breath coming in wheezing gasps.

The girl wanted to carry her.

The entire situation was preposterous. She needed to get a grip, to concentrate, orchestrate a response, but before she managed a single word, a man's voice cut through the storm, shouting, and heavy steps came clamoring down the dock.

"Alex! What the—what's happened?"

A man appeared through the curtain of rain, his blonde hair matted to his forehead, a grey Clemson University t-shirt drenched through to his skin. He appeared to have been running for some time, his face red with exertion.

"What's going on?" His eyes swept between them, taking in the situation.

"She was in the water." The girl took his arm, pulling him beside her. "Her boat—it doesn't matter, help me get her to shore."

It was clear he had a dozen questions—half as many as Catharine herself —but he had the sense to table them. Catharine tried again to speak, but found herself victim to another fit of coughing, another miserable round of spitting up fetid salt water.

"I'm sorry," she managed between heaves, mortified by her ineptitude to help herself.

Again the girl was squatting by her side, quieting her with a gentle wave of her fingertips.

"We're going to carry you, okay?" It was clear from her tone she wasn't looking for permission. And despite Catharine's embarrassment of the ordeal, she was in no position to protest.

With no further discussion, the man slipped an arm under Catharine's knees and around her shoulders, effortlessly lifting her to his chest.

"Where should we take her?" They were already halfway down the dock, moving quickly with his long, hurried stride. The weather had turned to a full force gale, the wind battering the three of them with a spray of sand as the man slowed to ease his way off the slippery wood to the beach below.

"There, please." Catharine's voice was a rattling wheeze, hoarse and strange to her own ears. She pointed toward the towering wooden gate barring access to the drive of Cleveland Manor. There was no point in the back garden door now. No point in trying to make a covert entrance. "My husband..." A rising tide of darkness was sneaking up on her, the pounding in her head becoming violent, almost unbearable. She opened her mouth to try again, but the darkness won, and she felt herself slipping into unconsciousness.

Chapter Nine

"I don't know what she was thinking!" Carlton Cleveland paced his study, feverish in his attempts to light an Arturo Fuente cigar with a lighter that would not hold a flame. His fingers fumbled on the spark wheel in frustration. "In this weather! Without a word! She's got no common sense! I didn't even see her leave! Did you?" Flinging the unlit cigar into a pen holder on his desk, he wheeled on his heels to look at Jerome, his valet. "With all these guests!" He waved a heavy hand toward the door, indicating the people still waiting for him in the library down the hall. "Why in the hell would she leave when we have all these guests?"

The valet did not answer. It was known the senator needed no reply to his rhetorical questions.

"She's fortunate Dr. Murray was among our callers today, elsewise we would have had to ferry to Hilton Head! In this storm!"

"Did he say if the missus would be all right?" Jerome kept his eyes downcast, careful with his question, yet unable to hide his concern for Mrs. Cleveland.

The question snapped Carlton back to his senses. It would not do for him to appear to have no consideration for the wellbeing of his wife, even if it was only Jerome.

"A concussion." He rubbed his temples, feeling as if he were the one who had suffered a heavy blow. "Took in a bit of water, though he didn't think much. Said her lungs sounded good overall." Carlton returned to his pacing. "And some skin off her shin. God!" He burst, slapping his fist against his open hand. "If those kids hadn't been there, if that girl did not see her…" His voice trailed off. What a rigamarole that would have been—*Senator's Wife Found Drowned on Island Beachfront*. The press would have loved to eat that up. It was bad enough as it was.

He'd need to do something for the couple who brought her to the house. It would be expected of him to reward their bravery.

And if he was fortunate, he could buy their silence. No one else needed to know about the situation. It was exactly what those media sharks would be looking for and he did not need his wife's name plastered across the front page of the *Wall Street Journal* in a near-drowning incident. He could see the headlines now: "Senator Cleveland's Wife: Folly or Foul Play?" There would be too many questions, too many things inferred. It would get convoluted and look poorly on him; the media at its finest.

"I must see to my guests." He stopped in front of the fireplace and looked at Jerome. "I'll tell them she was out walking and got caught in the storm. That she's taken a chill." This was more to himself than the valet.

"Yes, sir." Jerome averted his eyes to the floor. Carlton paid him no mind. The valet was accustomed to keeping secrets for the Clevelands.

Carlton crossed to his desk and snatched up the cigar, deliberating.

An hour earlier, the groundskeeper, Edmund, had come running up the drive, shouting for Senator Cleveland. Carlton had been taking scotch with Congressman Chisholm, Assemblyman Palmer, and Dr. Murray while their wives chatted in the sunroom. He'd noted Catharine's absence when they were driven inside by the summer storm and reckoned she'd gone to change for supper. It wasn't unlike her to disappear when they were entertaining— if only to get under his skin, to make him look bad.

As the situation was later explained to Carlton, Jerome had heard Edmund's calls from the courtyard and intercepted him at the front door, knowing Senator Cleveland would not wish to be disturbed. But as soon as he saw the groundskeeper was accompanied by a man carrying the unconscious form of Mrs. Cleveland, he'd rushed to fetch the senator.

And that was where the nightmare of the evening had started.

Jerome had appeared in the threshold of the library, his voice wavering, his placid face unsteady. "Forgive me, sir. There is a minor development."

It was so unlike Jerome to interrupt Carlton in his library, especially when guests were present. He'd stood, faster than intended, and sloshed scotch from his glass, soiling his vest, and drawing the attention of his guests.

"If you'll excuse me, gentlemen. I'll be but a moment."

There'd been a brief summarization of the scene outside before Carlton pushed past Jerome and took the stairs two by two to the foyer, where the groundskeeper was waiting with a pair of beach bum kids dripping water across the entry. And at the center of it all was his wife, semi-conscious, held in the arms of the stranger.

"What on God's green earth—?" He charged, then quieted, worried his guests would overhear. The women were in the sunroom a short hallway to the right, and though the battering rain on the windows muted their voices, he feared the disturbance would bring someone to the hall to see what the row was about.

The young man, half a head taller than Carlton, stepped forward with Catharine, but it was the girl who did the speaking. "Is there a doctor on the island? She—"

"Who the hell are you?" Confused, he looked to his wife, who was beginning to show some signs of sentience. "Catharine, what the devil is going on?"

She tried to speak, but her words were weak, unintelligible, and the girl cut in again.

"Your wife was in the water—her boat capsized—she hit her head. She needs a hospital." She placed her hand on Catharine's back as his wife was overcome with a raucous round of coughing.

"The hell she does!" He spat, his agitation growing in fear that Congressman Chisholm's wife would appear in the hall at any moment. "What do you mean she was in the water?" He couldn't wrap his mind around it. Was it even possible she'd set off on the damnable dinghy while he was entertaining their guests? "Jerome!" He searched for his valet. "See these—see them—" He forced himself to slow down, to steady himself, to take a breath. This would not look good for re-election. "Please see them to Catharine's sitting room." He motioned down the hall, then stopped, realizing it would take them directly past his library. He turned the other direction. "Take the west wing, around the kitchen. I—I will—" He was at a loss. This was nonsense. It was just like her to do this to him. He glanced at his wife, drenched, her blouse indecently clinging to her skin, a wash of blood trailing down her forehead, disappearing into the mess of her flaxen hair.

It was an absolute clusterfuck of a situation.

He smoothed his lapel, aware of the scotch staining the silk of his vest.

"I will have Dr. Murray look in on Mrs. Cleveland."

Jerome nodded, turning to address the couple and handle the disaster. It was the benefit of the exorbitance of the wage he commanded. He knew how to put out fires. And keep his mouth shut.

Carlton turned to the groundskeeper. "Edmund—find Ellie—make sure she gets this mess cleaned up." He took a careful step out of the water pooling on his Calacatta floors. "Quickly now!" He needed this to go away, and go away at once.

An hour later, after the initial shock had worn off and it had been established Catharine was in no immediate medical danger, Carlton could focus on nothing more than damage control.

Dr. Murray was a good man; a longtime friend. Loyal. Devoted. And more than anything, he was a man who knew how to keep his lips sealed. He took pride in the privacy he afforded his patients—all high-class, notable clientele—and regardless the fact that he had been at the manor as a guest, taking scotch and cigars in the library with the boys, he'd assured Carlton no mention of the incident would leave Catharine's sitting room.

"Your wife is a strong woman." Murray had conferred with Carlton in the hall after tending to Catharine in her private rooms. "And a lucky one. That could have ended in tragedy." He gave instructions on what to watch for after near-drowning and a concussion.

Carlton tried to appear sympathetic. To promise she would be well looked-after. But there was so much more to worry about than Catharine suffering a headache. Especially when she was the one who had placed herself in the imbecility of the situation. "Thank you, Roger." He'd laid a hand on the elder man's arm, stilling him from his departure. "Your discretion—and of course your medical advice—is dually appreciated."

A nodded agreement had passed between them, and then the doctor returned to the library and Carlton had called Jerome to his study.

Now, satisfied the catastrophe was averted, Carlton stepped through the door to see to his company.

"Sir," Jerome followed him into the hall, "shall I have Edmund see the couple back to their hotel? They are waiting in the foyer."

Carlton paused. He'd forgotten about the damn kids. Did he need to speak with them tonight or could it wait until morning?

He finally decided tending his own guests was imperative. Given his wife was in no condition to do her part, to entertain them, someone had to handle the situation. The kids could be put off until tomorrow. He couldn't keep Chisholm and Palmer waiting any longer.

The senator turned to Jerome. "Drive them yourself. Make it clear how grateful I—*we*—are, and insist they join us tomorrow night for dinner. Do not take no for an answer." Pacified, he strode down the hallway, preparing his best nonchalant, debonair demeanor.

Chapter Ten

The next morning Alex was up at dawn. She'd slept little with the shutters of the inn banging against the windowpanes, but the storm broke with the rising of the sun and she stepped onto the porch to find a beautiful summer day.

The ocean, not a stone's throw from the Civil War–era wraparound porch, was wondrously still, a bed of rippling glass, the only disruption in its sleek surface the occasional seabird that dipped from the sky, hunting its breakfast while the sun rose over the water.

She rubbed her temples, pressing her palms to her eyes. She couldn't get the events from the day before out of her mind.

It wasn't the actual circumstances of the accident that bothered her. It had been unexpected, and the *what-ifs* were plenty, but she'd simply been in the right place at the right time.

It was the strangeness at the woman's residence that was troubling. The lack of concern or caring from the husband, his complete indifference at his wife's state of wellbeing. Who the hell worried about water on the floor when their wife was on the brink of unconsciousness—half-drowned?

She and Caleb had been ushered back to the grand foyer after the woman —Mrs. Cleveland, apparently—was left in an elegant bedchamber that Alex could only compare to the overblown hotel in New York where she and three of her teammates had shared a presidential suite the previous year. The hotel had sponsored Rage FC when they were favored to win the playoff final and put the players up in extravagant rooms usually reserved for celebrities and politicians. A publicity stunt for Women's Sports, it was all over-the-top with exaggerative luxury, ridiculous and excessive, but they laughed their way through the experience with endless champagne and obscene orders of room service.

The entire Cleveland Manor had been like that—lavish and exorbitant. Uncomfortable and cold.

Alex settled into a wooden rocking chair on the porch, drawing her knees to her chest and wrapping her arms around them, still wrapped up in thoughts of the night before. The bizarreness of it all.

The two of them had been shown to a settee by the penguin-suited, expressionless attendant, Jerome, where they were asked—*instructed*—to wait. A woman had just finished wiping down the glassy entry floor, curtsying to them before she disappeared.

"Did we just walk into the nineteenth century?" Caleb mocked, his loud voice echoing across the marble. "Do people really curtsy these days?"

Alex cringed, shushing him, but couldn't help but secretly agree. The place was a scene plucked out of *Gone with the Wind*. Clark Gable and Vivien Leigh would appear any moment around the Antebellum archway.

With the passing minutes, Caleb grew impatient. They were sitting in silence on a cream silk sofa, Alex painfully aware of the seeping water stain spreading from their soaked clothing. An antique grandfather clock ticked out the seconds with its golden pendulum while Caleb drummed his fingers on his knees, eventually turning to foot tapping. He was not known for his patience and ability to sit still and his attention span was at its breaking point.

"Should we just walk back?"

"What if she needs something?" Alex was reluctant to leave. Not without an update on Mrs. Cleveland. "They may need to take her somewhere—to a hospital or something."

"They won't need us for that." Caleb was on the verge of annoyance, but for once Alex made no move to pacify him, so he resigned to settle back down. He crossed his arms. "I swear we're going to find out this whole thing is a prank on hidden camera."

The clock chimed the passing of the hour, drawing Caleb to his feet.

As if on cue, Jerome—the butler? Did people still have butlers?—entered the hall.

"If you will follow me," he was stone-faced, succinct in his manner, "I will drive you to your hotel."

"We can walk." Caleb unfurled himself toward the door. "It's barely a half mile."

"The weather—"

"—we're fine. Really." He turned to Alex, a pulse ticking at his jaw, blaming her for making them wait for nothing. "Let's go."

She wasn't as eager to get to her feet. She knew she should follow his lead, make her exit, listen to his I-Told-You-Sos all the way back to the inn. She felt flagrantly out of place in the extravagance of the foyer, her hair damp with seawater, her thighs sticking to the silk of the sofa, the teal of her toenail polish in glaring contrast with the cream tones in the rest of the room. For the hundreth time that evening she was grateful she had been wearing the modest, one piece suit she preferred for swimming, instead of the bikini she'd brought to sunbathe.

"The woman...?" She didn't feel right using a name she'd only overheard.

"Mrs. Cleveland." Jerome gave a nod of acknowledgment. "She is resting and will make a full recovery. The Clevelands are profoundly indebted to you for your assistance and efforts. They request your presence at dinner tomorrow evening." He paused, clearly realizing his words did not reflect any deep feelings of appreciation. "It would be their honor," he added with what Alex thought was meant to be a smile.

"That won't be necessary," Caleb was already halfway across the hall, but the man in the suit was quick to intercede, blocking his exit from the towering double doors.

"The invitation is not of necessity but gratitude." Standing in similar impressive height to Caleb, he met the younger man's challenge calmly, with impassive eyes. It was obvious he would not be taking no for an answer.

"We'd be happy to." Alex didn't know why she said it—she had no desire to return to this dismal place with its cold, hostile aura—but she wanted a scene even less, and Caleb was on the verge of making one. She crossed to the threshold, her bare feet forgotten, and rested a hand on Caleb's tense forearm. "*And* we would be grateful for the ride." She pinched his arm in a vise grip, silencing his protests. She was not about to let his ego and irritation turn into a pissing match with the real-life Jeeves.

To her relief, with little further conversation, she found herself in the back of a black luxury sedan, one of the few cars on the island, for a two-minute drive through the pouring rain to the bed-and-breakfast less than a mile down the road.

Now, twelve hours later, it felt like a disjointed dream. If they weren't committed to dinner with the modern day cast of *Pride and Prejudice* this evening, she could almost believe she hallucinated the entire thing.

Alex uncurled from the rocking chair and leapt to the ground, skipping the four wooden steps that led from the walkway to the century-old porch. She had some time before Caleb woke. He was not an early riser and wouldn't emerge from his room for at least a few more hours. A run along the sand sounded like the perfect way to enjoy the brief gift of morning solitude. The hour just after dawn was always her favorite.

Overhead, a flock of pelicans navigated their V-shaped formation along the water's edge. Alex jogged across the dirt road and onto the sandy beach to follow in the wake of the majestic birds.

Chapter Eleven

South Carolina in July was sweltering. The heat clung to the air as if risen from the internal bowels of Hell, and when there was no sea breeze to relieve the muggy atmosphere, even the mosquitos found the air too thick to spend much effort on flight.

Usually, Catharine was west-bound long before summer arrived on the eastern coast. May through November, when her schedule permitted, she could be found alongside the Pacific Ocean, where the air was crisp and she could enjoy beautiful seascape views from the balcony of her bayfront home in San Francisco.

If she had her druthers she would spend the entire year on the West Coast but Carlton wouldn't have it. It didn't look good for a South Carolina senator to have his wife residing in the liberal, communist, hippy hellhole of California—his words, not hers—so she compromised with long summers and filled the rest of the time with travel; mainly work, sometimes pleasure. She relinquished much of the day-to-day business to her management team to delegate but kept her hand in the larger contracts and expansion projects with her personal staff. Carlton never quit badgering her about her hands-on role in the company, but she refused to take the back seat position he demanded. He couldn't stand having a wife more successful—more influential—than he was, and were it only for that purpose alone she would have maintained her control. But the truth was, she loved her career. She had a mind for growth and innovation, loved building and expanding, orchestrating mergers, giving life to offshoot companies beneath the umbrella of Brooks Corp. She was one of few women in the male-dominated transportation industry and highly respected amongst her peers. After being invisible in her father's household for so long, it gave her satisfaction to know she was regarded as a kingpin in her field.

Her work was something she excelled at, and she refused to give it up for a man to alleviate his pathetic insecurities.

For the past few years she'd turned her focus to expansion of the humanitarian and charity organizations she'd launched across the globe. She was no mind-bending philanthropist, but she reveled in having the means and ability to change the lives of those needing a helping hand. A chance at a better, brighter future.

It got her out of South Carolina, away from the small, dogmatic minds— offered her a freedom she was never able to find when she was at her husband's side. Unshackled from the same constraints that had followed her from London all those years ago.

So she spent as little time on Daufuskie Island as was socially acceptable. As long as she was present for Carlton's most prominent rallies and beside him at state and national events, no one made mention of the dysfunctional relationship between the South Carolina politician and heiress to the British business dynasty.

This year, however, Catharine was late to leave for California. She'd spent the better part of May on business in South Africa, working out a contract for a shipping dock that would drastically impact the traffic of exportations from the Port Elizabeth coastline—a project that had been under negotiation for years and was finally coming to fruition.

She'd wanted to go straight from Algoa Bay to the American West Coast, but Carlton had an upcoming charity fundraiser in Charleston, so she'd opted to stay on the island in order to attend the event. San Francisco would have to wait.

Now, after her near brush with death, her regrets to stay on Daufuskie magnified. Not due to the incident—it could have happened anywhere; the ocean was no more forgiving in California than it was in Carolina—but because it would reignite Carlton's conviction that Catharine needed monitoring; that she ought not be left to her own devices. He would rally that her independence and freewill were going to be the ultimate demise of her—*of them*—and she needed to plant her feet, stay in South Carolina, quit galivanting across the globe as if she were a man. She'd heard it all before. And after the afternoon debacle, she knew she'd hear it all again.

As she'd anticipated, he barged into her bedroom after the remainder of the guests departed late in the evening, full of scotch and vengeance. He'd made no effort to check on her since Dr. Murray left her rooms, disappearing to his world of cigars and shop talk, without ever so much as an inquiry as to her wellbeing. But as soon as they were alone, without the obtrusive ears of his precious friends to overhear, the night was an entirely different story.

"I'm sick of it!" He stumbled through the threshold, his eyes glazed and pallor of his cheeks ruddy from the liquor. "God damnit, Catharine, *sick of it*, you hear!" The repetition of the staccato words hung heavy in the hot summer air. "I mean it! I won't tolerate it a second longer." He crossed the room to where she was sitting up in her bed, flipping through a copy of *The Guardian*.

"Not tonight, Carlton." She set aside the melted bag of ice that had done little to curb her raging headache, and drew a long, tired breath, her lungs still rattling with fluid. "Let's table it until morning."

"Tell me, do you spend every waking moment of your days thinking up ways to make a fool of me? Or does it just come natural to you? Your imbecility?"

"I'm feeling much better, thank you for asking." She would have risen to walk away from him, but she didn't trust that the nausea would not return, so instead she turned her eyes back to the magazine, having no wish to engage with him this evening.

Livid, he snatched the periodical from her hands and flung it to the floor.

"You brought this on yourself! What the hell were you thinking? In the middle of a damned dinner party! Our guests—"

"*Your* guests!" She'd had enough. Enough of his tantrums. Enough of his belittlement and castigation. Catharine swung her legs over the side of the bed and forced herself to her feet, heedless of the wave of dizziness that threatened to overcome her. "Your inane friends and their vacuous conversation! God forbid I not want to be part of it, Carlton! Hour after hour of listening to you pat each others backs and kiss each others arses!"

The outburst took Carlton by surprise, his face flashing a moment of sobriety as he stared at her, dumbfounded. Seldom did she argue with him, especially when he was heated.

"Catharine." It was his patronizing tone reserved for contentious political debates and children. "You know it's part of the job, part of the commitment."

His job. *His* commitments. She had supported him for over twenty years, bowed to his commands, adjusted her life to live around him. And never once had he supported her in her own career, abetted her own undertakings.

It was all about Carlton, all the time.

"It's been a long night." Her will to fight drained as exhaustion took over. "Please, let's discuss it in the morning. I need to get some sleep. We both do."

To her surprise—and immense relief—he conceded, an action so unlike him in the midst of a battle.

"Goodnight, then." His eyes were glassy once again, the moment of sobriety fleeting. He patted an awkward hand on her arm—an attempted display of concern for her wellbeing—but never said as much.

His steps swayed as he crossed the room, where he paused to steady himself against the doorjamb, and then he was gone, leaving Catharine to her isolation.

The following day she woke to the misery of a windless, sultry Carolina morning. The skies were clear, the sea still, without a ripple to break its surface. She sat on her balcony, looking out across the manicured gardens and marble gazebo, to the dock across the sand. It looked empty without the dinghy tied beside it. Somber. Lonely.

She wondered what had become of the Sunfish? Had it drifted across the channel to Turtle Island, washed up on the beach? Or had it made its way to the bluer waters of the North Atlantic, where it would eventually succumb to some trauma that would leave it at the bottom of the ocean?

Somehow, she preferred the latter. She thought about the barnacles that would grow on its hollow mast; the sea life that would take up residence in its hull. She closed her eyes, wondering what it would be like to lie beside it, the sand and silt shifting beneath the water, covering the striped sail, deteriorating the smooth lines, swallowing her lifeless limbs.

Disturbed, she blinked away the macabre image, and reached for her tea.

What a fool she'd been to get herself in such a predicament. Not even a quarter mile from shore on a vessel so easily tended single-handed. She was a cautious person, controlled, meticulous. How she'd let it come to such asininity was inconceivable.

She was told a vacationing beachgoer had swam into the rough surf to rescue her—that the girl had dragged her to safety. She didn't recollect any of that. She didn't recollect being in the water at all. Vaguely she remembered being on the dock, the waves pounding the pilings, a dark-haired girl kneeling beside her, her voice calm and reassuring.

She remembered a soothing hand placed on her back, another holding her hair back from her face as she retched out the contents of the sea.

It was that which she remembered most of all—a kind gesture from a stranger.

Carlton had invited the girl and her boyfriend to dinner.

It wasn't out of any deep appreciation for their heroics in saving her life. Catharine wasn't ignorant enough to fall for that. He was only concerned with damage control. He would spend the evening wooing them—bribing them, if necessary—whatever it took to buy their silence. If there was one thing her husband hated above everything else, it was bad media. He could not bear the thought of the sidelong glances in Congress a poor headline attracted, the resulting whispered criticisms. He lived in fear his colleagues were talking about him behind his back; that they'd found reason to laugh at him.

Which meant any mention of a brush with death linked to the Cleveland name—no matter how innocent the circumstances—would send him into orbit. He'd worry the accident would reflect poorly on him in one way or another. That people might think he'd tried to kill his wife—or worse—that he had no control over her.

Catharine took one last look at the empty dock before setting aside her untouched tea and rising to her feet. Afternoon was approaching and she needed to make arrangements for supper. She was still battling the pressure of a headache, and in no mood to entertain, but it was the least she could do in return for the enormous debt she owed the couple. Regardless if Carlton was grateful for their efforts, it was she who owed them her life. The least she could do is prepare for their arrival.

Chapter Twelve

The Cleveland Manor looked strikingly different in the cloudless Carolina sky. Less Battle of Bull Run, more Antebellum. The uncanny feeling of a false pretense of peace whitewashing the stunning three story walls.

Alex watched the grounds unfold through the tinted window of the black Bentley as they pulled into the gated drive, mesmerized by the grandeur of the estate. They came to a stop on the cobblestone landing encircling a bronze life-sized statue of a rearing horse in the center of a fountain. It was reminiscent of the old plantation mansions but modernized and rebuilt without consideration of cost.

The place didn't have a friendly air.

She stepped past Jerome, who held the door for her, immediately feeling awkward in her sandals and peach cotton sundress. She hadn't come to Daufuskie anticipating a dinner party with the deep-pocket South.

Beside her Caleb was uncharacteristically tense. "Feels more like a walk to the Spanish Inquisition," he bent his head close to her ear, his gray eyes alight with teasing, before offering his arm in mock gallantry to lead her up the marble stairway.

As Alex passed through the double doors, she kicked herself for not having thought to Google the name Cleveland. No doubt there was an entire Wiki page dedicated to this bizarre, chilly place, and its peculiar inhabitants.

As they waited in the foyer for Jerome to close the doors, Caleb wandered across the entry, looking up at a painting hanging at the foot of the staircase. It was an old man in period garb, a white collar around his neck, his head turned in profile. Harsh. Baroque.

"Let me guess," he turned toward Alex with a stage whisper, wagging his eyebrows, "an original Picasso?"

Alex cringed at the incongruous comparison, but before she could hush him, a warm voice greeted them from the second landing, settling down into the foyer.

"Rembrandt, as it happens. A favorite of my husband, though I doubt even he could venture to say why. I myself find his work dark and somewhat dreary." Mrs. Cleveland appeared at the top of the stairs, pausing, her gaze on the painting, before starting down to greet them. "Mr. Anderson. Miss Grey." She smiled as she approached, with none of the coldness of her surroundings. Her voice was low, vibrant, with no sign of the weak, debilitated struggle from the previous afternoon. "We are so pleased you could join us."

Alex let out a slow breath, still frozen in the overwhelmingness of the manor. She had none of Caleb's confidence when it came to meeting strangers, preferring her tight knit group of friends and controlled social settings. The media attention and demands of public engagements that came with her budding NWSL career had lessened her shyness and forced her to develop a persona from behind which she could take cover, but it didn't assuage the discomfort she still found in in-person appearances where she couldn't hide behind short post-game interviews and pre-season podcasts.

But as the woman swept gracefully onto the marble entry, her eyes finding Alex's with the warmth of a smile, she felt some of her trepidation alleviate. There was a genuineness to her demeanor, a cordiality that expelled the hostility of the hall.

She was a stunning woman. The kind of woman who illuminated a room, who drew attention to herself without ever even trying. The kind of woman that belonged to the glamour of the silver screen, the cover of the latest fashion magazine, the lavish luxury of a Southern Plantation mansion. She made sense here, surrounded by glimmering marble, polished mahogany, Rembrandt hanging casually on the walls. There was nothing of the disheveled, insentient being from the day before, washed in blood and salt and sea.

Clad in the simplicity of summer white—pearls hanging blithely above the Queen Anne neckline of her tencel twill dress—she brightened the room with her welcoming presence, the easy warmth she exuded.

Yet, despite her beauty, despite the assertive self-confidence she wore like a glove, she appeared neither arrogant nor assuming—perhaps, Alex thought, watching her glide to the floor, she was smothering a hint of apprehension herself, covered behind her gracious smile.

"I—" Alex opened her mouth, but her brain was slow to offer her tongue a further command. "You look well," was what she finally settled on, stumbling obtusely over the words. This opulent place was outside her wheelhouse. Miles outside her comfort zone.

The woman extended a manicured hand. "Much improved since you last saw me, I imagine." Her lips turned up at the corners in an engaging smile. She had the lull of an English accent, posh and pleasing. "We have not been properly introduced. Catharine Cleveland."

Alex shook her hand. "Um, Alex. Grey." As if it were two separate names.

The stupidity.

She rushed on. "And CalebAnderson." One awkward jumble of syllables.

If Mrs. Cleveland noticed her discomfort, she didn't let on, instead simply pressing Alex's hand in hers, before turning to acknowledge Caleb.

"It is a pleasure to meet you both. I hope it goes without saying how utterly grateful I am—*we* are, the senator and I—for your selfless heroics yesterday afternoon."

The senator? Alex got stuck on the word, hardly hearing Caleb's nonchalant reply, the absolute ease at which he dealt with strangers. He was never at a loss for words, indelibly programmed to say the right thing, to fit in to the situation. People were his natural gift. He harbored none of Alex's awkwardness.

Whatever he'd said made the woman laugh—musical, pleasant—and Alex found herself drawn back to the conversation.

"I doubt that very much, Mr. Anderson—you give yourself too little credit—but in any case, you both are to be commended." The woman— *Mrs. Cleveland*, Alex reminded herself—returned her eyes to Alex. Blue eyes, the same color as the Carolina sea on a cloudless morning. Eyes that held hers openly, unwaveringly, an inquisitive depth behind them.

Alex found herself unnerved behind the gaze, as if the woman could see right through her.

Caleb was ever to the rescue, even if it was unwittingly. "Forgive me, ma'am, but did you say senator?"

There was merit to his blunt candidness, for which Alex was grateful. She never would have voiced the question.

"My husband?" She seemed taken aback by the question. "Senator Cleveland? I'm sure you must have met him last evening—though I suppose there was no time for formal introductions. I imagine it was quite a scene." Her face shifted seamlessly to a practiced mask of decorum, some of her warmth receding. "He will join us shortly on the terrace."

Senator.

Alex reflected to her brief meeting with Mr. Cleveland the night before. His pompous, arrogant attitude and complete lack of interest in his wife's wellbeing still weighing on her mind. It made sense now. A US senator, full of self-importance and disdain for those he felt were beneath him. She should have known he was a politician. If she'd only taken a few seconds to search the name, she would have recognized him immediately. Loud-mouthed. Belligerent. A pillar amongst the staunchly conservative Deep South society.

A man appeared from the hall, waiting ramrod straight in the shadows, until Mrs. Cleveland acknowledged him. He was tall, thin, the spitting image of Jerome, only his hair was graying and the skin around his eyes and mouth held deeper creases.

Mrs. Cleveland gave a cursory tilt of her chin.

"Ma'am," he bowed at her recognition, "Senator Cleveland would be most pleased to have Mr. Anderson join him in his library for spirits. Mrs. Hathaway has set tea for you and Miss Grey in the garden."

Alex felt the sudden urge to laugh at the absurdness of it all. This was a world far outside her realm of reality. Tea. Gardens. Senators. Spirits in a library. But her own amusement was cut short as she caught Caleb's eye, aware he was preparing to make a joke, voice his own entertainment at the bizarreness of the afternoon. She tried to silence him with a glare, to beg him, just for once, not to make light of the situation. It was not the time. This was not the place. These were not the people.

The corner of Caleb's mouth flickered. "I would be most pleased," he sang out the words in a heavily accentuated drawl, then winked at Alex, allowing for a pregnant pause, before turning to face the somber servant. "Lead on, Jeeves!"

Alex contracted inward, wanting to disappear.

Lay on, MacDuff.

If he was going to mock their hosts, he may as well get his literary context correct. But at this point, what did it matter?

Without missing a beat, the older gentleman nodded. "A fan of P.G. Wodehouse, I presume?"

There was no chance Caleb knew what he was talking about. Alex knew for a fact he hadn't picked up a book since high school—the last thing he'd read had probably been Lord of the Flies.

"I must say, however," the older man continued as he led Caleb away from the foyer, a good-natured amusement in his tone, "*I* am a butler. My son, Jerome, is a valet—same as Reginald Jeeves."

Alex couldn't hear Caleb's distant reply but was relieved to hear the butler laugh as their steps disappeared down the hall.

"I'm not sure about you, Miss Grey, but currently a cocktail sounds more reasonable than tea."

Alex looked back to the woman, suddenly realizing her lifeline of Caleb was gone, that she was now expected to navigate this evening on her own. She felt a rise of panic. She wasn't equipped to tread the waters of the Carolina elite alone. What would they talk about? What stupid thing would she say to make this woman realize she didn't belong here—that they should have tipped their hats to her the evening before, and called it said and done?

"That is, of course, only if you drink." Mrs. Cleveland filled the silence in her amicable way, her level eyes reading Alex once more. "It would be understandable if you did not. I hope you will forgive me, but I delved a bit into your history. The occupational hazard of having a husband as a senator, I'm afraid." She smiled, an apparent attempt to soften the revelation of having her privacy invaded. "I understand you are a top tier athlete?"

Alex tried to brush away the shock of being investigated in order to attend a dinner invitation she hadn't even wanted to accept. No good deed went unpunished. But she couldn't hold it against the Clevelands. Mrs. Cleveland was right—as a senator, her husband would no doubt be cautious who they invited into their home.

It didn't matter, anyway. Alex had nothing to hide. Not so much as a parking ticket. And no matter how private of a life she lived, in the world of professional sports, the athletes were subjected to a torrent of fan critique and speculation on a daily basis—even for players like Alex, who hadn't overtly caught the public eye.

"Soccer. I play for a local team. Rage FC." She could have kicked herself. A *local* team? She made it sound like she was playing for AYSO. Hardly a "top tier" athlete. But then again, she doubted this woman in her heels and pearls had ever heard of the NWSL. WoSo—the affectionate tag for Women's Soccer—wasn't exactly on the forefront of the political elite.

"I understand your football team is one of the winningest clubs in the country."

Regardless that Alex had played with numerous international players—all of whom referred to the sport as *football*—she still found it quaint coming off this woman's lips. Endearing. Coupled with the fact that she'd actually researched Rage, taken time to look at the stats...

Mrs. Cleveland continued, the tilt of her head leading to an ironic smile. "I have to say, however, I was surprised to find swimming was not your profession."

Alex couldn't help but laugh. "A hobby only, I'm afraid. I wouldn't recommend testing my skills a second time."

A layer of ice melted away, a fragile comfortability emerging in its wake. Alex found she didn't mind when the senator's wife slipped her arm through hers and led her into the hall, through a brightly lit sunroom, down the back of a cobblestone staircase that spiraled to the ground level before unraveling into a lavish garden extending colorfully inside the manor walls.

"Let's have that drink, shall we?"

Chapter Thirteen

Carlton had ordered his assistant, Matthew, to run backgrounds on the couple. Anything to give him ammunition to silence their tongues. When he'd come to Catharine that afternoon with the report, she could tell he'd been disappointed with the results.

Nothing incriminatory. Nothing leverageable.

Alex Grey was twenty-six years old. She'd attended Clemson University on a combined athletic and academic scholarship and graduated salutatorian five years earlier. Her father was an architect, mother an artist—both deceased. She'd been raised by relatives, was unmarried and presently employed by the National Women's Soccer League. No arrests. Excellent credit.

Caleb Anderson was twenty-eight. Newly hired by Markel Sporting Industry. Didn't hold a passport. Was raised in the foster system. Mediocre student. Attended Junior College. No known family. Misdemeanor at sixteen that had been redacted from his record. Credit below par.

Nothing too interesting on paper.

"Just a couple of punks encroaching on the private beaches," Carlton had grumbled at Catharine over breakfast, shoving the paper to the floor.

Nothing about what they'd done for Catharine. How they'd been in the right place at the right time. No mention that she'd be dead without them. But then again, perhaps the alternate scenario would have been his preference. Bad press aside.

She sat across from the Clemson graduate in the garden, studying the self-conscious way the young woman perched on the edge of the wrought-iron chair, her eyes—amber in the sunlight—averted to the rows of rose bushes, hands tucked neatly at her sides.

After Carlton's sleuthhound report of the morning, she'd spent a few moments looking up the NWSL, familiarizing herself with the league. It hadn't come as a surprise that the girl was an athlete. From what she'd been told about the conditions of the water from which she'd saved her, it was a wonder they both hadn't drowned.

She was surprised, however, to find the young woman so unsure and self-effacing. She was nothing of what she expected from someone who'd been willing to risk their own life to save a stranger. She'd predicted someone brash. Cocky. Overweening. Someone more like the boy, with his self-assured swagger and lofty certainty.

This girl was the opposite. Yet, even with her nervousness, and despite her clear discomfort in her surroundings, she maintained a quiet air about her, a stillness and reserve Catharine found refreshing. She was a pleasant enigma. A bit of a mystery.

"How long are you and Mr. Anderson on the island?" Catharine hated small talk. Cocktail parties. Fundraisers. Political palaver that droned on and on. Everything her life was made of married to Carlton. Everything outside her career. She wanted to ask the girl what had possessed her to run into the ocean when the majority of the world would have watched from shore, unwilling to wet their feet.

But she didn't. Decorum frowned upon deposition of ethos without banal introduction.

A bottle of aged Hennessy sat between them, two snifters upturned, ready to pour. Catharine turned them over, pouring an even measure into both.

"We head home tomorrow afternoon. Caleb—Mr. Anderson—has an early flight to Puerto Rico Monday morning."

"Cognac?" Catharine offered, raising a brow as she set the bottle down. The girl hesitated, then nodded. Catharine doubted she'd ever sipped brandy neat.

"Puerto Rico? Lovely time of year for the Caribbean. Business or plea-sure?" She slid the snifter across the table before lifting her own in a toast. "To the great kindness you paid a stranger." She saluted, sloshing the brown liquid clockwise around the glass, careful the contents remained below the rim. "May it be returned two-fold in your future."

The girl raised her own glass a hand width off the table, a flush of embarrassment touching her cheeks, and acknowledged her with a nod. "To your good health, Mrs. Cleveland."

"Call me Catharine, please." She set the glass to her lips and her guest followed suit. Other than the hint of a grimace, the young woman sipped the heady drink without pause.

"It's his first business trip for a new job." She cleared her throat as she set the glass down, her fingers steepled in front of her. "Markel Sports. They design world-class sports complexes."

Catharine was unfamiliar with the company. She wasn't an avid sports enthusiast, with little knowledge of team competition. She'd fenced, rowed, and shown equestrian sports throughout her teenage years, but the only sport she'd continued into adulthood was sailing. Though many would argue it wasn't a sport at all.

"It sounds like the start of a successful career." She took another sip of the brandy. If she was honest, she wasn't terribly interested in Caleb Anderson. Based off her limited interaction with him, he appeared just another cheeky, arrogant young man; handsome, self-admiring, a personality that swallowed the air in every room he entered. She knew the type well. Charming, but with a lack of cultural education. Affable, until his temper ran short.

"You must be very proud. How long have you been together?"

The girl had braved another sip of cognac, but now set the snifter down too quickly, causing the glass to ring sharply in the stillness of the thick air.

"Oh, we're not together." She tripped over the words. "I mean, not—well, not like—we're just—we're friends. We've been friends since we were children."

The young woman's fingers went self-consciously to her dark hair, fiddling with a strand that hung loose behind her ear. It was evident the question had embarrassed her.

"I shouldn't have assumed." Catharine sought to change the subject, hoping to put her at ease. "Tell me about you, Miss Grey."

"Oh, it's just Alex, please." She waved off the formality before interlocking her fingers around her glass. She clearly didn't enjoy talking about herself. "There's not much to tell, honestly. I kick around a ball for a living and run in my spare time. I'm very boring."

Catharine couldn't help but smile at the self-deprecation. She was out of her element.

"Somehow I doubt that."

The girl's color deepened, a warm flush traveling up her cheeks. She was naturally pretty—dark hair, intelligent hazel eyes, smooth skin bronzed by sunshine. Lithe in the way only an athlete can be. There was nothing synthetic about her. No plastered on facade. No attempt at a pretense to hide her uncertainty. Just a shyness that leant her a certain charm, the subtle presence of humility.

"Tell me about Rage FC."

At once there was a change in her demeanor, a settling relaxation as the conversation turned in a direction where she maintained her mastery. Her expertise.

She told Catharine about the history of the NWSL, how it had come to be one of the most stable, successful leagues in the history of women's soccer. The only women's league that had enjoyed relative longevity in the United States. She explained they were in mid-season, brightening with a competitive keenness as she mentioned her club's favored prediction to reach the playoffs for the fifth consecutive year—and blushed again when Catharine drew a linear relation to the fact that Alex had joined the team five seasons prior.

"A testament to your talent."

"Oh, it's not that, trust me." She laughed over the rim of her brandy glass. "I've only been lucky to have the honor to play with such a gifted group of women. We've a truly talented team, with some of the most accomplished players in the world."

They talked about how Alex had found her love of soccer—how the sport had saved her from her heartbreak after losing her parents at a young age—how she'd played through all her collegiate years. Catharine enjoyed listening to her talk about her passion. She enjoyed watching the quiet, reluctant demeanor vanish and a vibrance take its place, drawing her out of her shell, away from her hollowed answers and uncertain apprehension. There was a freeness to her when she talked about her game. A weightless enthusiasm.

Catharine knew the feeling. It was how she felt when she was on the water. When she left the chains of her every day life behind. When she unleashed herself from the burdens of societal expectations and demands; the never ending requirement to be someone other than herself. Someone who was never quite enough. Not proper enough, not talented enough, not dutiful enough.

On the water she was always Cate Brooks again—twenty years old, full of life and freedom; happy.

What a breath of fresh air it was to see someone actually living their dream.

"And when do you play next?" Catharine asked, shifting away from her reverie. Away from long days on the Thames, cool nights enveloped in an English autumn breeze. Back to the sunshine of Carolina. The harshness of its endless summer heat.

"We play in Portland in two weeks. It should be a great match. They're currently the number one team in the league." She took another sip of brandy, her body loose, her thumb tracing a mindless loop around the rim of her glass. No sign of her previous rigidness, the unease of when she'd first arrived.

"And what about you, Mrs. Cle—Catharine?" She corrected herself, a slight hesitation at the familiar form. "What are your passions?"

It was Catharine's turn to find herself at a loss for words, thrown off by the candidness of the inquiry. She couldn't remember the last time someone asked her about herself beyond the query of polite conversation—the last time someone was actually interested in her, rather than her money or influence or ability to do something for another person. It always revolved around whatever service she could provide, whatever favor could be done. It was never about her as a person.

"Passions?" She tried to laugh to soften the staleness of the word as it left her mouth. Her passions died in London over twenty years ago. But that was something she would not explain.

She had her work. The responsibility of the corporation. Her humanitarian efforts and charities. But they weren't her passions.

"I suppose my passion remains the sea. Regardless of its recent attempt to kill me." She smiled to make light, but Alex only nodded, waiting for her to go on.

Catharine didn't know why she felt she owed her a more elaborate answer, but she continued all the same. "I don't spend as much time on it as I once did—as much time as I would like. Between work and Carlton's political career, I guess there never seems to be enough time."

"Does the senator enjoy the water?" Alex's gaze swept around the garden, raising to the sea birds calling overhead. "That's probably a stupid question. I imagine when you live in a place like this, you can't help but love the ocean. It's practically at your front door." She toyed with the stem of her glass, a touch of awkwardness at Catharine's silence. "I'm not sure I could live on an island. I'm afraid I would feel too closed in."

Catharine did not tell her being closed in had nothing to do with where you lived. That "closed-in" was what came from a series of life choices and that every choice you made concreted the path along the way. That each choice—big or small—affected your happiness. Affected your freedom.

No, it had nothing to do with where you lived and everything to do with who you were surrounded by, what thoughts you allowed to fill your mind, what risks you were willing to take.

Instead, she diverted. "I spend little time on the island, honestly. I suppose Carlton finds it peaceful, though he hates the water, but the estate has been in his family for generations. Otherwise I've no doubt he would keep permanent residence on the mainland, taking comfort as far from the water as he could get. But," she shrugged, "there's no convincing Southern men away from their traditions. There's some truth to being unable to teach an old dog a new trick." She offered a flippant gesture to the lawns around her, hoping to put the subject to rest. She didn't want to talk about Carlton anymore. "Would you care for a tour? I expect dinner won't be ready for another hour."

Chapter Fourteen

Alex was fascinated with the senator's wife. There was something about her —a magnetism, an underlying current—that was enchanting. It was as if there was an unspoken familiarity between them, regardless of the vast disparity between their worlds, or the reality that they had just barely met.

She enjoyed listening to the gentle lilt of the English accent, the poshness of her voice with its pleasing cadence and warm tones. There was something awe-inspiring about the woman—more than just the immensity of her beauty and exorbitance of her lifestyle—something that pulled at Alex, made her want to find the right questions, to slip behind the rehearsed perfection of her carefully donned veneer. There was an air of intelligence about her; a sophistication, a genuine sense of enlightenment that radiated in her conversation, captivating Alex, drawing her in.

It was more than the headiness of the cognac. More than the besetting aura of the atmosphere. More than the harrowing experience they'd shared the previous afternoon.

But Alex couldn't determine what.

They wandered through the garden, along the cobblestone path set between rows of vibrant flowers, their petals threatening to wilt in the hot afternoon sun, before venturing to the spacious lawns rolling out past the pool and gazebos. Aside from the sporadic acknowledgement of a particular type of plant, or the mention of the history of a sculpture or fountain, an amicable silence had fallen between them, lending a tranquility to the afternoon, an easiness which Alex reveled in.

She loved Caleb like a brother—enjoyed his company and humor—but there was a certain relief in not having to fill every moment with idle talk and continuous chatter. To just be present with another person, yet still allowed the privacy of her own thoughts, her own contemplations.

Catharine must have felt the same as she strolled along, content in the silence, as they came to a gated archway in the outer stone wall that ran along the front of the property. She lifted the latch, pressing the door open to reveal the ocean sprawling out before them, mere steps across the private road.

The dock stood erect in the stillness of the water, the unrelenting sunshine casting narrow shadows off the low pilings. It was such an unalarming sight, so placid and still, postcard perfect of the coastal waters and silky smooth beach, with no indication of the traumas of the previous day.

Beside her Catharine drew a small sigh, her own gaze fixed on the scene before them. "It's almost like being trapped in a parallel universe, don't you think?" She spoke quietly, perhaps more to her self than anything else, her thoughts echoing Alex's same.

Without another word the graceful woman kicked off her heels with reckless abandon, and set off across the hot sand until she came to the edge of the old jetty, where she waited for Alex to join her.

"Come sit with me."

Alex obediently took a seat beside her at the end of the dock, the two of them dangling their feet over the edge, dipping their toes in the sun warmed surface of the water. Below the hem of Catharine's dress Alex could see the angry abrasion running the length of her shin, the only real testament to the catastrophe twenty-four hours earlier.

It seemed quaint that this woman—elegant and refined, dressed for supper on a secluded island, the wife of a US Senator, a clear pillar of conventional society—would have such a carefree side to her. She was a paradox. There was something more that lay behind her perfected manner and polished poise. More than the lavishness of the oppressive manor could hide, more than her overbearing husband could deny. It was that part of her Alex found fascinating. That glimpse of mystery that drew her in.

They sat for some time overlooking the water before Alex broke the silence.

"Aren't you worried they'll notice we've gone?" She hated that her voice was thin and unsure, but she didn't want to be the cause of another outburst by the senator. "Yesterday, Mr. Cleveland seemed quite..." she hesitated.

"I learned a long time ago that there would be no pleasing Carlton Cleveland, so I don't go to extensive efforts to try. Fortunately, I've found with enough scotch flowing, it's rarely noticed I'm gone." Catharine smiled, continuing more reassuringly, "but we won't stay long."

"Doesn't it bother you," she didn't know where the question came from —it wasn't like her to pry—but it was too late to turn back now, "that he was more concerned with his guests than with you? You nearly drowned." Her voice trailed off and she worried she had overstepped her bounds. But the events of the day before hadn't quit bothering her, and she knew there might not be another time when she could ask.

From the corner of her eye she could see the silhouette turned out toward the horizon. The sun glistened off the tear drop pearls that highlighted the high cheekbones, framing the chiseled features and flawless skin. Her blonde hair was pulled back to a low ponytail at the nape of her neck, her blue eyes reflecting the color of the sea. With perfect stillness, her slender, elegant hands sat clasped in her lap, a faint scattering of freckles across her knuckles, bronzed from the sun. She looked as natural there, on the salt crusted dock, her feet buried in the water up to her shins, as she would in the sitting room of the upper-class circles of the Southern elite. It was as if there were two different women, neither less captivating than the other, both at ease in the persona of Catharine Cleveland.

In the silence that followed, she drew behind her mask of impassivity. Wherever her thoughts carried her, she once again became the senator's wife, aloof and detached, hovering just out of reach. Gone was the relaxed, easy-going woman of the garden. But almost as fast as the facade was raised, the mask was lowered, the defense gone, and the amiable expression returned.

"It would only bother me," she said at last, her voice even amongst the quiet murmur of the lapping sea, "if it came as a surprise. But I assure you, there is no new revelation that Senator Cleveland cares more about his reputation than his wife's well being."

Alex turned to look at her, somewhat taken aback by the frankness. She wasn't sure what kind of answer she'd anticipated, but it wasn't that.

"Surely he must love you?"

Catharine laughed and Alex looked away, embarrassed at her blunder. She had stumbled on a subject she hadn't meant to broach.

"Oh, my dear, we were not married for love. Love has never taken any part in it." There was a bitterness behind the word, a disdain, but it was not directed at Alex. She lifted her feet from the water, disturbing the glassy surface, offsetting a ring of droplets that slowly disappeared back into the sea. "That was never part of the deal." She hesitated, on the cusp of saying something more, but then gave a gentle pat to Alex's shoulder before rising to her feet. "We'd best get back."

The woman took a moment to look around her, surveying the dock and empty beach, her thoughts once again her own. "I just wanted to thank you once again, Miss Grey." Her formality was returned. "If there is ever a way to repay your kindness, I hope you will not hesitate to ask." She offered her hand to help Alex to her feet.

Alex took the proffered hand, shaking her head as she rose. She didn't want repayment. She didn't want anything. All she could think was how much she hated the way *Miss Grey* sounded on this woman's lips. So cold. So detached.

"Please," she stepped down from the dock, "Just call me Alex."

Chapter Fifteen

The sky was bright with the burning lights that illuminated the thirty-thousand seat stadium the Portland Warriors shared with their fellow men's team, Tridents FC.

The rivalry between the Warriors and Carolina Rage had a history tracing back to the inception of the league, resulting in a highly anticipated match that broke attendance records for a regular season game in the NWSL.

In contrast to Portland, a roster stacked deep with a squad full of seasoned players and international superstars, Rage was a relatively young team, comprised of talented rookies and newly minted starters eager to prove their worth and make their name in the growing success of the women's game.

As a fifth season starter for Rage, Alex was considered one of the veteran players, regardless that she was just twenty-six years old. But she held two championship titles under her belt, and six straight postseasons, an accolade only a handful on the Portland roster could boast.

But regardless the variance of experience between the two teams, statistics held them evenly balanced, promising an exciting match.

Amidst numerous chances, and several well placed shots on goal, the score remained zero-zero until the 75th minute, when Portland subbed on one of their star wingers who'd been recovering from a minor injury and hadn't started the game. But her fresh set of legs and impressive movement off the ball immediately shifted the velocity of Portland's press, exposing Rage's defensive line, and finding space for a beautiful header to the back of the net.

Rage found no answer for the late game goal until three minutes into stoppage, when Lexie Hoover, a rookie midfielder from Stanford, made a dazzling cross into the eighteen, finding Alex's left foot, allowing a one-touch tap into the near post between the Portland goalkeeper's splayed legs.

Forgetting her burning lungs and cramping muscles, Alex flung herself into the arms of her teammates, the squad raucously celebrating the hard-fought equalizer. It wasn't the win they were looking for, but with less than a minute left in added time, they could enjoy the satisfaction of silencing Portland's thirty-thousand fans in their home stadium. A draw still gave them a point—a decent outcome against a rival team on the road—and put Rage FC in second place in the league's standings.

After signing autographs and taking photos with what seemed to be an endless parade of young fans, Alex jogged toward the tunnel that led to the visiting locker rooms, ready to hit the showers and call it a night.

Had they pulled off a win, she would have given in to her teammates insistence they head downtown to celebrate, but tonight she just wanted to get to the hotel early.

Usually Caleb would have been at the game; his grinning face standing out in the front row of the visiting supporters section, wearing a Rage jersey with her name and number on its back, his shouts of encouragement and celebration ringing across the field.

But for the first time in her professional career, he'd missed a match—off on his business trip to Puerto Rico—and she was all alone.

It felt strange, him not being there. And yet, somehow, a relief.

Entering the tunnel, her mind was back on the last day they'd spent together—two Sundays earlier on Daufuskie Island.

He'd drank too much scotch—a gift from Senator Cleveland before they left the manor Saturday evening—and was still hungover as they'd walked toward the ferry that would return them to the mainland.

"We'd be a good pair, Grey." His voice was languid with liquor as he tried to take her hand, approaching the landing. "You and me."

Alex had feigned misunderstanding and gently removed her hand from his, patting it with sisterly affection. "We are a good pair, Caleb. We've always been a good pair."

He pulled away, frustrated. "You know what I mean, A!"

Her heart fell at his aggravated disappointment. She'd known for a while that he desired more from their relationship than she wanted to give.

Somewhere down the road things had changed for him, but her heart had not followed and she was left behind, stuck and content with their past.

"I love you like a brother, Caleb." It felt like an apology. She tried to take his arm. "I've always loved you."

But he'd heard enough. Embarrassed by her refusal, he'd withdrawn, hurt, and they'd boarded the ferry in silence, watching as the island of Daufuskie slipped away and the Carolina shore appeared. It wasn't the end to the vacation celebration Alex had wanted. She hated seeing him disappointed and felt guilty—angry at herself, even—that she could not return his affection.

But she couldn't force her heart to want what he wanted. She couldn't evoke feelings she didn't have, and she didn't want to pretend that she could.

He would understand. He would come around. He had to.

"Hey, Grey! Hold up!"

Alex slowed at the entrance of the tunnel, turning to see the tall, loping form of their keeper, Erin Halsey, waving her down.

"Some lady flagged me down from the seats and asked me to give you this." She held out a small piece of paper—a folded over ticket stub—with a few short words peeking out in black ink.

Without opening it, Alex tucked the note away into the palm of her hand. "That was some save against McCutchen," she slapped Halsey on her shoulder, ignoring the note. "Saved us from a loss for sure!"

The broad-faced keeper brushed off the praise and trotted toward the locker room. "We're going to D'Laney's for drinks," she called over her shoulder. "Bring your secret admirer!"

Alex watched her go before glancing down at the ticket stub.

She didn't know anyone in Portland outside of soccer. No one who would be sending her notes from the stands. A fan, maybe, asking for a follow on social media. Or a phone number—she'd gotten more than a few of those over the years, though they'd all come from hopeful college boys and creeping older men. She wasn't exactly the type to draw in the WLW crowd.

She unfolded the stub. The handwriting was neat and flowing, just a few short words squeezed in above the printed *Warriors* Vs. *Rage*.

"In the area. Great match. Dinner?" Beneath the QR code for admission was the careful, elegant signature: "C Cleveland" and a phone number.

Alex read it over several times, still standing in the tunnel. Behind her, the groundcrew were beginning to tend the field and the bright stadium lights switched off to the dull glow of work lights.

She finally refolded the ticket stub and drifted toward the lockers where most of her team had showered and cleared out for the evening. They had a late afternoon flight the following day back to South Carolina, so a majority of the girls planned to make the most of their night in Soccer City USA and meet at a nearby bar that catered to the local sports teams.

After taking a long shower—unusual for her—and changing into her street clothes, Alex packed her bag and pulled out her cell phone. She doubted Catharine would have waited around this long to get a response. She honestly didn't know why she was dragging her feet to reply. Or why the thought of joining her for dinner made her nervous. The senator's wife had been nothing but pleasant at their meeting on Daufuskie. More than pleasant. She was genuine and thoughtful. And kind. Incredibly kind. Alex couldn't remember the last time she'd met someone who seemed so real.

After they'd left the dock and headed back to the house to meet Caleb and Senator Cleveland, all the conversation had turned benign and casual. Small talk, mostly from the senator, who regaled Caleb with stories from DC and self-important accolades.

Alex had found herself lost in thought most of the evening, wishing she could go back to the shore, wishing she'd had more time to talk to the fascinating woman without the constant soliloquy of her husband.

That evening as they'd said their goodbyes, Senator Cleveland casually remarked one last time—for the hundredth time over the course of dinner—how he and his wife would appreciate it if the events from the day before remained confidential. And once again, both Alex and Caleb had assured him they would keep his confidence. There was no reason to mention it to anyone else.

As they left, Catharine had invited Alex to come see her in California if she was ever in the area during the summer. Alex said of course she would, knowing it would never happen. The lovely Englishwoman was only being polite.

And that had been it. A chance meeting in a strange place, a brief encounter Alex knew she would never forget. But nothing more.

Yet here she was—in Portland of all places—just a couple weeks later. Alex opened a new text message and punched in the numbers.

Sorry it's so late, I'm just leaving the stadium. If you've already headed out for the evening I completely understand. Thank you for coming to see the game!

She hesitated, rereading the message, and finally hit send.

Almost immediately the text tone chimed.

Pick you up at the west entrance? 10 minutes?

This time, without hesitating, Alex sent back an "ok" and grabbed her gear bag, slamming the locker door and hurrying toward the back exit. Her teammates were gone—either to the city or back to the hotel—and the only personnel Alex passed on her way out the door were the night staff, preparing the venue for the men's game the following evening.

The main entrance was still backed up with cars filing out of the parking lot, but the west gate was mostly vacant, with just a few straggling fans and tailgaters.

Despite being the middle of summer, the evening had a crisp Oregon chill that made Alex wish she'd grabbed something warmer than the old Clemson sweatshirt she'd stuffed in her bag. She stopped on the curb by the pillared entrance and dropped her duffle to rummage for the tattered pullover. It wasn't a flattering sweatshirt and she suddenly felt self-conscious as she pulled it on, wishing she'd packed more appropriately.

But more appropriately for what? It wasn't like she'd planned to go anywhere other than the stadium and potentially the raucous sport hangout downtown if her teammates had been able to drag her there. She'd never have thought twice about the old sweatshirt then.

There wasn't more time to dwell on her attire, however, as a sporty black two-seater Porsche pulled up to the curb and the tinted window rolled down.

"Care for a lift?" The distinctly English lull was warm amidst the briskness of the evening.

Alex stooped to peer into the window, finding her apprehension vanishing at the sight of the amiable expression on Catharine Cleveland's face.

"If you're going my way." She surprised herself, teasing, a smile creeping onto her lips. Her nervousness had been for nothing. She didn't know why she'd been so hesitant to see her. It wasn't that she hadn't wanted to—on the contrary, she'd felt a lingering despondence at the thought that she would never see her again. A feeling that had stuck with her the past two weeks. Which, frankly, she felt was ridiculous. She had no ties to this woman, no claims on a friendship that was unwarranted. They'd shared a momentary harrowing experience, and Alex had done what any able-bodied human being would do for another person in Catharine's situation. In the aftermath, she'd been amply thanked for her actions by both the senator and his wife. There was nothing left to link them together.

And perhaps it was because of Alex's desire to see her again that she was so reluctant at the meeting, because it seemed fruitless and odd to want to reconnect with a stranger so badly.

The trunk opened and Alex tossed her bag in the small compartment before climbing into the coupe.

"I must admit," she fumbled with the seatbelt before looking up, "I did not pin you to be a big soccer fan." She'd forgotten how blue the woman's eyes were.

"My first match, actually." Catharine spoke through a close-lipped smile. "Surprising, really, since football is practically a religion in England." She extended her hand. "It's wonderful to see you again, Alex. I'm glad you got my note."

Alex felt her face flush as the Englishwoman pressed her fingers warmly in greeting and averted her eyes out the windshield to the dark stadium sign in front of them. "I wish it had been a better game," she stumbled, feeling some of her awkward tension returning. "But I'm glad you decided to say hello."

"Are your friends gathering somewhere specific? Should we join them for a drink?" Catharine shifted the car into gear and rolled away from the curb toward the exit.

Alex wasn't sure if she wanted to go somewhere alone with Catharine or if it was better to join the loud, bustling joint where her team was celebrating. Her teammates were an ornery lot—they'd want to know who Catharine was, how they'd met. They'd wonder why on earth the sophisticated, classy, beautiful woman would ever bother to seek Alex out—a question Alex still wondered herself.

But she couldn't think of a better place to go this late in the evening—she didn't know Portland very well—and the comfort of her friends sounded welcoming.

"It's a sports bar a few miles from here. I'm afraid it can be a little loud and chaotic." She motioned to the left from the complex entrance. "If you'd rather—"

"—it sounds perfect." Catharine steered the agile car onto the street, speeding to the center lane.

Chapter Sixteen

D'Laney's Pub was overflowing with young, obstreperous Portland locals intermixed with players and staff from Rage and Warriors, the two clubs showing up to blow off steam and catch up with friends. The place was cleaner than a dive bar but still had the raucous, rowdy vibe and dollar-bill-covered walls reminiscent of a downtown college hangout.

A poster on the door advertised free shots on "Tata Tuesdays - Titties for a Cure," the rest of the writing covered by the bouncer—a burly, overmuscled individual with a V-shaped goatee and eyebrows that ran the distance of his forehead. He jutted his chin at Alex, apparently determining her to belong to the variety of athletes the bar drew in, and then turned his eyes to Catharine, eyeing her up and down in her lambskin jacket and designer slacks. She looked like she belonged on the cover of Fortune 500 or headlining an article on World's Most Influential Women. Not the usual suspect for D'Laney's.

"ID?" He demanded, stepping away from where he'd been leaning against the door. It was a clear power play—Catharine had a good ten years on nearly every other patron in the bar—but his calloused, stubby fingers were outstretched, palm up, waiting.

With an acquiescing gesture of agreement, Catharine pulled her ID from her purse and handed it over to him.

"You've got to be kidding me—" Alex started, annoyed, but Catharine quieted her protest with a hand on her arm.

He spent a moment squinting, reading the name, flipping the ID over as if there was some remote possibility this polished woman had offered him a counterfeit, and finally, realizing his authority was coming near an end, handed it back with a begrudging grunt, side-stepping the threshold to let them pass.

"I'm sorry—" Alex began as they passed into the loud main stage area of the bar where an energetic rock band was doing a remixed cover of Ellie Goulding's *Love Me Like You Do* with a dozen couples bobbing back and forth on the dance floor, but she was cut short by shouts of "Grey! Grey!" and some frantic waving across the room by the back patio.

Through the throng of bodies Alex could make out Rachel Parsons and Erin Halsey, both with a long neck bottle clutched in hand, waving her over.

She steered them through the crowd, glancing over her shoulder every few steps to make sure she did not lose Catharine in the chaos, until they were within earshot of her teammates.

"Y'all are late!" Rachel greeted cheerfully, her Texas twang thick with alcohol.

One of the more conservative athletes, Parsons wasn't much of a drinker, and a single light beer was known to turn her into a blubbering fool.

"Who's your hot friend?" she started without preamble, shoving her non-Coors hand toward Catharine.

Alex felt her stomach turn a somersault—her teammates could be the biggest idiots! It was a terrible idea to bring her here. She wanted to apologize to Catharine, but didn't even know how, so instead she shot the lanky, outspoken sweeper—who apparently had no brain or filter—a seething look that went entirely unheeded.

"Rachel Parsons," the girl was drawling, crushing Catharine's hand in hers. Then, without pause, "you are gorgeous!"

"And you are drunk." Erin Halsey stepped forward, draping an arm over the sweeper in annoyed sisterly fashion, sensing Alex's embarrassment and trying to salvage the situation. "I think we met in the stands." She tried to change the subject. "I'm Erin."

To Alex's surprise, Catharine seemed neither annoyed nor embarrassed at Rachel's outburst and instead graciously shook both hands in turn. "You are very kind," she said to Rachel and addressed Erin with a smile. "Thank you for delivering my message. I'm sure I seemed peculiar." Her melodic laugh clashed with the sharp racket of the room. "I'm Catharine," she added with a friendly finality that closed off the introductions.

"Sawyer's on the patio." Erin jerked a thumb behind them. "I think Santos may be back there, too. I'm not sure where the rest of the squad's gotten off to."

Abby—who went almost exclusively by her last name, Sawyer—was Alex's closest friend on the team. She was an attacking midfielder and well-loved team captain. She and Alex had gone through the draft together and were selected in succession. They'd hit it off in their first professional training and been fast friends ever since.

Alex felt a surge of relief that Sawyer was still around. As well as Catharine had taken in the whole college bar, drunk friend, crowded boy-band environment, she still regretted that she hadn't insisted they go to dinner elsewhere. Without the questions and awkward inquiries. But at least Sawyer would offer some normalcy to the locale.

Outside, Alex spotted her friend perched up on the block wall surrounding the patio, a half-finished glass of wine balanced on a knee and her attention turned casually toward a pair of young men standing in front of her, both settled in poses only vain college boys could pull off, trying their best to appear suaver than they actually were.

Little did they know they were barking up the wrong tree.

"Excuse me, boys." Sawyer hopped off the wall when she saw Alex, landing as gracefully as a ballerina, the crimson contents of her glass never breaking its flat, still surface. "I thought you were going back to the hotel." She gave a gentle admonishment, "I would have waited for you!" Her eyes flicked past Alex and found Catharine, dim in the tiki torch light of the patio bar. She glanced back, curious, waiting for an introduction.

"I wasn't." Alex paused, aware of how loud her voice suddenly sounded. The cooler weather and gentle Oregon mist had driven most of the patrons back into the roar of the crowded main bar, leaving the few outdoor stragglers in relative peace and quiet. "I just—I had an unexpected visitor." *Visitor.* It sounded so lame, but she didn't know how else to explain it. She could hardly go into the details of the situation here on the patio of a college bar, with Catharine standing an arm's length away. She glanced over her shoulder to make the introduction. "Sawyer, this is Catharine," it felt so strange to call her that, instead of the more appropriate *Mrs. Cleveland,* "Catharine, our team captain, Abby Sawyer."

"Everyone calls me Sawyer." The tightly coiled spirals of black hair swung with the cadence of Sawyer's steps as she drew forward to greet Catharine, her predictable high-wattage smile donning her lips. It was only the flash of a glance in Alex's direction that promised she had questions, but remained polite enough to table them until they were alone. Alex had always kept her life outside of soccer close to the vest, but Sawyer was no outsider—and other than Caleb, she was probably the person who knew Alex best in all the world.

"I appreciate you ladies allowing me to interrupt your celebration," Catharine's voice was warm through the chill of the drizzle as she caught Alex's eye. "I'm afraid I turned up without warning. I had the pleasure of meeting Miss Grey a couple weeks ago while she was on holiday. She mentioned she played for Rage FC, so when I happened to be in Portland, I thought it might be a perfect time to attend my first football match."

Alex felt herself unwind, grateful for Catharine's effortless way of handling introductions. She didn't want to say the wrong thing—to give something away she shouldn't. Not after the senator had been so clear about his desire to keep the incident confidential.

But Catharine appeared entirely at ease with her friends and their inquiring glances, so Alex let the tension slip from her clenched hands and began to take in the evening, still completely bewildered how this night had come about but determined to enjoy it nonetheless.

Within minutes she found herself seated beside Catharine at the stone fire pit, joined by Sawyer and Sylvia Santos, who'd wandered back out to the patio with Rachel and Erin.

Rachel had regained some of her sobriety, and with it an ounce of common sense, though she still seemed awe-struck by the alluring Englishwoman. But Alex couldn't blame her—she herself found it almost impossible to stop sneaking sidelong glances toward Catharine, who leisurely answered questions about life on Daufuskie Island, how long she'd been in America, what part of England she was from. She wasn't perturbed by the attention she drew, but still managed to never really reveal anything about herself, while still satisfying the curiosity of the inquiring minds around her.

Alex couldn't tell if she withheld the information about her husband's occupation because she didn't want anyone to know or simply because it wasn't part of the conversation. She was just grateful Catharine handled any questions about herself and that as the evening went on her friends moved to other topics—the biggest plays of the night, who was likely to be traded come winter, what the postseason might entail.

"Did Marty tell you all about Turner's slip up?" Sylvia was leaning forward, her voice low, swinging a glance around to each of her teammates.

"About the California team?" Sawyer scoffed, waving the secrecy off with an amused eye roll. "That's old news, Syl. I'm pretty sure you and Halsey were the only ones unaware it was public knowledge! *SheBallz* has been tweeting speculation about it for weeks."

"It's not public knowledge—" Sylvia protested, but Sawyer laughed, her brown skin glowing in the firelight, her palms raised in defeat.

"Okay, not public *knowledge*, just the most widespread "secret" in NWSL history." She winked, using her fingers to make air quotations.

"California?" Alex's ears pricked to the topic. For years there had been rumors about an expansion team taking shape in the Golden State, but it had never come to fruition.

All eyes turned to Alex.

"Seriously, Hollywood?" Sawyer drawled out the nickname in jest. "Of everyone at this table, *you* are the one still clueless? Where have you been the last few weeks! It's plastered all over social media!" She spread her hands, incredulous. "HEG's been courting you for an endorsement next season—they have to have said something to you…"

She shrugged. "I'm supposed to fly out to Sacramento in a couple weeks to meet with Hargrove's grandson. They didn't say anything about a new team."

HEG: *Hargrove Entertainment Group*—one of largest corporations in sports—majority owner of numerous professional teams around the globe, from the NBA to the NFL to the EPL.

There had always been talk that Sampson Hargrove was interested in establishing a California team for the NWSL. He owned the LA Sharks, an MLS team in Southern California, and the West Coast state was anticipated to be a Mecca for women's soccer.

"Hollywood will finally get to play in Hollywood," Rachel teased, making a face at Alex. "Sounds like you can kiss Carolina goodbye. You'll be one of the first players HEG is after."

"Don't get ahead of yourself." Alex dismissed her, trying hard to hide her annoyance. She didn't like being caught off guard. She was usually up-to-date on the latest league rumors. The hole she'd crawled into over mid-season break was proving detrimental. It was ridiculous to have missed something so groundbreaking. Especially with the ties to HEG. It was no secret the sports industry powerhouse was on the search for a new female athlete to promote their latest athletic brand, *Kickstar*, and Alex had been on their radar.

For a fifth season NWLS veteran making less than $50,000 a year, taking on a sponsor like HEG was life changing.

Though she wasn't sure how she felt about the prospect of getting traded to another team. After her initial three-year contract with Rage ended, she'd been signed yearly, so each season there was always the possibility of being floated. But she always assumed Sawyer would be the first to go, given her commitment to the USWNT often interfered with club level games, frustrating the management for the Carolina team. Alex didn't have the luxury of that problem, so her longevity with Rage was on less shaky ground. But HEG's involvement changed things.

On one hand it was an exciting possibility, getting to help shape and cultivate a brand-new team out of its infancy. Finding herself in a position to make soccer history. With HEG at the helm, the team was sure to rise to the top of the league, even in its first season. With that kind of financial backing, it could finally be the move that put women's soccer in the headlines. And—God willing—the change could have the potential to stir up Alex's career, give her another shot at the National Team, open a door she'd worried might be closed forever…

But that was all something that could be dwelled on later. After all, everything was still a rumor. And she had no way of knowing if HEG would even want her. The cart was lumbering ahead of the proverbial horse.

Returning to earth, Alex found Catharine's attention on her, an amused smile flitting the corner of her lips. "Hollywood?" She raised her pristinely shaped brows in question.

"Their idea of stupid humor—trust me, I'm the least *Hollywood* person alive." Alex tried to wave it off, but Rachel Parsons, true to fashion, could never let anything go.

"It would only be stupid if it wasn't warranted." The Texan winked at Catharine. "Somehow, whenever ol' Grey here does anything—hell, she could miss a PK with a keeper knee-deep in molasses, fire an own goal from outside the eighteen, hand a Championship over on a silver platter—

and the press would still hoist her on their shoulders. Praise her style, her flare, her energy—"

"Her *pizazz*," Santos cut in jovially, her Brazilian accent rolling out the Z. "Wasn't that the word the Carolina Chronicle used last match?" The other girls all laughed.

Sawyer grinned, joining the roast. "No Nat caps, no international league play, not even an NCAA championship—just Clemson and good 'ol Rage FC, and yet here amongst us sits the golden child of soccer. The media loves her pretty white girl, All-American, God-fearing, Southern Baptist ass. Ladies, may I present to you, Do-No-Wrong *Hollywood*."

"Hey, you're supposed to be on my side!" Alex admonished, but she couldn't hide her smile, regardless the flush burning on her cheeks in embarrassment.

"I wouldn't be your friend if I passed up an opportunity to tease you," Sawyer defended, her hickory brown eyes sparkling with mischief. "Oh, the stories we could tell…" She glanced at Catharine and arched a brow, drawing a laugh from the lovely lips. "But of course, I'll save those for another time. Our little Alex is bound to melt away if we embarrass her too soundly." She hopped to her feet and grabbed Alex's arm across the fire pit. "Come on, Grey, you haven't even offered your guest a drink, and Lord knows a person needs one to tolerate your company!" She looked at Catharine. "What can we get you?"

"Brandy." Catharine answered. "Thank you."

Alex rose to go with Sawyer. "Cognac?"

"You're a good study, Miss Grey," Catharine regarded her beneath the length of her blonde lashes, a smile dancing behind her discerning blue eyes. There was the sensation of an unspoken language lingering between them, same as Alex had sensed back on the island. It brought a rush of heat to her cheeks, and sent her quickly through the patio threshold toward the bar.

After ordering drinks, Sawyer rounded on Alex, her hands firmly planted on her hips and head tilted at an angle that forced her black ringlets to slip from behind her ear. "Okay. Spill it." Her eyebrows shot up in expectation.

Alex tried looking confused, uncertain of the question, but Sawyer wasn't having it.

"Seriously, girl, I've known you six years and never seen you with anyone other than Caleb and now you suddenly expect me to believe some woman you just met a couple weeks ago mysteriously shows up to watch your game and you invite her to an after-party? I'm not buying it." She pursed her full red lips, making an admonishing smacking sound.

Alex couldn't help but laugh at the irony. "As crazy as it sounds, it's exactly as you just described." There was nothing to refute. "I met her on the beach on Daufuskie, Caleb and I had dinner with her and her husband, and tonight she showed up at the game."

"Her husband?" Now it was Sawyer who was surprised. "Ain't no way Miss Thing out on that patio has a husband—at least not in the marital sense," she said flatly. "Your friend from across the pond hasn't taken her eyes off you since you both walked through the door."

"Oh for God's sake, *Abby*." She fell back on the surefire insult of using her first name, a rush of anger spiraling at her friend's insinuation. Anger, mostly stemmed from embarrassment. "It's not like that at all! Stop trying to turn everything into more than it is."

"Take it easy, sugar." Sawyer rolled her eyes, "I'm not saying it is *like* anything. I'm just calling it as I see it. And as I see it, there's a lot more going on here than meets the eye."

"I'm not a lesbian, Sawyer—" Alex practically choked on the word, her face hot with humiliation, trying to find a fine line between defending herself and not insulting her friend.

"And Lord knows all us gay girls are grateful for it," Sawyer broke in, her own dark eyes hinting at indignation. "We don't need your flawless, pretty girl face playing on our side. You'd make it hopeless for the rest of us to ever find a date again." Her eyes softened a little and she reached out, taking Alex's hand in hers. "You should be flattered, Alex." She half-smiled, trying to diffuse the situation. "That woman looks like she walked off the cover of *Vogue*—or owns *Vogue*—one of the two." Her laughter was good natured, easy again. She patted Alex's hand. "I'm pretty sure the first woman who ever had a crush on me was my freshman PE teacher, who was about as round as she was tall, with ear hair that outshined her eyebrows."

Alex tried to laugh but couldn't force the sound from her throat. "I promise you're wrong," she said, regaining her composure. "You've read way too much into this situation." She lowered her voice and subconsciously glanced around. They were alone at the end of the bar, most of the patrons still on the dance floor or hanging around the standing tables, drinks in hand. There was no one within ear shot. "She was in a boating accident and I happened to be there and pulled her from the water. She nearly drowned. The next day she and her husband invited me and Caleb to dinner at their mansion—in thanks for saving her life. It was nothing more than that." She hesitated, and when Sawyer didn't immediately say anything, Alex continued. "It turned out her husband is a South Carolina senator. They asked us to keep everything quiet. They didn't want the accident in the press." She squeezed Sawyer's hands in earnest finality. "That's all there is to the story. Today she was in Portland on business and saw our team was playing, so she came to the game and sent a note to the locker room inviting me to dinner. And here we are."

"And here we are," Sawyer shook her head, smiling. "Of course you saved some senator's wife while on vacation. Only you, Alex."

"Please don't say anything—no one else knows. I don't want to embarrass her or the senator. I promised I would never speak a word of it." She didn't need confirmation from Sawyer that her secret was safe—Abby was the most trustworthy person she knew, along with Caleb. And an ardently loyal friend.

"I still say she has a little crush on you." Sawyer gave her a sidelong grin as their drinks arrived, turning toward the patio. "You're her hero, after all."

Alex shushed her and took up the cognac—who knew Hennessy was so expensive?—and a pint of local brew the bartender recommended. "You just wish she was batting for your team."

"Who wouldn't," Sawyer shrugged in agreement. "She'd certainly be a win. Bringing a big wig Southern politician's wife over to the dark side…"

But the teasing ended as they crossed back onto the patio to join their small party.

Chapter Seventeen

It was after midnight when the gentle Portland mist turned into a steady rain, forcing the patio dwellers up from the fire pit and into the main bar.

The cover band was busy with an enthusiastic rendition of *Sweet Caroline* as several dozen drunk, discordant voices hollered out the chorus, raising drinks into the air that spilled down their arms and onto the dance floor. A particularly intoxicated young woman—the goalkeeper for the Warriors, Alex informed her—had taken off her t-shirt and was twirling it around like a victory flag, her strident voice rising above the others. *"Hands touchin' hands, reachin' out…"*

Catharine held onto Alex's arm, not caring to get separated in the hustle of the bar. It was packed now and so loud the beat of the music felt permanently engrained in Catharine's bones.

"Let's get out of here," Alex yelled close to her ear, clutching her hand and pulling her toward the door.

Catharine nodded and turned to say goodbye to the other women from the Rage, but they were lost in the commotion and the faces around them were just a sea of strangers.

She let Alex lead her through the throng of bodies, desperate for fresh air and space. It had been more than twenty years since she'd found herself packed into a pub filled with university students and a sub-par live band lending to the deafening atmosphere. She never thought she'd find herself in that scene again.

A cool blast hit them as they elbowed their way out the door and onto the city sidewalk, the relief as palpable as the first breath of air after coming up from a long dive.

"Holy cow!" Alex was breathless, giddy with the same wave of claustrophobia Catharine had been fighting. "Where did all those people come from?"

"It would seem we're the only two people in Portland who turn into pumpkins after midnight." Catharine laughed, welcoming the steady rain on her face, no longer caring that it was flattening her hair and permeating the soft leather of her jacket.

"I'm so sorry, I had no idea it would get that crazy." Alex pulled the hood of her sweatshirt up over her head in a futile attempt to stay dry. "I don't think I've been in a bar past nine p.m. in more years than I can remember."

"And here I am, corrupting your good behavior already," Catharine teased, gesturing toward the car parked at the curb.

"Something tells me this isn't much your scene, either." They climbed into the Porsche, Alex shaking the water from her tennis shoes.

Catharine pressed the ignition and the engine roared to life while she flicked through the controls until she figured out the heating module. "There." She held her hand in front of the vent. "Who knew it would get so brisk in August!" She lifted her eyes to Alex. "Well, maybe not my scene, but I certainly had a good time. Your friends are a pleasure."

"My friends are a pain," Alex's smile was broad, with a sincerity Catharine had not seen from her before. It was no wonder a company like HEG would pursue her as the face of their newest brand. She had a model perfect smile, a dimple creasing the corner of her left cheek—a compelling countenance for an athletic advertising campaign: young, beautiful, successful, well-loved. Every girl on the pitch would want to be like Alex Grey.

"They're charming," Catharine countered, finding Alex's good mood contagious. "I can't remember the last time I laughed so much over the course of an evening. Unfortunately, *my scene* is a bit more… reserved. Are you hungry?" she asked without pause, shifting the car into gear. "I'm afraid I didn't have time for lunch today and I'm famished."

"I think the only places open will be burger joints and dive kitchens. The hotel we are in has a restaurant but I think it closed at ten."

"Have you ever been to The Nines? I have a suite there. And a kitchen that never closes."

She watched Alex in her peripheral vision, expecting the girl to decline. The hotel was across town and it was after midnight. No doubt she was ready to get back to her own hotel with her friends. They were practically strangers, after all. No matter how much Alex reminded Catharine of a life she had long placed in a dormant memory, this girl wasn't part of that life, she wasn't part of those memories. Catharine couldn't will herself back in time. And Alex Grey couldn't revive the life she'd thrown away—decades ago—that now enslaved her to the world she lived in today.

"Well," Alex said, pulling at the sleeves of her sweatshirt in consideration, "I'm not sure I'm dressed for anything too fancy." She gestured at the wet Clemson sweatshirt with a self-conscious laugh. "I hadn't really packed for a night on the town."

"No one will mind. I guarantee it."

Alex met Catharine's eyes with a surprising candor, holding their gaze for a moment before tilting her head in a well-then gesture. "In that case, I have never been one to turn down a kitchen that never closes."

Catharine pulled away from the curb and shifted through the gears without another word.

Chapter Eighteen

A pair of valets rushed through the rain to open the doors, umbrellas held overhead, offering curt salutations of deference. "Welcome back, Mrs. Cleveland." They greeted her by name.

"Are there any bags, Mrs. Cleveland?"

Alex stepped awkwardly around the valet at her door, glancing over the roof of the coupe to see Catharine handing off the keys. "Thank you, no. Keep it up front, please." She held two fingers out toward the man who received the fob, a folded bill stuck between them. "We'll be down after dinner."

Alex thought the valets might give her looks—dressed in a wet sweatshirt and road grime splattered jeans, a pair of well-worn Vans on her feet, clearly not of the class this hotel was meant for—but if they had any questioning glances, they were disciplined enough to hide them behind her back.

The doorman greeted them with the same warm, accentuated pleasantry, again acknowledging Catharine by name.

"You must stay here often."

"Once before, I believe," Catharine tilted her head, not understanding the correlation. "Quite a few years ago."

Who the hell did you have to be to have the staff recognize you on sight at an establishment you had only visited once before? This world was out of Alex's league.

The elevator attendant was waiting for them. Catharine opened her clutch to search for the keycard that gained access to the floor of her suite, but the liveried man shook his head. "No need, Mrs. Cleveland." He swiped his badge for the top floor beside block letters that read *The Nines*.

A few minutes later, Alex found herself seated at a long high top table in a kitchen competing in size with the entirety of her apartment.

The suite was a mix of modern high-tech luxury and classic downtown history, bathed in designer detail. From the Italian marble counter tops to the wide custom molding lining the vaulted ceilings and polished wood floors, it was extravagant, at the least, but still offered a sense of warmth, unlike the rooms Alex had glimpsed at the Cleveland Manor.

"Do you come to Portland often?" Alex watched as Catharine sorted through the mini bar—*mini* was a relative term, in consideration to the rest of the suite—and retrieved a short, triangular bottle of Hine Triomphe and two snifters.

"Nightcap?" Catharine either hadn't heard or ignored the question.

Alex hesitated. She wasn't much of a drinker, especially during the season, but tomorrow was a travel day and Monday a day off, so she would have a few days to recover.

"Thank you." She took the drink Catharine poured.

"We have two options. There is a chef who can come make us dinner, or, if you're feeling particularly brave, I can fix up something." She indicated a pantry off the side of the elongated room. "I read somewhere that they grow all their own produce here at the hotel."

"Let's leave the chef to his sleep," Alex started to get up from her chair, but Catharine objected.

"You are my guest! Sit, please." Despite her obvious lack of expertise around the kitchen, she looked optimistic. "It might not be gourmet, but I won't poison you, I promise."

She went to work, sorting through the fridge and pantry. Twice she refilled their glasses, and Alex didn't object. The liquor was relaxing and there was something soothing about the quiet kitchen and familiar sounds of chopping and running water and the sizzle of a pan at high heat.

It was a peculiar feeling, having this woman who wanted for nothing—who was accustomed to the best money could buy—waiting on her. Serving her.

But for however wealthy Catharine Cleveland was, here, alone, without the rest of the world looking in, she had a self-effacing quality that Alex never would have expected. A modest, unassuming demeanor that was separate from the public perception of the prestigious politician's wife.

She seemed lonely, and a little sad, now that Alex could study her without distraction. It was almost palpable, despite her smile and easy conversation about the events of the evening—not small talk, really, just a distracted exchange as she contemplated the ingredients she'd laid out on the counter.

"I did warn you it wouldn't be haute cuisine," she cautioned, her exasperation at the plate before her endearing in her frustration.

Alex was presented with a very ordinary turkey and bacon sandwich on a bread that appeared to have every grain known to mankind. Beside the sandwich was a variety of chopped fruit, meticulously sliced and arranged with delicate precision.

"It's perfect," she said honestly, taking the last sip of her brandy and unfolding the cloth napkin that lay before her. Alex was grateful to get something in her stomach. The room seemed a little precarious after so much alcohol, and she could feel her cheeks flush with a slight unsteady lilt to her voice. She poured them both tall glasses of water from the carafe and drained half the contents in a long swallow.

"Are you in Portland often?" she asked again, though she figured she already knew the answer based on the number of times Catharine had stayed at The Nines. She didn't seem the type to break a routine once it was established.

"Portland, no." She took the chair across from Alex. "Not often."

"What brought you here this weekend?" Business, she imagined. But beyond a brief mention that she—or her husband, Alex wasn't sure which—owned some kind of shipping company, she had no idea what she did in her line of vocation. Other than the fact that it was clearly a lucrative enterprise.

"I was on my way to California," Catharine said simply, lifting a piece of fruit to her mouth with the heavy, polished cutlery.

Alex laughed, finishing the glass of water before picking up her sandwich and flattening it between her fingers. "Portland's not exactly a straight shot to California from South Carolina. How'd you end up here?"

Catharine took another sip of cognac. "A football game." She set her glass down and looked at Alex, her gaze unfaltering with almost a hint of a challenge in it—daring Alex to show surprise, to find herself alarmed at the sincerity behind her answer.

But Alex did neither. She just held the woman's study for a moment longer than was comfortable before flicking her attention to the large dining room windows that covered the majority of the wall behind Catharine, capturing a dazzling view of the Portland cityscape and the brilliant night lights that lit up the black, early morning sky.

Little time passed, but the silence felt like an eternity as Alex contemplated what to say.

If Sawyer hadn't made such a fuss during their conversation at the bar, she wouldn't have thought twice about it. When money and time weren't an issue, why wouldn't someone go out of their way to see a new friend? She and Catharine had shared an inordinately traumatic experience, and with it came an air of familiarity cultivated by the situation.

It was flattering, really. That this woman who lived in a dimension beyond Alex's wildest comprehension would want to spend any effort engaging in her life. This woman who traveled the globe, lived a life few even caught a glimpse of, the life you read about in magazines of celebrities and movie stars—she found Alex interesting enough, relatable enough to let down her guard, to allow her behind the curtain of rigid propriety and acquiescing deference she had shown in the presence of Carlton Cleveland on Daufuskie. The perfect hostess, the politician's wife, well-spoken but not outspoken, friendly but not warm. Alex had seen a little of the lifted facade on the dock that day, but this evening she'd unraveled an authenticity of character she never expected from the English socialite. This vulnerable, humorous, open side of her was even more engaging than the woman she'd met on the island. This woman was pragmatic. Sincere.

Sawyer had filled her head with nonsense.

"Well, the next time you come to a game, I'll make sure we win," Alex offered at last, matter-of-fact, her attention returning to the plate in front of her, her lips turned up into an involuntary smile.

"I'll count on it." Catharine spoke in the same level tone before allowing herself to smile, her eyes catching Alex's as she looked away from the skyline view.

"Tell me," she changed the subject, "we've heard plenty about me tonight—tell me about you. How did Alex Grey come to play professional soccer?"

They talked into the early hours of the morning. Alex, her lips loosened with cognac and high from the events of the evening, spoke at length, answering the various questions Catharine put to inquiry—everything from her childhood and how she met Caleb, to her education at Clemson and her journey to joining South Carolina Rage. Catharine wanted to know her professional goals and where she saw her career in soccer taking her. Was soccer an Olympic sport? What was the National team and how did the World Cup operate? Did she have ambition to play at the international level? How she felt about HEG and their potential sponsorship and the possibility of a new team on the West Coast. Was it an opportunity she would accept? Did she see it as a lateral move or something more?

Alex answered verily, touching briefly on her disappointment at having not been given a chance at a senior national team call up, and admitting the news about the California team had caught her off guard. She hadn't had time to think about what it might mean for her future.

"HEG is a bit of a mogul in sports, are they not? I assume a contract with a company of that caliber is a favorable endorsement for an athlete?"

"Favorable, indeed," Alex half-laughed, "but nerve-wracking, also. With sponsorship and endorsements comes pressure—ownership, in a way. I don't know if I'm ready for all that."

Catharine had folded and unfolded the thin cardboard drink coaster half a dozen times, changing it to one shape or another. Her hands worked idly, unaware of their occupation, automatic and mechanical. Not too unlike the rhythmic drumming Caleb did with his fingers when he had been sitting too long. A routine release of energy—nervous energy, in the case of Caleb— but Catharine did not seem nervous. It was just custom for her. Everything about her presented as structured, practiced, militant. Alex imagined most of her life was like that—either from birth or raising. No doubt it was part of what made her such a successful businesswoman: she was a pedant; habitual, punctual, meticulous.

Catharine noted Alex's fascination with her hands and dropped them to her sides with a self-admonishing shake of her head, but made no mention of it.

"The pressure of delivering on the field?" she questioned, still on the endorsement.

"Oh, hardly." Alex waved a hand through the air, brushing off the sentiment. "The field is where I'm comfortable. I'm sure I should be more worried about giving them the results they want there, but honestly, that is the least of my concerns. It's the rest of the expectations I worry about." She stared out the window at the cityscape. Everything had been such a whirlwind over the summer, she hadn't really had much of a chance to focus on HEG or the league transfer window—or what any of it would mean for her.

The few meetings she'd had with the company representatives had been hasty, one-sided conversations from men in suits and women in low, sensible heels and bob haircuts that had been out of style since the eighties. They'd called her 'darling' and 'hun' and patted her hand as one would reward a puppy for sitting quietly at the dinner table.

Be a good dog.

They reminded her of the parishioners from her uncle's church: straight-faced, devote, too holy for their own sanity; their gaze always turned down the curve of their nose, chin held in proud, martyred deference.

"HEG is known for the very specific set of standards they expect their athletes to abide by. When they endorse you, they own you, and they own the image of you. They demand a certain persona and lifestyle, both on and off the field."

That *lifestyle* was why they had passed up Abby Sawyer, who was arguably the best central midfielder playing for the league. Closing in on a hundred national team caps, having played for the US Team beginning with the U-16s, her stats placed her on par with some of the greatest players in the game.

But aside from being black and coming from a drug ravaged skid row in Chicago where her mom had ODed when she was twelve, forcing her to raise her five-year-old brother on the streets, she was also an outspoken civil rights advocate and out-and-proud lesbian, unafraid to stand up for what she believed in.

A liberally moderate company would have had to handle Sawyer with kid gloves, let alone the famously conservative, Christian-based, right-wing HEG, who frequented headlines for their contributions to the Republican Party and their funding of socially controversial programs, from abstinence outreach to pro-life legislation, conversion therapy, and beyond. They wanted only the Tim Tebows and Allyson Felixes of the world—a voice like Abby Sawyer's was not welcome.

Of course, they hadn't said as much directly to Alex, but the implication was clear. They had a specific set of attributes they were seeking—ones that an openly gay, agnostic, woman of color did not meet.

The blatant discrimination against her friend infuriated Alex, but Sawyer had laughed it off and told Alex she would box her ears if she turned HEG down on her behalf.

"Their dollars are as green as anyone else's!" She'd shown no hint of betrayal. "Only a fool would turn them down. And I won't let you be a fool, Grey! This is a career changing opportunity."

And so, after heavy consideration, Alex had continued the relationship with HEG and accepted their courting. This coming trip to California would seal the deal. And elevate her career. Something that was needed when youth was no longer on your side of the sport with your mid-twenties trailing behind you. She did *need* this.

She just didn't know if she *wanted* it.

"It's owned by one of the most conservative businessmen in the world. They want their athletes to emulate that—him." She laughed, though the sound was more derisive than cheerful.

"I don't know Sampson Hargrove personally, though we've met a time or two. He's supported some of Carlton's legislation over the years." She paused. "I realize I barely know you, but I can't imagine you have much to worry about when it comes to their expectations."

Alex felt a rush of air escape her lips—another attempt at a laugh—but once again the sound was mirthless and dry. Of course she'd met Sampson Hargrove. No one ever met Mr. Hargrove himself. But she was Catharine Cleveland.

Usually reticent and tight-lipped regarding her feelings, the alcohol had lured Alex into a state of candor, and for some reason she didn't mind telling this woman her weighing apprehensions. Things she hadn't even told Caleb or Sawyer.

"I hate being the pastor's niece, the Baptist architect's daughter. And I'm afraid, sometimes, that's all anyone ever sees in me."

And why would it not be? She'd been schooled since birth to be obedient, agreeable—to not make waves. It was not a woman's place to question superiors, to challenge authority, to disagree with those who controlled their lives. Her parents. Her aunt and uncle. Her professors at Clemson. Her coaches. So why would Hargrove Entertainment not expect the same?

She should simply be grateful for the opportunity—that's what her aunt would tell her. Forever reminding her any "blessing" in her life had been put there by God.

Not by hard work. Not by perseverance. Not by sheer grit and will.

By God.

And, perhaps, there was truth to it. She'd been unquestioningly fortunate. She lived a life few ever dreamed of, she'd made a career out of something she loved.

But there was more to it than that. More to *her* than that, and she didn't want to be peddled as the poster child for the Southern Baptist conservative upbringing.

"I hate being the one they always expect to be perfect—the grades, the games, always expected to say the right things, to dress the right way—to be the role model for every girl sludging her way through Sunday morning Bible study or trying to find her place on the church soccer team."

She swallowed away the tightness that snuck into her voice, her eyes cast to the empty plate in front of her.

It was what she loved about soccer. The open field. The ninety minutes of endless opportunities. The unpredictable chaos of the beautiful game. It was the one place she could entirely be herself. The one place she was in charge of her own life. A place where she was welcomed—encouraged—to be bold, assertive, demanding. A place that set her free.

But the game always ended. And the pressures of her life were always waiting just outside the touchlines.

And now there was HEG perched as a frontrunner at the helm—opening the door to an even more demanding, restrictive authority than she had ever known. A door she had willingly left open, invited them in. A door she began to wonder if she should have slammed shut months ago.

But how could she say no? Like Sawyer had said—only a fool would turn them down.

"I'm sorry." She looked up from the table, forcing herself to stop chewing on her bottom lip. "I sound like a total ingrate. And I promise I'm not. I think I'm just tired. And the alcohol…"

Catharine's face was unreadable through her tranquil stare. She'd listened silently, and Alex had the uncanny feeling she'd heard far more than what she'd actually said.

At length, Catharine's fingers resumed their subconscious busywork with the coaster. "Having reservations about the weight of expectations placed upon you is a far step from ungrateful. At the minimum, it is a respectfulness leant to your employer—but more importantly, it is a fundamental responsibility you owe to yourself as a person. I think you will find I am very understanding when it comes to feeling the pressures of expectations and the weight of constant scrutiny from the world around you." She slid her fingers down the freshly folded seam in the center of the coaster, gathering her thoughts to continue, but the unexpected ringing of the telephone jarred them both from the quiet atmosphere, and brought Catharine abruptly to her feet.

"Excuse me." She appeared as surprised by the interruption as Alex as she crossed through the threshold to scoop up the living room receiver.

"Hello?" She was unmistakably annoyed, and the caller must have felt the same, for Catharine listened a moment and then responded, more civilly, "No, Carlton, it's just three o'clock in the morning here." Another pause. "Yes, I had a change of plans. I will be in San Francisco in the morning." There was a long silence while the caller spoke and Catharine stood staring out the window, her face impassively still.

"I would prefer you didn't," she said at last, glancing toward the kitchen, her voice lowering. Her mouth was drawn into a thin line and a hint of anger had slipped into her tone.

Alex looked away, trying to ignore the call, realizing whatever turn the conversation had taken was clearly private and Catharine was not pleased.

When Catharine had her back turned, she quietly slid from the high counter chair and found her way to the restroom, hoping to give her privacy to finish the call.

Chapter Nineteen

Catharine brewed two cups of tea with water from the electric kettle—oh, how her mother would have disapproved—and slid a steaming mug across to Alex, who had reluctantly returned to her seat.

She'd offered to take an Uber, but Catharine admonished her for the suggestion, insisting she would take her back to her hotel, but a cup of tea was first in order.

"My mother lived by the code that there was little in the world a cuppa couldn't cure." Catharine scoffed at the notion, lifting the Bone China to her lips to test the temperature, before setting it back down. "She was wrong, of course—but the sentiment is there." She offered a wry smile, trying to take the chill out of the air.

Her mother had been wrong on so much more than tea.

"If you'll tolerate a few words of unsolicited advice, let me just say this," she fixed her gaze on Alex, but kept her tone light, almost in jest. "Never allow someone or some thing to control you for too long, because the habit becomes difficult to break—not on their end, but on your own." It was her way of both addressing and dismissing the interruption of the phone call. She was still trying to put it from her mind. She wouldn't let Carlton ruin what had been a perfect evening. Not again. Not like he always did.

He had been unable to reach her on her cell, so had instead phoned her assistant, Nicole, in the middle of the night, to demand the location of her whereabouts.

It hadn't been Catharine's intention to withhold her travel plans from her husband. It had just never crossed her mind to tell him. They lived entirely separate lives. When they were not both on the island they would go days—weeks, even—without any form of communication. Carlton would only call when he eventually needed something.

Portland had been a last minute decision. It was nothing she'd given great consideration, but it had certainly struck a chord to ignite an undesired consequence.

For whatever reason, Carlton had suddenly become overtly suspicious, enkindling a newfound jealousy she'd not previously encountered.

He was drunk on the phone—fueling his typical belligerence—berating her for her secrecy, accusing her of dubious behavior. He was going to fly out to California. Stay for a couple of weeks. It was his duty to keep an eye on her, he'd slurred through the receiver

On another night, in another time, Catharine may have humored him. She may have allowed him to force his way into her peace, to topple her privacy. She would have placated him, agreed to his demands, hoping he would forget them in the sobriety of morning—but she no longer had the energy for it. She'd had enough. And even in his drunken rant, he seemed to sense the change. To sense the finality of something. The shift in the domineering imbalance of their lives.

"I'm done, Carlton," she told him calmly at the end of the conversation after he'd spewed his ultimatum about coming to San Francisco. "I'm finished."

He'd paused a second, clearing his throat in aggravation, before demanding to know what she meant, an underlying tremor of unease sneaking into his bullying.

But Catharine would elaborate no further. She told him they could discuss it when he was less drunk and she less tired, which had fueled a new barrage of insults and accusations, but for once, she cut him off.

"I'm hanging up now." It was something she had never done in all their years of marriage. "Please don't call me back."

And she had done just that.

Her tolerance of his bullish behavior was at an end. She would deal with his wrath tomorrow, but not tonight. And this time she knew—they both knew—she would no longer tolerate the way it had been. The way it had always been. She'd finally had enough.

And for whatever good sense he had, he'd believed her, and hadn't rang again.

Now, sitting back at the table, Catharine was grateful for Alex's polite courtesy in excusing herself from the room. She was embarrassed by her husband, and the last thing she wanted was for the young woman to have to listen to her fight with him on the telephone. It was maddening enough he'd ruined what otherwise had been a perfectly enjoyable evening.

Catharine looked down at the tea, realizing in her frustration she'd forgotten milk and sugar. She laughed, running a hand across her brow, and shook her head as she rose to go to the fridge.

"In all my life of drinking tea—and let's be honest, I'm English, I was raised with it in the bottle—I don't think I have ever forgotten milk and sugar...especially for a guest." She returned with the condiments, distributing both appropriately, before settling back down.

The brandy had worn off and the call from Carlton brought a strain to the conversation she regretted. She didn't want it to end like this. Not when she'd had more fun and felt more herself than she had in decades. She didn't want to ruin that. Didn't want to let *him* ruin that.

"On a better note, you said you are coming to San Francisco?"

Alex withdrew from her silence, setting her cup down and toying with her ponytail. "Yes, I'm supposed to meet with Hargrove's grandson to finalize the contract."

"Will you be in the city long?"

"A few days, I think. I have to look at my tickets—HEG made the arrangements. I just know I had to beg my coach for an excused absence for two training days, and she wasn't happy." Alex's expression soured slightly. "I don't even know where I am staying. Caleb booked the hotel."

"Oh, will he be joining you?" Catharine was annoyed at her inability to hide the flatness in her voice. It shouldn't matter to her what her plans were with the boy.

Alex shifted uncomfortably on the chair, taking up her cup, turning her focus to the steaming liquid. Catharine realized she'd brushed onto a sensitive subject.

Something had not gone well for Alex and her friend on the island. She'd mentioned earlier they'd had a disagreement—one that clearly played into her plans for San Francisco.

"Sorry, that's none of my business—"

"—no, no, nothing like that. I just don't know. Between his new job and my uncertain plans for the future, I hadn't considered it. I guess he probably won't."

"Well, whether he does or doesn't, my home is by the bay. I've been meaning to have a summer gathering with some of my friends, so if you, or you and Caleb—however that plays out for you—would like to join me, it's in the city but still a lovely area. A small gathering, nothing special."

She stopped talking, realizing she sounded like a fool. She didn't know why she couldn't just ask if Alex would want to visit. There was a part of her that feared her rejection; that she wouldn't want to see her again. That Catharine had misread her willingness of friendship. But she had to ask. She enjoyed her. Her company. Her intelligent conversation. It made her feel alive again. Made her realize she was missing so much more to her life than what she'd resigned herself to. She gave her a sense of hope—for what, she didn't even know—but for more than what she'd settled for.

"I sound like a dolt. I'm sure the last thing you have time for—"

"I'd love to see the Bay," Alex cut her off, saving her from the miserable awkwardness that was so unlike her. "I'm not sure of the itinerary with HEG, but if it isn't conflicting, I would love to see your home. I've really enjoyed this evening." She smiled, easing Catharine's discomfiture, and the burden of Carlton's call slowly dissipated from the night.

Chapter Twenty

Coming off a 4-0 win over the DC Capitol Tyrants, the locker room of the Rage was pumped and loud, both players and technical staff celebrating the additional three points that tied them in first place with Portland for the regular season. It would take an all out turn of terrible luck to strike them from postseason.

"Don't get complacent, ladies," the assistant coach, Melanie Wu, shouted above the din, picking her way through the high-fiving, laughing girls that were stripping down to hit the showers.

Melanie was a stringent, stoic, self-proclaimed realist who rarely celebrated, even when the scoreboard was deserving and the team was on fire.

"Oh, give it up, Mel," the head coach, Marty Bales, slapped the petite, sparrow-like woman on the back. "Smile for once. We're on track to win the Shield." The Shield—NWSL's coveted award that went to the team that finished with the most points before entering playoffs. Rage FC had won it three times over the years. A fourth win would be a league record.

"Unless—"

"Unless the apocalypse hits!" Erin Halsey hollered, her booming alto voice drowning out the protests from Wu, unapologetically. "Let loose a little, Coach," she tossed a discarded jersey in the woman's direction, aiming it just right to land on the frowning woman's head.

Several of the girls laughed as Melanie yanked it off, training her narrowed eyes to Erin, fuming at the indignation.

But no one paid her any mind and the celebration continued unabated.

In the corner of the room, Alex quickly stuffed her boots and gear into her locker and packed her duffel, pulling her hair back in a pony tail, still dripping from her rushed shower.

"What time is the flight?" Sawyer bent to pick up a dropped shin guard and tossed it into her friend's locker.

"Nine." She glanced at her watch. It was just after seven.

"Nothing like cutting it close," Sawyer said wryly, zipping up the bag while Alex tugged the heels of her Vans up after stuffing her feet into them, still tied.

"Did you call him?" Sawyer held the bag aloft, just out of Alex's reach.

"Seriously, girl—did you call him?"

"No." Alex reached a hand out. "I'm in a hurry, Abby."

"Oh, don't start that *Abby* shit with me." Sawyer gave her a pointed look, pulling the bag behind her back, ignoring Alex's grabs for the handle. Alex only ever called her Abby when she was annoyed. "Whip out that damn phone of yours and call him back, for God's sake."

"Look, don't—just don't! I'm late!"

"He's your best friend!"

"That's the point!" Alex hissed, finally managing to snag the denim bag, jerking it into her arms. She felt her eyes involuntarily well with tears, infuriating her even more. She was not about to cry in this locker room with her whole team in mid-celebration.

"Sugar, you gotta fix this." Sawyer set a gentle hand on Alex's arm, staying her. The sincerity in the low, midwestern tone Alex loved to tease her about was the final straw and she felt the first tear slip down her cheek.

"He wants something more than I have to give," she half whispered, half choked, hastily wiping the tears from her face and pulling a faded baseball cap onto her head.

She glanced up at Sawyer, who was uncharacteristically quiet. Even with the clamor of voices carrying across the room, the brief silence between them was deafening.

Caleb had returned from Puerto Rico a week earlier. They'd texted a couple times while he was gone— beachfront photos of the location where he was working and stupid sloth memes from Alex that had always been the long standing joke between them—but not more than that. She couldn't remember any other time when they hadn't talked every single day. The lack of communication was agonizing. She convinced herself they were both just busy. Nothing more than that.

But no matter what she'd convinced herself, she was still overwhelmingly relieved to find whatever tension had built up between them had diminished when she came to pick him up at the airport. He had morphed back into the good-natured, teasing boy he'd always been, regaling her with humorous anecdotes from his trip, and the adventures he'd found on his first out-of-country travel.

For a boy who'd once struggled with confidence and self-assurance, it was a relief to see him thriving under his newfound sense of responsibility, and the eagerness at which he was approaching his career. It was a good change for him. For *them*. Alex hoped it might turn his focus elsewhere; help alleviate the dependency he'd felt for her since they were children. Because she was certain that reliance was the root of their problem. He might feel like he wanted more from her than their friendship allowed, but Alex suspected with all of the changes in their lives, he was just afraid of losing her. Which was an unfounded fear—something that would never happen—he was the best friend and closest family she had ever known, but in the turmoil of their lives, something he'd forgotten. All he had to do to come to his senses was realize that would never change.

At least she hoped that was all it would take.

So, that night, when they'd stopped at one of their favorite beachside hangouts to grab an early dinner, Alex wasn't prepared for Caleb's sudden, sober and ardent declaration of love. Something he had hinted at a half dozen times before but never fully laid bare in earnest.

She sat across the plastic checkerboard tablecloth at their table for two on the patio and shook her head mechanically, her eyes fixed on the fading light of the horizon disappearing over the ocean.

"Don't do this, Caleb." Her voice shook through her breathless whisper, a tightness creeping into her chest she could not dispel. "Please don't do this. We've been through this."

"We haven't!" He reached across the table, taking hold of her arm with strong fingers, pressing fervently into the bones of her wrist when she tried to pull away. "Please, Alex, we haven't. Just look at me." He slid his grip down to capture her hand, gently entwining her fingers in his. "You can try and deny it all you want, but you know I love you—"

"Love me, yes! But you aren't *in love* with me, Caleb! You don't know what you are saying—"

"I do! I have been in love with you for as long as I have known you—"

"Caleb—"

"Please! Just hear me out." His voice was wavering, entreating. She relinquished her hand to his, unsure what else to do, but kept her eyes on the water. She couldn't bear to look at him for fear she would find he truly meant what he said, and it broke her heart.

"I know you think I'm just going through a phase—that I'm confused, desperate, whatever it was you said on the island. But you're wrong, A. You couldn't be more wrong." He squeezed her hand. "I've spent the last three weeks thinking about it, sorting out my feelings and everything I want in life. And I know now there is nothing I want more than you—"

"Caleb, please!" At that Alex did pull away, feeling smothered by the urgency in his touch.

"We are perfect for each other, Alex! We're good together—"

"And we will continue to be!" She had to take a deep breath to try and calm her voice, to blink away the tears that threatened to fall. "We will continue to be! But as friends—the friends we have always been!" She paused. She had to do something. Anything to fix this.

"I think I'm getting transferred to California," she blurted, knowing she had no actual confirmation of a trade, but not knowing what else she could say to deter him. "And—"

"It doesn't matter!" He wasn't swayed, though the glance she shot at him was enough to see the declaration had surprised him. With their lack of communication since Daufuskie, he knew nothing of the developments with HEG and the recently confirmed expansion team that was set to begin at the start of next season. But he had clearly scripted this conversation time and again and no matter what she threw at him wasn't going to be put off. "Markel has offices all over the country—the world! No matter what region they put me in, I can make my home base anywhere—"

"You can't keep following me across the country!" The words were out of her mouth before she had a chance to think about what she was saying— or tame the harshness they implied—and she immediately regretted them. But from the wounded expression on his face, she could tell she finally had his attention, and she was going to hold it for as long as necessary—until he understood. "You can't, Caleb. Both of us are at the prime of our professional lives. Neither of us know what will come next or where we will end up. The one thing I know for certain in this life is that you are the best friend I have. You are the one person I can count on, and we will always be there for each other, but I—"

"I want more than that, Alex! It's not enough!" He leaned his elbows on the table, staring at her in silence until she finally resigned to look at him, uncomfortable under the insistence of his unblinking gray eyes. "It's not enough." The words were barely audible, his breath coming in short heaves as he tried to fight away his own tears.

In all the years she had known him—in everything they had been through together—she had never seen him cry. And she didn't know what to do to stop it. An insurmountable weight was being forced on her shoulders, one she wasn't certain how to escape. The stability of her world was crashing down around her and she feared something was breaking that could not be fixed. No matter how hard she tried.

"I'm not in love with you, Caleb," she finally whispered. There was nothing left to say. "I'm sorry."

They stared at one another in silence while the world continued to turn on its axis, as if her whole life hadn't just imploded. The gulls sang out their greedy cries as they swooped low over the water, feathers silver in the last rays of sun setting over the sea, their song disrupted by the chatter from a nearby table between a waiter and tourist from out of town—all unheeding as the walls of Alex's neatly conscripted life went crumbling to dust. And in the aftermath, she watched as Caleb's eyes shifted from hurt, to anger, to despair.

"I won't give up on you, Alex." His voice was flat, dead, devoid of emotion. He stood, his face masked in the shadow from the flickering patio light behind him, and snatched his hat into his hand.

He didn't wait for Alex to beg him to stay and she made no effort to keep him from leaving. She only watched his broad shoulders—heavy with their own invisible weight of disappointment—disappear down the sidewalk before cutting across the street to the beach, where he set off down the sand, his head bent and hands stuffed in his pockets, staring at the ground ahead of him.

She knew she didn't need to wait for him by the car. He would find his own way home. She just prayed whatever damage had been done would be reparable. That somehow, some way, things could go back to the way they used to be—to the way they'd always been. But she knew deep down it would never be the same. There were words that could not be unsaid. Feelings that could not be mended.

In the week that had passed since their dinner, Caleb had finally tried to call her, several days earlier. Alex hadn't picked up the phone and he hadn't left a message.

Yesterday, she'd confided in Sawyer about all that had transgressed between them and her friend hadn't left her alone about it since. Sawyer knew all too well how important he was in Alex's life.

"He'll get over it." Sawyer finally concluded, her voice muddled between the thump of the bass echoing from inside the showers, several of the girls shouting out lyrics to Ice-T's *6 'N the Mornin'*. "But you have to call him. You have to reach out to him."

"Right now, I have to get to my plane." Alex felt defeated. It was more than a matter of getting over it. She slung her bag over her shoulder. "And focus on this trip." She forced herself to smile, reaching over the bench to hug her friend. "I'll call him," she promised, hugging her tightly. "Thank you."

"Don't come back here without that contract," Sawyer winked, letting the subject of Caleb go, and squeezed Alex's hand. "And don't let those Dark Ages white men scare you into anything less than you deserve! Now get, girl! You'll miss your flight!"

Chapter Twenty-One

A bitter northwesterly had whipped up along the coastline, spilling over the break wall and sending icy sprays of salty bay water onto the deck of Pier 39. The tourists had scattered to the safety of the pubs and eateries packed along Fisherman's Wharf, leaving only a few brave souls on the water facing side of the wooden pier, their jackets fastened snuggly around their ears, faces turned away from the sheet of mist that rolled over the railing.

Catharine paid them no attention. They were mostly marina workers and restaurant cooks who stepped outside for a smoke and breath of fresh air. None of them so much as cast a glance at the woman perched on the highest step of the wooden platform overlooking the bay. There were all sorts of oddities in the city—especially along the waterfront—an affluent woman dressed in Burberry and heels with windblown hair on the cusp of tears was the least peculiar of scenes that could be witnessed in the tourist district in the evenings.

Catharine was grateful for the anonymity. She had planned to get off the ferry and catch a cab straight to her home a few miles down the shoreline, but by the time the boat docked and she made her way to the landing it was all she could do to find the nearest quiet place and sit to collect herself for a moment. She didn't notice the wind or the ocean spray or the chill that crept into her bare fingers, despite the pair of cashmere gloves tucked, forgotten, inside her coat pocket.

She hadn't expected to find herself emotional. For forty-eight hours she'd been prepping for her meeting with Carlton. Prepping ever since he'd called to announce he was flying to the city.

California was her domain. That was their unspoken agreement. Daufuskie Island was his world and the City by the Bay hers. He traveled to San Francisco off and on, but never to their—*her*—city home. He preferred the quiet, secluded peninsulas across the bay, staying in Belvedere or Tiburon, claiming the sounds of the city and the chance of being recognized was too uncomfortable and risky. After all, he was an all-powerful senator from South Carolina, he liked to remind her.

On Wednesday, however, he'd called and announced that he would be flying in for a couple of days, and no, no need for her to make arrangements for him to stay in Belvedere, he would suffer through the Marina House so long as she had a driver arranged to pick him up at the private terminal. He hated traveling through the city.

But Catharine had declined.

They'd spoken a handful of times since his middle-of-the-night phone call in Portland and she'd told him several times they would need to sit and talk—she would fly back to Daufuskie before the end of the month so they could have a discussion in person—but he'd shown little interest.

Which made the sudden trip to California unexpected. And inconvenient.

"I'm having a gathering Saturday for some of my city friends. They aren't people you enjoy." She was sharp and unapologetic. He didn't like any of her friends, so the declaration was unsurprising.

"Cancel it, Catharine. My plans are set."

"Fabrice DuPont has flown in from Paris and is staying with me with one of his assistants," she said flatly, knowing well that Carlton detested the Frenchman. He was disgusted by his flamboyant, arrogant expression and extravagant demeanor. Fabrice was an artist, famous for his abstract portraits of many of the royal families that commissioned him for his eccentric, visionary talents.

His "assistants" were always young, blonde, slightly built university-age boys from whatever country Fabrice had most recently freelanced. Often, he traveled with more than one.

The Frenchman wasn't actually staying with Catharine, though he had on many previous occasions, so Carlton had no reason to suspect otherwise. The artist was in town, and likely to come to tea, but he and his latest companion had arrangements across the city where Fabrice was working on a mural for the mayor of San Francisco. But Carlton didn't need to know that.

"I don't know how you can tolerate that abomination in our house! It looks bad, you associating with those kinds of people—"

"I can meet you in Sausalito on Friday afternoon," Catharine cut in, offering a compromise. "At The Spinnaker. Four p.m."

Two days later she'd waited impatiently at a seaside table overlooking the bay, watching the minutes tick closer to five-thirty.

He was always late, and Catharine knew to expect him to arrive on his own time, with no concern for the people he constantly left waiting, but today she was more aggravated by his insolent dilatoriness than usual. She was painfully punctual—always fifteen minutes early—and known to expect her staff to be seated and settled for meetings no less than three minutes prior to the start time. She'd ended business partnerships and fired high level executives for being minutes tardy. She found it intolerable. Insulting. One of the few things she had carried over from her father. Punctuality and accountability were everything. And she always suspected Carlton's remiss tardiness, especially toward her, was intentional. It was his way to exert power over people. Waste their time. One of his favorite "tactics," as he liked to call them.

On another day she might have left. She didn't like to be toyed with. But today she couldn't. This afternoon could not be put off. It was time.

At a quarter to six he finally sauntered to the table, an Old Fashioned clutched in one hand and a half smoked cigar in the other.

"I ran into a fellow from McLean at the bar," he said in way of greeting, kicking back the wooden chair and setting down with a heavy sigh, a bit of the brown bourbon sloshing over the rim onto the white linen tablecloth. "Lives next door to Gingrich. Said the country club annuals were—"

"I want a divorce, Carlton."

"—on the rise." He finished his sentence, the last words tapering off slowly. "I'm sorry?" He raised his coarse, graying eyebrows in interest, the heavily wrinkled creases between his eyes drawn up in moderate consternation. "What did you say?" His thick Southern drawl was moving toward the verge of vexation.

"A divorce," Catharine repeated evenly, steeling herself to keep the waver out of her voice, "I want one."

Of all the reactions Catharine had prepared herself for from her husband, the one she hadn't planned on was his sudden, loud, bellowing laughter. It was the kind of laughter that turned all the heads in the room, a deep, booming sound that shook his belly and jowls until tears ran from the corner of his red rimmed eyes.

"Oh, my dear," he said between breaths of a guffaw, slapping his fleshy hand on the table, almost upsetting his low ball glass and its contents. The thick gold university ring from Blue Hose clicked gratingly on the tabletop as he patted the white linen in amusement. "I thought for a minute—" His voice trailed off as he continued his laughter and wiped his ruddy, streaming cheeks with the back of his hand. "Oh, my." He coughed, trying to catch his breath, and finally took a sip of his bourbon.

A hint of composure returned, his eyes moist from his hysterics, he turned his dark gaze to her and smiled a smile that sent a chill icing its way down her back. "I thought for a minute you said you wanted a divorce." He chuckled once more and took another sip of his cocktail. "But then I thought to myself—my wife is a sensible, intelligent woman. She could never make such an—*unfortunate*—decision."

Now they traversed into the territory Catharine had prepared for. His thinly veiled threats she anticipated.

All around the dining area heads had turned in their direction, but she nor Carlton paid them any mind. They were in a stand-off—and this was one Catharine intended to win.

"Enough theatrics, Carlton," she said coolly, her poised hands steepled on the table in front of her. "Do not pretend this has come unforeseen. We have been on this path for many years. Until now we have just avoided the unpleasantry."

"Unpleasantry?" His voice was low and scathing, his dark eyes beginning to smolder deep in the thickness of his brow. "*Unpleasantry?* Let me tell you this, you little twit," he hissed, his knuckles turning ghostly white on the table in front of him, his breath coming in ragged, sputtering gasps, "if you think for one moment that you will waltz in here—that you will come in here and treat me like one of your business puppets—like a discarded bit of refuse... I promise you, you do not yet know the meaning of the word *unpleasantry!*"

"Carlton," Catharine started quietly, empathetically, trying to diffuse his anger, "it is not a business deal. But it is a bad arrangement. One we have both been unhappy in, and—"

"Unhappy?!" The word thundered across the room and the eyes shot back to their table, which this time he noticed. "Unhappy?" He dropped to a searing whisper as he leaned forward in his seat, his mottled, sweating face inches from hers, lips trembling and pulse pounding at his temples. "If you think for one iota of a second that I give a fuck about your happiness you are more dimwitted than I ever imagined possible." He sat back hard against the chair, almost tipping over backward, but regaining his balance at the last moment. "This conversation is over." He went to stand and reconsidered, taking up his glass and downing the contents in one swallow. "You go on to your little tea party, Catharine," a menacing smile turned up the corners of his mouth as his eyes hooked onto hers, blazing despite his pseudo-amicable tone. "Have your friends, have your fun, and then take a day to regain your senses. And then we'll pretend this conversation never happened. Because I promise you," again he leaned forward, his acidic breath hot in her face as the diabolical smile spread across his mouth, the sting of the liquor blushing his forehead, "whoever—whatever—put this idea into your hollow head... it isn't worth it. Nothing is worth it." His voice was barely audible. "I will destroy you, you little bitch." He continued to smile, his gaze never leaving hers, his voice even and words staccato. "I will destroy everything about you. Your life. Your business. Your friends. Everything!" He chuckled, returning to rest against the back of his chair, his composure morphing into a mask of tranquility. "You just think on that, my dear. Because you know I am a man of my word." He winked and lifted his empty glass in a mocking toast.

Catharine could feel the years of pent-up rage boiling inside of her, the aggravation and degradation and humiliation she had suffered at his hands, all while continuing to live up to her promises as a wife and partner—both in business and in marriage. She had given him so much of her—everything he had asked for—and he had taken it all, offering nothing in return. She had made him, while all he had ever done was try and tear her down.

It didn't matter that he didn't love her. They had never loved one another. She had never imagined they would. But it was the lack of respect, the endless belittling and bullying and utter disregard for her as a human being that she could not—would not—tolerate for a single moment longer.

As a businesswoman and negotiator, she knew she should leave the conversation where it was. It would be best to let him depart and consider the situation. Then, in a couple weeks have her attorney write up a fair and honest offer that she would present to him when his temper had time to cool and he was able to think more clearly about the inevitable deliberations on the horizon. The request for a divorce could not have caught him as off-guard as he presented. He had to have seen the writing on the wall. The end of a contract. Nothing less, nothing more.

But Catharine didn't feel like negotiating. She was tired of him berating her and expecting her to just walk away, giving him time to settle down, to pretend it never happened. All the insults, the name-calling, and deprecating remarks he used to boost his own pathetic, fragile ego. She was finished.

She stood from the table, gathering her coat and hat as he sat back in his chair, smirking as if he'd won. He was about to signal to the waiter to bring him another bourbon when Catharine stepped forward and swung her arm across the distance between them, connecting the back of her hand hard against his corpulent, simpering mouth.

"Go to hell," she hissed between clenched teeth, watching his smug expression change from disbelief and shock to blinding white rage. She had no doubt had they not been in a public setting he would have leapt to his feet and strangled her then and there.

Not waiting for him to react, she quickly strode from the restaurant and hurried to the boarding dock where they were making a last call for the ferry.

A half hour later, back on the mainland, she sat on top of the platform built for tourists to catch a better look at the sea lions, and glanced at her watch. It was 7:19.

She would give herself until 7:30 to collect her emotions. She'd battled off the tears of fury that had arisen on the ferry, and sat dry-eyed in the harsh evening wind with the sting of the cold settling into her cheeks and fingertips, chapping her lips and making her nose run. She was a mess. And she would allow it for eleven more minutes.

Eleven more minutes to process the evening, to process the last twenty-two years, and then she had to push it aside. File it away. Leave it behind and let it go.

Tonight she had business to attend and a gathering to arrange for the following day.

Chapter Twenty-Two

Contrary to popular belief, San Francisco's Marina District didn't boast the most extravagant homes in the city. That honor was reserved for Pacific Heights—several blocks up the hill—where the lavish locality was home to *Billionaire's Row*, a street featuring thirty-million dollar mansions and brimming with the Who's Who in the Tech Industry.

But the Marina District held the indisputable upper hand when it came to location. A stone's throw from the water. Stylish. Historic. Home to a great many successful artists and high-class business professionals: doctors, lawyers, CEOs, painters, photographers, and authors.

Catharine had looked at homes in Pacific Heights. It was a gorgeous area, set high on the tallest of San Francisco's hills, offering breathtaking views of both the city and the bay. The homes were mostly ostentatious—huge 15,000-square-foot Tudor mansions, unique Italianate masterpieces, Beaux-Arts architecture, flamboyant Queen Anne Victorian works of art, Gothic Revival estates fully equipped with parapets and pinnacles and battlements. Every type of architectural design one could dream of… it had been done, without factor of expense.

But none had suited her fundamental requirement: she wanted to be *on* the water. Not just enjoying a view of it. And, having grown up in the center of London, her home needed to be in the city. The towns across the bay were too remote. Too quiet.

The Marina District was quaint and the houses on Marina Boulevard unique and gorgeous and original, but most importantly, they were feet from the sea, adjacent from Yacht Harbor, where Catharine could berth L'lune Alouette, her beautifully restored classic wooden ketch she'd purchased two years earlier for her fortieth birthday.

It may not have been the most prestigious neighborhood in the city, but Catharine's waterfront home was unquestionably the most magnificent in the district.

When Alex arrived in front of the three-story, coastal modern residence sitting luxuriously on a corner lot across from the harbor, its forward-facing facade bathed in rich sunlight that was beginning to cast long shadows across the wide glass staircase leading to the second story entrance, she almost turned around. The home was built with floor-to-ceiling walls of glass overlooking the bay—mirrored by views of the Golden Gate Bridge and Alcatraz—and accented with a palette curated with natural materials of wood, artisan glass, and hand-textured stone. A warmth of light spilled out through the open windows, carrying with it the deep, resonating notes of a cello, before fading into the surrounding sounds of the late afternoon.

It was the illuminance of the stunning beauty of a lifestyle Alex knew nothing about. One she wasn't certain she should dare to invade.

Her own parents had been well-off. As a prosperous, world renowned architect, her father had provided them a comfortable, want-for-nothing lifestyle, but it had ended so quickly, with Alex at such a young age, she could hardly remember it now. And even the things she could recall had been nothing like this. She knew the senator and his wife were affluent—an understatement—based off their island mansion and Catharine's extravagant taste she'd been given a glimpse of in Portland, but she'd somehow attributed that in connection to the standards of the political elite.

This was something different all together.

There was something mesmerizing about the beauty of the home, with its proximity to the bay and doubtless iconic views it garnered from the height of its rooftop patio, or the balconies of glass jutting from each lavishly designed floor. It was a showcase of sophistication, a paragon of perfection.

Alex didn't belong here.

She belonged across the street, along the San Francisco Bay Trail, where a steady stream of runners were breezing along the dirt path, headphones on, eyes trained forward, oblivious to the opulence of the neighborhood around them, lost in the exhilaration of the run, high on adrenaline and the flood of endorphins.

She stepped off the staircase and onto the sidewalk, looking up again at the gleaming reflection of the bay off the sleek walls, the glow of light pouring onto the balconies from the open sliders, allowing the gentle notes of the cello to float down to the street level.

She would have left, jogged across the street and disappeared into the anonymity of tourists and locals that had come out to enjoy the warmth of the late afternoon sun along the water, but a voice from the rooftop called her name, halting her in her tracks.

It was a cheery voice, almost sing-song, and one Alex did not recognize.

"Up here!" It came again and Alex found a dark-haired, round-faced woman—of similar age to herself—leaning over the glass balcony, smiling. "I'm assuming you're Alex," she trilled, her elbows propped on the railing. "I've been on the lookout for you."

Alex froze in place at the strange statement. She hadn't expected anyone to be watching for her.

"Yes," she managed an acknowledgement, nodding stiffly. There was no escaping now.

"Well, come on up, the door is open!" The young woman disappeared from view.

Alex hesitated on the steps, fighting the urge to sneak away, but found her feet forcing their way up the glass staircase against her will.

Before she could step across the threshold the woman from the balcony was there, silhouetted by the light of the door.

"Catharine's been expecting you!" she said by way of greeting, stepping aside to make room for Alex to enter. "I think she may have given up on you. She'll be thrilled you're here."

She wasn't much taller than Alex. Black, curly hair bounced freely in ringlets just above her slender shoulders, and flawless olive skin complimented her dark features. Her face was round, like a cherub, and she reminded Alex of one of the porcelain dolls her aunt kept in her curio cabinet: beautiful, exotic, with brightly painted lips and green eye shadow that made the dark eyes dance with light. But unlike the dolls, this young woman had a warmth that was palpable. Alex instantly liked her.

"I'm Juliet." She stretched out a hand, revealing strong fingers and a muscular forearm that Alex typically only found common in fellow athletes. "Juliet Sweeney. My friends call me Jules."

"Alex Grey." She shook the hand, lifting her eyes to the entry around them. To the left there was a floating staircase leading to the floor above where a mixture of voices were interspersed with laughter, accompanied by the opening notes of *Viva la Vida* resonating from the cello.

The home was lavish, but contrary to the manor in Carolina, it offered a welcoming atmosphere, designed with a free flowing interior that drew the eye seamlessly from one room to the next, providing the ideal environment for entertainment.

"I hear you are an athlete," Jules motioned for Alex to follow her up the suspended staircase in the direction of the muffled voices. "A football player?"

"Yes."

The staircase let off into a posh living room, exquisitely furnished in cream. The furthest wall was made of transparent doors that were slid open to reveal a sprawling deck overlooking the backyard, and adjacent to it, down an open frame hall, there was another living area and a wall of glass that let out onto a balcony overlooking the bay. There was a biophilic style to the architecture Alex had not seen before, melding the modern continuity of the interior with the beauty of the natural elements of the bay. It was something her father would have loved.

To the left of the staircase a young man sat atop a wooden stool, a beautifully varnished cello cradled between his legs, his head bent and eyes shut while his fingers and bow deftly drew out the Coldplay classic in a manner that gave it a life of its own. Several people sat on nearby settees, enraptured by the melody of the musician, while another small group stood near one of the sliding windows at the opposite end, sipping drinks and chatting quietly, so as not to disturb the music.

Catharine was not in the room.

"Can I get you a drink? Or call for tea?" Jules stopped at an ornate cart filled with a dozen bottles of various scotches, brandies, and wine.

Alex thought about the manilla folder tucked into her shoulder bag containing the contract she was supposed to sign and return by Monday to HEG. There were dozens of dos and don'ts outlined throughout the agreement, ranging from termination upon indictment of criminal charges, to the lesser ramifications of suspension for being photographed or videoed drinking in public. It was no secret that Samson Hargrove was a recovered alcoholic, and the company's no-drinking clause was infamous amongst its endorsed athletes.

Since she'd never been much of a drinker, the clause hadn't initially fazed her, but it suddenly seemed tedious and restrictive. She'd never hesitated to sip a glass of wine before, especially at a dinner party.

"Seltzer and lime would be great," she gestured toward the bottle of sparkling water on the cart.

"My drink of choice, too," said Jules with a laugh, using the silver tongs to pluck a few ice cubes into a crystal glass. "I'm a dancer. Whenever we are on tour or within a few weeks of a performance I lay off the alcohol all together."

A dancer. That made sense as to the woman's strong, graceful physique.

"Where do you dance?"

"I'm currently on tour with the Melbourne Repertory. We're on a two-week break before we start up in Canada for an autumn campaign. But I'll be back in December with the San Francisco Dance Company. That's my real home."

Behind them the cellist brought his piece to an end and there was soft, polite clapping from the captivated audience.

"Truly brilliant, Lukas!" A high tenor cooed, and Alex turned to see a bald, very thin, hawk-like man dressed all in black clapping his gloved hands vigorously. "You have the most remarkable way of turning even the tritest of tunes into absolute masterpieces! Perhaps you will indulge us with an original off your latest album?"

"Fabrice DuPont," Jules tilted her chin toward the man in black, handing Alex her seltzer. "Artist to the elite," she mocked in an exaggerated French accent, winking one of her umber eyes. "Over there is his *assistant*," she flitted a finger in the direction of a slightly built blonde boy standing alone by the window, aimlessly staring out over the bay. "Sven, I think. Or Severo. Something like that. They never last long and he has a new one with him every time I see him."

Alex laughed, not sure what to do with the information. "And the cellist?" she asked, watching the black-haired, soberly handsome musician smile politely at Fabrice, who continued to shower him with praise.

"Lukas Krajnc. Named this year's most influential European musician under the age of thirty." She chewed her bottom lip, her eyes alight with the flickering flame of the wall mounted fireplace encased in glass behind her. "Have you ever seen a more beautiful person?" Alex didn't have time to respond before Jules continued. "From Slovenia. A friend of Victoria Woodrow." She indicated a young, withdrawn, sulking girl sitting back against the settee nearest the musician, scowling. "Well, I should really say a friend of her father's, Richard Woodrow." She paused, waiting to see if the name was familiar to Alex, and when she could see it wasn't, resumed, "Real estate mogul from Australia. Think Forbes 500 from Down Under. A good friend of Catharine's. Victoria is a real ass. She brought Lukas here as her date—ironic, really, because he can't seem to stand her much more than anyone else, he's just too polite to say so. And," she added sotto voce, "they aren't exactly one another's type." Jules smirked to indicate some kind of joke Alex didn't catch and proceeded, "Lukas has hardly taken his eyes off Fabrice's little blonde friend all night long. But then, Victoria's only criteria in a lover is at least seven digits in their bank account—so Lukas doesn't really fit the bill, anyhow. She'd screw a dog if it came with a title and inheritance. Last year her father got tired of her antics and cut her allowance down to a maximum of one wrecked Maserati a month and only half a penthouse. So, now she's practically desolate and heavy on the search for someone who won't treat her so unfairly." She rolled her eyes. "She certainly won't find that on a musician's salary, no matter how highly rated. But type or not, Victoria can't handle not being the center of attention, and Lukas hasn't given her the time of day since they arrived. She only brought him to impress Catharine, no doubt, but still, she can't stand the fact that he's not taken his eyes off the Swede all evening." The dancer made a little tsk tsk sound between her teeth and leaned in closer to Alex. "All this simply to say—*beware*—because Victoria is a nightmare when she's in a good mood, so you can imagine the tempest brewing in her rage. There will be a scene before the night is over; mark my words."

Alex tried to process all the information and remember the names, but it was futile. Everyone seemed so foreign and unique and extraordinary.

But she was grateful for Jules and her friendly chatter. It made her feel less awkward and alone in the room.

"And Mrs. Cleveland?" Alex asked, seeing no sign of the woman who suddenly felt like a complete stranger. Surrounded by Catharine's friends and in her home, she was reminded how little she actually knew the senator's wife. The hostess she met tonight would undoubtedly be nothing like the woman she'd spent a fun, casual evening with in Portland just a couple weeks prior. This was not a sports bar, and these people were not her loud, comforting, boisterous squad. Exotic dancers, famous painters, musicians, and old, old money. No, this was very different than Portland.

"She's bidding Nathalie adieu. She was supposed to stay on for the weekend but got called to Bordeaux unexpectedly. Too bad, really. Nathalie is my favorite. She's one of us." Jules glanced up to clarify. "Normal. *Mortal*. Knows what it takes to make rent, you know?" She gave an arch lift to her brow.

"Ah, yes," Alex couldn't help but smile. "Yes, I certainly do know."

"She's an actress. Classical. Shakespeare. Ibsen. Chekhov. She and Catharine went to Oxford together many years ago."

Alex heard her named called from across the room and turned to find Catharine standing at the bottom of the floating glass stairway that led to the floor above.

"You came!" Her expression was lit with genuine delight.

Alex watched her cross the floor, her eyes drawn to the silken red scarf tied loosely about her neck, sharply contrasting her white, high-waisted boiler suit and matching heels. Her hair was down around her shoulders and longer than Alex remembered it. She was reminiscent of one of the glamorous Hollywood film stars of the 1930s. Katharine Hepburn. Vivien Leigh. Greta Garbo.

How she could manage to look so formal while simultaneously maintaining an immense measure of unaffected ease, it was hard to understand. It was in the lightheartedness of her smile, the fluidity of her gait.

Momentarily Alex forgot about Jules and the cellist and the brooding girl on the sofa. She forgot about the party and the discomfiture she felt in the grand townhouse surrounded by art worth more than every collective penny she'd earned in her lifetime. And she forgot about the manilla envelope stuffed in her purse with the contract to sign by Monday.

She was once again as transfixed by the beautiful wife of Senator Cleveland as she had been that day on Daufuskie Island. How such a misfortunate event—what seemed a lifetime ago—led to the afternoon in the manor garden and the evening at D'Laney's and the small hours of the morning in The Nines hotel where she'd begun to see a glimpse of a woman she had never expected to get to know. A woman she doubted many in Catharine

Cleveland's life ever saw: a fascinating, brilliant, genuine woman who had built an admirable facade to hide a vulnerability at her core.

Alex thought of how the senator had treated her the night of Catharine's accident, worried only for himself and his reputation, and again how he'd berated and belittled her on the phone in Portland, a call that had quickly sobered the evening they'd enjoyed.

But here, in this townhouse, in this company and this setting, she didn't remotely resemble the woman she had met on a dreary, constraining island in a home that lacked warmth and life and vivacity. This woman was radiant, relaxed, entirely herself. She was the complete version of the woman she'd caught glimpses of in Portland. Happy and at ease.

She still maintained the air of gracious hostess, but it was genuine and lacked the affectedness she hid behind in her husband's domineering presence.

"I had given up on you." She leaned in to kiss both of Alex's cheeks in greeting. "I am so pleased you came!"

Alex awkwardly held her seltzer aside to receive the Englishwoman's welcome, acutely aware of the quieting of the room and the eyes that turned in their direction. On her own, she'd made no impression to those in attendance—but Catharine was the kind of woman who drew the attention of a room as a moth was drawn to flame. They all looked now to see who it was their enchanting hostess was greeting.

"I see you've met Jules," Catharine continued, oblivious to the eyes she'd attracted, setting an affectionate hand on the shoulder of the dancer. "She is about to leave us for the autumn."

"The misery of a Canadian fall," Jules laughed, crossing her arms across her chest to ward off the charade of a chill. "I'll be jealous of you all in California long before winter rolls around."

"I've helped coach a few youth camps during winter off-season in Canada," Alex offered sympathetically, "I don't envy you one bit."

"As long as the Canadian dollars are easily exchanged to US currency— I'm happy to welcome the chill," she smiled, tossing her head in a way that made the dark ringlets around her face bounce to-and-fro. She was easy to picture center stage, on pointe, a spotlight warming her bronzed complexion and highlighting her lustrous eyes. Everything about her was suited for performance.

Jules's gaze flicked passed Catharine and her mouth turned to a wry smile, her finely shaped eyebrows arching in amusement as she nodded behind them. "Incoming."

Across the room, the girl—Victoria—had risen from the sofa and was strutting toward them, her sharp features clouded in annoyance.

"Catharine," she called, forcing a smile onto her thin, plum painted lips, "surely you will introduce the rest of us to your new friend." She glided up to them, extending a hand toward Alex, which she withdrew as though having been burnt when Alex went to shake it. Apparently a handshake was not the fashionable greeting she had been looking for—just the brush of fingertips.

"Victoria Woodrow," she didn't wait for an introduction, "I'm assuming you're the college athlete—tennis? Volleyball? Sorry, athletics aren't my thing."

It didn't take Jules's earlier warning to realize there was a vileness behind the smile that surely fooled no one.

"Football—" Catharine began to interject.

"Football?" Victoria gave a derisive laugh, "I didn't even know that was a thing for women... how quaint—"

"Soccer, *Victoria*," Jules seethed between clenched teeth, clearly tired of the game and the girl. "Alex plays *professional* soccer in South Carolina."

"Oh, of course," the thin lips simpered, her jade eyes devoid of a smile, "how silly of me. *Soccer*. I'd no clue that was a professional sport. How nice that you could join us, Alexandra. Better late than never, isn't that what they say?"

Alex didn't bother correcting her on her name, nor did she show any indication of annoyance, unwilling to give the girl that satisfaction. Instead, she smiled. "There are indeed women who play American football, but they are far tougher than I."

"I doubt that very much," Catharine took Alex's elbow, plainly accustomed to the petty, churlish behavior from the young woman and choosing to ignore it. "Victoria, be a dear and have Grace bring a fresh kettle. This one has surely gone cold."

She steered Alex away, leaving Victoria smoldering at the request of such a menial task. But the girl clearly knew her limits and petulantly complied.

"She's a spoilt brat, but harmless, really. Come, let me introduce you to the others."

After the rounds were made, Catharine received a call she couldn't put off, but Alex assured her she was fine on her own.

The other guests were all affable, if not a bit odd, but welcoming all the same. It was the painter, Fabrice DuPont, who took the most interest in her. The eccentric, hollow-cheeked artist was fascinated by her career and had dozens of questions regarding the American league versus the women's side in France. He was a fan of Olympique Lyonnais Féminin and knew the game surprisingly well. He inquired about the national team and if she desired to play for her country.

Alex assured him that was the ultimate goal for every professional player, but one that was hard fought in a highly competitive atmosphere.

"There is nothing in this life worth having if it is not hard won, mademoiselle," he displayed a row of tightly packed teeth, reminiscent of a fox, suiting his angular face and dark, unblinking eyes. But there was passion to his heavily accented English, and despite his otherwise stoic countenance he had a kindliness hidden beneath his eccentricities. Alex could see why Catharine enjoyed him. Even his young, reticent companion, Sven, did his best to include Alex in the conversation, though his English was limited and they were all disappointed to learn Alex did not speak French—the apparent common language amongst them.

Victoria returned to catch the end of the conversation and did not miss the opportunity to point out the inadequacy of Alex's monolingualism.

"Funny, is it not, how Americans place so little value on language? I mean, nearly every educated citizen in Australia speaks two languages; most more than that."

Jules poked her head in from the balcony where she'd been taking a photo of the sunset behind the Golden Gate. "I don't know what *educated* circles you've ever actually familiarized yourself with in Australia, but I assure you, bilingualism is no more a thing in Oz than it is in the States."

"I'm Australian," Victoria snapped. "I think I would know."

"One would think." Jules rolled her eyes. "When was the last time you were there for more than a few days on holiday?"

"That's irrelevant."

"I've done seven tours with the Melbourne Repertory. I know a little something about the Australian elite." She slipped her phone in her pocket, giving up on the sunset, and stepped into the brightly lit room, unwilling to miss the chance to spar with the haughty socialite. "Besides—isn't your mother American?"

Victoria bristled. "Yes, but she met my father on holiday in Bristol—"

"Oh, that practically makes her Bristolian," Jules drawled out dramatically, sliding onto the couch where Alex was sitting with Fabrice. "And how many languages does she speak?" She turned her oval eyes to the arrogant young woman in feigned anticipation.

Alex smothered a smile, amused at Jules's boldness and unabashed repartee. She would usually have been shocked by the onslaught of belittling remarks from this girl she didn't even know, but Victoria was so over-the-top hostile—to such a ridiculous extent—she couldn't help but find it amusing.

Victoria's pale green eyes flashed between Alex and Jules before settling back on the dancer. "My mother is a *very* accomplished woman," she spat dumbly, clearly lacking a defense. "She may not be as well versed in language as some, but she is far more cultured and educated than the average American, and—"

"And that still makes *her* unilingual and *your* point moot," Jules brushed her off with a flippant gesture of her expressive fingers, turning dismissively toward Alex to reengage in conversation, but the pompous debutante would not be put off.

"Do tell us, Miss Sweeney, just how many languages do you speak? Undoubtedly your New York education puts the rest of us to shame?" She smirked, certain of her upper hand.

"Four." Jules didn't bother to look back at Victoria, who was still standing front and center in the room, her hands perched firmly on the place her hips should have been had she any curve to her sparse frame. "And I was educated in Italy, where I was born. I didn't move to New York until I attended Julliard when I was sixteen."

"What languages do you speak?" Alex asked, impressed, hoping to steer the conversation in a different direction.

"Italian is my first language. And then of course English and French."
She paused lengthily, her back still turned to Victoria, but a small smile
played at her lips. She was baiting. Waiting.

And like the fool she was, Victoria fell straight into her trap.

"That's three," she practically snickered, looking around at Fabrice to try
and engage him in the quarrel, but he was uninterested with her rant and
never lifted his eyes from where he had busied himself in a sketchbook he'd
pulled from his blazer. "Pray tell us, what is the fourth language, Juliet?"

Pausing for effect, Jules turned back toward Victoria and smiled loftily
before calling across the room to Lukas, who was meticulously tuning his
cello while immersed in conversation with Sven.

"Lukas—ali nam boš zaigral še eno pesem?"

The musician looked up in surprise, a brilliant smile crossing his handsome face. "Govorite slovensko, gospodična?"

Jules cast a sidelong glance at Victoria, aware she had struck the chord
she was aiming for, and rose from the couch with a curtsy, pirouetting
playfully about on her toes before trotting across the hardwood floor toward
the Slovenian. "Play us another song, will you?" she repeated, this time in
English. "Something we can dance to?"

The cellist gallantly took the hand she offered, pressing it to his lips and
bowed his head in acquiescence. "What shall I play, Miss Sweeney?"

Alex watched the proceedings from the comfort of the couch, waiting for
Victoria's head to explode. The entire evening the girl had been desperate to
try and garner the attention of Lukas or Catharine or even Fabrice, but here
she was again, the most disregarded person in the room—a foolish child,
scolded and forgotten.

Alex almost felt sorry for her—she was brimming with tears of frustration—but the angry blush and thin-lipped scowl that crossed her otherwise
attractive face was all too telling of the ugliness of her character. There was
no sympathy to be had. She glared in Juliet's direction before leaving the
room in a huff, but no one else noticed.

"Do you know any Cole Porter?"

Alex's gaze lifted off the retreating form of the storming socialite and
found Catharine's silhouette in the shadow of the balcony. How long she'd
been there, Alex wasn't sure, but from the amused smile touching her lips
she gathered she'd heard most of the exchange between Jules and Victoria.

"Madam?" Lukas tilted his bow toward Catharine as she moved into the light of the room. "What song should you like to hear?"

Jules clapped her hands in delight. "Oh, yes! What about *Let's Misbehave*? Something we can dance to!"

"On cello?" Catharine laughed and looked to Lukas. "Mr. Krajnc?"

"For you, Gospa, anything!" The Slovenian grinned with a boyish charm, his stubbled cheeks displaying two perfectly placed dimples only adding to his indisputable attractiveness.

"Dance with me, Catharine!" Jules caught hold of her white sleeve before she could pull away, laughing.

"No, Juliet, absolutely not!"

Alex watched as Jules cajoled Catharine to dance with her, not taking no for an answer. She was relentless in her persistence, and by the time Lukas's masterfully delicate hands started the intro to the 1920s classic, both women were laughing and swirling around the floor in an improv swing step to the rich melody the talented musician brought to life.

It was no surprise to find Catharine was a graceful dancer, easily following Jules's lead as they laughed their way through the impromptu choreography. There was a radiance that exuded from her in the comfort of her home, amidst the solace of her friends. In the moment she seemed as young and carefree as her dancing partner, shedding off the burden of the rigid businesswoman, the politician's wife.

"You missed your calling, Mrs. Cleveland," Jules teased merrily as the song came to a close, bowing in deference to Catharine.

As Lukas drew out the ending notes of the coda, Alex realized Jules was going to begin looking for a new partner to persuade onto the floor, so in the brief moments the dancer was negotiating the next tune with Lukas, she quickly excused herself from Fabrice and slipped out to the balcony.

The sun had sunk below the level of the horizon, leaving behind the brushstroke of a crimson glow that painted the darkening sky. In the distance, the Golden Gate Bridge was swathed in the pastel of an orange hue, the magnificent red towers enveloped in shadow. The air was cool and laden with mist that settled in crystal droplets along the glass railing, pulling in the last flecks of light through the filter of a thousand tiny kaleidoscopes.

Alex ran her fingers through the dew, drawing out a meaningless serpentine as she breathed in the peace of the empty terrace.

Behind her, through the lambent light of the living room, she could hear Fabrice and Sven bidding farewell to Catharine, promising to visit before they returned to Paris. She knew she should step inside and say goodbye—it would be the polite thing to do—but she couldn't bring herself to leave the privacy of the balcony and revitalizing feeling of having a few moments to herself.

As the glow over the water disappeared, an inky darkness taking its place, the notes of the cello faded, replaced by the indistinguishable murmur of Jules and Lukas speaking blithely in the musician's native language. With the threat of being asked to dance over, Alex drew in one last breath of the Pacific Ocean air, and prepared herself to return to the dwindling party, but stopped short when she found Catharine standing in the doorway, watching her.

"I didn't mean to startle you," Catharine's lips turned in an apologetic smile, a hint of embarrassment at her intrusion. "You looked so peaceful, I didn't want to interrupt your thoughts."

"Oh, no interruption," Alex assured her, glancing toward the bay. "I was just taking in the view. It's truly remarkable."

Catharine smiled. "I've had the pleasure of witnessing the sun set on six continents, in more countries than I can even remember, and I will say that none can hold a candle to the sunsets along the coast of California." She stepped beside Alex, setting her hands on the railing, and leaned forward, closing her eyes and inhaling a deep breath of sea air.

Alex snuck a sidelong glance at Catharine, studying the serenity of her elegant face as the gentle breeze from the bay lifted the hair around her shoulders. She thought about what Jules had said earlier when she'd first pointed out Lukas.

Have you ever seen a more beautiful person?

She'd not given her an answer—the question had been rhetorical—but as Alex watched Catharine on the balcony, she knew her own answer was simple: yes. Because Catharine Cleveland was unequivocally the most beautiful person she'd ever seen. There was no denying it. And she knew, somewhere in the back of her mind, that it was absolutely ridiculous to be so taken with the woman—but she couldn't help it. There was something about her that Alex was inexplicably drawn to. She could hardly admit to herself that she'd waited all evening to find a moment alone with her, away from the other guests who all seemed to seek the same attention from the charming woman. It was embarrassing. She felt like she had a schoolgirl crush—the same silly way she (and half her teammates) had crushed on her middle school soccer coach who'd looked like Kate Beckinsale but kicked like Mia Hamm. But this was different. She wasn't a child anymore. Yet at the same time, she didn't care. It was harmless. And perhaps it wasn't so different from middle school after all. Catharine was no ordinary woman—wealthy, powerful, brimming with sophistication and unparalleled beauty. It was natural for Alex to find her enchanting. No doubt as did Jules and Victoria.

Only Alex knew it wasn't Catharine's fortune or elevated social stature or prominent political husband that caught her attention. It was so much more than that. It was her refreshingly intelligent conversation, her uniquely cultured outlook on life, her surprisingly empathetic view of society. She was different than anyone she'd ever met.

Catharine opened her eyes and Alex swiftly averted her gaze to the darkening backdrop of the bay, where the silhouetted sailboats swayed, docked inside the marina.

"I'm assuming the seventh would be Antarctica?" She said, trying to fill the silence that fell between them.

Catharine looked up, puzzled at the question, then laughed. "Ah, yes. Unfortunately the only time I have been to Antarctica was during the short period where the sun did not rise at all."

"I can't imagine having seen so much of the world. It must be magnificent."

"The benefit, I suppose, of a career born in shipping. I can name every major port between here and Mauritius." She sighed. "Though I'm afraid much of my sightseeing has been limited to business: seawall jetties, boat landings, harbor dredging and conveyor access." She offered a hollow laugh that held no mirth, before turning to look at Alex, her smile warming. "I imagine there will be a great deal of travel in your future when you are on the national team."

"Ha!" Alex scoffed. "That's a big *if*, I'm afraid. There's a lot of talent out there, all younger, stronger, faster every year."

"You must be doing something right if HEG sent you home with an offer." Catharine reached forward, taking hold of the small silver soccer ball charm Alex wore around her neck, examining it between her graceful fingertips before slipping the necklace clasp that had fallen forward around to the nape of her neck. Alex felt her cheeks flush and prayed the light was too dim for Catharine to notice.

Subconsciously, she reached her own hand to the pendant, rubbing the smooth little ball between thumb and forefinger, an action she resorted to when she was nervous or flustered. It had been a good luck charm Caleb had given her the day before she was selected by Rage FC in the first round of the draft. She'd worn it every day since as a talisman. Her *worry stone*, Caleb called it.

"Did you bring the contract?"

Catharine had called Alex the day before in order to give her directions to her home and had inquired how her meeting with HEG had gone earlier in the morning. Alex had told her about the contract and how she had the weekend to review it and was relieved when Catharine suggested she bring it for her to look over. Having an experienced set of eyes look over the binding agreement was exactly what she needed. But now she felt badly about seeking Catharine's advice. No doubt it was the last thing she wanted to do after an evening of entertaining.

"I did, but I don't want to impose—"

"Don't be silly. Most everyone has gone, and those who haven't are making ready to leave. I will see them out and then we can go over the agreement."

"Honestly, you don't—"

"Have you had an attorney or agent review it?"

Alex had neither. She'd been approached by several agents this season, but it had seemed futile while playing for the NWSL. There was so little money involved. And the deal with HEG had come together so quickly she'd never had time to seek out an attorney.

"No."

"Then let me look it over. Contracts with large corporations are never in the best interest of the individual party. Trust me on that." She touched Alex's forearm with finality. "Come, let's tell the others goodbye, put on the kettle, and have a look at your contract."

Without waiting for a response she turned for the threshold and disappeared into the light of the room.

Chapter Twenty-Three

"It was a pleasure, Mr. Krajnc," Catharine stood on the landing of her staircase while the musician gallantly stooped to kiss her hand in farewell. "I hope I will see you again before you return to Europe."

"It would be my honor, čudovita dama."

Beautiful lady. Catharine smiled as he released her hand and shouldered his cello, glancing toward the cab on the street where Victoria was waiting impatiently. Catharine considered offering to have him driven to his hotel—the girl was in a state and would be outright boorish—but she figured he could handle himself. He did not appear concerned by the girl's sweeping moods or inane behavior. Anyone who had spent any amount of time with her knew what to expect.

As he cleared the last stair to the sidewalk, Juliet came rushing out the door, pausing to kiss Catharine's cheeks. "The perfect evening, as always," she sang out, making certain Lukas knew she was there. "I will see you soon?"

"I may have to go to Carolina, but yes. I will see you before you leave to Canada." She squeezed the girl's hands, shaking her head. "You are beyond redemption, you know?" she whispered, knowing exactly what Jules was up to. Lukas had paused to wait for her.

"Would you have me any other way?" She winked and trotted down the stairs two by two until she reached the handsome Slovenian. "You wouldn't be going downtown, would you?" Catharine heard her say as she pulled the door closed behind her. Jules was fully aware the young man was staying at the Fairmont and would be obliged to offer her a ride. Victoria would certainly feel otherwise.

She shut the door reluctantly, half tempted to watch the scene play out to its conclusion, but she'd had enough of Victoria's tantrums for one evening.

Why she put up with the girl, she wasn't sure. Richard and Melanie were dear friends, but they had raised a monster.

She stood in her foyer, reveling in the sound of silence. She'd sent Grace, her house attendant, home early, insisting there was nothing so pressing to attend that could not be cleaned up in the morning. It was a relief, after the afternoon of festivity, to have the house quiet.

Catharine stopped in the downstairs kitchen and drew hot water from the fancy espresso maker someone had flipped on over the course of the evening—an appliance Carlton insisted remain as a fixture, regardless that it got put to use less than once year. She watched the automated machine fill the teapot, amusing herself to think about how appalling her mother would find the shortcut. She wondered if her mother had ever embraced the twenty-first century, employing the convenience of an electric kettle, or if she still filtered her water into a clay urn, allowing it to sit for a day prior to scooping it into a pot with her bamboo ladle, before being brought to a boil over charcoal embers.

The only acceptable way to make a proper cup of tea.

That was perhaps true, when you had Colonel Benjamin Brooks to please, but Catharine was finished with moving mountains to please the men who felt they ruled the world.

She dropped a tea infuser into the pot, wondering if her mother could sense the abomination of decorum across the Atlantic, and then snapped the ceramic lid closed, frustrated by the harmless turn of her thoughts.

She heard so seldom from her mother now, her last four letters going unanswered. She should call her this week, but she knew she wouldn't. There was so much left unsaid and unaddressed for so many years—too many years—their conversations had become strained and futile. But it didn't stop her from missing her. From missing the relationship they'd once shared.

She shoved off the lingering threat of nostalgia, grabbed the kettle and two cups, and headed up the stairs. Those memories were no longer here nor there.

Half an hour later, Catharine slid the contract back across the surface of her desk toward Alex, sitting adjacent to her, watching quietly as she highlighted and made notes along the photocopied pages. With Alex's consent, she'd put in a call to her attorney, Gordon, catching him before he boarded a flight to South Africa. There were several clauses revolving around extension opportunities and commission bonuses she wasn't certain how to interpret, and though he was a business attorney and unfamiliar with the specific athletic contract elements, he'd suggested a handful of language changes he felt would better protect the client.

Waiting for Alex to re-read it, she pulled her reading glasses from her nose and tapped them thoughtfully against the smooth oak finish of her desk.

"They're quite specific," she mulled, impressed with HEG's legal department. "No drinking in public, no physical appearance alterations without prior consent, no swearing or offensive language, no suggestive photos on social media, no politics, no blatant displays of affection outside of marriage—really, who demands that?" She laughed. "I always thought my contracts were a little 1950s. My father would approve of their solicitors." She smiled at Alex, then leaned forward to peruse the document in earnest, pointing out a few sections she had asterisked. "I'm not familiar with allocated payment options, but I am versed in the extension offers and general agreements on the business side." She tapped a highlighted section on the third page with the frame of her glasses. "The Morality Clause—is this common for athletes?"

Alex picked up the page to review the section.

The spokesperson agrees to conduct herself with due regard to public conventions and morals, and agrees that she will not do or commit any act or thing that will tend to degrade her in society or bring her into public hatred, contempt, scorn or ridicule, or that will tend to shock, insult or offend the community or ridicule public morals or decency, or prejudice Hargrove Entertainment Group in general. Hargrove Entertainment Group shall have the right to terminate this Agreement if spokesperson breaches the foregoing.

Catharine fiddled with the silk of her scarf, deliberating over the provision. "It's a broad statement allowing excessive room for interpretation. I'm sure they discussed it with you?"

"Extensively," Alex's lips disappeared into a tight line. "We have similar clauses in our player's contracts, but they rarely come into action, even for the women who go out of their way to bring attention to themselves—and not in an attractive manner." She looked up. "I don't think it will be much to worry about."

Still, Catharine could tell she was concerned about signing the contract in general. Something was weighing on her mind more than she let on.

"Gordon felt the core of the contract was upfront. It's very cut and dry without excessive filler. Mainly boiler plate clauses and specifics in the addendums. The deadline is Monday?"

"Eight a.m." Alex rubbed her jaw and sat back in the chair with a sigh. "I know they have quite a few candidates for the—"

"It's you they want." Catharine discarded her glasses onto the desk and stood to stretch her legs. "They've signed the contract and extended you an offer. The pressure of the deadline is just a game. A way to make you believe they have a dozen other considerations lined up if you don't cave to their every demand. It's the shortest route to get what they want."

"Do you think it's a good deal?" Alex picked up the stack of papers, thumbing through the lot of them. "The right thing to do?"

Catharine stepped around her desk and came up behind her, setting her hands on the girl's shoulders and leaning down to see which page she was currently stewing over. It was the signature page—signed by the Hargrove executives—the only blank lines waiting for Alex and a notary.

Alex stiffened at her touch, an action that seemed involuntary, but relaxed again when Catharine spoke, returning the attention to the agreement. "On what front? The right thing to do for your career? Your finances? Your life?"

"All of it, I guess," Alex dropped the papers onto the desk, agitated in her frustration.

To Catharine it was a trivial contract, an inconsequential sum of money —but she was well aware of its significance to Alex. It was a deal, if negotiated appropriately, that could be life changing. It could give her a leg up in her career, a financial stability she'd likely not known before—a way to move forward for the future.

But she also understood the responsibility that came with it. Corporations like HEG didn't hand out sizable sums of money without expecting a yield in return, and they would hold Alex firmly to their contract. Everything from policing her way of life to demanding results on the field, the obligation had the potential to quickly turn something she loved into a burden of profit. But it seemed like there was more to her reluctance than the simple concern of living up to expectations.

"I guess what I don't understand is—there's not a woman on my team—in the league, even—that wouldn't kill for this opportunity. I'm under no delusion as to how lucky I am to even be considered. But the truth is, it's Sawyer who should be signing this contract. She's the better player, the more successful person, the hardest worker I've ever known. She's the epitome of who aspiring young athletes should look up to. And the only reason it's me sitting here, and not her, is because she doesn't fit their mold. She's not the look they want. She's too outspoken, too original, too…"

"Much of a minority?" Catharine gently suggested when Alex struggled to find the right word.

"Too much of a minority. Yes." Alex let out a derisive laugh, shaking her head in disgust. "Yet here I am, not even sure if this is what I want. I love the sport. I love the challenge and the camaraderie and the game itself. I love the girls I play with—they're like my family. I just don't know if I want the publicity—the attention that it comes with. No one even knows my name outside the hardcore soccer fans… and I'm good with that. And yet, ironically, HEG's biggest selling point was the fame and notoriety the endorsement would garner—the chance to become every little girls' hero. But it's made me think twice about it now. And I feel so ungrateful, knowing it shouldn't even be me—so… undeserving." She covered her face, pressing the heels of her hands into her eyes, groaning in exasperation.

Despite the young woman's obvious distress, Catharine couldn't help but laugh, squeezing her shoulders when she felt Alex bristle defensively. "Oh, Alex," she reached to gently pull her hands from her face. "There is nothing undeserving about you. The very fact that you take the opportunity so seriously, that you have weighed the pros and cons and given it so much consideration—*that* is exactly what makes you deserving." She pivoted to perch against the arm of the chair, facing her. "HEG knows what they are doing. They chose the person best fit for their needs. Even if there are other players you feel are more worthy, *you* are the one they are courting. Don't sell yourself so short on what you have to offer. Turning them down won't change the outcome of what they are seeking. But accepting the opportunity could shape your future. You just have to ask yourself if it moves you in the correct direction. If it brings you closer to your goals. If you can use the platform to do good—to help better the world around you. And if the answer is yes, take their offer and embrace the opportunity."

Alex drew a long, slow breath, tipping her head back to stare at the ceiling.

Catharine studied her troubled face, creased in consternation. She sympathized for her and the moral turmoil she was battling. But even if it weren't for the ethical conundrum, she imagined Alex would have difficulty seeing the value she brought to the table. She seemed that sort of person; humble and self-effacing.

There was part of her that wanted to persuade her to sign. If Alex's teammates were correct, the affiliation with HEG would lead to the likeliness of a trade from South Carolina to California, and though Catharine hadn't allowed herself to dwell on the hope that Alex might find herself on the newly announced West Coast team—a topic she'd recently followed on Twitter—she couldn't totally dampen that part of her bias toward her accepting HEG's offer.

Which was a ridiculous sentiment. She hardly knew the girl. They'd only the slimmest cornerstone of the incipience of a friendship. Yet she quietly hoped she would accept the endorsement, all the same.

Alex's gaze shifted away from the ceiling, her thoughts returning from wherever they had taken her. The tension had eased from her expression, replaced with the subtle hint of a smile flickering in the green and gold flecks scattered throughout the honey brown of her eyes.

"I'm held to no accountability until I sign?"

Catharine wasn't sure where the question was headed, but she at least knew the answer. "You are under no obligation until it is signed and recorded."

"Our goalkeeper, Halsey—you met her in Portland—her aunt, she's like the team mom, was born in San Francisco and made me promise I would go to The Buena Vista for an Irish coffee." She paused. "It's not far from here, is it?"

The Buena Vista was a historic cafe near Ghirardelli Square. Catharine had never been inside the corner pub, but she passed it frequently and Jules had unsuccessfully attempted to convince her to go with her a time or two. It was a huge tourist draw, but a favorite venue of locals alike.

"About a mile away."

"Would you go with me?"

Catharine was mildly taken aback at the invitation, given Alex's habitual diffidence in all their previous interactions, and it must have shown.

"I mean—" The bashfulness returned as she struggled between committing to the invitation and backpedaling to her former shyness. The former won out. "I could use a drink. And if I'm going to sign this thing, it sounds like it might be my last one for a while. In public at least."

When Catharine didn't immediately answer, Alex turned her gaze toward the darkened windows, her insecurity getting the better of her. "If it's too late in the evening, I totally understand—"

"Would you prefer to walk or drive?"

She looked back at Catharine, her lips slow to lift in a smile. "Walk."

Catharine couldn't remember the last time she'd walked any memorable distance in the city. Carlton wouldn't allow it. His fear of abduction for ransom due to his political profile and their financial status had gripped him with a paranoia Catharine had never felt up to challenging. She found his rules and restrictions pointless—any vigilant criminal would know well enough that Senator Cleveland wouldn't pay a dime for his wife's safe return—but she'd lived under the weight of his shackles all the same.

But not anymore. He no longer had a say in what she did.

"I feel like a truant teenager," she admitted as she drew her arm through Alex's, steering their steps down Marina Blvd. Like all Saturday nights in the city, the streets were busy, teeming with tourists and transients, cyclists and delivery drivers.

She had little concern of being recognized. Opposite her husband, who sought media attention and basked in the glow of the limelight, Catharine did not enjoy the glare of publicity. She kept to herself, and despite Brooks Corps widespread success, maintained a low profile in her private life. Unlike the tech industry giants and flamboyant business tycoons—Musk or Zuckerberg or Bezos—she did little on social media, and enjoyed the anonymity of so few people knowing her name.

It was somehow exhilarating to turn off the well lit waterfront pathway and onto the uneven sidewalk that curved away from the bay and traversed through the darkness of Great Meadow Park. How Carlton would have detested the looming canopy of trees and shadowy figures that lurked amongst them, or the solitude of the San Francisco Bay Trail where it arched along Aquatic Cove, before returning to the blinking lights and cacophony of sounds emitting from the shorefront block of Ghirardelli Square.

Catharine felt like she was seeing it all for the first time, despite having lived in the Marina House for over a decade.

"Safe to say we aren't the only ones who needed a reprieve," she said as they passed the historic cable car depot where the line was at least a hundred deep. Across the street the bright red neon sign hung above the double doors to the Buena Vista, where upbeat, mediocre piano music filtered through the open windows running the length of the building. A handful of men in suits lingered around the entrance, exhaling long breaths of billowing smoke.

"I'm batting 0-2 when it comes to choosing the bars we go to," Alex half teased, half apologized, holding the door for Catharine to step into the crowded cafe. "If you'd rather go somewhere else—"

"Then what would you tell your goalkeeper's aunt?" Catharine countered with a smile, glancing around at the beauty of the wood varnished bar with its copper accents and colorful pastel tile backsplash. Clusters of vacationers in Alcatraz hats and Golden Gate t-shirts sat sipping cocktails around heavy round tables that lined the front of the room, while the bar appeared the preferred location for the local businessmen clientele, their ties loosened and cuffs unbuttoned on wrinkled dress shirts.

Alex picked her way through the crowd until she found a table that had been abandoned by the previous patrons, their drinks and dinner plates left in place with no busser in sight. Quickly she pushed all the plates to one side, wiping down the surface with an unused napkin to remove the condensation from the drinks and debris of the meals. Catharine could tell she was embarrassed, much the same way she had been at the sport's bar in Portland, worried she would be put off by the atmosphere or the people. What she didn't realize was that the normality of the evening was exactly what Catharine was enjoying. The ordinariness of spending an evening out in the city, packed in amongst the weekend crowd, where no one knew her name—where nothing was required of her—where she wasn't expected to look, to act, to respond a certain way.

"Let me get the rest of this." She set a hand on Alex's arm, stopping her halfway through cleaning the table. "You get the drinks. I believe you owe me an Irish Coffee."

When Alex returned with the goblets of the famous cocktails, she drew her chair close to Catharine so they could hear one another over the din of the room.

"A toast to the endless prospects of your future," Catharine lifted her glass and touched Alex's. "May whatever decision you make bring you everything you hope for."

They sipped and Alex set her goblet down, cupping her hands around the warmth of the clear crystal, and looked candidly at Catharine. "What toast shall we make for you?" Her hazel eyes had lost their glimmer of green and gold in the dim lighting. "I feel like you have asked so much about me, and I know nothing about you at all."

"And what should you like to know?" Catharine tilted her head, reserving the trace of a smile. As a rule, she preferred to be the one asking questions, not answering them. But it was seldom that anyone ever actually asked her anything meaningful about herself. "How about this: I will give you three questions. They may be anything you would like to know, and I will answer them honestly. But in return, you shall answer the same questions for me."

Alex's eyes held hers, brimming with a challenge, her lips hovering over a smile of her own. "Anything at all?"

"Anything at all."

Alex broke the gaze to finish her drink. "All right, then. Fair enough."

A cocktail waitress walked by and she flagged her down for another round.

"Three questions is not very many." Alex sat back in her chair as the waitress set down two more steaming goblets. Somewhere behind them the live band began a poor rendition of Amy Winehouse's *Back to Black*. She ran the tip of her finger along the rim of the glass before finally picking it up to draw a long sip.

"Something easy to start." She set her drink down, resting her forearms on the table and steepled her fingertips. "What brought you to America?"

It was ironic the question Alex felt was simplest was probably the one that actually had the most complex answer. There was nothing *easy* about it. But it was simple on the surface.

"It has to be something I can ask you in return," Catharine teased, "but I'll give you this one for free. Marriage."

"To Senator Cleveland?"

"He was Assemblyman Cleveland at the time. But yes." Alex seemed disappointed in the plainness of the answer but did not question further. Part of Catharine wanted to elaborate, to tell her how it had all come to pass—to lay it all out in the open for the first time—something she had never told to anyone before. But she didn't. It wasn't the time or place.

"What is the best decision you have ever made?"

Catharine thought for a moment, considering her reply. "It's funny," she said, still contemplating the most honest answer she could compile, "I have asked that question countless times over the years in interviews and evaluations, to an endless number of employees and associates, but I don't think I have ever been asked it myself." She could think of dozens of poor choices she had made over the years, things that affected her entire life in ways she never knew were possible, but the good decisions did not come to mind so easily.

There was one thing, though, that felt like the right decision. "I've told Carlton I want a divorce."

The admission of it, saying it out loud to someone else for the first time, suddenly made it much more final. Much more real. She'd wanted to tell Nathalie this afternoon when they'd found a moment alone, away from her other guests, but her friend was having troubles of her own and she didn't want to add her personal worries to the weight on her dear friend's shoulders. Nathalie was an empathetic worrier and had been there for Catharine in so many moments of need. The news could wait for another time.

Alex didn't hide her shock very well. "I—I didn't know, I'm sorry."

"I'm not sorry," Catharine said, uninterested in sympathy. "It's all happened so quickly I haven't had much time to process it. But it has been a long time coming." She thought about the twenty plus voicemails sitting in her inbox from the last twenty-four hours. The first ones started off threatening and ranting, but as the calls continued unanswered, they turned to apologies and pleading. Part of her had feared he would show up at the

Marina House uninvited, skipping his flight to Carolina, but that would have been brazen, even for him.

"I… wow," Alex didn't know how to respond and Catharine almost regretted telling her. She didn't want to change the mood of the evening.

"It's a good thing, Alex," she said reassuringly. "You asked what the best decision I have ever made was and I can answer with absolute certainty that this is it. It is something I have needed to do for a long time. I just needed the courage to do it."

"Was that what the call was in Portland?"

"No, no. That was just daily life with Carlton." Catharine laughed dryly. "Twenty-two years of daily life with Carlton Cleveland." She shook her head absently, dozens of scenes running through her mind from the last two decades. Finally there was a light at the end of the tunnel.

"And you? What is the best decision you have ever made?"

Catharine expected her to say something about her soccer career—or her education. Something that got her to where she was today. But instead Alex answered, without hesitation, "Jumping into the sea to help a stranger."

It was Catharine's turn to find herself at a loss for words. The simple response caught her off guard. She took a sip of her drink to busy her hands, finding the whiskey in the coffee comforting as it burned down her throat. "I guess I can't dispute that," she said after a minute, looking over the girl's inscrutable face before finishing her drink. "Carlton might, however," she teased, to lighten the mood. "I'm relatively certain he was counting heavily on my life insurance policy. Especially now."

Alex humored her with a tight smile, shaking her head. "I guess it would be funnier if it didn't seem so true. I know you said on Daufuskie that you didn't marry for love… but were you ever in love?"

Catharine thought about that first conversation she'd had with Alex on the dock just a short month earlier. It had been such a passing statement at the time.

"Is this your second question?" she asked as matter-of-factly as she could manage, still trying to maintain control of the conversation. Alex lifted her fingers off the table to acknowledge her agreement, indicating she should go on.

"Then no. The answer is no. I have never been one moment in love with Carlton Cleveland."

"But with anyone?" Alex urged, unsatisfied with the answer. "My question was if you were ever in love. Not just with him."

"So it was," Catharine acquiesced, self-consciously folding and unfolding the cloth napkin on her lap, creasing each pleat to perfection. "Then yes. I have been in love. And you, Alex Grey?" She said without pause, leaving no room for speculation. "Undoubtedly you have found yourself in love on many occasions in your young life?"

"No." Alex arched a shoulder in indifference. "I don't think I have."

It was not the answer Catharine expected. She narrowed her eyes quizzically. "Never?"

"Never." The girl was so pragmatic and casual, Catharine was inclined to believe her. But she still pressed on, her curiosity piqued. "How does a beautiful young woman—talented on multiple fronts—get through high school—university—life—without ever falling in love?"

"Is that your third and final question?" Alex teased, trying to cover her blush with a pointed stare.

"You catch on quickly, Miss Grey," Catharine conceded, pushing her empty glass to the edge of the table and reaching for Alex's, which was still half full. "May I?" She indicated the glass and set it to her lips with Alex's consent.

"I'll give you this one for free," Alex said with playful smugness, referring to Catharine's earlier quip about the question of what brought her to America. "It's easy to go through life without falling in love when you have never found anyone worth falling in love with."

"Touché." Catharine slid the glass back to Alex. Fair enough. She wanted to ask her about Caleb—if they had sorted out their disagreement—but she refrained. "And your last question?"

Alex took her time finishing the rest of the drink.

"May I save it for a later date?"

She meant to see her again, then. Catharine smiled. "A raincheck it is."

"Can we walk back by way of the water?"

Chapter Twenty-Four

The bike path leading from the Maritime Museum toward East Harbor was empty, save for a few lone runners padding along in the dark, immersed in the world of their headphones and runner's high.

Catharine and Alex walked side-by-side in a comfortable silence, both lost to the privy of their thoughts, neither in a hurry to reach their destination. As they approached the Municipal Pier, Alex noticed the chain wrapped around the wrought iron gates to keep the public out after dark was only dummy locked. She paused in front of it, glancing around. They were alone.

"Let's walk the pier!" She jiggled the lock loose from the rusted chain. She wasn't ready for the night to end.

"Alex—"

"Oh don't," she laughed, pulling the gate open just enough to squeeze through. "I know that tone. That's the *this-is-a-terrible-idea* tone."

"Very perceptive," Catharine acknowledged dryly, but she didn't resist when Alex caught her hand, pulling her toward the gap and onto the other side.

"I'm fairly certain that contract has a clause specifically related to public misconduct."

"Then it's a good thing I haven't signed it yet." Still holding Catharine's hand, Alex drew her down the concrete pathway that arched out into the bay, lit only by a few pillared lampposts. Her head was still light from the effects of the whiskey, giving her a boldness she would otherwise not have possessed, and it wasn't until they reached the end of the pier that Alex finally allowed Catharine's hand to slip from her own, uncertain as to her reluctance to end the touch. There had been a shift in the air sometime over the evening—a current running between them—and Alex was beginning to feel like she wasn't the only one who felt it.

Trying to ward off the threat of awkwardness that crept in between them, she turned to look out across the bay toward Alcatraz, sitting solitary in the distance, little more than a luminous shadow rising out of the water.

"It looks so swimmable from here." She cast her eyes the short distance between the jetty and the island.

"It probably is for you."

Alex could feel Catharine's smile through the dark, the two of them standing so close their hands brushed at their sides.

"There's an annual swim each year—the Sharkfest—if you ever care to try it out."

Alex turned to look at her through the dim glow of the lamplight to see if she was teasing.

"The Sharkfest?" Alex raised her brows, skeptical. "The name itself does not sound too inspiring. I prefer my swims shark-free, as it is."

"I'm serious," Catharine laughed, "it takes place every August. You just missed it. I love to watch the swimmers from my balcony. You really should try it."

"Watching from your balcony or making the swim?" Alex was surprised at her own coquetry, knowing it was only the tipsiness talking, but enjoying it all the same. She hopped onto the low guardrail, unconcerned with the twenty foot drop into the frigid water below.

"Either." Catharine reached to take hold of her forearms, uncomfortable with her perched on the railing. "But if you decide to do the swim, please don't start your training for it tonight."

"Would you jump in after me?" Alex baited, leaning further over the water.

"No." Straight-faced, Catharine pulled Alex forward until she slipped to her feet from the wall. "Because the sharks would have eaten you long before I ever made it to the water. It's not called Sharkfest for nothing."

"Sometimes I can't tell when you are serious or just teasing." Alex knew she should step away from where she stood—too close to Catharine to be comfortable—but she couldn't bring herself to move; to pull away and expand the distance. She was heady in the closeness of her, aware of the fragrance of her hair, the smoothness of the fingers that held her wrists. It was absurd to even notice such things, to find herself so intoxicated, but she found she couldn't help it.

"Ten years of sailing on this bay and I've never seen a shark," Catharine conceded, but her voice had grown quiet, the teasing tone lost while she struggled with her own unspoken dilemma.

Alex tried to summon a witty remark to alleviate the tension, but she couldn't find a single word. The effect of the whiskey was dissipating, draining her bold coyness of moments before, stealing from her the courage to ask the question that had been lingering on her mind.

But she knew if she didn't ask now—if they resumed their walk back toward Catharine's home—the night would be over and she might not find another opportunity.

"Was it a woman?" She immediately wanted to recapture the question, erase the words, find a way to turn back three seconds in time. It was no business of hers who this woman had shared her heart with. She had no right to pry. Catharine had been nothing but gracious, generous with her advice and time. Who was Alex to intrude into her secrets of another life, long passed by? But there was no rewinding the moment, so she felt the need to follow through, since she had gone this far. "That you were in love with?" Her voice was lost in the gentle lapping of the water against the pilings, the hum of electric coursing from the lamppost above their heads. She wanted to look away, embarrassed at her own audacity, but didn't. The least she could do was have the courage to look Catharine in the eye.

To her surprise, the woman appeared neither shocked nor offended, though she said nothing for an agonizing length of time.

"I hope you realize this is your third and final question for the evening," she broke the silence at last, "because I'm not sure I have many more in me tonight."

"Catharine, I—" Alex was going to tell her not to answer, to apologize for her insensitivity, but Catharine reached up, silencing her with the press of a finger against her lips.

"Yes. A very long time ago. A lifetime ago, really."

Alex didn't know if she was surprised at the answer or was surprised at the simple candor of the answer. Or maybe it was both. Nor was she certain what exactly prompted her to ask. Ever since Sawyer made the comment in Portland, she hadn't been able to shake it from her mind. It had made her unduly observant to every gesture, every touch, every glance. But up until tonight, she'd felt like she was reading too much into something that wasn't there. Now, however, standing as they were, she could no longer deny the truth that there was an unspoken energy between them—an unmentionable attraction she didn't know how to confront. And on some level, it scared her.

Alex had never considered herself attracted to women. She'd had a handful of "boyfriends" over the years, but none of which grew too serious or lasted very long. She just hadn't been that interested in them—and of course there was soccer. It took precedence to everything in her life and left very little time for anyone else, except Caleb and Sawyer.

But in the month since she'd met Catharine, she had to admit, however absurd she found it, that she was attracted to her. She'd tried to pass it off to herself as admiration—fascination with a woman who came from a world she couldn't begin to comprehend. Wealth. Power. Beauty. An intrigue built on the mystery and ambiguity that surrounded her. Captivating. Charming. An enigma that grew more complex the more she got to know her.

Yet she was certain now that it was so much more than intrigue. So much more complicated than admiration. It wasn't something she could rationalize, or begin to understand.

"How did you know you were in love?" Alex had to swallow away the tremble in her voice, praying Catharine could not feel the shaking of her hands. They were standing so close she could feel the warmth of Catharine's breath against her already burning cheeks, smell the sweetness of the whiskey on her lips. It would be so easy to lean forward, to kiss her—but just the consideration of the action sent her thoughts in a tailspin. What the hell was she thinking?

"How did I know I was in love with a woman?" Catharine let out a surprised laugh, her eyebrows lifting, but there was no mockery behind the tone, just a thoughtful intake of breath. "I guess the same way you know you're in love with anyone. When you find someone who makes you feel different... someone who lingers on your thoughts, day and night... someone who—when apart—you count down the seconds until you are together again. Someone whose simple existence makes you feel more alive than you've ever been..." Her voice trailed off, her thoughts far away.

Alex didn't speak, not wishing to interrupt her private counsel. She couldn't help but wonder what great love she had known to experience those things. What she must have given up, left behind, in order to marry Senator Cleveland. And what it must have done to her in return.

They stood in silence for some time, the only sound the water against the break wall and the occasional murmur of the nightlife in the city. Alex looked away, cycling through a dozen things she could say, but none of which seemed likely to ease the strain she'd inflicted on their evening. The quietness between them had grown nearly palpable, strumming with tension.

A breeze picked up over the blackness of the bay, catching the wisps of hair that had been tucked behind her ear, blowing them across her face. Catharine reached up, brushing the strands free of her eyes, her fingertips lingering against her cheek. "It's getting late." There was the trace of melancholiness lying beneath her tone.

Alex turned back, reaching to take hold of the hand against her cheek, and they stared at one another for a moment, both having more to say, but leaving the words unsaid. Another time. Maybe. Someday.

At length Catharine carefully withdrew her hand, breaking the tensity of the moment, and looped her arm through Alex's, turning them back toward the entrance of the pier, the conversation closed.

Half an hour later, Alex found herself at the foot of Catharine's grand front entry staircase—the same steps she'd considered retreating from hours earlier—but the events of the afternoon seemed so far removed from the evening, they barely felt connected to the same day.

They'd walked back from the pier without speaking, all sense of the easy contentment they'd enjoyed on their way to the cafe lost, neither knowing how to assuage the strain of silence.

Without ascending to the terrace, Catharine stopped. "Would you care for a cup of tea?"

Alex wanted to accept the invitation. For the second time in as many weeks, she didn't want to finish their evening with the uncomfortable lull of unfinished conversation. Without knowing if she would ever see her again. She wanted to go inside, sit on the bay front balcony, to ask her the thousand questions lurking around in her head. She wanted to listen to the beautiful lilt of her voice, to find something to say to make her smile, to simply enjoy the nearness of her, anything to keep the night from coming to an end.

But she also knew she was making another decision—beyond tea and conversation. Something unvoiced, but understood. Leading her on—leading them both on—for the hope of something she knew was impossible. Something she could not do. No matter how much she wished she could.

"I can't." The words didn't sound like her own. Like they belonged to someone else.

And in truth, they *did* belong to someone else. *Something* else. They belonged to decorum and society. To HEG and her pastor uncle and Sunday school teacher aunt. They belonged to Caleb. To the deep, impenetrable roots of the South. To the years of Sunday sermons and bedtime Bible studies. To the looks she'd seen Abby Sawyer and Erin Halsey and any number of other girls on other teams ignore. To the covered smirks and raised eyebrows that never were quite hidden. And to the contract in her bag —the contract she knew she needed to sign for a company that expected her to fit their cookie-cutter guidelines and "wholesome family values" of the standards they sermonized. The *values* that did not include women like Sawyer or Erin. And the values that did not include the way she found herself feeling about Catharine Cleveland.

"It's late, and I…" she stumbled over her words, feeling a surge of anger toward herself, followed by an unexpected rush of tears that clouded her vision. She turned away, unable to bring herself to look at Catharine.

"It's okay, Alex." A gentle hand settled on her arm. "I understand. I truly do."

Alex believed her that she did, but still couldn't meet her eye.

"Let me drive you to your hotel."

"I need the walk." She pressed her lips firmly together to keep from quivering, trying to smile, but failing miserably. "Thank you, honestly, for the evening. It was—it was a wonderful night." From the corner of her eye she could see Catharine's own smile falter, and just for a moment Alex thought about asking her to please offer again—that she would stay—the rest didn't matter. But even as she thought it, Catharine, too, seemed to read her mind and gave an indiscernible shake of her head before leaning forward and pressing her lips to Alex's cheek. "Goodnight, Alex," she whispered against her ear, squeezing her arm softly. "It was a wonderful night."

And then she was gone, up her stairs, disappearing onto the landing of the terrace, and a moment later there was the sound of the lock of the door sliding into place, punctuating the finality of the evening.

Alex stood on the sidewalk, staring across the street toward the marina, barely able to breathe. She wondered if she would ever see Catharine again, if their paths would ever cross? But why would they? They lived in two completely different worlds and led drastically variant lives. There was no reason to see each other again, and the realization brought the tears anew, this time unabated.

Without knowing where she was headed, or even which direction it was to her hotel, she stepped off the curb and jogged toward the waterfront pathway, picking up speed as her feet hit the trail. Suddenly she needed to put as much distance between herself and Catharine Cleveland as quickly as possible.

Chapter Twenty-Five

By the end of September, Rage had secured a position in the playoffs. With only two games left in regular season, the only question remaining was if they would earn enough points to beat Portland for the Shield.

It had been a whirlwind month for Alex. She'd signed the contract with HEG, accepting a one year endorsement pledge, with a three year extension option—one of the negotiating points put in place by Catharine.

Before the ink had dried on the initial agreement, a second negotiation was put in motion by HEG: a trade deal with Carolina. It should have come as less of a surprise to Alex that the next move from the powerhouse corporation would be to secure her rights for their team in California, but the news had still come as a shock. Five seasons with Rage—an established senior roster fixture—and she'd been sold for expansion draft immunity, a $100,000 in allocation money, and the first round natural draft selection for the coming season. It was a big deal, a sizable trade, proof of the value HEG placed in securing her for their roster, but Alex had still received the news with mixed emotions.

Her whole professional career had been spent in Carolina. Her fanbase, her support system... Sawyer. The trade uprooted her entire life, everything she'd ever known, and sent her into the abyss of the unknown. Was she even worth everything HEG had paid for her? Would the success she'd found on Rage transfer to a new team? A new coach? A new management staff? A new home?

Another national team call-up had come and gone, and once again Alex had not been invited to attend the camp. Despite being tied for the Golden Boot for the NWSL with eleven season goals and two games left to play. Despite the attention her career had drawn with the interest from HEG and the move to the West Coast. Despite the certainty of her teammates that this

The Senator's Wife

would be her year—that the National team coach would finally look her way.

She'd had to set the recurring disappointment aside. Save it for another day. Turn her focus to the changes ahead.

Sirens FC—the newly revealed name for the Oakland club—had hit the ground running. HEG had pulled out all the stops to build their roster and enter the league the following season with a high-powered team. It was clear they had no intentions of sitting at the bottom of the pack, fighting for draws and the occasional win, while developing their roster, as was the history of most expansion sides. With the money they'd spent, the international players they'd lured, the star power they had garnered, they hadn't come to mess around. They were in it to win it.

Boasting the promise of an ownership group willing to spend the money to create a successful club, pledging a highly experienced management staff, and the guarantee of a world-class stadium built exclusively for soccer (a project well underway), securing a place on the California team was considered a privilege throughout the league.

Despite the success the NWSL had garnered coming into its ninth season, there were still teams playing games on high school soccer fields and training grounds that would be considered unfit for AYSO standards, let alone a professional league.

So, playing for a stacked club on the West Coast—the "Best Coast"— was far from the worst thing that could happen in Alex's career.

Coupled with the fact that she would soon be spearheading HEG's latest brand, *Kickstar*, a sports apparel line intended to rival *Nike*, it was impossible to dwell too long on the disappointment of leaving her comfort-zone of Carolina Rage FC. The opportunities unfolding seemed almost too good to be true. Things the shy, insecure girl who had once kicked a ball around the dirt lot of a back alley sport's therapy program in the tiny town of Carlisle, South Carolina, had never dreamed possible.

Professionally, her life was on track.

After returning from San Francisco, she'd thrown herself into training with a single-mindedness she'd never known before. She pushed herself harder physically and mentally than was probably beneficial, but it had been the only way she'd found to keep her entire focus and energy on the game.

She'd wanted to be exhausted. She'd wanted to feel depleted by midnight runs and pre-dawn swims and anything she could find to keep her mind from returning to San Francisco. From lingering on whatever madness had taken hold.

Inadvertently she'd forced herself into the best shape of her life, and in doing so, had found her name on the shortlist for the season MVP. A career highlight she'd never considered achievable at the beginning of the year.

It was only Sawyer who suspected there was more to Alex's sudden drive than the simple preparation of readying herself to secure her position as a starter on the Sirens roster the following year. She'd tried to talk to Alex about her trip to San Francisco—to ask her what had happened—what had stemmed the shift in her demeanor upon her return, but Alex had closed her out.

In truth, she'd wanted to talk to her about it. She'd wanted to tell her everything. Sawyer was the one person who could possibly understand. But she hadn't been able to bring herself to do it. To open up about the way she was feeling—the way she had *felt*. Felt, because whatever it was, it was in the past now. A fleeting moment in time.

At least that was what she told herself over and over again.

She insisted to Sawyer her only motivation was to arrive in California in the best possible form—and perhaps, if the stars ever aligned, find herself an invitation to train with the US National Team. And Sawyer got the message. She knew, the more she pried, the further Alex would withdraw, so she'd closed the topic with the simple acknowledgment that she would always be there if Alex needed a listening ear. And all the conversation had remained on soccer ever since.

It was only in the waking hours of the morning that Alex found herself questioning her decision, wondering if she had made the right move? Wondering, if, by choosing the best interest of her career—the easy road ahead—if she'd thrown something else away in the process, something she might never get back?

But it was her *career*! Her *dream*! Nothing was worth risking that.

Was it?

Either way, it didn't matter anymore. That ship had sailed. She'd forced its departure with another strategic maneuver she'd set in place shortly after signing the contract for HEG.

Caleb.

She'd stepped off the plane in Savannah, entirely decided on the path ahead. She would give him the chance he wanted—see if she could find more to give. She missed his friendship, missed the comfort he provided with the history they'd shared. She loved him, and hoped, if she gave herself the opportunity, she could learn to fall *in love* with him, as well. He was a good man. Devoted. Hardworking. He would do anything for her. And even if it wasn't everything she longed for, she knew she could do far worse than Caleb Anderson. She just had to try.

The first weekend in October, Alex was invited to attend the US Soccer Federation's annual conference in Dallas, TX with several members of HEG management. It didn't interfere with the last game of regular season, so Alex felt obligated to make an appearance—her first official representation of *Kickstar.*

Following the conference, there was going to be a black-tie dinner, which her HEG representative, Tom Eicher, suggested she attend with a "plus-one." Oozing with good ol' boy vibes from his native Georgia, he'd called her up, inviting her to the conference, offering his suggestion about the dinner, and closing with "no one likes to see a pretty girl by herself, you know."

A contrary approach to their no-public-displays-of-premarital-affection clause, but Alex had held her tongue.

It had made her anxious to ask Caleb. It was a step in a direction she wasn't sure she was ready to head. It made them more official. More *real.*

Up until then, she'd gotten by with hands held and goodnight kisses. Late night texts of *I love you.* Morning texts of *I can't wait to see you again.* He'd been willing to take the relationship slow, to give her the time she needed.

But this felt like a shift into a different realm.

She'd known from the very beginning that their relationship was only a diversion. No different than the endless hours of sweat and tears she'd poured into the gym. She was running away from something she didn't know how to handle, and if she was honest with herself, she'd found the entire experience exhausting—forcing herself to muster feelings toward him she didn't know how to feel.

But it was what it was, and so she asked him to attend the conference with her in Dallas.

It wasn't so much the distance, or the dinner, that made it feel so binding, but rather the fact that it was such a public event. With word abuzz about the high-rolling team in California, and her recent publicity with *Kickstar* making headlines, she'd found herself thrown into the limelight of the sport, her name popping up on feeds previously reserved for superstar players, instead of flying under the radar on local WoSo news. She'd done more interviews and podcasts for *Kickstar* in a month than she'd done her entire career. Her game worn jerseys were showing up on eBay. She'd been asked for autographs at the supermarket. Photos with an Uber driver. Had to do a speaking engagement at a local elementary school where a dozen voices had chorused the sentiment that they wanted to grow up to be just like her.

Which meant as soon as she and Caleb were photographed together at the conference in Texas, her love life was bound to be paraded all over social media. It happened to all the women in the league—but up until now, she'd managed to keep her relationship status strictly private. After this, she'd have to acknowledge the role he played in her life. Accept that they really were a thing.

She'd chastised herself for worrying what Catharine would think if she were to come across it. Would she know the moral struggle Alex put herself through? Would she understand why she'd done what she'd done?

And then she'd reminded herself it didn't matter.

Sawyer was the only person in Alex's life who'd shown any interest in the relationship between her and Caleb. And that was only to make her disapproval known—a sentiment Alex could have felt from half a mile away. She knew Alex well enough to know Caleb wasn't what she wanted. She'd told her she didn't feel it was healthy to date her best friend, just to fill a void. That she hoped Alex knew what she was doing, because sooner or later, one of them was bound to get hurt.

And then she'd closed the subject, and they hadn't discussed it again.

In the end, the trip to Dallas was less stressful than Alex anticipated. One of Caleb's shining qualities was the extreme ease in which he dealt with people. He was the type who had never met a stranger. There was no one he couldn't engage in conversation, regardless to their walk of life, or the differences between them. His people skills were superb, his confidence overbrimming. Where Alex was shy, uncomfortable in the presence of strangers, Caleb deftly controlled the conversations, rescuing Alex from the monotony of small talk and endless introductions.

At dinner he held her hand under the table, teasing her with an encouraging wink out of view of the other guests, swathing her with his unspoken support, knowing how far she was out of her element.

She found a new appreciation for him in that moment, taking in his boyishly handsome face as he engaged in conversation with Tom Eicher, smoothing out all the rough corners of the inadequacies she felt. She thought, just maybe, she had made the right decision. That she could possibly find herself a little in love with him. In love with the steadfast support he gave her, and his undeniable pride in her accomplishments. There was no question that he loved her—truly loved her—and for that, she owed him.

That night after they'd stepped off the elevator to return to their respective rooms, Alex caught his hand before he could leave her at her door.

"Stay with me tonight."

The words were all jammed into a single utterance, as rushed together as the hammered beating of her heart. She'd rehearsed the moment all through dinner, going over the scene a hundred times in her head, hoping maybe she'd feel the stirrings of desire—find the spark to ignite a kindle that refused light. But now that she was here, the only thing she felt was the need to get it over with. To face the inevitable outcome and put that aspect of their relationship behind her. It wasn't like he would be the first man she slept with. It couldn't be that different than the underwhelming experience of her boyfriends in college.

But at the same time, she wanted it to be more than that. She wanted to be able to give him more of herself than she'd given anyone else. He deserved that. She wanted to prove to him—prove to herself—that she could do this. That she *could* love him. No matter what was wrong with her.

He hesitated a breath, searching her face with an earnestness that was endearing, the wrinkles of concern crisscrossing at the corners of his gray eyes.

"You don't have to, A." He cupped her chin between his thumb and forefingers, leaning down to brush her lips with his. "There's no rush—"

"I want you to stay." It came out more forcefully than she meant it, worried she would lose her nerve and change her mind.

She needed to know that she could do this. That she could make this work. For both of their sakes. Like Sawyer said: she needed to know she knew what she was doing.

Chapter Twenty-Six

Catharine brushed past Carlton's executive assistant, Matthew Stellar, who'd come to receive her from security, and strode down the familiar hall of the Russell Senate Building toward her husband's office. The spectacled young man, clad in his habitual argyle sweater vest, struggled to keep up with her fast pace, pleading with her to take a seat in the waiting area until Senator Cleveland was off his phone call, but she paid him no mind.

Carlton's secretary, Eleanor, had recently retired—Catharine had sent her a card in lieu of attending her retirement party, something she'd been genuinely sorry to miss—and was replaced by a young, coy blonde with large, blinking doe eyes. She was beautiful, despite her dull expression, and could not yet be twenty-five.

Just Carlton's type.

Catharine passed the surprised woman's desk without a word, Matthew in tow behind her.

"Mrs. Cleveland, if you would just—"

She pushed open the door to her husband's office, ignoring the young man's desperate pleas, and marched to the desk where Carlton sat, both feet propped on the thick oak surface, leaning back heavily in his padded executive chair with a cigar slowly burning in one hand and the receiver of the phone in his other. With a flick of her wrist, she dropped a file folder onto the desk, impassive as he lurched upright, surprised at the intrusion, and kicked over a stack of papers as he flung his feet to the ground.

"Damnit, Stellar!" He growled at Matthew, who immediately rushed to gather the fallen papers. "I told you I was not to be interrupted!" He snubbed out his cigar on an engraved silver ashtray and dropped the remainder of the butt in his trash can. He was the flawless caricature of the Southern politician. A mouth-breathing, doltish swine. She couldn't fathom how she'd put up with him so long.

"Catharine," his tone of contempt for his assistant turned to one of caution toward his wife. "I was not expecting you so early." He held up a finger to pause their conversation and spoke quickly into the receiver. "Bill, I need to call you back." Then hung up.

"Leave it, leave it, Jesus," he waved his hands at Matthew who was restacking the papers on his desk. "Close the door behind you!"

When they were alone, Carlton jammed an accusing finger at the file folder but didn't pick it up. "What is this?" he demanded, then seemed to recollect he was no longer the one with the upper hand and his tone softened. "Thank you for coming."

They had not seen each other since their unpleasant meeting in Sausalito, more than three months earlier, but over the past weeks Carlton had successfully persuaded her to speak with him over the phone, which was a step up from the curt, perfunctory emails she'd previously used as communication.

"You look well," he said when she said nothing, and again glanced anxiously down at the file folder. "What is this?" He tentatively thumbed the outside corner of the papers.

"The divorce paperwork, Carlton." She stood ramrod straight in front of his desk, her gaze steady and devoid of emotion.

Furious, he lunged forward in his chair. "You said—" he growled, then caught himself, starting again more quietly, a hint of nervousness in his tone. "You said you would hold off—"

"I said I would table it until you announce your candidacy." She turned brusquely, taking a few steps to the liquor cart he kept on the far side of his desk. "That is the best I can give you, Carlton."

"What about the primaries!" His low drawl was shrill with unease. "What if—"

"As I told you on the phone, anything past the spring we will have to play by ear. I won't make any promises beyond that. If that is not suitable, we may as well just continue with the process—"

"I have waited my entire life for this, Catharine!" Spittle flew from his mouth as he shouted, but the anger was gone, replaced only with an immense despair. And it was exactly that despair that brought her to DC, despite her better judgement.

He had been talking about making a bid for the presidential seat for as long as she had known him. It was his obsession—his ultimate drive and dream.

She doubted he would ever make it to the primaries. He wasn't presidential material. He was neither a great orator nor a strategic businessman. He was vainglorious, frequently put his foot in his mouth, spoke out of line, was careless of the toes he stepped on and the bridges he burned. He had no military experience, his ethical and marital history was less than stellar, his resume was a laundry list of failed businesses attempted over the years, and if it hadn't been for Catharine's money, he would never have made it as far as he had in the political arena.

He was no more savvy in his seat as a senator than he was as a husband. His race for a presidential nomination would likely be as futile and unremarkable as the rest of his mediocre career. But Catharine did not want the weight or burden of being the "cause" of his unsuccessful election, nor did she wish to shoulder his wrath if it all fell flat and she was all he could find to blame. He'd made plenty of threats, most of them idle, over the last couple of months, but if he truly felt she was the root of his failure, she wasn't sure what extent he would go to for retaliation. In his position he knew just the right people to be dangerous.

And in truth, despite her disgust at how he treated her and the complete demise of what had always been a fragile relationship to begin with, she still harbored enough good will that she was not anxious to see him fail at the one thing he wanted most in the world. Their divorce would already be widely acknowledged in both the business and political circles, but for it to come just months before he put his name in for candidacy—it would turn into a three-ring circus in the media—which neither of them needed.

"I know, Carlton." She sighed, a modicum of agitation disappearing from her shoulders, her guard diminishing at his exasperation. She uncorked the bottle and poured them both a finger of whiskey, setting the glass in front of him before sitting on the very edge of the leather upholstered chair, unwilling to get too comfortable.

The primaries were sixteen months away. In the spring he would announce his candidacy and begin the slow trudge of a campaign trail across the States to lead up to the early voting in South Carolina the following year. Almost a year and a half away. An impossible amount of time. But, if she were to go to court with him, to bully and battle him through a contested divorce, the war could wage over the course of a decade. Maybe even longer.

"Listen." She sighed, certain she would regret the decision, but continuing anyway. "I will stand by you with this election—same as I have done for all the others—until it has been determined one way or the other; win or lose."

He started to interrupt her, but she held a hand up to stay him until she'd finished. "But no matter which direction it takes, no matter the outcome, you must promise me you will let me go without a fight when it is done." She leaned forward, hands flat against the desk, the whiskey still untouched. "I will have your word, Carlton."

He was hesitant to answer, which didn't surprise her. It didn't matter much either way. His promises were worthless. He'd boasted on countless occasions that he enjoyed making promises simply for the pleasure of breaking them. But she wanted him to say the words. She wanted them to both know, when the time came, that he was the one breaking their agreement. Because he would. It was just his nature.

"I promise," he muttered, tipping the contents of the glass back in one swallow. He hated being told what to do, especially by women, and most especially by his wife. But right now, she held the cards, and there was nothing he could do about it that wouldn't burn him in return. "I will not fight it." He pushed the glass away, doing his best to hide his disgust for the situation.

Sulking, he swept the file folder into one of his lower desk drawers. "I'll look this over later. Did you get the usual rooms at the W?" He changed the subject, visibly relieved to have the folder out of sight. "Matthew said he tried to reach Nicole to confirm your reservations, but she never got back to him."

"Nicole could not join me—her father passed away," she said shortly. "But yes, I have my usual rooms."

"Ah," he contemplated, "I'm sorry to hear it. Give her my condolences." He tapped his fingers thoughtfully on the desk. Catharine knew he had never liked Nicole, but oddly enough he did respect her. She was efficient and driven and incredibly loyal to Catharine. She had been working as her personal assistant since she was straight out of Emory—over ten years now

—and was practically part of the family. Catharine also knew he still found her a bit of a challenge, given that she was certain he'd tried to sleep with her on more than one occasion. But Nicole was not some wilting, apprehensive wallflower easily manipulated. She was no nonsense, black and white, and honest as the day was long. Even Carlton Cleveland had to respect that kind of backbone.

"You are by yourself then?"

She nodded.

"I will change tonight's dinner to the POV, then, so you don't have to leave the hotel after dark."

Usually Catharine would have told him not to bother, but she liked the POV at the W. It was hip and contemporary and the rooftop views unparalleled of the city.

"Thank you," she stood from the chair, preparing to take her leave. "Eight o'clock?"

"I'll call Bill and Tina and let them know. Do you need a ride back to the hotel? Matthew can take you."

"No, I'm fine."

He stood, pulling a handkerchief out of his pocket to mop at his brow, his hands fiddling with the square of fabric. "Catharine, I—" he paused, stuffing the silk into his pocket, and cleared his throat uncomfortably. "Thank you," he finally managed, his dark eyes glancing to her before darting back to the whiskey, hidden beneath his furrowed brow.

Catharine couldn't remember the last time he'd thanked her for anything. It wasn't a term readily available in his vocabulary.

She stared at him, thinking back to the day they'd first met in London at a luncheon arranged by her father. He'd been slender back then, with black hair and strong, square features. His skin had been clear, his eyes bright with endless ambition.

The man before her now resembled almost nothing of that young man. Broad chested and thick around his middle, his black hair peppered with grey and his face soft and fleshy, with only a hint of the strong jaw that had once given him an almost handsome countenance. He'd told her that day he planned on becoming President of the United States—as matter of factly as one might mention they'd had trout for dinner the night before. She hadn't laughed at the time—rather, she'd hardly spoken at all, spending the entire meal trying to avoid her father's glowering stare—but thinking back, it had been a laughable statement from the ambitious Southern man who'd graduated near the bottom of his class at Presbyterian College. Other than his old name, he'd been nothing, no one. Yet here he was, decades later, still whittling away at his goal. The DC political arena had been brutal. It had aged him probably twice what the years should have done, but he'd climbed the ladder and paid his dues. She respected that.

"We'll get through this, Carlton." She didn't touch his arm like she once might have, or offer him a smile, but her words were genuine. Somehow, they would get through.

Without another word she turned and left the office.

Chapter Twenty-Seven

The rooftop nightclub was packed on the Friday after Thanksgiving. The line in the lobby waiting to gain access to the elevators transporting patrons upstairs was wrapped around the building. Despite the rain, people stood huddled under umbrellas, coat collars upturned, waiting for a party to exit so the next guests could enter.

"Did you ever think we'd have our names on the A-List?" Caleb wondered, draping an arm over Alex's shoulders as they walked past the line and approached the host who stood behind a small podium next to the velvet rope.

The narrow-faced man looked up from his list, eyeing the couple suspiciously, his eyebrows knit in anticipation.

"The line is that way," he said with a nod of his chin toward the door, his thick accent—Russian or Ukrainian, Alex wasn't sure—gruff with annoyance.

"I don't think you know who you are talking to," Caleb smarted with a lofty air, his lopsided grin causing Alex to bristle beside him. She hated his inappropriate jokes at the most indecorous times.

The host was equally unamused. "Enlighten me." His lips barely moved, his somber features frozen on his face. Undoubtedly he dealt with smart ass comments all night long and found Caleb no more clever than the rest of the aspiring social climbers in line, waiting in the torrential downpour for their chance to rub elbows with the glitterati that bypassed them without so much as a glance.

"You're looking at this year's NWSL Golden Boot winner, Alex—"

"Grey," the host finished, only the quiver of a smile touching the corner of his thin lips. "I'm a fan, Miss Grey," he was almost pleasant. "You are a competent footballer. It's unfortunate Americans do not place as much value on their women's league as they do their men's. The women are far superior. Especially your National team."

"If only the powers that be who cut the checks felt the same way," she smiled. "Though it's the plague of women's sports across the globe, I'm afraid."

"True, Miss Grey," he nodded, his hand drifting to the velvet rope. "Congratulations on the championship. I was of course rooting for the Tyrants," he added unapologetically, referring to the playoff final between DC's team and South Carolina Rage after the Capitol Tyrants had knocked off Portland in the semi-finals. "But I can appreciate a good match, no matter the outcome."

"I take it you have us on your list?" Caleb tapped a finger on the podium, his agitation mounting.

The slender man turned his eyes to him, his expression inscrutable. "I have Miss Grey on my list," he said, his unruly black brows arched in defiance. "I am assuming you must be her plus-one?"

Alex squeezed Caleb's hand in warning, knowing the dig would be sure to elicit a rise out of him. He didn't like feeling like her tag-along.

"Yes." She offered the man a beseeching smile, wanting to make it through the doors without a scene.

The man relented, unclipping the rope and gesturing for them to step inside the hall. "Mr. and Mrs. Wright arrived about twenty minutes ago," he said, referring to the couple who had invited Alex and Caleb to join them at the exclusive club.

She thanked him, before dragging Caleb toward the elevator.

"He was just goading you," she whispered as the door slid open and several men in tuxedos filed out, their faces ruddy with liquor and their laughter thick and raucous. She waited for them to clear out then stepped inside, pressing the button for the rooftop terrace that said "POV."

"It's so easy to get your goat," she teased, poking him in the ribs above his cummerbund, "your name was on the list next to mine. He was just having a go at you."

Caleb rolled his eyes, catching both of her wrists in one of his big hands and pulling her toward him. "*I was of course rooting for the Capitol Tyrants,*" he mocked, imitating the host's heavy accent. "Of course a little weasel like that would be cheering for the losing team."

"He lives here! How could he not root for the Tyrants!" she chided, pulling one of her hands free from his grasp to push back the twisted curl that fell into her eyes. "Remind me next time we are invited somewhere that requires me to wear my hair down and a floor-length dress to politely decline." She fussed at the tendril futilely until the elevator dinged and the doors opened to the crowded terrace.

Somewhere in the throng of tuxedos, Armani suits, and evening gowns, Mr. Emil Wright, the architect for the soon-to-open Sirens stadium, and his wife, Helen, a congresswoman from Colorado, were waiting for them.

The Wrights were significant shareholders of Markel Sports, Caleb's employer, and had politely invited Alex and Caleb to dinner after meeting them at the Championship after-party the previous weekend.

"You could have worn your jersey," Caleb teased, reaching for her hand as they made their way through the crowd, but Alex subconsciously drew it away, finding the room stifling enough without being tethered to his presence.

"The booth by the window," she said over her shoulder, catching a glimpse of the white-haired architect before carefully picking her way around the scattered tables and chairs, Caleb trailing at her heels.

Caleb was the first to notice the South Carolina senator.

It was shortly before eleven p.m. and they had just finished their farewells to Emil and Helen. The older couple had an early morning flight to Wales, where they planned to spend a couple weeks before Christmas, so they'd called it an early night.

Alex had been thankful to see the evening end. It had been a whirlwind week of parties and photoshoots, interviews and awards ceremonies, and she was exhausted. The Wrights had been lovely. Over the course of the evening, Alex discovered Emil Wright had collaborated with many of the same builders as her father, and even worked—years apart—on several of the same projects when they first entered the field of design. His wife, Helen, was reserved, but pleasant, speaking little about herself—the complete opposite of most of the politicians Alex had ever met. True to his nature, Caleb did the majority of the talking, and by the end of the evening had somehow garnered an invitation to join the Wrights in their Colorado home for Christmas.

"I'll grab our coats," Caleb said, before stopping in his tracks, his eye catching a familiar figure at the large corner booth beside one of the floor-to-ceiling windows overlooking the Washington Monument.

"Isn't that..." He touched Alex's shoulder to get her attention, but his voice trailed off before finishing his sentence. "I'll be damned, it is. What was his name? Clemson? Cleaver?"

It took only a single sweep of the crowd to find the face he was referring to, and immediately Alex felt her heartbeat quicken and her mouth go dry. She wanted to grab Caleb's arm and pull him to the door—get out of the room as quickly as possible, or rewind the night by five minutes and leave with the Wrights, casually chatting about Christmas on the way to the lobby. But her feet refused to move.

"Senator Cleveland." She uttered the name under her breath, feeling the same distaste of it as she had a half year earlier, stuck on Daufuskie Island. But the racing of her heart slowed as she scanned the booth and found the face she was looking for absent. Despite her relief, she felt a twinge of disappointment, but immediately brushed it away. Why would Catharine be here? She was divorcing the senator—they were a long way from California and South Carolina and there was no reason for her to be in DC. Which was best, anyhow.

"Yes, that's it! Cleveland!" Beside her Caleb was completely oblivious to the tumult of her emotions. He took a few steps in the direction of the senator, stopping only when Alex grabbed his arm, her fingers digging his cufflinks into the skin of his wrist.

"What are you doing?!" The sharpness in her voice brought several pairs of eyes to them from the surrounding tables, curious at the commotion. Alex didn't care. "Please, let's just go." She would have done anything to have him be reasonable, to have him listen to her, just this once. "Please." She lowered her voice and the onlookers slowly shifted their attention back to their drinks and conversations, losing interest in the little scene.

"I want to say hi," Caleb shrugged from her hold, taking another step toward the booth. "He was an interesting fellow. Surely after that weekend he remembers us." He laughed, perplexed at her urgency.

"Caleb, please." Entreating, she tried to reclaim his arm. She would beg if she had to. "I'm tired, it's been a long week, I just want to go back to the hotel."

"I'll just be a minute, A," he yanked his arm away, annoyed. "You don't have to come."

Alex dug her fingernails into the palm of her hand, fighting off the urge to shout at him as he turned and strode toward the table where the senator sat with his entourage. Lately, when it came to Caleb, it no longer seemed to matter what she wanted, or didn't want. With the *Kickstar* ads in full force and her nomination for the NWSL Most Valuable Player of the Year—despite losing the award to a striker on the Bluebells—she'd found herself battling the limelight in the sports community more than she'd anticipated, finding the intrusion to her privacy more invasive than she'd ever imagined.

But for as much as she hated it, Caleb thrived off the attention. He was addicted to it, seeking out opportunities to have Alex interviewed, promoting her to the agents and managers that now came sniffing around, each promising a better offer than the last. He loved posting photos on social media, getting her name—and quite often his, too—in print. He masterfully worked his way onto A-list parties and sought invitations to restricted events Alex had no interest to attend.

She knew Caleb thought he was doing what was best for her. For them. In his mind the money and fame and notoriety *were* the ultimate achievement. They were the endgame. The goal. He never heard her, or at least didn't believe her, when she told him it was the sport she loved. It was for the love of the game that she'd taken on HEG and the Sirens and sacrificed her privacy and quiet lifestyle. It was the fellowship of belonging to a team —a squad that was as passionate and dedicated as she was.

The irony wasn't lost on Alex that since signing with HEG, and the approaching transfer to California, the camaraderie she valued so much with the women she'd played with for the last six years had taken a toll, especially with Sawyer. Part of which—maybe most of which—was due to Caleb's desire to promote her as an individual, inadvertently dividing her from the rest of the women she'd devoted the greater part of her adult life to.

To Caleb the game was a steppingstone. A means of climbing the social ladder, bringing in the commercial contracts and sponsorships, raising the salary and securing the bonuses. And no matter what she said, Alex couldn't seem to make him see otherwise.

She watched the crown of his golden hair weave in and out of the crowd, making his way toward the corner of the room, and resentfully forced herself to rush after him. What if he said something inappropriate to the senator? What if Catharine had mentioned seeing Alex in Portland or San Francisco? She never told Caleb she'd seen Catharine again. There had been no reason to. He wouldn't have understood, and somehow she wanted to keep those visits to herself. They didn't belong to Caleb. They were one thing that was hers and hers alone. She wanted to keep it that way.

Alex caught up to him as he was approaching the booth, only to find an impassive-faced, muscular man dressed in a plain black suit step in front of them, barring the way.

"This area is restricted," the man—on par with the height of Caleb—said coarsely, his arms crossed in front of his broad chest. He was a brawnier version of Will Smith's character in *Men in Black*, sans the sunglasses.

"No threat here," Caleb laughed, dramatically holding his hands up in the air to show his innocence. "I just want to say hello to the senator."

A few feet away Carlton Cleveland looked up from the edge of the gold upholstered booth, glancing over with vague interest. From where Alex stopped—an arm's length behind Caleb—she could see the senator trying to recognize the young man, but was clearly unable to place him.

The situation was growing even more embarrassing than she'd imagined.

"Senator Cleveland," Caleb spoke over the bodyguard's shoulder before Alex could determine how to end the burgeoning humiliation. "Caleb Anderson," he continued, as if that would jog the politician's memory.

"Go on," the man in the suit ordered, stretching his arm out to bar the path. "This booth is restricted from public access. These guests do not wish to be disturbed."

"It's okay, Miles."

Behind Alex, a distressingly familiar voice pacified the security detail, before a gentle hand was placed on her shoulder in passing.

"Mr. Anderson is a friend of ours. You can let them through."

Catharine stepped between the bodyguard and Caleb, offering her hand to the latter. "How do you do, Mr. Anderson?" she greeted politely before looking beyond him to Alex. "Miss Grey. What a surprise to run into you both. Won't you join us?"

The man—Miles—obediently moved aside and Caleb brushed arrogantly past him before Alex could find her voice and decline the invitation.

How could she be here? With him! In the Capitol.

She momentarily forgot the absolute horror of the situation. They were supposed to be getting divorced. Had it all just been talk? Had Catharine lied?

She felt a stirring of anger—betrayal—slip beneath her skin, before realizing how ridiculous it was. She had no claim on Catharine. Was she not here herself with the man she swore was nothing more than a friend?

Her thoughts tumbled through a whirlwind of emotion before regaining traction to the awareness of the sheer embarrassment the next few minutes were bound to entail. She could have killed Caleb and his inability to listen to her for a single second. They should have been in the elevator, sinking down to the safety of the lobby, where she could have walked away from this night primarily unscathed.

That was never going to happen now.

When she finally realized the senator, Catharine, and Caleb were all staring at her, she came crashing back to her senses and forced herself forward to where Caleb stood beside the L-shaped booth, the senator still leaning against the glimmering gold vinyl, recognition slowly registering in his eyes.

"Ah, our friends from Daufuskie," he crooned out of the side of his mouth, clearly unprepared to see either of them again and worried he would need to explain their acquaintance.

"Mr. Anderson. Miss Grey," Catharine seamlessly took over the introductions, "may I introduce you to the former Vice President and his wife, Mr. and Mrs. Sherwood."

The couple sharing the booth with Cleveland nodded politely in a half-hearted, indifferent manner before the man—acutely familiar from his early 2000s campaign ads—turned back to the senator, clapping a hand on his back. "We're off, anyhow, Carlton," he said, adding, more obscurely, "I will think on your proposal and get back to you. It's certainly unique."

"I'll be in town for the rest of the month. I hope you and Elle will join us for dinner," the senator drawled through the smoke of his cigar.

The men rose and shook hands and Catharine kissed the cheek of the older woman before extending her hand to the former vice president.

"It's always a pleasure, Bill," she said, stepping aside and looking toward Caleb, who, by the grace of God, had enough sense to stay quiet.

Whatever they just interrupted had clearly been important and Alex wished, more than ever, that she could close her eyes and disappear into the twilight of an abyss.

Chapter Twenty-Eight

Halfway back from the ladies' room, Catharine recognized Caleb. She'd been preoccupied with finding a way to gracefully bow out of the after-dinner conversation and wouldn't have noticed him at all—just another suit in a sea of tuxedos—but as she was passing alongside the bar in the crowded lounge, her attention was drawn to a voice raised in agitation, and she glanced over to find herself just feet away from the unmistakable form of the flaxen-haired boy she'd met on the island. And, even more to her surprise, Alex. She was clutching onto his arm, some disagreement between them, resulting with the boy shaking free of her hold and heading across the terrace.

Catharine waited beside a table of boisterous, intoxicated young lobbyists too wrapped up in their slurred ideations to change the world to ever notice her presence. Alex was standing half a dozen feet away, jostled by the surge of evening partiers, but very much alone. For a faltering moment, Catharine almost approached her. There had been several times over the past months when she'd considered calling—after the first mainstream commercial for *Kickstar* came out on national television, or when Juliet texted her a photo of the cover of a Canadian sports magazine that had a small sub-article photo of Alex at the bottom with the caption "No *Grey Skies* Ahead for American Soccer." Or most recently when the banner of her homepage flashed with a headline advertising South Carolina Rage's Championship win over the Capitol Tyrants. She'd wanted to congratulate her. And why shouldn't she? They had not departed on unfriendly terms. There were no misgivings or hard feelings. There was no reason not to call and offer felicitations.

But she couldn't. It was so much more than that. So much more than could be put into simple words or offered an easy explanation.

For that reason Catharine hung back, waiting for the woman to move on. POV was packed for the holiday weekend. It would be simple to avoid Alex and her friend until she could reach Carlton and the Sherwoods and bid them good evening.

To her surprise, however, the young man headed straight for the booth her husband occupied, trailed shortly after by Alex, who appeared to have reasonable misgivings about approaching the senator uninvited.

After stepping forward to intervene, preventing the boy from getting thrown out of the lounge, Catharine regretfully found Carlton to be in an amicable mood, inviting the couple to sit with them.

Continuing to avoid eye contact, Alex declined. "We don't want to interrupt your dinner, but thank you—"

"Don't be silly, sit, sit," he patted the sleek upholstery beside him, "have a drink. The night is young."

She began to repeat the refusal, but Caleb cut her off, pressing his hand into the small of her back, pushing her toward the table. "We'd love to," he said, and Catharine watched Alex's body go rigid at his touch, the muscles of her bare shoulders tightening above the cut of her gown.

"It's late—"

"We have time for one drink, Alex," he superseded, gesturing for her to take the cramped seat facing the window so he could sit directly across from Carlton.

Catharine knew that tone. She knew the aggravation of being overridden by a man determined to have his way while there was no decorous means to refuse him. She observed the scene with keen eyes, well aware much more was going on than the display on the surface. Alex hadn't looked at her once and she felt for the girl and her discomfort, but wasn't sure how to alleviate the unease of the situation.

"What a surprise to run into you here," Carlton jawed on, oblivious to the underlying facets at play around him. "I barely recognized you. You clean up quite nicely, Miss Grey," he said with a guffaw that made Catharine wince. He was on the brink of being drunk, and now with the Sherwoods gone, he was bound to fall into a much more uncouth demeanor. He'd been on his best behavior with the former vice president in attendance—a glaring indication he was intimidated by the man, though he would never admit it. "What brings you to the District?"

Caleb accepted the cigar offered to him and never blinked an eye at the waiter who appeared out of nowhere with a lighter, despite the no-smoking signs plastered all over the terrace. Carlton cared nothing for rules he considered beneath him.

"Business," the boy drawled, drawing a long toke and letting the smoke out slowly. He looked very arrogant—unerringly fitting the setting—and little resembled the young man she'd met over the summer.

"Miss Grey had a championship game at Audi Stadium last weekend and I've had some local business to handle, so we stayed over."

"Oh, that's right," Carlton mused, "soccer, wasn't it?" Uninterested, he continued, "let's have a drink, shall we?" And with the lift of his fingers the waiter returned. "Two Old Fashioneds?" he said in Caleb's direction, but it wasn't really a question. "And a pair of Gin and Dubonnets for the ladies."

"None for me, thank you," Alex spoke up and out of the corner of her eye Catharine saw Caleb press his fingers into her knee, hushing her.

"Mr. Hargrove would hardly deny you one drink with the senator." He laughed, but his tone was more dismissive than teasing.

There was something different about Alex since Catharine had last seen her. For all of her on-field successes and accomplishments, she seemed less self-assured and more withdrawn, her face hollowed under a mask of impassivity. Catharine wasn't sure if it was due to her discomfort in the presence of the current company or if something else lay beneath it. She would have suggested they take a breather on the balcony, leave the men to their cigar argot, and found a moment to speak to her alone—but she wasn't sure Alex would allow it to happen.

"Just the old fashioneds," Catharine said to the waiter, who took a darting servile glance back to the senator to see which order he should follow. "That'll be all, *thank you*," Catharine accentuated, a slight tilt of her chin daring the waiter to defy her.

Beside her Carlton lifted a brow, his eyes catching hers, a challenge amidst them. She could see him wavering on the decision to let it go. But he simply couldn't.

"You see, son," he arched toward Caleb, pulling on his cigar and exhaling a pungent cloud of smoke, flicking ash onto the table, "let this be a life lesson. It's always the most beautiful women who are the most controlling. My beguiling wife, for example…" He tipped the cherry of his Montecristo toward Catharine, nodding with mock deference. "You'd be hard pressed to find a more attractive woman than Mrs. Cleveland, but the same could be said for her unfaltering... *intransigence*." He let the word roll off his tongue as he once again met her eye, the corners of his churlish lips twitching. Pausing a beat, he allowed the air to smolder between them, before offering his bellow of a laugh to dissipate the tension, and returned his gaze to Caleb, chucking his fleshy chin in Alex's direction. "Though I dare say it looks like you've got your hands full already," he smirked, rolling the cigar between his fingers. "Like I said, it's always the pretty ones that do you in."

The waiter, forgotten, shifted restlessly, drawing Carlton's attention.

"You heard the lady," he stubbed out the end of his cigar on the table directly outside the ashtray, "just the old fashioneds."

Catharine could feel the shakiness of her breath as she willed herself to control her tongue. Soon enough, this was all coming to an end.

"How long are you in DC, Mr. Anderson?" Catharine forced herself to inquire.

Alex stared out the window in front of her.

"We head home Sunday night. Now that the season is over Alex has to begin packing for California. Her contract was purchased by a new team coming to the Bay Area."

"My condolences," Carlton cut in with a mixture of sarcasm and disapproval. "Terrible state. A scarcity of upstanding, God-fearing people. Don't get me started on the jackass politics—"

"We won't," Catharine interjected, and he laughed, his gaze piercing beneath his heavy lids.

"Ah, my dear, your misplaced love of the West Coast is nothing short of pitiful. There is plenty of beauty all over this nation, you need not suffer that liberal cesspool to find it."

"Perhaps it is not the beauty I am seeking, but the distance," she marked, her sarcastic smile matching his. "And you, Mr. Anderson? Are you also moving to California?"

For the first time since she'd sat Alex looked directly at Catharine. "No," she answered, beating Caleb to it. "He's been assigned to the southeast, so he will stay around Carolina."

"Well, for now," Caleb said, "I'm hoping to get a position in the west next year."

Catharine held Alex's eye for a moment, ignoring the boy. "It sounds like quite an adventure. I wish you much success." She despised how trivial the words sounded when she wanted to say so much more. But what more, really, could be said?

When Alex once again shifted her gaze out the window, Catharine stood, suppressing a sigh, and motioned for the nearby attendant to gather her coat. There was no point in making the evening any worse for either of them.

"It is a pleasure to see you both," she said, "I hope you will excuse me, I'm fatigued after a long day of travel."

"If you're anywhere near Oakland, you'll have to come to one of Alex's games next year," Caleb rose to his feet. "The new stadium is truly impressive."

"Perhaps," she gave a noncommittal shrug, turning to allow the attendant to help her into her cashmere.

"Don't count on it," Carlton scoffed, tipping back his whiskey with a flick of his wrist. "I'm afraid soccer doesn't fit in much with the posse of painters and poets and dancers she entertains out there." He swirled the remaining contents in his tumbler. "You'll be more likely to find her at the opera or ballet," the words rolled off his tongue in disgust, but he threw in a chuckle to lighten the tone, as if that made it all acceptable. "Not really a sporting fan, my wife." With a final swallow he finished his drink and set the glass down with a near-shattering clink. "Two more, boy," he called for the waiter.

Alex looked up, shaking her head at Caleb, but he brushed her off, picking up the lowball and downing the whiskey to level with the senator.

"Goodnight, Miss Grey. Mr. Anderson." Catharine nodded at Caleb. "I wouldn't try to keep up with him. He's a professional at this—you'll regret it in the morning."

She turned and didn't look back.

Chapter Twenty-Nine

Overnight the District of Columbia had turned white with snow. No significant amount, just a dusting to blanket the buildings and monuments, but with the steadiness of the continued downfall it was enough to drive the locals and tourists indoors, leaving the streets around the White House in a lull.

Alex woke early, as usual, and slipped noiselessly into her running clothes and a warmup jacket, taking care to pad silently across the hotel floor, determined not to wake Caleb.

It was unlikely he would have heard her even if she'd marched the entire Philharmonic Orchestra through the bedroom, he'd been so drunk the night before, passing out fully clothed at the end of the bed as soon as he'd stumbled through the threshold. It was all she could do to drag off his dress shoes and convince him to slide under the covers before he was asleep once more, snoring a raucous, unvarying rhythm that undoubtedly kept more than just Alex awake through the night.

But she didn't want to take any chances. She needed the morning to herself and embraced the blast of cold air that stung her face as soon as the doorman swung open the double doors.

He tipped his hat, his eyes peering out above a checkered scarf. "Morning, Miss. It's a touch nippy out," he warned, acknowledging her lightweight jacket and running shoes.

"It'll keep me moving," she smiled, slipping her earbuds in and taking off at a jog down E Street as the snow fluttered through the faint light of the gray morning.

The doorman hadn't been wrong. The large thermometer in Freedom Plaza read twenty-eight degrees, a solid thirty degrees colder than the weather she'd left in South Carolina. Made only worse by her shoes that were immediately drenched, leaving her feet in a state of numbness—an improvement, however, from the ache of the heels she'd worn to dinner the night before.

But she didn't care. She welcomed the burn on her cheeks from the bitterness of the morning. The slush of snow that stuck to her hair. The heaviness of her steps as she picked her way along the salt-strewn sidewalk. Her mind—even more than her overstrung body—craved the monotony of the run. Down E Street and up 14th until she came to New York Avenue, doubling back to 15th.

She saw the large white W approaching ahead, hanging above the lobby entrance to the hotel where they'd had dinner the night before. She knew Catharine was staying there. The senator—three sheets to the wind with Caleb—had fleetingly suggested they continue their bottle of Dalmore in his wife's suite, displeased last call had come so soon. But to Alex's immeasurable relief, by the time he struggled to his feet he'd forgotten the idea, and she'd managed to steer Caleb toward the door while the senator's security detail deftly handled their charge.

Alex quickened her pace past the glass canopied entrance. She didn't know why she'd chosen this route. Had somewhere in the back of her mind she hoped she'd turn and see Catharine through the grand foyer doors? Had she imagined the woman would be sipping tea in her corner suite and happen to look out the window as Alex ran by, like some mawkish Audrey Hepburn classic?

She was embarrassed by the foolishness of it. Ashamed to know a part of her hoped it would happen.

Rounding the corner, careful to avoid the wettest spots on the sidewalk concealed by the increasingly heavy snowfall, Alex turned down E Street and sprinted the last half mile to her hotel. Her lungs were blazing from the cold air and her legs were threatening to cramp from the effort, but as she reached the front door her mind felt the clearest it had in weeks. Or the numbest. It was growing hard to tell the difference.

"Change your mind, Miss?" The doorman said cheerfully, holding the door to welcome her back to the lobby.

"Trimmed it short, three miles," Alex puffed, peeling off her damp jacket and tucking back the wet hair plastered to her cheeks.

"You just ran three miles?" Wrinkles creased across his forehead. "In the snow? You can't have been gone twenty minutes!"

Alex glanced at her watch. "Nineteen minutes, forty seconds."

She laughed when he looked impressed, it wasn't an overwhelming feat. The ice had added over a minute to her average 5k, and she was only the fifth fastest woman in the league.

The doorman was intrigued. "Track and field?"

"Soccer, actually," she dried her face with the towel he offered and apologized for the wet footprints she left on the way to the stairs.

As soon as she stepped in the room, she could tell Caleb had woken. The comforter was on the floor and the blackout curtain across the window had been pulled open, allowing the muted glow of the stormy morning to cast dull shadows on the carpet. She felt a sense of disappointment, knowing the quietude of her day had ended.

Caleb appeared from behind the kitchenette with a glass of water and flopped onto the bed, still wearing his tuxedo pants—his vest and shirt piled in a heap on the armchair.

"Oh, hey." She hung her jacket on the door knob. "You're up early."

"So are you." His smile was crooked as he lifted the glass to his lips, draining it in a single swallow, his cheeks splotchy and deep purple bags accentuating his red-rimmed eyes.

"How are you feeling?" She took the empty glass and refilled it at the kitchen sink.

Grinning, he at least had the courtesy to look sheepish. "I've felt better."

"I imagine you'll have quite a hangover today." She couldn't hide the coolness in her voice. She was angry about the night before. She hadn't even wanted to go over to the senator's table, let alone face the awkwardness of sitting there with Catharine, and then being forced to wait while Caleb got sloshed with the small-minded, arrogant, bigoted prick, until they closed the bar down. But what she wanted never seemed to matter anymore.

She handed him the water and he caught her hand as she went to walk away.

"Are you mad?" he laughed, pulling her to him, careless that the water was spilling onto the mattress.

"Caleb, don't—"

"Come on, A." He set the glass on the nightstand and dragged her beside him. "I got a little carried away. I'm sorry." He didn't sound very sorry.

"You were shit-faced, Caleb." She struggled from his grasp to sit on the edge of the bed.

"I admit, I went a little overboard—that Scotch was my downfall."

"Well, now you can pay for it with your hangover." She didn't look at him.

"You know what they say the best cure is for a hangover?" She could hear the smile in his voice as he slid a hand under her shirt, trying to slip his fingers beneath her waistband. His morning breath was rancid at her neck, and the feel of him against her sent an involuntary shudder down her spine as she jerked away, managing to get to her feet.

"Yes—water and sleeping it off."

"Come on, A. Don't leave me hanging." He rubbed at his tired eyes with the heel of his palm. "You're no fun."

"Neither were you."

He slumped against the headboard, continuing to smile. "Only a sadist would leave me like this, with you looking that good," he motioned toward the damp running shirt that clung to her skin, prompting her to awkwardly turn away. "Fine, fine, I'll sleep it off. Oh," he added as she headed for the shower, "I almost forgot. You had a phone call."

She paused in the doorway.

"Your cell rang—that's what woke me."

Alex's eyes trailed to her phone sitting on his nightstand, the screen open and unlocked. She'd never cared before that he answered her calls or flipped through her texts, but this morning it bothered her. "Who was it?"

"The senator's wife." He raised a brow. "I was dead asleep and saw the name flash C. Cleveland—I thought it was the senator calling, so I answered it. I actually thought I was dreaming." He laughed, amused with himself. "She seemed a little surprised when I picked up. Thought she had the wrong number." He tossed Alex her phone. "No clue what she wanted. She's an odd gal. Smoking hot for a middle-aged housewife, but strange all the same."

"She's not a housewife."

God, he could be an asshole. She thumbed through her notifications, her palms suddenly clammy.

"Whatever you want to call those folks that don't work a day in their life, yet still have the world handed to them." His eyes were shut as he settled back against the pillows. "Wake me around noon, will you? I have a Zoom meeting I can't miss."

Once she was certain he was asleep, Alex decided to skip her shower, stripping off her damp clothes and dressing for the day—jeans, sweatshirt, beanie over her wet hair—and grabbed her wallet and hotel keycard. She didn't know where she was going, but she knew she couldn't stay in the room a minute longer. Not with him. She suddenly felt trapped—suffocating inside a life of her own making, the neat little box she'd constructed herself —four tidy walls and a glass ceiling, where she could look up and pretend she could still reach the sky.

She took a last look at Caleb's sleeping face, his disheveled hair and the dark stubble growing on his cheeks. He was barely recognizable to her anymore. The man who sat last night with the senator, smoking Cuban cigars and ordering high dollar whiskey while making senseless, vulgar conversation, was nothing reminiscent of the boy she'd known for the last sixteen years. How anyone could change so much in a matter of months seemed impossible. But then—hadn't she changed, too? How could she expect to know someone so well when she felt like she barely knew herself? There were times, when they were alone, that she glimpsed that comfort and happiness she'd known with him for so many years. Where they both felt like themselves. But those moments came further and further apart now, and no matter how hard she tried to keep it together, the gap between them was expanding, cleaving a rift she feared could never be repaired.

She slipped out the door and into the hallway. It was early and the long corridor was empty, the other guests still sleeping off their Friday night. Fighting the urge to cry, Alex leaned against the door and slid to the floor, drawing her knees to her chest. She turned her phone over and over in her hands, trying to decide what to do.

She doubted Catharine would call again. They'd barely spoken the night before, she'd hardly been able to look at the woman, let alone hold a conversation. The initial shock of seeing her brought back all the doubts and questions she'd spent the last months trying to bury—but here they were, clawing their way to the surface, threatening to upset the fragile sanity she teetered on.

Alex opened a new text and selected Catharine's number from her contacts. She'd wanted to erase the contact—she'd spent too many hours staring at it, wanting to make a call—but had never been able to bring herself to hit the delete button. Besides, what good would it have done? She knew the number by heart.

She needed to talk to her. To close this chapter of her life and move forward with the future she'd designed. Too much had been left hanging; left unsaid.

Zeke's Coffee, 9AM?

She read the simple text over and over before forcing her fingers to hit send.

She had to do this. It had to end.

Chapter Thirty

The one-room coffee house was packed with businessmen in long coats and tourists in DC sweatshirts and cellophane-thin yellow ponchos hustlers on the corner were selling for a ridiculous price. The snow began to taper off, but the chill had not lifted, driving all the usual sightseers and travelers indoors, caught off guard by the drop in the weather.

Catharine arrived at a quarter to nine, picking her way through the cramped room to stand in line behind the half dozen people ahead of her, ordering triple shot caramel mocha lattes and pumpkin spice holiday drinks disguised as coffee. It was a few minutes before the hour when she finally picked up her black house blend and found a spot nearest the window to nurse the hot brew.

She'd been surprised to get Alex's text. From the slurring, groggy state in which Caleb answered the call, Catharine doubted he would even remember the conversation, let alone tell Alex she had rung.

She shouldn't have rung.

She tried to convince herself she was calling to make sure they'd gotten back safely the night before. The boy was on the brink of being soused by the time she took her leave—undoubtedly Carlton pushed him well past his limits after. But she knew her call was not a simple hello; a check-in. If it was, she would have called to say hello months ago.

When Caleb answered, she'd almost hung up. She doubted Alex would take her call, but she certainly hadn't expected the deep voice of the boy to come on the line in her stead. It hadn't dawned on her that he would be there.

In her room.

Apparently things had changed since last they spoke.

Now, waiting in the crowded coffee shop, she wished she had hung up. It would have been better that way.

She watched halfheartedly out the window a few more minutes, sipping the bitter brew, until she saw Alex round the corner, her arms crossed, hugging herself against the cold, head down and steps slow. About fifty feet from the front door she stopped, looking up at the coffeehouse door, and then disappeared beneath the covered awning of the building next door.

Ten minutes passed and she didn't reappear. Finally, deciding she must have gotten cold feet, Catharine pulled out her phone to text her—to tell her she was sorry, but wouldn't be able to make it—to give her an easy exit, since she was obviously vacillating with her decision to meet. But before she could hit send, Alex shouldered her way through the door and pulled off her beanie, looking around until her eyes found Catharine.

"I'm sorry," she said after working her way to the window. "I almost didn't come."

Catharine's lips tightened in what she meant to be a smile, but she couldn't force it to her eyes.

"I understand." She looked around the room and Alex followed her gaze. The seats were all taken and the noise level was dissonant between the din of chatter and the cheerful Christmas pop tunes playing on the radio.

"I didn't know it would be so crowded."

All of Alex's awkwardness was returned, her eyes avoiding Catharine's as she took in their surroundings, unsure what to do. There was no possibility of holding a private conversation in the small cafe. If a private conversation was what she wanted.

"Will you walk with me?" she said at last. "It's not as cold as it looks."

Catharine smiled despite herself. "I'm not sure I'm the one who should be concerned about the cold." She eyed Alex's sweatshirt and bare hands. "Where is your coat?"

"In a box somewhere in Charleston. I'm fine, honestly. Can we walk, please?"

Catharine pulled on her beret and gloves. "After you."

Outside the snow had slowed significantly, coming down in flat, soft flakes that melted as soon as they fell on Catharine's face and hair. Travel had taught her to appreciate nearly every kind of weather—but there was always something magical about the first snowfall of the year. Perhaps the charm of it was stored in nostalgia from a time long forgotten. The winters before the summer when her father had turned everything upside down.

They were silent as Alex chose a route down H St. and turned into Lafayette Square, away from the pedestrians that were beginning to brave the streets to hurry to their destinations.

The brick paths were blanketed in undisturbed snow and the historic ginkgo and cypress tree branches were weighted down by their heavy loads, standing out like stark, white sentries lining the park.

Alex came to a stop in front of the famous Andrew Jackson equestrian statue, her gaze turning up to the towering bronze.

"Have you ever been here?" Catharine ran her gloved hand along the top of the low spiked railing encompassing the landmark before looking around at the empty square.

"No," Alex said, tucking her hands into the pockets of her sweatshirt, her cloud of breath betraying the chill of the air. "It's beautiful. Other than the weather." She stamped her feet.

Catharine unwound her vacuna wool scarf and pulled it free of her coat. "There's a saying we have in England: *There's no such thing as bad weather, only unsuitable clothing.*" She reached forward and brought the scarf around Alex's neck, feeling her shoulders go rigid against her fingertips. "Relax, Alex. It's just a scarf. It won't bite."

Alex started to pull away, but stopped, allowing her to finish tying it around her neck, embarrassed by the admonishment.

"Now, tell me," Catharine took a step back, giving her space, and folded her gloved hands into her pockets. "What are we doing here?"

Alex averted her eyes back to the memorial, her face as cold and set as the figure in bronze. "I just—" she took a breath and let the air out slowly, composing herself. "I can't do this."

She shut her eyes and Catharine waited, watching her expressionless face.

"And what is it you can't do?" She asked at length.

"This!" Alex came alive with the sharpness of the word, her voice wavering with emotion. She turned to Catharine, pulling her hands from her pockets and gesturing between the two of them. "This! This here, whatever this is. I don't even know what this is." She covered her face in frustration, and Catharine wanted to reach out to touch her, to console her, but she dared not.

Instead, she waited for her to go on.

"I can't—" Alex started again, still hiding behind her hands. "I can't be the only one—whatever this is between us—it can't just be me that feels this."

"Alex—" Catharine reached forward to draw her hands from her face, but as soon as she touched her Alex jerked away as if she had been struck.

"Please, don't!" She shook her head, wrapping her arms around herself defensively. She looked like she was about to lose her battle against the tears threatening at the brim of her eyes. "You don't understand!"

"I *do* understand!" Catharine cut in sharply, her own anger piqued. "I understand far more than you will ever know!"

Alex tried to turn away but Catharine caught her arm. "I understand, Alex, that none of this fit into your scripted, perfect plan. I understand how easy it is to make decisions based off what you think you are *supposed* to do —not what you *want* to do. And I also know how quickly making decisions based on what others want can turn your life upside down."

"My life is already upside down!"

"But it doesn't have to be!" Catharine squeezed her forearm hard. "It doesn't have to be! That's what I'm trying to tell you."

"And what would you have me do?" Alex choked over the words, the first frustrated tear stealing down her frost burned cheek. "Just throw everything I have worked for away?"

"I wouldn't have you throw anything away," Catharine said softly, trying to find the right words. She had been in this position. She knew this conversation inside and out. And she knew the consequences it held. "I would just have you reconsider where you are headed. To think about what you are willing to give up to get where you are going. If it is worth the cost."

Alex drew her arm away, some of her anger fading, and wiped at her tears with her sleeve. Her lips were quivering, dry and chapped from the chill, but her voice resumed its steel.

"I was raised by a Southern Baptist pastor in a small town in the heart of Union County where I knew every person in our parish by name. I went to Clemson instead of Stanford or UNC because my uncle felt the smaller university would better preserve the Christian principles. Every church in the county donated to my high school soccer team because of my family name. HEG didn't choose me based off my talent. They chose me based off my image." Her voice had dropped to barely a whisper, as if she were afraid of her own words.

"HEG is temporary. Even soccer is temporary. It won't be there for your entire life." It wasn't the right thing to say. Catharine knew it wasn't as soon as it was out of her mouth, but it was too late to recover.

"But it *is* my life! Can't you see that? It's everything important in my life. It's all I have that's mine. All I know. All I have worked for. And I know it sounds pathetic and," she faltered, searching, "and *small-minded*, but I can hardly bear the publicity and lack of privacy as it is. I can't imagine what it would be like if I were to have some—some—" the tears began anew, "immoral... scandal... attached to my name."

Catharine was silent. This wasn't about her or what she wanted. It was about Alex, and Alex alone. She didn't want to see her make the same mistakes she had made in her youth, to go down the same path that led her to where she was today. But she knew from experience she couldn't change her mind. No one—not even the person she'd loved most in all the world—had been able to change her own mind when she was forced to decide what life she would choose all those years ago. It had been futile to try.

"Do you love him?" she asked at last, breaking the brittle silence that fell between them.

Staring off into the distance, her face was once again impenetrable. "I don't know."

"Then don't do this."

Alex wheeled to face her, her face contorting with anger. "How can you stand there and offer me advice when you are every bit a hypocrite? All that talk of divorcing your husband—and here you are, at his side, as if nothing ever happened!"

"You have no idea what has happened!" Catharine snapped, defensive. "Or what I am dealing with! Separating him out of my life isn't as simple as a decree on paper—it goes so much deeper than that!"

Somewhere behind them a lone jogger trudged by and both women subconsciously moved apart as he passed, neither looking at each other.

When he was gone and they were alone again Catharine crossed to where Alex had stopped beside a bench facing the White House.

"I'm sorry," Alex said, not looking at her. "You're right. I don't know what you are going through."

Silence resumed, interrupted only by the quiet birdsong sung tentatively from the snowy trees, and the sound of cars passing in the distance. Catharine bent down and dusted snow off an engraved plaque beside the bench. It was a dedication she knew well and had read on many occasions while walking in the park.

"*The Inspiration Bench*." She ran her gloved fingers along the golden letters. "Do you know who Bernard Baruch was?"

Alex shook her head, her focus on the old park bench in front of her.

"He was an adviser to President Wilson during World War I. A truly great philanthropist of his time. He was famous for saying: '*Be who you are and say what you feel, because those who mind don't matter, and those who matter don't mind.*'"

Beside her Alex exhaled, her shoulders drooping as she turned from the bench, her cheeks stained with tears.

"I have to go." She said, defeated, unwilling to meet her eyes. She reached to untie the scarf Catharine had wrapped around her neck. "Caleb has a conference call and I have to wake him—"

Catharine placed her hands on top of Alex's, stilling her fumbling fingers that tugged at the scarf.

"Are you happy, Alex?"

Startled, the young woman looked up and stared at Catharine, as if the question was absurd. "I haven't been happy since the day I met you."

Now Catharine was the one to drop her hands—stung—and look away, for fear the girl would see just how much her words affected her.

"I didn't mean—that came out differently than I meant it," Alex tried to recover, reaching to touch Catharine's shoulder, but Catharine brushed her away.

"It's fine, Alex," she said, a doleful laugh escaping her lips. "No matter how you meant it, you got your point across." She was suddenly chilled and tired, without any relation to the weather. "I think we have both said all we need to say. Have a safe journey home tomorrow—"

"Catharine, please—"

"I do truly wish you the best." She forced herself to smile, before turning down the path, knowing Alex would not follow.

Chapter Thirty-One

Oxfordshire: 23 Years Earlier

The two girls strolled leisurely away from Kenton Theatre down to Thameside before turning east along the river, laughing merrily at one another's melodramatic imitations of the cast of characters from the matinee of Shakespeare's *Twelfth Night*. It was Sunday and the mariners that worked along the docks had all gone home for tea, leaving the girls alone in their journey down the shore.

"I think I would make a very good Cesario," the older of the pair—Nathalie—boasted, tossing her dark hair over her shoulder before twirling around in her best swashbuckling manner and extending a gallant hand to the blonde girl at her side. They passed the bridge on White Hill and were approaching the landing to Rod Eyot, the tiny island in the middle of the Thames, where their friend, Geoff, would be waiting to ferry them across the river.

With the same mock regality, the girl with the flaxen hair offered her fingertips to be kissed by the make-believe Cesario, laughing. "You might make a good Cesario," she looked up, coy through long lashes, "but I think I prefer you as Viola."

"You don't say?" Nathalie's French accent wrapped warmly around the words, her smile coquettish as she held the slender fingertips to her lips a moment longer. "Tu es parfait comme Cate." *You are perfect as Cate.*

"*You* are crazy," The sea blue eyes danced as she shook her head, her cheeks flushed at the compliment.

"Only about you." Nathalie slowly released the hand, taking a hold of her elbow and pulling her forward toward Rod Eyot. "Come on, we'd better hurry if we want Geoff to taxi us!"

A few minutes later they were climbing off a rickety wooden dock into their friend's rowboat—only designed to carry two—but the girls tucked easily into the single seat at the bow as the young man held the boat steady for them to settle.

"You're late," he chided, his crooked grin dispelling any real admonishment as he set off across the river with long, powerful strokes of his oars.

"Not hardly," Nathalie defended, slipping her arm around Catharine's waist as the boat bobbed and lurched along the current.

"You frogs never could tell time. You and your French sense of malleable punctuality." Geoff continued in good humor, "but all joshing aside, I can only take you as far as the Hartford place today and you'll have to walk the rest. My dad wants me in early."

"I thought you were off tonight?" Nathalie frowned, disappointed. "You were coming for supper."

"You'll have to blame her father on my absence," he jerked his chin toward Catharine as he brought the boat alongside the Hartford dock, wrapping a strong arm around one of the lower pilings to keep steady as the girls scrambled up the side. It was made for much grander boats than his simple dinghy, but with some effort they both managed to gain their feet without ending up in the river.

"I thought my father had the factory closed this weekend for the festival?"

Geoff shrugged up at her. "Colonel Brooks called and said to continue production. Some production deadline got accelerated."

"Tea tomorrow, then?" Catharine called as he pulled away, rowing upstream against the current.

"I'll let you know. I'll ring you from the shop."

They waved goodbye and the girls set off down the dock that belonged to the neighbors on the west side of the Brooks family estate. The Hartfords were never in Henley-On-Thames in the summer and Catharine often used their vacant dock as a rendezvous point with her friends when she wanted to meet in private, away from the prying eyes of her father.

But Colonel Brooks was back in London and wouldn't come to their country home with Catharine's mother, Emily, for another fortnight yet, so she had the estate to herself.

Almost to herself.

The house staff was ever present, but they had turned a blind eye to their young mistress's visits with her university mate, Nathalie, for the past three years. Whether the two girls had managed to hide their affair, or the staff were simply loyal to the girl—young woman now, having just turned twenty—whom they had all known and loved since she was toddling in nappies, Catharine never knew. But she was still careful whenever there was a possibility of prying eyes and begged Nathalie to do the same. If her father ever got wind...

They climbed over the low wooden fence marking the separation of the Hartford and Brooks estates and slipped into the acres of woods that ran between the properties. The sun was slowly creeping toward the western horizon, casting brilliant spindles of light through the canopy of trees, illuminating the summer leaves in all their orange and golden splendor.

Catharine led the way, picking around the low brush that caught at the hems of her skirt, cursing herself for not wearing trousers and sturdier shoes.

"Attends-moi!" Nathalie called, urging Catharine to slow down. "You are in such a hurry, Cate," she scolded, trotting up to catch her hand and pull her around. "Why the rush?" Nathalie brought her free hand to the long blonde spiral of hair that slipped from behind Catharine's ear, running the golden curl between her thumb and forefinger.

"Mrs. Ainsley will be expecting us for tea." A slow smile crossed Catharine's lips as she met the French girl's shining eyes.

Nathalie smiled in return. "Mrs. Ainsley has held tea late for us before," she challenged, running her hand down Catharine's cheek until her thumb came to rest on her lower lip. "What did Olivia say in Act III? *'love sought is good, but given unsought is better?'*"

Catharine pressed the warm palm against her lips. "I don't think I give you cause to seek love very often," she chided, entwining their fingers with a seductive slowness as she brought her other hand behind Nathalie's neck, pulling her face toward hers.

It didn't matter how many times she tasted the warm sweetness of Nathalie Comtois's lips—every time was as intoxicating as their first kiss.

Three years they'd been lovers, beginning when they were both first year students attending university in Oxford—Nathalie studying theatre and

Catharine honoring in business—and they'd been the best three years of Catharine's life.

This summer they'd both graduated, and Nathalie was returning to Paris to begin her career. It seemed unimaginable that their time spent together—weekend trips to the country, spur of the moment holidays across Europe, all the long nights and early mornings—would come to an end. They would still see each other—a promise repeated fervently—every opportunity they could find, but it wouldn't be the same.

Catharine pushed the looming future from her mind. They had come to Henley-on-Thames for a two-week holiday before the summer ended and she didn't want to spend the time moping about.

Nathalie slid her hands around to Catharine's back, her fingers finding the row of silk-covered toggles clasped at her neck.

"We can't," Catharine half whispered, half laughed into Nathalie's mouth, pulling reluctantly away. "Not here. The groundsmen will be out working until dusk."

The French girl's chestnut brown eyes were dark in the long shadow cast by the sun behind her, but Catharine could see she was smiling. "Act II, Scene I: '*But come what may, I do adore thee so that danger shall seem sport, and I will go.*'"

"If only I had studied theatre instead of business, I would be able to rattle off a quote to tell you, as romantic as it sounds to flirt with danger, the repercussions of one of my father's gardeners seeing us like this would be far more catastrophic than any death scene Shakespeare ever put to paper." She leaned forward to kiss Nathalie's lips again. "And so—to teatime we will go."

"You've lost your sense of adventure, Cate Brooks."

Catharine loved it when she called her Cate. Nathalie was the only person who did—it was something that was theirs, and theirs alone. Two years older, with endless confidence and an easy manner, the dark-haired French beauty was everything Catharine wished she could be. Free-spirited, self-assured, positive of her future. She didn't care for rules of decorum or the highly structured principles demanded of women of their time. She was just herself—whoever she wanted to be—and the only child of the famed business tycoon, Colonel Benjamin William Brooks was head over heels in love with every nanoscopic detail about her.

On another day she would have let Nathalie convince her to stay in the woods. Allowed herself to be swayed by kisses that clouded all other thoughts in her mind, won over by hands that knew how to persuade her to cast off the restrictions of her formal English upbringing. But an uneasy feeling had gripped her. Ever since Geoff had mentioned her father opened the factories for the weekend—she couldn't break free of the icy tentacles of fear that crept up her spine.

"My sense of adventure ends with bug bites and mildewed forest floors," she made light, and Nathalie conceded with only a hint of disappointment, settling for just the touch of fingertips to fingertips as they picked their way through the wood and came to the clearing that led to the rolling parkland surrounding the Brooks' estate: Honour Stone Manor.

As Catharine predicted, the groundskeepers were out, tending to the endless lawns and gardens, their eyes turned to their work, uninterested in the two girls who leisurely strolled toward the great Jacobean manor.

Late that night, long after the girls had hidden themselves away in Catharine's suite, smothering their laughter as they fed each other grapes and grew tipsy on blackberry wine, dancing barefoot to *Ne Me Quitte Pas*, lost to everything in the world except each other, Catharine woke with a start. She lay still, holding her breath, listening through the darkness for the sound that had woken her, but the house was silent. Mrs. Ainsley and her staff had retired for the night long ago, and it was well before dawn—well before the time she'd make Nathalie rise and sneak to the adjacent chambers, to sleep the last hours of early morning alone.

Nathalie chastised her for being paranoid—for all the precautions she made them take. "Mrs. Ainsley loves you like a daughter. If she were going to tell the Colonel, she'd have done so long ago."

But Nathalie did not understand the consequences of Colonel Brooks's anger—the burden of his wrath. And she prayed she never would.

Colonel Brooks was not an understanding man. He had never approved of his daughter's friendship with Nathalie—referring to her only as "the plebeian from Bordeaux." He considered a career in acting no different than a profession in prostitution—classless, immoral, deceiving. A vocation no upstanding individual would pursue. Had it not been for Catharine's mother, Colonel Brooks would have forbade the friendship from the start. Yet even with Emily Brooks's advocacy, Catharine knew they still walked a fine line and were playing with fire. If he ever found out… if he ever so much as suspected…

"Nathalie." The chill of foreboding from the afternoon had returned. She pressed her lips to the ear of the sleeping girl beside her. "Did you hear anything?"

Groggy, Nathalie stirred, turning on her side to face her. "Hmm?" She didn't open her eyes.

"I heard something."

"Cate," it was a singsong admonishment, her accent thick with sleep. "You were dreaming. Go back to sleep." She reached forward, slipping her arms around Catharine's waist, drawing her into the curve of her body.

"No, it woke me."

"The flutter of a butterfly's wings would wake you. You've been on edge all day." She found Catharine's mouth through the dark, the sweetness of blackberry wine still lingering on her tongue. "Now go to sleep. We have a few more hours before dawn."

Catharine stared at the ceiling as the girl tucked her face into the nape of her neck, their bodies entwined. She told herself Nathalie was right. It was just a dream. But she couldn't shake the feeling that something was going catastrophically wrong.

"I saw a man at the theatre today," she ran her fingers absentmindedly through Nathalie's silken hair. "Watching us. I'd never seen him before."

"Every man watches you," Nathalie said sleepily, her voice muffled against Catharine's skin. "All other women fail to exist when you are in a room."

Catharine smiled despite the gnawing discomfort she could not shake loose from the pit of her stomach. "I think you may be biased."

"No," Nathalie murmured, "tu es belle."

A moment later her breathing was soft and rhythmic and Nathalie had resumed her sleep.

Catharine lay awake a long time, watching the moon traverse the sky, but eventually her weariness won her over, and she drifted into an agitated unconsciousness, filled with dreams of masked faces and high-pitched laughter encircling her as she sat blinded by a spotlight on a stage.

A hostile rapping jarred her from her sleep, forcing her breathless as she sat up, blinking away the fading visions of her nightmare, dazed to the world around her. She was surrounded by light.

She waited, frozen in terror, for the sound to come again. This time she was certain it had not been from her dreams. Beside her, Nathalie had bolted upright, and in the split second of silence Catharine realized the light was coming from the window, the sun high in the sky—it was well after dawn. They had overslept.

The pounding came again.

"Open the bloody door, Catharine!"

In the dawning of her clarity, the moment turned ironically surreal, the room taking on a fantastical feel. Time seemed suspended. For years she would relive those seconds, replaying the scene in her mind, waking from her sleep with the gripping panic that always lingered behind.

There was the scrape of a key in the lock, and she remembered catching Nathalie's eye—holding it for a heartbeat, no longer—but the expanse of understanding that passed between them could have filled a lifetime.

And then the door was swinging open and the rage of Colonel Brooks swallowed the room. He was still in his evening attire, but disheveled in a state of disarray Catharine had never fathomed possible for the perfectionism her father endlessly sustained. His cheeks were dark with stubble, his collar open and tie loose around his neck, his blonde hair—peppering with silver—wild and unkempt.

"So the rumors are true." His strides stopped short in the center of the room, his gaze falling leaden onto Catharine. She had never in her life imagined the level of hatred a man could feel for his daughter. The absolute disgust. The propensity for loathing.

There was a quietness about him that terrified her. A silent brewing violence unlike anything she had known before. Even from him.

"I'd thought it might be that boy—the factory foreman's son—but I should have known."

Beside her Nathalie had pulled the comforter up over her bare chest, her eyes darting from Colonel Brooks to Catharine, before landing on the door. Deciding if she should run.

But to Catharine's dismay, she didn't move. Whether out of simple shock, or loyalty—the unwillingness to leave her on her own. Later, Catharine always felt it had likely been the latter.

"*You*—" his voice shook, rising in volume as his face contorted with rage, "you are a disgrace. An *abomination*." Shaking himself free of his bewilderment that had left him frozen in place, he charged across the room in a handful of strides, arriving at the side of the bed. He bent, snatching up the blouse Nathalie had carelessly discarded the night before, and flung it in her face. "Get out of my house!"

"Father! Please!" Catharine was crying before the words even left her mouth, struggling to the side of the bed. Before her feet had found purchase on the floor, he'd slammed her cheek with the back of his hand, sending her sprawling against the headboard.

"You will *never* address me as such again. You are no daughter of mine!"

He'd raised his hand to strike her again, but Nathalie, half-dressed, flew at him to intervene. "*Bâtard*!"

Dazed from the blow, Catharine watched, horrified, as her father caught Nathalie's wrists midair and slung her to the floor.

"Get *up*, slag! Get *out*."

Her head still reeling, Catharine forced herself out of the bed, falling to her knees at Nathalie's side. "Please…" She was looking at Nathalie, but pleading to her father, terrified he would turn his wrath toward the French girl. "She hasn't done anything!" She could taste blood in her mouth—her lip split from his wedding ring—and feel it dripping down her chin.

Colonel Brooks reached down, wrapping his fist in Catharine's hair, and dragged her to her feet. "Put on your clothes," he hissed between clenched teeth, his hand still tangled in her hair. "We are leaving."

Her eyes found Nathalie's, still kneeling beside her.

Go. She begged her wordlessly, praying she would understand. She could not stay and fight for her. It would only make things worse.

Nathalie hesitated, holding Catharine's gaze, but in the end she seemed to realize it was a battle neither of them would win. She pushed herself to her feet, her eyes never leaving Catharine's, before she finally turned and ran for the door.

"You filthy, unnatural whore," Colonel Brooks averted his eyes from her naked body as Nathalie disappeared into the hall. "You will *never* see her again. Do I make myself clear?"

When she gave no immediate answer—too terrified to speak—he slammed his fist into the side of her head. The second of many blows to follow over the coming agonizing weeks. "Get dressed," he hurled her toward her closet, sending her sprawling to the floor. "We leave for London immediately."

Chapter Thirty-Two

"Do you know it's been twenty-three years since I spent Christmas in my own home?" Catharine set down the tray of tea she'd collected and settled into one of the wicker chairs on her balcony.

Without invitation, the woman beside her took up the kettle and began pouring the brew.

"You realize you are the only Frenchwoman I would ever trust to stir up a proper cup," Catharine nettled her, begrudgingly permitting her to take over the task.

"That's only because your domineering English heritage has falsely dictated an inferior method of fixing a decent cup for centuries, and I'm the only Frenchwoman on earth willing to lower my standards to please you."

"You are incorrigible, you know? You always were."

"You would never have loved me otherwise."

Catharine shook her head with a smile but glanced away as she took the tea from Nathalie. It was still a tender subject sometimes, even after all these years—the way things worked out. But that was all long ago now.

Her onetime lover—now longtime friend—had shown up unexpectedly the night before Christmas Eve, letting herself into the townhouse and surprising Catharine when she returned from her downtown office that evening. She had planned to spend Christmas alone, having already given Grace the week off, enjoying the solitude. For the first time in her life she did not have to answer to anyone or commit to anything. There were no holiday parties Carlton could force her to attend, or campaign trails to travel. No DC political functions or donor charity balls. Just her own agenda.

She had moved the remainder of her life to San Francisco, though was still obligated to fly to South Carolina or DC every week or two to maintain impressions at Carlton's side. But aside from that, her complete focus was on her own work; rebuilding a life of her own. Come spring, she'd reluctantly agreed to make appearances on the campaign trail with Carlton. He would announce his nomination in January and begin the slow march across the country with rallies and fundraisers shortly after. It would be a long, tedious year—but then it would be over. Regardless the campaign outcome, there would be no more delaying the inevitable. One way or another, by the following summer, she would be free.

As long as Carlton stuck to their deal.

"Twenty-four years, actually," Nathalie said, drawing Catharine's attention back to the balcony. "You forgot Cairngorm Mountain. The year before."

Before what, Nathalie didn't say. They both knew.

Before everything.

"Ah, yes," Catharine conceded with a hollow laugh."How could I forget? My mother was fit to be tied not having me home for Christmas. I told them it was a mandatory university trip, you remember? To Hamburg. God," she shook her head, her smile genuine. "What fools we were."

Nathalie held the tea to her lips, her brown eyes turned to the fog that had settled on the bay. She was a classically beautiful woman with a renaissance appeal—her soft, expressive features easily portraying a gamut of emotions —a trait that had worked markedly to her advantage as an actress. Where she had been unquestioningly beautiful in youth, she'd grown only more elegant with age. *A fine wine*, Catharine teased her. *Sour grapes*, Nathalie refuted. But the one thing that never changed were her smiling eyes, always on the brink of laughter. It was Catharine's favorite thing about her—there was a thoughtful, understanding, empathetic depth to them that always made you feel welcome and always made you feel heard.

"Me, maybe," Nathalie said, reflective, "but you were never a fool. You warned me so many times."

"We were so young, Nat. And full of ourselves. We felt invincible."

"I've been thinking about that morning recently," she said, and Catharine knew there could be only one morning she was referring to. She herself had it on her mind lately—more than she had in many years. But the two of them had never spoken about it to each other.

"I've always wondered how different life would have been if I had just listened to you. Even that night. You knew. You warned me and I refused to believe anything bad could ever happen. Where would we be today, I wonder, if I had not been so obstinate?"

Catharine drew her knees to her chest and rested her chin atop them, her untouched tea still balanced in her hand. "We would have been caught eventually. If not that day, another. Even if we hadn't—you would have gone back to Paris and in due course written me some heartfelt, melodramatic missive about how you found someone new. And I would have cried for a month before burning your letter, resigning myself to life as Colonel Brooks's daughter—femme tragique." Her lips pressed together in a tight, sad smile. "It was destined to be so. We never were meant to last."

"No," Nathalie sighed, "I don't think we were. But I don't regret a moment of it, do you? Those were some of the best days of my life."

Catharine absently ran her finger along the rim of her cup, saying nothing. Memories of those three years with Nathalie had been all that got her through her first years of marriage. They were the only antidote to her lonely misery—her daydreams of moonlight walks along silver riverbanks and long, slow kisses with hands exploring sun-kissed bodies—recollections of the happiness she once enjoyed and the obsessive, overwhelming, smothering love she'd felt for Nathalie Comtois.

It was two long years after being shipped off to South Carolina to become Mrs. Carlton Cleveland that Catharine first returned to Europe—a business trip to the Port of Marseille. Against her better judgment, she'd tracked Nathalie down and found her playing Élise in a production of The Miser at the Théâtre du Châtelet. Her biography in the programme listed an impressive start to her career—all roles she'd daydreamed about with Catharine while lounging on the riverbank in Oxford—planning out their futures and all they would hold. Nathalie was living the life she'd imagined, chasing the dreams that fueled her passion. And Catharine had traded in a controlling, abusive father for a manipulative, jealous, micromanaging husband. One set of chains for another.

Throughout all five acts, Catharine had thought about the ultimatum she'd been dealt and the terrible choice she'd made. There was not a single day since that pivotal morning that she did not regret choosing to please her father over her own chance at freedom. The cliche stood true: all the riches in the world could not buy happiness.

Catharine waited by the stage door after the play. In twenty-four months she had not been able to bring herself to write or call. The upheaval of her life had mentally taken a toll and in her anguish she had feared that Nathalie might not want to hear from her again. It had all gone downhill so agonizingly fast. First, the horror of the morning in Henley-on-Thames, and then the following day when Nathalie had hazarded showing up at the Brooks's London home, refusing to leave until she saw Catharine. It was only after the threat of the girl making a terrible scene that Colonel Brooks sent his daughter to the foyer, looming ever-present in the background as Catharine numbly told Nathalie she was promised to marry an American and would be moving to North America within the fortnight. Nathalie had cried and pleaded, begging Catharine to come away with her, but there had been no reaching Catharine. She'd been so downtrodden, so defeated, she'd barely had the strength to ask—and then beg—Nathalie to leave, and never contact her again.

It was in the best interest of them both, she'd said, and closed the door. And that had been the last time she'd seen her. Until the Théâtre du Châtelet.

After the play, when Nathalie came out the stage door to greet the small crowd gathered in wait for the actors, she was laughing and hanging off the arm of the pretty young actress who had played Mariane, sharing an affection with her that Catharine recognized all too well. She'd watched them for a moment, anonymous in the shadows, and then quietly slipped away without ever looking back.

It was the following year that Catharine had finally found the courage to reach out to her former lover. To write to her of her many regrets, and beg her forgiveness for all her wrongdoings, and the pain she may have caused. Lengthy, heartfelt, sincere.

"More than anything, I miss the dearest friend I have ever known," the letter said in closing. Her return address on Daufuskie Island.

It was months before she got a reply, but the correspondence was warm and forgiving, filling Catharine in on all the time that had passed and the adventures she had encountered—from back-alley theatre troupes to the grand stages of Paris and beyond. She wrote about a woman she had met—a Spaniard—and of the love they now shared.

It was a blow to Catharine. Despite knowing they would never have what they once had, somewhere in the crushed ruins of her heart she knew she had harbored a fraction of hope Nathalie still loved her... and by some stroke of fortune they could somehow go back in time and regain what they had lost.

But it was a fool's fantasy, nothing more. She'd made a vow to her husband and a promise to her father, neither of which could be broken. And Nathalie had moved on.

But it didn't make the hurt any easier to bear.

At the end of the letter, Nathalie wrote that she was coming to New York for the summer—a Shakespearean theatre festival—and if Catharine had an inclination to come see her, she would be delighted.

And so, it was on a humid, cloudy afternoon in Central Park that the spark of their friendship was rekindled. They spoke little of the love they'd once known, but the closeness they had experienced—the ardent bond of friendship that only two like-minded women can share—was still there. And thus it had grown and blossomed over the past twenty years—through Catharine's tumultuous relationship with Carlton and Nathalie's unstable career—they had been there for each other for the good, the bad, the exhilarating, and the heartbreaking. Catharine counseled Nathalie through at least a dozen lovers—some serious, some just passing through—and Nathalie had long listened to Catharine's frustrations in her marriage and acted as the voice of reason when it came to making difficult decisions with her company. It was a comfortable, familiar friendship they enjoyed; one that simply fit, like an old, worn glove, without complication or hidden agenda.

The two women sat silent for a time, sipping their tea, lost in thoughts of the past. After a while Nathalie set her cup down and stretched back in the balcony chair, fixing her gaze on Catharine.

"While we are on the subject of forbidden secrets," her eyes were alight, despite the dullness of the morning, "what is it you are not telling me?"

Catharine offered her best look of perplexion, but Nathalie waved her off. "Don't you stiff-upper-lip me," she scolded, crossing her arms, "something's brewing, and I can't quite put my finger on it. So—spill it."

Turning her face to the cloud covered sky, Catharine shut her eyes, contemplating whether she wanted to open this can of worms with Nathalie.

On one hand, it would feel good to get the weight of it off her chest and Nathalie was the only person in her life she could trust—but on the other, she knew she would never hear the end of it if she did confide in her friend.

"If I tell you," Catharine said at last, returning her gaze to meet Nathalie's over-perceptive eyes, "you have to promise not to get too carried away. You can't dramatize the situation the way—"

"You've met someone!" Nathalie lurched forward, unfurling her crossed legs, dropping her elbows to her knees, her chin in her hands, the way she always did when she was wholly engrossed in a topic. "Mon Dieu! Just when you think something's impossible, the walls of Jericho come tumbling down!"

"God, you're so dramatic." Catharine rolled her eyes. "Look, you have to promise—"

"I'll make no such promises I can't keep! Now, carry on!" She was as giddy as a schoolgirl. "You must tell me all."

"Honestly, there isn't much to tell—"

"Is this the reason for your divorce? I knew something had to push you over the edge—"

"*No*," Catharine said firmly. "My divorce with Carlton has been a long time in the making—"

"Exactly! So, something finally got you to act! Are you having an affair?!"

"Nathalie, Jesus. No! I knew it was a terrible idea to tell you…" She let out a sigh. "I mean it when I say there is not much to tell—"

"—But there is *something* to tell." The Frenchwoman's flair for the dramatic was part of her charm and Catharine couldn't help but hide a smile behind her cup.

"To prevent your utter disappointment at the end, I'll preface it by saying whatever this was—it's over now—in honesty, it never even began."

Nathalie twirled her finger in a *hurry up* motion, bored with the disclaimers. "Yes, yes. Whatever you say. Back to the details."

"In July—"

"*July*!? This has been going on since *July* and you said nothing—"

"Jesus, Nathalie, do shut up!" Catharine unfolded her legs from the chair and got to her feet to pace the balcony.

Unfazed by the admonishment, Nathalie waited expectantly, her hands steepled beneath her chin.

"In July," Catharine reluctantly began again, "I got myself into a bit of a situation sailing my old dinghy and nearly drowned. Fortunately, there was a girl who happened to see me capsize and came to my aid."

"You almost drowned?" Nathalie furrowed her dark brows, confused. "You never said anything—"

"Do you want the story or not?" Catharine said pointedly. "I swear, Nathalie—"

"Yes, yes, I'm sorry. Go on. My lips are sealed." She made a zipper action across her mouth and sat back, trying to feign nonchalance.

Catharine paced across the front of the balcony once more before turning and leaning against the glass balustrade, resigning herself to the telling of proceedings of the last six months of her life. She spoke candidly, leaving out nothing, and covered the gamut of events, both significant and irrelevant, from the beginning in Daufuskie Island to the ending in Lafayette Square a few weeks prior. When she finished, she stepped away from the railing and took up her cup of tea, trying to busy her hands.

"Well," Nathalie said at last with great, mock gravity, "you must truly be smitten."

Catharine narrowed her eyes, suspicious, waiting for the trap she was certain was being laid. Very rarely did Nathalie have anything to say in great seriousness.

The Frenchwoman continued. "In all the years I have known you, I don't think I have ever seen you drink a cold cup of tea. She must be impressive."

Annoyed, and mildly embarrassed, Catharine set down the porcelain with a clatter. "That's all you have to say? That's your great insight?"

"I'm serious," Nathalie was indignant. "I mean it, Cate." She smiled at Catharine's frustration. "You really are quite taken with her. How old is she?"

"Young." She sighed. "Twenty-six? Maybe twenty-seven now? I'm not certain."

"I see. She is young." Nathalie nodded, calculating. "Sixteen years…"

Catharine bristled. "Not much different than me and Carlton. Amazing how no one notices when you are a man."

Nathalie waved her off. "And the boyfriend?"

"What about him?"

"What's he like?"

Catharine shrugged, indifferent. "Handsome. Appears driven. A bit—a lot —pompous. I don't know, I've spent very little time around him. They have known each other since childhood."

"But you don't think she loves him."

"I can't begin to claim I know her mind, Nathalie," Catharine snapped, swiping up her cup to take it inside then changing her mind and setting it back down, sloshing half its tepid contents onto the serving tray. "Damnit!"

Nathalie laughed, which only annoyed Catharine more.

"You really are in a state," she dropped a napkin atop the spilled tea, "I think I need to meet this girl."

"Oh, sod-off, Nat! You know me well enough to know I will *never* allow that to happen. Have you meet her and cause some unnecessary embarrassment on both our parts? Not bloody likely."

"Oh, it's going to happen," the woman's eyes twinkled as she swatted Catharine's hands away from the tea. "Let me get this, you've made enough of a mess already."

"I told you, it's quite over!"

"If it's over, why are you so flustered?"

"It's your incessant desire to turn something into something it isn't." Catharine sank into her chair, drawing one knee up to hug to her chest. "You know what the last thing she said to me was?"

Nathalie quit mopping at the tea and looked up, realizing Catharine wasn't as finished on the subject as she feigned to be.

"That she hadn't been happy since the day she met me."

"The context, please."

"In the square. She was upset and getting ready to leave. I asked her if she was happy. That was her reply." Catharine looked away from her friend, still feeling the sting of Alex's words in the park.

"I'd say she's about as over you as you are of her, then," Nathalie shrugged, going back to gathering the tray. "Or," she continued, not bothering to look up from her task, "she's about as over you as I was for the first twelve months after I unexpectedly found myself alone and cut off from the one thing I wanted most in the world. I'm confident I would have had a similar response to you that first year had you put the question to me." She looked up, all sense of her previous teasing cast aside. "I know you don't see it, Cate, but you're not..." she hesitated, trying to find the right words. "You're not like most people. Loving you is a double-edged sword. On the one hand, to have your love is the most magnificent feeling in the world. It's this—this magnetic forcefield drawing you in, and your heart wants to follow with reckless abandon, but on the polar side your mind is screaming at you to stop. Because it *knows*. It knows casting its lot with you is a wager fit only for the most temerarious... falling in love with you is like Icarus and the sun... and I believe I can speak from firsthand experience that the fall into the ocean far surpasses the expectations of concerns your mind was warning your heart about along the journey."

Catharine stared at Nathalie, unblinking, her face blank and still as stone. At length she shook her head, her brow creasing in confusion. "I'd be more likely to translate Sophocles's *Oedipus Rex* into Latin than I would to interpret whatever it is you just said."

Nathalie was not put off and did not laugh. "The *CliffsNotes*, then." She sat forward and stared straight at Catharine. "I can see where someone could find themselves acutely unhappy falling in love with you while not actually knowing if they could ever attain you. It's a fair enough concern."

Catharine was quiet, ruminating the words.

"I don't believe I have ever led anyone on in false pretense or with feigned intentions."

"No, not false at all. That's part of your greatest charm. But falling in love with anyone is scary, naturally—but falling in love with someone like you is downright terrifying, and it's not easy to recover from, I promise you that. Because no one wants their heart broken, especially not by the likes of you."

"Oh, for God's sake, don't be so melodramatic, Nathalie. You're not up for a Tony here. I'm no different than anyone else—"

"I know you can't really believe that, Cate." Nathalie stood, tea tray in hand. "But all of it aside, the simple fact that you have the power to make someone unhappy speaks volumes as to your importance in their life." She shifted the tray under one arm so that she could rest a hand on Catharine's shoulder as she walked by. "I haven't seen you show interest in someone in over twenty years, and it's not been due to your frigid marriage to that *trou du cul* husband of yours. Perhaps it's worth stepping off your ethical high horse for just once in your life to pursue something for yourself."

Catharine kept her attention forward, her lips pressed into a frown. "I'd be lying," she said quietly, "if I said I wasn't a little afraid—afraid of letting this go anywhere beyond a secret, childish fancy. It's been a tremendous risk demanding a divorce from Carlton. The only real leverage I have over him is this election—he needs me right now. He needs me to be the dutiful, quiet, supportive wife at his side. Nothing to disturb the waters. And I have agreed to it until the election is decided, one way or another. I will leave him with what is fair—the papers have been drawn up—and in return for my cooperation he has agreed to the divorce without contest." She looked to see if Nathalie understood. "But if it ever got out—if it was ever found out that I—" she couldn't bring herself to say the words. They were still such blasphemous memories of her past. "My father remains the majority shareholder in Brooks Corp. He may be dormant, but he is there. And those percentages never let me forget it. He could force me out—take everything."

"You could fight him. You've built this empire while he sits silent on his throne, thousands of miles away, living like a king off your labors—"

"They were his labors first," Catharine cut in, "built on the back of my grandfather before him. And the numbers don't lie. A majority vote isn't contestable. I made a deal with the devil all those years ago. I would not bring shame to our family and he would hand over the control of the corporation to my judgement. Upon his death his shares will be mine, but until then…" Her voice trailed off.

"You haven't spoken to him in years. He knows nothing about you."

Catharine laughed, bitter. "On the contrary, I'm sure he knows everything about me. His last little stronghold of control. He'd never give that up. It will be a battle enough to have him learn I have requested a divorce, but I can work my way around that. But if he suspected for even a moment…" She took in a slow, steadying breath. "It sounds so petty, saying it out loud. But it does terrify me. Brooks Corp has been my entire existence. It's the only thing I have to show for a life that feels less than lived. I don't want to lose it."

Nathalie was contemplative, unrushed to respond.

"Then don't lose it," she said finally, as if it were as simple as that. "There are plenty of secrets the world never needs to know. And you, my dear, know how to keep them better than most. But don't throw something else away out of fear. You've already done that once. The risk may be worth it."

Before Catharine could respond, Nathalie disappeared through the open glass panels without another word.

After a few minutes, Catharine stood and walked to the balcony, looking down across the street at Marina Green and the harbor beyond it. The fog was still low along the shore, hiding all but the tops of the tallest masts in the marina. The streetlights were wrapped in tinsel and lights to celebrate the holidays and somewhere down the boulevard one of her neighbors had Christmas music blaring through open windows.

"It's beautiful," Nathalie said behind her, pressing a hot cup of tea into her hands when she turned to face her, "but it's certainly not Paris at Christmas."

"When do you head home?" Catharine suddenly felt the weight of her loneliness press heavily on her shoulders. She knew Nathalie had only stopped by on her way back to France to visit her family and could not stay long. She had a two-week holiday before beginning rehearsals for an original play opening in New York in February.

"I should really go tomorrow," she said, wistful, sensing her friend's melancholia. "But I'll be back Stateside for rehearsal soon, and you'll have to come see me in New York. If the show doesn't flop."

"I highly doubt it could," Catharine pressed her shoulder against Nathalie's with a smile. "I heard it was cast quite brilliantly."

The two women leaned against each other, sipping their tea and watching the cargo ships navigate the bay. Catharine was grateful for the company. She got to see Nathalie so seldom she enjoyed any time she could get with her.

"We'll see. The critics certainly felt differently last summer." She referred to the early closing of the show she had done in Amsterdam in August. "Are you still holding the charity gala at City Hall this year?"

"It's scheduled. I'm sure Carlton will try to turn it into a campaign event somehow."

"You should invite the girl."

"Alex?"

"Are there others?" Nathalie asked with mocking incredulity. "Are you leading some double life I don't know about?"

"Dozens. It's a regular bordello around here."

"I should have known. It's always those quiet Londoners you have to look out for. Yes, *Alex*. Invite her and I'll come down for the weekend. It's before my show opens. I want to meet her."

"I doubt she'd come. If she's even in town. Her season will be starting up about the same time."

"Invite her, and if she doesn't show up, I'll drop the topic and never pick it up again. I swear it." She held out her hands to show her fingers were not crossed—something she'd done for all the years Catharine had known her.

"Fine. If it will shut you up, I will extend the invitation. But that's the end of it, understood?"

Nathalie's eyes shone, victorious. "Understood. Now get dressed! I want to go out on the water!"

Chapter Thirty-Three

Alex was a half an hour late to her own birthday dinner. She'd told Caleb she didn't want to go out, but he'd flown all the way to California to see her, so she'd finally agreed to a brief, low-key celebration not too far from her new apartment.

As she climbed out of the Uber, she realized she should have walked. At least then she would have had an excuse for running late.

Caleb had her car. He'd arrived early in the morning from a job he'd been on in Atlanta and could only stay two nights before he had to get back to the worksite. A new high school stadium or gymnasium, Alex couldn't remember. She'd left her keys tucked up in the bumper and told him she had a PT appointment in Berkeley, but could catch a ride with a teammate and wouldn't be back until evening. Then she'd jogged across the street to the waterfront cafe and watched out a rain streaked window for him to arrive and drop his bag at her third story apartment before leaving with her car.

There was no physical therapy session in Berkeley. She didn't even have training that afternoon—it was their first day off since preseason camp had started a week earlier—but she didn't tell him that.

Not that Alex would have been doing much in training, even if it hadn't been a rest day. She'd come up sore the second day of camp with swelling in her left ankle. Nothing serious, the medical staff assured her—a touch of tendonitis (undoubtedly a result of overtraining during off-season; a fact she chose to ignore)—but Rodney Collins, the new head coach for the Sirens, didn't want to take any chances. With preseason less than eight weeks away, he needed the squad sound and healthy. With the amount of money riding on the success of the team, Collins had been placed under an immense amount of pressure to perform. But even still, the former Youth National Team coach placed his players well-being as top priority. So he'd pulled Alex to low intensity workouts until the tenderness abated.

Her disappointment at being unable to give a hundred percent to her new squad was ironically dissipated by a call she received the morning after she'd been placed on the injury list. It was the morning before New Year's Day.

It was Isabelle Atwood. The iconic, no-nonsense, famously hard-nosed coach for the US Women's National Team. The senior squad manager minced few words to tell Alex she'd been impressed with her productivity throughout the end of the previous season, and if her performance continued as it had been, she'd be extending an invitation for her to train with the team at their late winter camp in Colorado. She didn't have to tell Alex that it was the camp that would help determine the roster for the SheBelieves Cup—the last major tournament before beginning CONCACAF qualifying for the following year's World Cup.

"This conversation is not an official call-up," the woman had finished the phone call curtly, "but consider it a call-up. You're on my radar, Grey. Don't let me down." And then she'd hung up.

Alex had soared out of the coffee shop—her ordered cortado forgotten—and found herself in Estuary Channel Park before she'd returned to earth to even realize she had no idea where she was going or what she was doing.

Dropping onto one of the ketchup-stained picnic benches facing the marina, she took a moment to rest her head in her hands, surprised to find her palms damp with tears.

It was happening.

It was finally happening.

A week before her twenty-seventh birthday, she'd finally gotten the call. The call of a lifetime. A call she'd begun to worry might never happen.

From her days of hand-me-down shinguards and cleats two sizes too small, to the devastation of her uncle refusing to allow her to attend the U-16 or U-17 camps in high school, she'd finally found a weak spot in the ceiling of her career. Another chance. An opportunity she wouldn't blow.

Suddenly, a few days on the injury list for a sore ankle didn't seem such a catastrophic event in the long run.

She'd wanted to call someone. To share the news. To have them congratulate her—to be on her side. She knew most of the girls would have immediately sought out their boyfriends or girlfriends or spouses. They were who you were meant to call when you received life-altering news, were they not?

But Alex couldn't bring herself to call Caleb. She told herself she didn't want to interrupt him in the middle of the workday, but she knew it went much deeper than that. The truth was, she didn't want to share the moment with him because she knew, as soon as he got involved, he would take it over—he would consume the excitement and the joy and the lifetime of dedication and struggle—it would become *theirs*, not *hers*. And sometimes not even *theirs*, but *his*. And she couldn't let it go just yet. This was her hard-won achievement. It was her accomplishment. He would have it soon enough.

She scrolled through her short list of "favorites" and stopped at Abby Sawyer. She hadn't spoken to Sawyer since she'd packed her car to make the twenty-eight-hundred mile drive to the West Coast the week before Christmas. It wasn't that they *weren't* speaking. They just *hadn't* spoken. And the more time passed, the harder it got to make the call.

Alex tapped the number, holding her breath, but before it could connect she hit cancel. She had no right to call Sawyer after weeks of silence just because she'd had good news.

She looked at the other numbers. Caleb. Erin Halsey. Uncle George and Aunt Pamela.

The number she really wanted to dial wasn't listed. And that silence was even harder to break than the one with Sawyer.

She finally settled on her Aunt Pamela, who answered on the fourth ring, as she always did, and addressed her as Alexandra—despite the fact her parents had legally named her Alex. But it wasn't feminine enough for Pamela. So she refused to use it.

"Well, that's very good, my dear," her aunt said, no more impressed than if Alex had called to tell her she scored a B on her Spanish test or her car had passed smog on the second attempt at a less-than-reputable test-only facility. "I'm sure you must be very grateful for the opportunity to express your God gifted ability."

Alex assured her she was, then tried to say goodbye before her aunt decided they should close the conversation with a prayer, but wasn't fast enough. The last ninety seconds of the call were dedicated to Pamela thanking the Lord for the blessings He bestowed upon her niece and asking Him to help keep Alexandra humble and mindful that her true purpose was in serving the Good Lord, however He saw fit.

As if He'd been the one to put in ten-hour days at the gym and full-fledged effort for ninety minutes every time she stepped on the field.

She hung up and walked the half-mile back to her apartment where she fixed herself a dinner she never ate and eventually called Caleb to tell him about her conversation with Coach Atwood.

That had been a week ago.

Now she stood in front of The Gallery Art Bar, thirty-three minutes after seven p.m., and took a meditative breath before pushing the double doors open to enter the small, retro building.

To Alex's utter horror she was greeted by a chorus of discordant voices shouting "surprise" as the low-lit interior of the room was simultaneously flooded with light from the overhead chandeliers, making it difficult to focus.

Her first instinct was to turn and run back out the door. She had hardly wanted to have a private dinner with Caleb, let alone spend an evening with the two dozen or more faces washed over in bright light leaping out at her from chairs and tables around the room. But she managed not to run. She forced herself to smile—at least what she hoped came across as a smile—and brought a hand up to shield her eyes so she could look around.

In addition to the small crowd—a combination of teammates, a couple vaguely familiar faces she thought might be Caleb's western region co-workers, and two HEG administrative reps, Matt and Erick—she saw posters had been plastered all over the walls that said "Way to go, Grey! USWNT!" along with Happy Birthday graphics and decorations.

Her cheeks flared. She should have known this was what he was up to. It had all seemed too simple and unpresuming. He had respected her wishes for a quiet night out without enough of a fight.

"Hey, babe!" Caleb greeted her, his voice loud over the background music, and stepped out from behind the door where he'd been videoing. His phone was still recording. "What do you think, is a call up for the National Team the best birthday present a girl could ask for?"

"It wasn't a call up," was all Alex could manage, feeling the flush extend from her cheeks to her collar bone.

This couldn't be happening.

"Well, the promise of one," he laughed.

Alex held her hand in front of her face. "Please stop recording," she mumbled, very uneasy in front of the camera. She knew he would post the video on his Instagram and Snapchat—his latest obsessions—and it would get shared far and wide, her fans and critics analyzing her response and expression and demeanor.

"Yes, but first a couple questions," he said, his voice mocking the low, serious tone of a sport's commentator. "What team do you anticipate the USWNT will face in the final of the next World Cup?"

"Caleb, enough—" She pushed his hand aside, forcing him to turn the lens to the ground. "I wish you would have warned me—"

"You can't warn someone about their own surprise party, babe," he laughed, taking another wide angle sweep of the room before ending the video. "But before I forget—I have another surprise for you." He was completely oblivious to her discomfort and embarrassment. "Halsey!" He yelled over the Bruno Mars song that was pounding over the chatter in the bar. "Where is she?"

Alex followed the direction he was looking to see the tall, brawny form of Erin Halsey—the former keeper for the Rage—standing at the end of the bar, ordering a drink. The day before the trade window closed, Halsey had been the Sirens most notable American acquisition. Touted as the number one goalkeeper in the world—the starting keeper for the USWNT—her move from Carolina had been monumental.

And an absolute welcome relief to Alex. To start the season off with a friendly face, a player with whom she had an excellent rapport both on and off the pitch, had been a soothing balm to the rawness of her nerves at joining a new team.

If only she'd been the answer to overbearing boyfriends who didn't have a clue how to read the writing on the wall when it came to respecting wishes for privacy. But even she didn't hold the antidote for that.

Still, Alex was relieved to catch her amiable gaze as she sauntered toward them. Everyone loved Halsey. It was impossible not to. She had a knack for making every situation bearable through her good natured humor and harmless pranks.

"Heya," she grinned, her freckles glaring in the flash of color from the disco ball that had come to life above them. She strolled over to Caleb and

Alex, beer in hand. "We've got a rival in the house! Cheetah! The guest of honor is looking for you!"

Cheetah—the nickname was reserved to tease only one woman in the league, earned by not only her immense speed but high predatory success rate in the box. Abby Sawyer.

Before Alex had time to process what Halsey was saying, the familiar face appeared at the goalkeeper's side, a reserved smile touching her brightly painted lips.

"Hey, Hollywood," Sawyer stepped forward, a half-empty glass of wine in hand, and hugged her old friend warmly. "I've missed you, sugar." The low, midwestern accent was palliative to Alex's overstrung nerves and she felt her throat hitch with emotion. She hadn't realized just how much she'd missed the tranquil soul of Abby Sawyer, or how terribly lonely she'd felt without her friend.

"What are you doing here?" Alex broke away from the hug, holding her at arm's length, still trying to wrap her mind around her unexpected appearance.

"I'd heard a pal was receiving her AARP card today, and when Halsey mentioned there'd be a retirement party, I couldn't not be here."

"Ass," Alex quipped at the old-lady-joke, but still had to brush her hand across her eyes. "I can't believe you're really here." She hugged her once more before reluctantly letting go, wishing they could just disappear into the crowd. "It's the best birthday gift I ever could have asked for."

"I don't know," Caleb cut in and Alex turned to see he was holding the camera again, videoing her hug with Sawyer. "The night is young! And surprises are abound! The best gift may be yet to come!"

"Caleb, honestly!" Alex placed her flat palm over the lens. "Enough with the video."

"It's for the Vlog!" he responded, as if that made it all okay.

"No more surprises tonight," she took hold of his wrist, squeezing it hard to make sure he was listening. "No more surprises, please."

"It's your birthday, what can I say," he waxed indifferent, a smug smile on his face. "Some things are out of my control."

"I mean it." Alex started to turn back to Sawyer, but Caleb caught her chin between his thumb and forefinger, turning her face toward him. "Hey, I haven't even had a hello kiss yet," he said with a fake pout.

Alex tried to muster some real affection toward him, telling herself he had gone to all the trouble to come and be there for her birthday, and that in his mind a surprise party was something everyone wanted—he loved celebrations and the chance to socialize—it wasn't his fault she didn't feel the same. But her kiss still fell short, she knew, as she stood on her tip toes and quickly brushed her lips to his, before pulling away to turn back to her friends.

"All right, I get it," he teased, "I can't compete with your girls. Just remember to save some time for me tonight, won't you?" He winked and moved away to talk to some of the other guests and Alex felt the vice-grip of anxiety lessen.

"I still can't believe you're here." She took Sawyer's hands in hers, before looking over to Halsey. "Thank you. Truly."

"I'm glad this punk called me," Sawyer patted Halsey's back. "Feels like the old days again. I miss this."

"I want all the gossip!" She slipped her arm around Sawyer's waist, steering her toward the back of the room where the music wasn't as loud. "You have to catch me up—tell me everything!"

It was only after reassurance from Sawyer that she would be in town until Monday—they would have plenty of time to catch up over the weekend—that Alex branched out to greet the other guests. The reps from HEG—only in attendance since they happened to be in town—left early, offering Alex a breath of relief. She always felt babysat by the company when they were present, making sure she was living up to the standards of a Hargrove Athlete.

"Nothing like having Big Brother always around, eh?" Alex turned to find Amelia Walker, the Sirens team captain—*her* team captain, she had to remind herself, the Sirens were *her* team—standing beside her, her gaze following the two stiffly suited men out the door.

Amelia was from Australia—one of several international players on the roster—and was without question the most talented soccer player Alex had ever seen. She was brilliant on and off the ball—arguably the most creative midfielder in the league—and her superior athleticism was nothing short of supernatural.

She'd been courted for the Sirens since the inception of the team, but her willingness to play across the pond had been hard won. Not only the captain of the Matildas—Australia's National Team—but a longtime megastar for the English Women's Super League (ostensively the most successful women's football club in the world), she'd been disinclined to sign for an American expansion team. But Hargrove Entertainment Group had been persuasive, and by the time the negotiations were settled, Amelia Walker had signed a two-year contract that made her the highest-paid player in the history of the league. Followed by an endorsement with *Kickstar*—without any of the restrictions and regulations instilled upon their other athletes.

Alex liked her. Amelia was all business on the field and a grueling captain who expected more from her teammates than was even sought by the coaching staff. But in turn, she was an uplifting voice of encouragement and the definition of a team player. Unselfish. Motivating. Reliable. A leader in every sense of the word. It was true—her excessive talent and natural ability was vested with a certain amount of arrogance, but it was not unmerited, and there was no question as to her ability to back up her words with equivalent actions.

A few years older than Alex and several inches shorter, she had a shock of short blonde hair she wore shorn on the sides, unruly in a way that always made her look as if she'd been woken unexpectedly and skipped the mirror on the way out of the door. It gave her a charming, roguish appeal that complimented the androgyny of her features—tomboyish and tanned— with lines creeping in from years of hard play in the unforgiving sun.

"Reckon we can have that drink now?" she raised her eyebrows as the shadow of the HEG representatives disappeared through the front window.

Alex laughed. "Do we dare?"

"It's your damn birthday, mate. What are they going to do? Fire us?"

Alex knew Amelia wasn't held to the same strict standards Hargrove demanded of their other endorsed athletes. She had all the same freedoms and diverse expression the rest of the rostered Sirens players enjoyed— protected by the NWSL. The conservative company had known from the start she didn't fit into their mold—and would give no effort to try. The endorsement deal had only been a buy-out to bring her to the States, but her skill set and contribution to the game had clearly been worth the deviation from the company's so-called values. They wanted a championship team and Walker was the woman to lead them there.

Still, tonight, for Alex's benefit, she embraced the term *we* with the obvious intention of putting Alex at ease.

"Besides," she glanced around the room, "if someone blows the whistle on us, you can blame it all on me. Tell 'em I didn't want to drink alone." She jerked her chin toward the bar. "What'll you have?"

Alex opened her mouth to respond when the music was abruptly shut off and a loud clapping sound silenced the room from the bar.

"Attention, attention," Caleb drawled, appearing from behind the bar where he'd muted the sound system before swinging up onto the counter to stand, towering over the partygoers.

At the soda gun the bartender looked miffed, but remained silent, waiting to see where this was going.

"So much for a drink on the sly," Amelia gibed, nudging Alex with one of her tattooed forearms. "I've got a fiver that says this becomes acutely embarrassing for you in a matter of moments."

Alex stared at Caleb, noting his moderately slurred speech and mild sway as he held a wrapped package out in front of him, scanning the room below. He was definitely drunk, and about to cause a scene, but Alex didn't know how to stop it.

Across the bartop she saw Sawyer turn from where she'd been chatting with Halsey and a couple Sirens players, her eyes narrowed in disapproval at the display. The rest of the party were looking up with curiosity.

"Ah, there you are!" Caleb waved when he located Alex, gesticulating grandly for her to come toward the bar. "Hiding out with our new friend from Down Under," he mocked in a poorly executed Australian accent, pointing a finger at Amelia. "You're kind of like a double agent, aren't you, Walker?" He was temporarily sidetracked from his mission. "I mean, if you think about it—you come here and learn our tactics, and then you go back and play for the Australian National team after stealing all our secrets— how's that work exactly, *mate?*"

"Caleb—" Alex started but Amelia touched her arm to hush her.

"He's drunk," she whispered with a shake of her head. "Don't bother."

Caleb went on. "Come, come, babe—I won't bite," he waved the package in her direction. "Well, at least not until you ask me to." This elicited a couple sniggers from his co-workers standing at the edge of the bar. Alex felt the blood drain from her face. Somehow she forced her feet forward—aware all eyes were on her—until she was within a couple yards of him.

"Please get down." She stared at the laces of his shoes.

"As you all know," Caleb addressed the guests, either not hearing Alex or ignoring her, "my little star here is on her way to play for USA!"

There was some mild applause and congratulations that Alex tried to drown out amidst her absolute horror of his exhibition. There was no way Isabelle Atwood was going to call her up after she got wind of this.

"So—I had a little gift made up for her," he waved the present in the air before tossing it to Alex, who, caught off guard, dropped it to the floor.

"It's a good thing you went with soccer instead of softball," he smirked as she fumbled to retrieve it from the ground, her fingers losing all form of coordination. The steady hand of Amelia Walker reached out in front of her, taking up the package, and placed it in her arms. "You can double my bet," she whispered with a glint of humor and Alex couldn't help but smile—though the sentiment was short-lived.

"Open it, babe," Caleb planted his hands on his hips, impatient, watching her with a lopsided grin.

With shaking hands, she slid her fingers beneath the tape, opening it to reveal a red, white, and blue US jersey with the number eleven printed on the front.

Relieved, Alex held it away from her to get a better look, grateful it had not been anything more embarrassing.

"Look at the back," Caleb hopped down from the bar and strode toward her, a hand reaching into his pocket.

Numbly, Alex turned the jersey around, immediately feeling the momentary respite of relief seeping from her body while a whole new level of mortification took its place. Above the blue outlined number eleven was the name *Anderson* in block lettering, glaring at her against the white polyester.

An unbearable pressure had begun to expand in her head, thundering between her ears. She wavered a little, unsteady on her feet, and it was Amelia who reached out a steadying hand.

"You see, A," Caleb continued, heedless of her dismay, "the name Grey is just far too short—too unremarkable—to wear on a jersey representing the USA. And so," he pulled his hand out of his pocket and dropped to a knee in front of her, "I feel compelled to change that." He looked up, holding his hand out toward her, displaying a small box with a diamond ring glinting in the fluorescent light of the hanging chandeliers. "Marry me, Alex Grey." As assertive and self-assured as he always was, he pressed the box into her hand.

Alex was silent. All of the sounds around her faded, disappearing into the erratic clamor of her heart. She stared dumbfounded at the ring, unable to bring herself to look Caleb in the eye. All of these people, all of the faces turned on her, waiting for her to say something. She wanted nothing more than to vanish, just disappear and wake up to find this was all an abhorrent nightmare.

It couldn't be happening.

"Well?" Caleb said, when the silence had drawn on a little too long, "We need an answer here. You don't want to keep your fans waiting." He flicked his thumb to the side, jolting Alex out of her stupor, where she turned and saw one of Caleb's co-workers—she didn't even know his name—holding Caleb's phone in her direction. "Smile," Caleb grinned. "You're live. All your followers are waiting with bated breath."

Alex turned back to him, speechless. She felt nauseous. He was still smiling.

How could he still be smiling? How could he not tell?

"I—" she shook her head very slowly, a feeling of claustrophobia over-powering her. "I need some air." She pushed the velvet box back into his stunned hands.

Self-conscious of the camera, she turned away, seeking out the clearest path to an exit. All around her the guests stared, silent, as she bolted in between them, unable to look anyone in the eye, and raced down the hallway, past the kitchen and into the ladies' room.

As soon as the door was closed behind her, she slunk down against the tile wall, her knees drawn up to her chest, head back against the porcelain.

This wasn't happening. This couldn't be happening. It was the repeated mantra in her head.

There was a soft knock before the door was slowly pushed open. Alex kicked a foot out to stop it, but recognizing the familiar brown hand with its pink painted nails, she drew her leg back to allow Sawyer entrance.

"Is there room for two in here?" Sawyer surveyed the two empty stalls and Alex on the floor. "I guess it's never really a party until someone ends up crying in the bathroom."

"I'm not crying," Alex said dully, staring at the wads of gum stuck to the bottom of the sink in front of her.

"I can see that." Sawyer shut the door and reclined against it with her shoulder, gazing down at Alex with an unreadable expression. "I take it that was unexpected?"

"Ha," Alex scoffed, forcing a mirthless laugh. "To say the least." She looked up at her friend. "He recorded all that live..." Her voice tapered off, still reeling with disbelief.

Heavy steps approached down the hall and there was a brief commotion. The bathroom door started to open against Sawyer's bodyweight, but was jerked shut from outside, followed by the low, angry curse of a woman.

"You fucking bogan—you can't have reached this age in life and not realized that if a woman hides herself in the loo, she doesn't want you to follow her." It was Amelia Walker.

"Get out of my way," Caleb was loud and belligerent. "This is none of your damn business." The door started to open but was slammed shut once more.

"Why don't you give her a few minutes before you—"

"I said get out of my way," Caleb hissed, and this time the door was shoved open hard enough to dislodge Sawyer from her sentry, nearly forcing her to the ground.

Alex leapt to her feet, placing herself between Sawyer and Caleb, holding a hand up to stop his entrance. Behind him, Amelia—who may have been petite in stature, but made up for it in strength and endless aplomb—had reached out to grab his arm, but held up when she saw Alex, waiting to see what she should do.

"Caleb, I need a little—"

"What in the hell is going on, Alex?" His face was blotched with whiskey and wrath. "You made me look like a fool—"

"You did that to yourself," Amelia slid between him and the door frame to squeeze into the bathroom, offering Alex a buffer from his rage. "You really need to go—"

The Senator's Wife

"Shut the fuck up, you pathetic dyke," Caleb growled, darting a hand out to grab the Australian's shoulder, but Alex intervened, her shock turning to outrage.

"Get out, Caleb!" She snatched her arm away as he tried to reach for her. "You need to leave me alone!"

"Alone!? I just asked you to marry me, for Christ's sake! I—I spent two months salary on that ring! I don't understand—"

"You wouldn't! You couldn't possibly," Alex's embarrassment was temporarily forgotten. "How could you understand? All you think about is yourself—"

"What! Alex—"

"I can't do this anymore, Caleb." Her eyes were dry and her voice was steady. "I can't. I need some time by myself—"

"You don't know what you're saying—"

"I know exactly what I'm saying! It's what I've been wanting to say for months—"

"Please," he shifted tactics, turning to pleading, his voice washed of anger. "Let's talk in private, away from here." He motioned at Sawyer and Amelia. "You're not thinking straight—"

"I'll leave your bag at the lobby."

"We need to talk in private, Alex!"

"I'm done talking." She tried to step around him but he thrust an arm across the threshold, blocking her path. "This is all just a misunderstanding."

"Get out of the doorway, *mate*," Amelia spat through clenched teeth when he once again disallowed Alex to pass.

Caleb whirled on her, all his previous rage returning, and for a moment Alex thought he might actually lunge to strike her—a challenge to which Amelia had not backed down.

But before she could do anything a strong set of hands grabbed Caleb by the collar, pulling him backward into the hall.

"Time to go, buddy," the stern voice of the bouncer said, subduing the taller man with a twist of his arm. "Party's over."

Caleb struggled for another moment before finally complying, moving a few steps away from the door. "Alright, alright," he shook himself free. "I'm going." He looked back at Alex. "I'll stop by in the morning."

Down the hall his friend was still holding the camera in their direction, a drunken grin plastered on his face.

Alex didn't say anything. There was nothing to say. As soon as the doorway was clear she walked stiffly into the hall, turning toward the emergency exit. She didn't care that the alarm blared as she shoved open the door. She didn't really notice. She just needed to find some air.

Chapter Thirty-Four

The HOPE Charity Gala was one of San Francisco's most talked about events of the year. Held at the historic City Hall in the heart of the city, the annual fundraising ball drew an all-star attendance from its celebrity audience, raising tens of millions of dollars for the HOPE Foundation—a non-profit providing free education to underprivileged youth, from primary school through university, in more than seventy countries across the globe.

Famous for its elite patronage—from A-list movie stars to technological giants, business moguls, nobility, and political leaders from around the world—it was heralded by *The San Francisco Times* as "the most prestigious gala this side of the Atlantic."

It was one of Catharine's pet projects. Hosted by WorldCargo—the US based corporation operating under its parent company, Brooks Corp.—it was an event she'd looked forward to organizing for the past eleven years. Successful. Consequential. Fulfilling.

Carlton had never felt the same. A colossal expense and undertaking, it had been a yearly point of contention between he and Catharine since its inaugural year.

"An astronomical misallocation of money and time," was his fall back criticism, regardless that he'd never so much as donated a single dime to its organizing and the only effort he put in was showing up to partake in the open bar.

But it hadn't stopped Catharine from enjoying the orchestration of the evening.

This year was different. With Carlton's official announcement for his bid for the White House, she couldn't bring herself to take much joy in the project. The gala had always been hailed as a neutral source for bipartisan camaraderie on both sides of the political arena, but this year her husband was bound to turn it into a GOP shit show, regardless his avowal to keep politicking to a minimum.

In response, she'd turned the management of the organizing committee over to her assistant, Nicole. One less headache to oversee. But there were still a few things she wanted to have her hand in, especially with the gala less than a month away.

Catharine called Nicole into her office.

She'd returned a few hours earlier on a red eye from Belgium—a meeting with the Antwerp Port Authority—and hadn't found coffee black enough to give her the energy to sort through the handfuls of messages posted on her desk or combat her overburdened inbox.

"Welcome home, ma'am. You asked to see me?"

Catharine turned from her view of the Transamerica Pyramid and greeted the girl with a smile.

"Nicole." New York born, transplanted to Georgia during her high school years—she still possessed the no nonsense, matter-of-fact, get-the-job-done qualities of an East Coast native, and even after ten years with Catharine maintained the same decorum for her boss as she had as a student straight out of university. "I hope all was well in my absence?"

"Nothing out of the ordinary. The permit issue in Guangzhou, but I believe Trent spoke to you about that already?"

"Yes. Gordon will touch down in Hong Kong later today. It appears that debacle is being narrowly averted."

"Very good." Her eyes flashed to the door. She was ever in a hurry to get back to her job.

"And the gala?"

"On track."

"Excellent. Will you send me a PDF of the confirmed guest list and seating chart?"

"Ma'am." Nicole nodded.

"Oh, and do me a favor—please place Senator Cleveland with Senators O'Riley and Chisholm at the north facing tables."

Despite her well-rehearsed poker face, Catharine caught the flicker of surprise in Nicole's perceptive eyes. It was gone as quickly as it had come. "Certainly."

"You can send the rest incomplete. I may have some changes."

"I'll have it right over."

Catharine dismissed her and returned to the window. Carlton would have a fit. It was outside propriety to seat the two of them apart, but she would use the excuse of seating him with the other Republican congressmen from Texas and Georgia to her advantage. She couldn't stand the thought of sitting beside him for the night, listening to his incessant, conceited dialogue about the election and the future he saw for America.

The notification dinged for Nicole's email and she dragged herself from the window to download the file.

Eight hundred invitations sent. Seven hundred fifty-six returned.

Catharine dragged the cursor straight to G.

Grey, status: unreturned.

She clicked out of the email, annoyed for being disappointed and doubly annoyed at Nathalie for forcing her to send an invitation she knew would not be answered. At least she'd upheld her end of the bargain. Now, if Nathalie would just stick to their agreement.

She rang her friend.

Nathalie picked up on the first ring. "Stateside?"

"Yes, I got in a couple hours ago."

"I thought you were going to stop in New York?" She was disappointed.

"Mid-flight we had an issue with a port in Guangzhou and I had to get home to retrieve some paperwork to send with Gordon to China. I'm sorry, Nat."

"I've found the best crepe shop in Manhattan. I was going to take you for breakfast. Next time, then. They're nearly as good as the ones at home."

"It's a date," Catharine promised. She felt badly. She knew Nathalie had been counting on her overnight visit. She was lonelier in New York than she thought she would be. But rehearsals were going well and her show was set to open the following month. "I'll come to your opening night. Then you can take me for breakfast."

"Is that to be penciled in or can I write it in ink?"

"You know I'll do my very best to be there—"

"—Barring any unforeseen circumstances," Nathalie finished the sentence, knowing it all too well. "Yes, yes, I know." She sighed. All of Catharine's life was *barring unforeseen circumstances*. "So," Nathalie switched gears, "any developments with Miss Grey?"

"No. It was as I told you it would be. She didn't respond to the invitation." It came out crosser than Catharine meant it.

"And you're sure you had the right address? You weren't even sure where—"

"Obviously I verified the address, Nathalie. Don't make it into a thing. I told you she wouldn't respond. Now that's that. I don't want to hear about it anymore. That was our deal."

"Well," Nathalie paused. "It's rude for her to have not responded one way or the other. No loss there."

It was too easy to get her off the subject—she knew Nathalie far better than that—but she let it go. Maybe for once she really wasn't going to make a mountain out of a molehill.

After a brief silence Catharine exhaled, tired. She'd not gotten any rest on the flight—she'd been too preoccupied trying to hold the China deal together—and the weariness was catching up with her. She should have stopped at home before heading to the office; there was just so much to do.

But it was more than a lack of sleep.

"You are going to be here for the gala, right, Nat?" She didn't want to be there alone.

"You can pull out that ink pen," Nathalie asserted and Catharine laughed at the jab.

"Touché."

They talked a few minutes more before Nathalie had to leave for an evening rehearsal, promising to call in a couple days.

Catharine resigned herself to the dreaded task of sifting through emails and returning her life to order after five days on the road. It was going to be a three-kettle kind of afternoon.

She wasn't through the first fifty emails when her phone buzzed. A text message from Nathalie.

—Did you see this? She sent a link to a video.

Catharine glanced at the title, *Proposal Gone Wrong,* and went back to her work. Whatever it was could wait.

A few minutes later her phone vibrated again.

—I take back what I said about being rude. I'd probably jump off the cliffs of Beachy Head if that happened to me.

Catharine clicked the link.

She found herself staring at a video of Caleb Anderson's face in a close up, whispering above loud music in the background, "she's here!" A moment later Alex appeared through dark doors, recoiling at shouts of *surprise*. The edited footage flashed to a clip of her repeatedly asking him to put the camera down, and then another frame of Caleb addressing the lens as if he were a talkshow host: "and here we are, friends—the moment you've been watching for. She has no idea! First the Nat Team, then her birthday, and now...dunt dunt dun..." He grinned with all the drunken stupidity of a frat boy. "I'd say it's been quite a good week for Alex Grey. Stay tuned for the big question." He handed the camera off to another man who then proceeded to film a slurred speech from the bartop, followed by an enormously embarrassing proposal that clearly mortified his intended prospective spouse.

Catharine watched long enough to see the camera follow Alex down the hall toward the bathroom, followed by the ranting form of the boy, but turned it off at that point. She didn't want to see anymore.

According to the YouTube link the video had been viewed over seven million times since it was posted two weeks earlier. The next video in queue boasted a highlights reel of the evening with a title that read *When You're Just Not That Into Him.*

Catharine swiped the screen closed, leaning back in her desk chair to stare at the vaulted ceiling of her sixty-first story office. She was tempted to research more. The video mentioned Alex making the US Team. No doubt there would an article about that on one of the women's soccer sites.

She refrained. Instead she texted Nathalie.

—No, I hadn't seen it.

—I guess you don't have to worry about the boyfriend anymore. You should invite her to the gala in person.

　　　　　　　　　　—*Brilliant timing. I'm sure I'm just who she wants to see. Give it a rest!*

　　　　　　　　　　—*You never know. She might need a friend.*

　　　　　　　　　　—*I'm not going to show up at her apartment uninvited.*

　　　　　　　　　　—*You showed up at my dorm room uninvited.* She included a shrugging emoji with a wink.

　　Catharine could feel her cheeks color and was glad Nathalie wasn't there to chaff her about it.
　　　　　　　　　　—*I was 17.*

　　　　　　　　　　—*And now you practically have one foot in the grave.* —an eyeball emoji— *Live a little. Go see the girl!! Off to rehearsal xoxo*

　　Catharine flipped her phone on silent and set it face down on her desk, going back to her emails. There was no way in hell she was going to show up unannounced at Alex Grey's apartment to invite her to an event she already declined by virtue of her disregard for the RSVP.

Chapter Thirty-Five

"God, you're out of shape." Amelia Walker was alternating jumping jacks with knee lifts as she waited for Alex to catch up in the parking lot of their apartment complex in Jack London Square. "It's only been, what, three weeks you've been sitting on your arse? How the hell can you lose your endurance that quickly?"

Alex came panting up to where the Australian was razzing her, shaking her head between breaths. "We just ran five miles in—" she checked her watch, "—under thirty-five minutes. That's less than seven minutes a mile!" She coughed, trying to clear her burning lungs, regretting the all-out effort she'd put in over the final mile. "Cut me some slack. I'm a striker—sprinting is my jam."

"Let's be clear—*you* ran five miles in 34:52. I ran them in 33:13." Amelia turned and proceeded to trot backward up the three flights of stairs, showing no signs of fatigue.

"Not everyone can be superhuman." Alex dragged herself up the concrete steps, paying special attention to her left ankle for any signs of weakness. There had been no more swelling or tenderness, but Collins still had her on light duty for another week. So the clandestine runs with Amelia probably weren't the wisest decision—but hey, Amelia was their captain, what could she say? She had her blessing—insistence, even.

"Nothing superhuman about it. You just have to want it." Amelia stopped at the third landing, folding over to stretch her warm muscles.

"I call bullshit." Alex plopped down on the top step, grabbing the toe of her tennis shoe, flexing her calf to keep from getting a charley horse. "I want it plenty badly enough. You just happen to be born with it. All the conditioning in the world couldn't make me as strong and fast as you, and you know it."

"I guess it's a good thing you can finish, then," Amelia teased, settling down beside her. "Because God knows it isn't your running game that will get us ahead."

Alex rolled her eyes. She was still one of the fastest players in the league, and despite her injury, one of the best conditioned players on the roster, aside from Walker, who was beyond any of their reach. "You just worry about how you're going to get me the ball, and I'll worry about netting us the wins," Alex countered, lifting the hem of her shirt to wipe the sweat from her eyes.

Ever since the disaster of her birthday a few weeks earlier, Amelia and Alex had developed a camaraderie extending beyond the friendly banter they'd exchanged since the first day at the Sirens training camp. They'd gotten on well from the start, but after the mortifying evening at the Art Gallery Bar, Amelia had become a fixture in Alex's daily life, even outside of soccer. They lived one floor apart and had fallen into the pattern of hanging out together in the evenings, watching pre-recorded WSL matches in England, analyzing film from previous NWSL seasons, dozing off to bad Australian soap operas and half-played games of Backgammon.

Alex knew Amelia had inserted herself in her life to take her mind off Caleb. Or, more accurately, off the aftermath of Caleb. The humiliation of his proposal in front of her friends and teammates had been only the beginning of the nightmare. The viral video that followed—ensuing in endless tasteless jokes, circulating memes, TikTok commentary and her name trending on Twitter (all for the wrong reasons)—had threatened the collapse of her spiraling mental psyche.

When HEG had left a vague voicemail the following Monday for Alex to call them, Amelia had told her to ignore the call. She would handle it. And whatever the Australian had done, HEG had never mentioned the situation again. Halsey'd been the one to talk to Isabelle Atwood, later relaying that the traditionally staid Welshwoman had admitted to laughing heartily at the video, and told the keeper to make sure Alex knew she had nothing to worry about—other than finding a less vainglorious boyfriend. Oh, and that *Grey* was as fine a name as any, and would look perfectly at home printed on the US kits.

With those fears abated, Amelia had steered Alex toward a public acknowledgment of the incident, suggesting she address it head on with her fans and supporters. Alex was never at risk of looking like the bad guy—Caleb's stupidity had crowned him the clown of the internet for a day (or week, or three)—but it was something Amelia felt might blow over faster if Alex faced it directly.

"Trust me, she'll be apples. The whole world can see that galah's a few kangaroos loose in the top paddock, but the chatter will go away faster if you own it."

Alex wasn't exactly sure what all that meant—Amelia's love of her Australian slang often flew over her head—but she took her advice and wrote up a carefully worded IG post of her own, thanking her fans for their support, and teasing that they owed her for providing a well-needed laugh to get everyone through offseason. She'd included a photo of her left hand with the caption "no rings attached," hit *post*, and then turned off all her social media for the two weeks following. She'd worried the joke would be too much a slap in the face to Caleb—even after everything went down, she hadn't wanted to hurt him any further—but then she'd remembered how he'd called Amelia a *pathetic dyke* on YouTube Live, and decided not to lose another second of sleep over any of it.

A task proven easier said than done.

"There's not a pro in the industry that hasn't dealt with some form of public debacle or another, trust me," Amelia'd told her, time and again. She'd had her own share of undesired limelight throughout her illustrious fifteen year career and had developed a hard-nosed approach to fan-based backlash and speculation. Alex could only wish she had a single millimeter of her thick skin. "We're all susceptible to it in our careers—and it eventually passes when the next unsuspecting internet victim has something go balls-up—but until then, you just answer them in the game. Give them something else to talk about. Shut their cakeholes with a banger of a goal or perfectly timed tackle inside the eighteen."

Alex had wanted to point out that getting shredded online for missing an open net while 1 v 1 with the keeper in added time, costing the team the game, was a little different than having your ignoramus boyfriend declare to the whole world that your name was too unremarkable to wear on a jersey, while simultaneously offering you a ring, but she'd left it alone. She knew Amelia was right. By the time the season started, it would all just be a bad memory.

And so what had started as a diversion from Alex's misery had turned into a fast friendship between teammates. A comfortable habit. A daily routine.

"Maintenance is still working on my toilet," Amelia peered over the railing to her apartment on the second floor. "I swear they must be paid by the hour. How hard is it to fix a simple leak?"

"They probably say the same thing about us when we miss a PK," Alex laughed, shoving herself to her feet. "I was going to make dinner anyhow. You can shower at my place."

"It's the principle of the matter. They've been at it all day."

Inside her apartment Alex tossed her keys on the counter while Amelia flipped on the kitchen lights. They were small one bedrooms paid for by the housing allowance for the team. While the complex was older, the apartments were safe and relatively well-maintained, with an ideal location directly next to the Oakland Estuary, where Alex could see Alameda Bay and the San Francisco city skyline from her Juliet balcony. About half her teammates lived in the same complex, with the others opting to take the allotted allowance and live further inland, pocketing the excess money.

She set her AirPods on the table and cleared her pockets, glancing at the opened envelope addressed to her in handwritten calligraphy.

Inside was an embossed invitation for her and a plus-one to a charity gala at San Francisco's City Hall sponsored by WorldCargo, a company she'd never heard of before. But tucked into the invitation was a folded piece of paper with meticulous handwriting she recognized immediately.

It read:

Miss Grey,

I would like to personally extend an invitation for you and a guest to join us at the HOPE Charity Gala. Your presence would be warmly welcomed.

Most sincerely,

C. Cleveland

Alex had been sitting at the table with Amelia when the envelope arrived shortly after her birthday. She'd been sorting bills and junk mail while they debated the benefits of ice baths when the WorldCargo envelope caught Amelia's eye mid-sentence.

"My dad works for WorldCargo," derailed from their conversation, she picked up the envelope to examine it. "He manages the stevedoring firm accounts out of Port of Melbourne."

"Stevedoring?"

"Longshoremen. Dockers."

"Ah," was all Alex said, taking the envelope Amelia handed her and running a dull butter knife along the edge of the thick paper. She pulled out the gala invitation and read it over, uncomprehending who it had come from. "It's an invite to some charity gala." Confused, she unfolded the slip of paper tucked in the center.

As soon as Alex saw the writing she knew her face would betray her, but Amelia had been focused on the card from WorldCargo.

She discreetly tucked the note between her cell phone bill and a re-election advertisment. It wasn't something she wanted to discuss.

"This is to the HOPE Gala," Amelia was as animated as Alex had ever seen her. "How the devil did you get an invite to that? It's like the White Tie Who's-Who of non-profits—invitational only. It's a big deal."

Alex tried to focus on what she was saying and not the note wedged beneath some Republican city councilman's cheesy grin. "How do you even know about it?" She tried to change the subject. "I've never even heard of it."

"And yet you're sitting there with an invitation to attend? You've got to be shitting me" Amelia turned the card over. "I mean, this looks official. It has to be real."

"Have you been before?"

"To the Gala?" Amelia was incredulous. "*No*. My father has a right important job with WorldCargo and has never been to an upper management Christmas party—let alone one of their White Tie events. I'm telling you, Alex—you have to be somebody to get one of these. Ronaldo. Kobe. Jeter. Woods." She flicked the card down on the table. "Someone like that. I mean, no offense."

"Well, I think I've had enough of invitation-only events with Caleb to last me a lifetime. Him and his obsession with getting on *lists*. There is no place I would rather be less than a public function right now." She stacked the card under the rest of her mail.

"No, Alex," Amelia said pointedly. "I don't think you understand. You can't turn that down. I'd kill to have an invite to that—and I personally despise invitational balls and parties and the whole nine yards."

"Take it, then. Go in my place."

Amelia's tanned face pinched into a frown. "Don't be a bogan."

Alex sat back, crossing her arms. "I have no interest in going."

"What if I went with you?"

"I appreciate the offer. But *no*."

Over the next week, Amelia pestered her about the gala a few times, trying to change her mind, but eventually gave up. Alex wasn't budging.

But she still hadn't been able to bring herself to throw out the envelope.

"Do you want to shower first?" Amelia was rummaging through Alex's mostly empty fridge. "I need to call my parents before they head off for the day. It's getting late in Melbourne."

Alex thumbed the crisp parchment back under the stack of mail and headed for the shower.

When she was finished, she grabbed her robe and opened the bathroom door to hear Amelia's voice coming from the kitchen. But as she started for her bedroom, she realized the Australian wasn't on her phone but was talking to someone in the doorway.

"Who is it?" She steadied the towel piled high on her head and moved to peek around the wall dividing the front entrance from the kitchen, curious who would have stopped by in the evening. It wouldn't be Halsey. She went to hot yoga at five p.m. But maybe Molly Rodriguez—one of the Sirens' fullbacks who lived on the first floor of their same building—or Jess Combs, the baby of the roster, an up-and-coming winger at just nineteen. Both stopped by frequently.

"If you wait just a moment, she'll be right out," Amelia was saying, blocking the view to the doorway. "Trust me, there's not enough hot water for her to be leisurely."

There was a muffled reply. Whoever it was was leaving.

Alex snuck a glance around the partition and then hurled backward, losing the towel on her head and nearly tripping over the fallen tie of her robe.

Of all the people on the planet she had not expected to see, the very last of them was Catharine Cleveland.

"Shit." She muttered to herself, listening to Catharine tell Amelia not to bother, she couldn't stay long.

What was she doing here—at her apartment?!

"If you want to leave your name and number, I can tell her you came by?"

"No, it's all right. Another time," Catharine was saying, and then Amelia noticed the bathroom door was open.

"Oh, she's out now!"

Damn Amelia.

Alex pressed against the wall, regathering her robe, her heart pounding.

"I'll grab her—"

"No, but thank you." From her hiding place Alex saw Catharine turn to leave.

She should let her. She *had* to let her.

"Catharine! Wait, please!" Before she could silence her tongue or stop her feet, she was out the threshold, standing barefoot on the third story walkway, doing her best to secure the tie of the robe still dangling at her knees.

The woman paused, looking over her shoulder. "I'm sorry, Alex. I shouldn't have just shown up without invitation. You're busy—"

"I'm not, really!" She swung an arm wide to show how *not* busy she was, and collided her hand with the stucco wall, scraping the skin from her knuckles, cursing internally. "We just—we just got back from a run. Give me just a moment—I'll get dressed—please."

"Alex—"

"Less than a minute, I swear!"

Uncertain if it was worse to leave her standing outside or invite her in, she compromised with leaving the door open, giving Catharine the option of either.

Without further acknowledgment she ran down the hall, slamming her bedroom door behind her. A few seconds later Amelia poked her head in while she was struggling into a sport's bra refusing to slide over her damp skin, tangling herself in a losing battle.

"I, uh…" Amelia was unsuccessful at swallowing her smile as she came up behind Alex to sort out the back of her bra. "I'm not even going to take a stab at whatever you got going on here, but… everything okay?" She was referring to Catharine, not the bra, though Alex would have preferred it were vice versa.

"I just—wasn't expecting anyone," Alex was hopping one-legged into a pair of joggers while blindly dragging a t-shirt out of her hamper.

"Yeah, I got that feeling." Amelia's lips twisted in a cat-that-ate-the-canary grin as she bent down to toss Alex her shoes. "I'm going to run down and call my parents and check on the maintenance crew."

"No! You don't have to go!"

"She doesn't look much like the dangerous type, I think you'll be okay here alone. Though it's always those classy ones who can be deceiving—so if you run into trouble, just holler—I'll hear you through these cardboard walls." Amelia winked, heading for the door.

"She's a friend from South Carolina." Alex wasn't sure why she volunteered information that wasn't sought. She just didn't want it to look like something it was not. Or at least less like whatever it was. "I was just surprised to see her."

"I'll wager that's one thing all three of us can agree on." Amelia teased, before disappearing down the hall.

Alone, Alex took a moment to pull herself together before returning to her front door. Catharine was at the railing overlooking the courtyard, but turned when she heard Alex's footsteps.

"I'm truly sorry to have interrupted your evening. Your friend didn't have to leave."

"Amelia lives downstairs. She's our team captain. Maintenance is working on her bathroom." Alex motioned toward Amelia's apartment below before reaching up to brush her wet hair back behind her ears. "We just got back from a run." She took a breath, and then laughed, despite the awkwardness. "I can't lie. I was surprised to see you here."

"I'm a little surprised to be here myself."

Alex gestured at her open door. "Will you come inside?"

For a second she thought Catharine would refuse—and part of her hoped she would. The apartment wasn't grand. It wasn't the world Catharine was accustomed to, with its cramped rooms and whitewashed walls.

There were dishes in her sink. Cleats and cones in her hall. A cheap leather couch she'd picked up at Ikea during the New Year's twenty-percent-off sale—a step up from the thrift store furniture she'd had in South

Carolina. She'd been stoked about it at the time—*moving on up*—but felt self-conscious about it now.

"Thank you," Catharine accepted, and Alex resigned herself to lead the way into her dismal kitchen.

"Can I get you a drink? I have water, Bubly, iced tea—hot green tea, but it's instant, so—"

"The tea sounds wonderful." Catharine stood in the threshold of the kitchen. Alex could feel her eyes on her as she fumbled through her cabinets and fridge, suddenly aware of every cheap oddity in the apartment: the plain white tile backsplash above the electric stove that needed re-grouting, the laminate countertops, the fridge that hummed too loudly to be in good working order, the lime build up that forced the water to exit the kitchen faucet at a funky angle. It was like seeing the place for the first time through a microscope. She should have continued the conversation outside.

"Would you like to sit?" She wanted to apologize for the plainness of her apartment—the thriftiness of her furniture and decor and lifestyle—but she didn't. This was her reality. This was who she was. And the truth was, after Caleb and HEG and everyone that wanted her to be someone she wasn't— she didn't want to apologize for being herself anymore. If anything had been gained from the last six months of her life, it was her realization that she could never please everybody—and there was no point in trying. *Those who mind don't matter, and those who matter don't mind.* Wasn't that what Catharine had quoted?

Catharine stood beside the table but didn't sit down. Alex couldn't find the box of tea and could feel her frustration building, though she knew it had nothing to do with the missing Lipton.

"What brings you here, Catharine?" she finally said, turning from her search through the cupboards to face the woman watching her silently, her hands resting on the back of one of the dining chairs that still had Alex's sweatshirt thrown over it from the night before.

"I don't have a good answer."

It wasn't what Alex expected her to say. She had been anticipating certainty. Eloquence of reason. The perfect poise that made up the entirety of Catharine Cleveland. *I don't know* didn't seem like it was something that would be in her vocabulary.

"I guess," she started again, "I wanted to see you. There was—," she deliberated, "I wanted to invite you to an event."

She had the same direct candor, ever maintaining her composure, regardless her own obvious discomfort at her uninvited intrusion.

"You could have called."

"Would you have answered?" The corners of Catharine's lips flickered, though it wasn't really a smile.

"Probably not." She closed the cupboard door behind her. "I can't find the tea."

"I didn't come for tea. So all's not lost."

Alex felt the stirring of a smile at the habitual dryness of her humor. Still, it didn't change her answer. "Unfortunately, I am afraid you drove all the way out here for nothing," she crossed to the table and pulled the sweatshirt off the chair, tossing it over the kitchen bar to the couch in the living room. "I can't go to your gala."

"The gala wasn't why I came." She finally decided to sit. "Though I still hope you will reconsider. I would love for you to be there."

"I'm afraid I'm just not the gala type." Alex couldn't hide the derision in her laugh. "I mean—look around." She spread her arms to their surroundings. "I think it's a bit out of my social standing."

"It's a fundraiser." Catharine was patient. "There will be a wide variety of guests in attendance, including many athletes."

"I'm not exactly LeBron James or Roger Federer."

"A fortunate truth."

Alex rolled her eyes. "I'm serious."

"So am I." Catharine drummed her fingers against the lip of the table. "But the gala is here nor there. The young man from last summer—Lukas Krajnc, the cellist—has a show opening at Symphony Hall. There will be a few people you've met before. I wanted to ask you to go with me?" She leaned against the back of the chair.

With me. There was so much context to those two words.

Alex watched her, marveling at how comfortable she managed to look sitting at her prefab table, away from the elegance of her bay front home and eccentric friends.

"When is it?" She wasn't sure if she was hoping for a conflict in schedule or not.

"Saturday. Eight p.m."

Even if she was medically cleared by then, training finished early on Saturdays and they were off on Sundays. There was no excuse.

"Caleb asked me to marry him." The admission fell out of her mouth and she didn't know why.

"I see." Catharine remained remarkably expressionless. "Are congratulations in order?"

"I guess, depending on how you look at it."

"Congratulations to you both, then."

"Just to me. I told him no."

There was the slightest lift of her brow. "Ah." The drumming of her fingers stopped. "And that is to be congratulated?"

"Yes. I think so."

Catharine reached forward and touched the sleeve of the t-shirt Alex had pulled on in her haste with one of her slender fingertips. The line of the hem was exposed and Alex flushed, realizing it was inside out.

"Come on Saturday, Alex."

Alex answered before she could overthink it. "Where should I meet you?"

Catharine stood. "Here. Six p.m."

"Okay."

"So, your mate from South Carolina left in an S-Class Benz. I half expected to see a chauffeur," Amelia said by way of greeting when she let herself into Alex's apartment and found her making a mess of chopping vegetables for a stir-fry. She hopped up on the kitchen bar, her heels rhythmically clicking against the cupboard below. "I swear, Grey—you have the most bizarre surprises up your sleeve. Who the hell can afford a car like that?"

"An impressively larger number of people than you would think," Alex tried to put her off. "Like every seventh draft fullback for the NFL, for example," she teased, referring to the least paid position in American football.

"I'm relatively adept at minding my own business—it's actually something I pride myself on—but, Alex... come on." She fixed her with a stare. "I can't let this one go."

"Let what go?" The vegetables were sticking to the bottom of the pan, burning on the electric stove.

"No, no, you don't get to play that game." Amelia hopped down from the counter and strut over to where Alex was, snatching the wooden spoon from her hand. "Give it to me—you're ruining it all!" She took over without much more success.

"Her name is Catharine." Alex didn't volunteer her last name. "I met her on vacation in Carolina last summer and we somehow, I don't know—became friends." She shrugged, pleased with the truth of her explanation. "She has a home here in San Francisco. She helped me with some of the language in my *Kickstar* contract."

Amelia twisted off the burner knob and removed the smoking pan, never taking her scrutinizing green eyes off Alex.

"Don't take this wrong," she said, without much hint of apology in her voice, "but why the hell would someone like that befriend someone like you? Can't say I see her as much of a soccer fan, dressed in those heels."

"She likes sailing."

"Of course she does," Amelia laughed. "On her hundred foot yacht with her twenty-man crew en route to the Bahamas. I might like sailing, then, too."

"No." Alex set a couple plates on the table. "You're wrong." She immediately looked away, trying to hide her defensiveness, but Amelia was hot on her trail.

"Am I?" Her smile was lopsided. "Tell me, if she is such a good mate, why were your knickers in such a twist when she showed up at the door?"

"I already told you—I wasn't expecting company."

"Remind me to never show up unexpected."

"I wasn't expecting to see *her*. As you already so eloquently pointed out, she's not exactly in my class of friends. Present company included."

"Salty," Amelia smiled. "A new side of you, Grey. I like it."

She spooned a heap of charred vegetables onto Alex's plate, quiet for a moment, thinking too hard. Alex was certain she wouldn't appreciate the next line of questioning before it even began.

"She's a right stunner, eh?"

Alex knew better than to deny it. "She is."

"Magnificent, really. Is she married?"

"Yes."

Amelia ran a hand through her wayward shock of hair. "Too bad," she set two cans of Bubly on the table. "I fell in love with a woman like her when I was in senior secondary. My soccer coach's wife, actually," she unceremoniously flopped herself into the chair across from Alex. "Didn't go very far," she laughed, spearing a blackened zucchini.

Alex wasn't taking the bait. "I'm sure your coach was grateful for that."

"I doubt he would have cared." Amelia shrugged nonchalantly. "I'm pretty sure he'd been shagging our keeper since Year eleven."

"Charming."

"Not really. He was a gronk. I almost quit the game over him."

"I guess it's good you didn't."

Amelia wasn't getting anywhere, so she took a different approach. "So, did Caleb know you fancied—what did you say her name was? Catharine?"

Alex looked up from her plate, unamused. "I'm not playing this game with you, Amelia."

"No game. Just an honest question." She had the good sense not to smile. "Don't take it so hard—it's not like Mr. Hargrove is going to walk in at any moment. I mean, unless you anticipate any more—interesting—company this evening."

Alex went back to her dinner.

"You know," continued the Australian, undeterred, "they tried to make me sign a clause that I would keep my private life—well—private. One of the polyester suits went so far as to suggest I grow out my hair, dress a little more—*delicate*, I think was the word he used." She laughed, but it lacked her typical sarcastic amusement, teetering instead on derisiveness. "Like there's never been a gay girl in soccer before. Hell, this game is won off the backs of the gays, most of them just do it with lipstick and their hair styled." She frowned. "Anyhow, I told them to fuck themselves, and I guess they were willing to forgo their 'Christian Values' for my playmaking abilities. But," she looked up from her fork, "I've no doubt there are a wide number of Hargrove athletes bound to such clauses."

Alex ignored the implication behind her statement. "I'm sure your girlfriend appreciates your authenticity."

She'd mentioned a girlfriend back in Melbourne but never spoke much more on the subject. Despite her defiance toward HEG, she did in fact keep her private life private.

"I guess." She was noncommittal. "You know, my fans were brutal when I left Arsenal. They considered me a traitor, leaving the WSL. Didn't matter that I was offered four times the salary to come kick a ball around an American pitch—not to mention the endorsement contract. But to the fans, it's not about the money. It's about the game. And I get it, I do. I love this game. But sometimes we have to make the best decision for ourselves—for our lives—not just for the sport. I'm sure you understand that?" She looked at Alex hard and Alex realized she was not talking about soccer anymore.

"I do understand it." She pushed away her plate. "It's just hard to know what the best decision really is sometimes."

Chapter Thirty-Six

The Bay Bridge traffic had inched along at an intolerable pace, backing up miles out of the city. It was worse than normal for a Saturday night, and by the time they reached the music hall, the valet lot was full and Catharine had been forced to settle for the parking garage a block over from the symphony.

Putting the car in park, Catharine glanced over at Alex, who'd been unsurprisingly quiet on the drive into the city. But despite their sparse conversation, she displayed none of the aloofness she'd harbored in both Oakland and DC. She was relaxed, more self-assured, and had seemed genuinely pleased when Catharine picked her up at her apartment across the bay.

Catharine watched the outline of her reflection in the passenger window for a moment before shutting down the engine. They were on the brink of being late, scheduled to meet Nathalie in the cocktail lounge at seven—it was a quarter 'til—but Alex seemed in no hurry to get out of the car, and Catharine had no desire to rush her. It wasn't the concert, or Nathalie— flown in for just two nights—or mundane conversation with her other friends from her box in the Davies Music Hall that was the culmination of her enjoyment of the evening. It was this right here—these moments alone —that she'd looked forward to. It was why she'd chosen to pick Alex up on her own, forgoing the comfort of a driver. And in just a few minutes the serenity of the night would be over.

"I'm glad you came."

Drawn from her thoughts, Alex turned from the window. "I'm glad you invited me." She seemed almost surprised after she said it, as if she had just in the moment come to that realization. She settled back in the seat, absently toying with the lace tooling sewn into the skirt of her dress. "You know, I assumed—after DC—that I wouldn't see you again. That you wouldn't want to see me again," her lips pressed together in a smile that fell short. "I know we're running late, and I don't know why I waited this whole drive to say anything—but I just wanted you to know... I'm sorry for what I said in the park. I was angry—*at myself*—for the mess I'd created, and I didn't know how to get out of it. I just wanted to close my eyes and duck my head and pretend everything was going to be okay—even when I knew things were bound to fall apart." She chewed on her lower lip, staring at her hands. "You were right—about everything. I just didn't want to hear it. And I feel like I've been entirely ungrateful for your kindness. I haven't deserved it from the start." She looked up abruptly. "Will you forgive me?"

Catharine laughed. "Let's see—you saved my life and in return I stuck my nose where it didn't belong, resulting in a well-deserved rebuke. I do not think we are on a level playing field. There is no forgiveness on your part to be sought."

"On the contrary—perhaps we are tit-for-tat," Alex returned her smile. "I saved you from drowning, and in another way, you've done the same for me."

"A liberal evaluation."

"A genuine assessment. There is more than one way to drown." Alex worked the material of her dress between her fingers, turning serious once more. "You made me realize I couldn't make anyone else happy if I wasn't happy myself. And without you—without your support—your friendship, I do not believe it is a conclusion I would have come to on my own. I owe you for that."

Catharine tried not to dwell on the word friendship. What its implication meant.

"It's hard, sometimes, to do the right thing for yourself. I think—as women—we are often programmed to try and please everyone else, but the truth is, in doing so, we often hurt more than just ourselves."

"I kept trying to explain that to Caleb. That I'm not what he is looking for—and I never would have made him happy in the end. But he doesn't understand."

Catharine wanted to tell her it wasn't her responsibility to make him understand; he would have to come to that conclusion on his own. But she didn't. The last thing Alex needed was more unsolicited advice.

Alex unclipped her seatbelt, but hesitated a moment more.

"What made you come to that game in Portland?"

Catharine examined the French tips of her manicured nails, as if she might find the answer there. "That afternoon in the garden on Daufuskie you reminded me of someone I had once been. Someone I thought I had lost."

"And have you found her again? Your lost self?"

Catharine looked up slowly, finding Alex's eyes on her, the provocation of a smile on her lips.

"I don't know," she tilted her head, maintaining Alex's bold stare. "Perhaps I have." She reached for her door handle, before looking back once more. "I suppose only time will tell."

Perhaps she had misconstrued the word *friendship* after all.

"You're late," Nathalie stood as Catharine and Alex approached her bistro table inside the Symphony lounge. "I'd begun to imagine the worst—the bridge collapsing, a deadly meteor shower, a plague of locusts consuming the land." She kissed Catharine's cheeks.

"Ever the dramatist." Catharine offered her own exaggerative sigh. "Four minutes."

"Four minutes later than I have ever seen you before," Nathalie intonated, her singsong voice—ever inhabiting the faint accent of her native language, regardless that dialects were one of her most natural talents—teeming with amusement. "Whatever have you been up to?" She pursed her lips, ignoring Catharine's withering glare, before turning to Alex with an elaborate show of airs. "Nathalie Comtois."

"Alex. Grey."

Catharine could see Alex withdrawing, folding into the shy girl who preferred the watchful vantage point of a wallflower, but Nathalie—true to her own gregarious nature—would not allow it. She brushed Alex's extended hand aside, leaning forward to kiss her cheeks instead, and regarded her with a smile.

"Catharine has spoken most warmly of you, but she failed to mention how positively lovely you are. Enchantée, Miss Grey."

Behind Alex, Catharine fixed Nathalie with an acerbic stare, which was blithely ignored. Nathalie had promised to be on her best behavior—it was the only reason Catharine had allowed this evening to take shape—but her *best* and *most flamboyant* were perilously intertwined. There was never any telling exactly what version of Nathalie might grace the evening. Tonight, it appeared, the actress was going for debonair. A step up, at least, from overprotective former lover.

"I understand you are a football star." Nathalie settled back into her chair, toying with the olive in her half-drank martini. "It must be an arduous career—rewarding, no doubt—but I must admit, I saw you recently on an advert on TV. With a look like yours, you were born for it. You should consider the profession—I imagine you'd make a lot more money."

"Ignore her," Catharine helped herself to a sip of Nathalie's drink. "She's an actress—she thinks everyone's ambition should be to grace the silver screen."

"False, and you know it," Nathalie snatched the drink from her hand, holding it out of reach. "I've certainly never suggested the art to you—your ingrained British stoicism would be far too depressing. When it comes to the apathetic genres, however, you could no doubt bag an Emmy." She shot Alex a wink, drawing an uncertain laugh, before continuing. "Miss Grey, on the other hand, practically had me rushing out to buy a pair of running trainers I positively do not need."

"She says *positively* only because the furthest she's run in the last twenty years is from the table to the bar."

"Touché." Nathalie feigned insult, before flipping directions. "Speaking of the bar—have you noticed your little pet over there?" She gave a slight nod across the room. "If you had mentioned her name was on tonight's guest list, I may have reconsidered the invitation."

Catharine followed her eyes to the glass bartop spanning the wall of windows, where Victoria Woodrow was leaning against the counter in a suggestive pose no doubt intended to magnify the limited assets of her chest. Her skintight scarlet minidress was little more than a patch of fabric, riding dangerously high up her thighs.

"Nathalie," Catharine chastised her.

"I will not apologize. She is an awful child."

She couldn't argue that. She watched her for a moment, coquettishly playing with a long sliver of blonde hair, while the young bartender paid her no mind.

"The curtain's in fifteen—if you force us to sit here while your darling ingenue waits for him to show her a modicum of interest, we may as well resign to miss the concert. In that dress he's undoubtedly mistaken her for une prostituée!"

"Nathalie!"

"Fine." The Frenchwoman slid from her chair, her heels clicking sharply on the marble floor, coinciding with the bell from the lobby indicating the final call for patrons to make their way to their seats.

Forfeiting her station at the bar, Victoria took up her martini and sauntered across the room, her nonexistent hips swinging with an attempt at sultriness that would have been laughable, were it not such an accentuating testament to her loathsome disposition. It was no wonder both Jules and Nathalie despised the child. But her father, Richard—a man Catharine admired and respected—was in attendance this evening, and would be sitting in Catharine's box. Victoria was the unfortunate appendage.

She greeted Catharine with an air-kiss and extended the minutest acknowledgment toward Alex, before clapping her gloved hands together loftily. "*Rapidement!*" she exclaimed in terrible French to no one in particular. "We don't want to be late."

Catharine dug her nails into Nathalie's arm as she felt her friend stiffen, forcing an ill-concealed smile of contempt to the Frenchwoman's lips.

"No, we wouldn't want that."

On the way to the loge, Jules found their small party in the hall, wasting no time in greeting Alex, slipping her arm through hers, as if she were an old friend. It was the nature of Juliet Sweeney—the warm and affable way she could make anyone feel as if they belonged.

As Jules and Alex chatted, Nathalie slowed her steps to fall in beside Catharine, allowing the two younger women to go on ahead.

"She is very pretty. Charming, really."

Catharine knew all the nuances of Nathalie's tones to know she was indecisive, her verdict still weighing.

"She is," she said, waiting for her friend to continue.

"She is not what I was expecting. As an athlete I imagined she would be more assertive. She seems very diffident."

"She is shy," Catharine dismissed the observation. "She is out of her element."

"Who wouldn't be, next to you?" Nathalie said, and when Catharine glanced to catch her eye, anticipating the goading of a jesting smile, she instead found only seriousness.

"Stop with that, will you?" Catharine flicked her arm just below her gloved elbow. "I thought you were meant to be encouraging."

"Encouraging I can be," Nathalie retorted, fixing her with a coy smile she could only imagine spelled trouble.

"You'd best remember our agreement," Catharine paused at the entrance to the box. "No theatrics. Play nice tonight, please," she whispered before slipping through the curtains to take her seat.

Chapter Thirty-Seven

The Davies Symphony Hall was sold out, all 2,743 seats filled with a conglomeration of attendees, from men in suits with boutonnieres and pocket squares, their Givenchy-clad wives laden by the weight of their jewelry, to college students with a bohemian flare, strutting about with avantgardistic irony.

As the house lights fell, Alex found herself seated between Jules and Victoria. She'd hoped to sit with Catharine, but in the rush to settle before the conductor stepped to his podium, she'd allowed herself to be whisked to the front row by the Italian dancer.

It was some minutes after the aisle lights had dimmed before Catharine came down the steps, taking a seat in the second row, and was joined by a slim, grey-haired man, wearing khakis and penny loafers. He looked out of place amongst the formal attire, but appeared entirely oblivious to his surroundings, spending the entirety of the first three sonatas whispering to Catharine about a coastal land development going up for auction by the Chilean government.

He was Richard Woodrow, Jules whispered. Victoria's indifferent father.

Alex tried to enjoy the performance, to focus on the handsome cellist sitting at the forefront of the orchestra who held both Jules's and Victoria's every raptured breath. But she struggled to keep her attention on the music, instead watching Catharine out of her periphery—a shadow of burgundy and silk—and had to force herself to keep her eyes forward, instead of wandering across the narrow aisle to where she sat.

During the lingering applause for *Prokofiev's Sinfonia Concertante, Op. 125*—an apparent audience favorite—she gave into the temptation to steal a glance over her shoulder, surprised to find Catharine's gaze on her, her interest turned only superficially to the Australian businessman's conversation. When she caught Alex's eye, she smiled, before Mr. Woodrow was insistent on returning her focus to him.

"Have you heard anything I've said, Catharine? It's an opportunity to win over New Zealand! Coscorn wants it—the Chileans like him, you know? You'd have to jump in the mix soon."

Catharine did not sound as eager. "South America is not my stronghold. I've spun too many wheels there in the past."

"This is a sure-fire investment. You won't find prime coastal land for this price again. Think of what we could do with it! The Shanghai of the South!"

"Richard," Alex could see Catharine smile from the corner of her eye, "if it is such a bargain, why not seize the opportunity yourself?"

"Because you know how much I prefer to spend your money," he laughed, the sound carrying across the diminuendo of the coda as the cellist brought another piece to a close.

"Shhh!" In a sudden fit, Victoria leapt to her feet, spinning toward her father on the aisle. "Will you shut up?! Some of us came here to actually listen!"

"Puis tais-toi et écoute," Nathalie—sitting directly behind her—snapped, reaching up to tug her back into her seat.

There was a half a breath of silence before Jules, unable to miss an opportunity to goad Victoria, leaned forward.

"In case you missed that, she said *then shut up and listen*—I know sometimes Nathalie's Bordeaux accent can be a bit—"

"I know what she said!" Victoria hissed, color rising to her heavily painted cheeks, livid to find herself the butt of the joke between the two women. She opened her mouth to speak, but thought otherwise of it, and lurched again to her feet before bolting up the steps on unsteady heels, disappearing into the hall.

"Mission accomplished," Jules whispered to Nathalie, the pair sharing a triumphant smile, before the dancer turned back to Alex. "Even her own father doesn't notice her tantrums anymore," she nodded toward where Mr. Woodrow hadn't missed a beat of his conversation with Catharine, before returning her attention to the stage.

At the intermission Richard Woodrow excused himself—he had a dinner meeting across town—but assured Catharine he would swing by her office before the week was over. And then he was gone, never so much as acknowledging the other guests in the box, including his own daughter.

Alex stood to stretch her legs while Jules made a phone call, and turned to find Catharine at the top of the stairs with Nathalie close by her side. There was a familiarity between the pair that Alex hadn't seen with any of Catharine's other friends—an affection amongst them that left Alex feeling on the outside. Nathalie was different. She wasn't vying for Catharine's attention; seeking her approval. She didn't have to. She was comfortable with whatever history they shared, confident in their relationship.

She watched as Nathalie reached up to fix the string of pearls hanging at the hollow of Catharine's throat, whispering something that made her laugh.

Before Alex could look away, Nathalie turned to address her, clearly aware of the attention she had drawn.

"Alex—come, you must be the deciding vote." She dropped her hands from the necklace and slipped her arm through the crook of Catharine's elbow, pulling her a step closer to the stairs. "I'm simply famished, and—as delightful as Mr. Krajnc's talents are—I vote we politely bow out of this engagement and grab some woefully divine take-out and play Quatorze at Cate's house until I have to catch my red-eye back to New York."

Cate. It was so intimate. So personal. Alex felt a ridiculous twinge of jealousy she attempted to brush aside.

"I—I'm fine with either." She refused to admit to herself that she'd looked forward to the drive back to Oakland; just the two of them. Nathalie was Catharine's oldest friend. Her *dearest friend*, she'd called her. Of course she would want to spend the evening with her when she'd flown all this way. It was pure selfishness to think otherwise.

"Ha! See, Cate!" Nathalie appeared to have won a battle Alex knew nothing about. "Quatorze and lamentable Chinese food from that little place in the Presidio—"

"Do you have training in the morning?" Catharine interrupted Nathalie. It felt like a small triumph of her own, that Catharine cared enough about her schedule.

Alex shook her head. "No." The Siren's preseason camp had just ended. They had two full recovery days before the first of their three preseason matches starting the following week.

"Fine." Catharine seemed as uncertain about the change in plans as Alex, but she shrugged it off with a smile. "Chinese and Quatorze it is then."

They bid goodbye to Jules, who was attending the opening night after-party as Lukas's date—a fact she could hardly wait to rub Victoria's nose in—and then collected their coats and headed for the parking garage.

Alex said little on the drive from the Symphony Hall to the Presidio—she'd offered to sit in the backseat (would have preferred to sit in the back seat) but Nathalie insisted otherwise.

She was hard to read, Nathalie. At moments Alex found her genuinely welcoming, embracing Alex's presence with a warmth that allowed her to fit right in. But then she would catch a glimpse of her in the rear view mirror or reflection in the window, and could feel a coolness in her gaze, a scrutiny she didn't understand. She would fall into French, teasing Catharine about something or another, as if Alex wasn't even there—drawing an immediate rebuke from Catharine, but continuing with the pattern all the same. She appeared thoroughly accustomed to Catharine's life—from ordering for her for dinner, to telling Grace, Catharine's house-keeper, that she could head home early—they would tidy up on their own. And Catharine let her. She didn't even seem to notice. By the time they climbed the stairs to the third story of the Marina House, settling into the living room, Alex was beginning to wholly appreciate the adage: two's company, three's a crowd.

"I hope you don't mind the change in plans overmuch." Nathalie kicked off her heels as she dropped herself onto one of the cream settees with an exaggerative sigh, not waiting for Alex to reply. "God, my feet are killing me." She rubbed at the ball of one foot.

Catharine had paused in her office to return a phone call, leaving the two of them alone.

Alex tentatively took a seat on the sofa across from her, silently cursing her own feet and their intolerance for heels, but feeling too awkward to follow the Frenchwoman's lead and kick them aside. The home was grander than she remembered it. Quieter. More immaculate. Classic, yet hi-tech. Both contemporary and antiquarian. A perplexing twist of modernism that fit Catharine well. Though, under Nathalie's watchful eye, Alex felt out of place—encased inside a museum with all its priceless art and modern sculptures, just another ornament on display.

As they waited for Catharine to join them, Alex turned her attention toward the floor-to-ceiling bookshelves inset in the wall beside the fireplace, filled with volume-after-volume of classics, historical publications, leather-bound first-editions and biographies. Nathalie followed her gaze.

"Do you enjoy reading?" She drew one of her stockings off her leg, tossing it beside her heels.

"Yes." Alex did not elaborate.

"Favorite genre?"

"A bit of everything, I guess." It felt like an interview. Like Nathalie was looking for answers to a question Alex hadn't been asked.

"As long as you don't say classics," Nathalie heaved herself off the settee, strolling stockingless to the rows of books, running a hand across the centuries-old spines. "God, how I hate them. Brontë, Dickens, Fitzgerald. Even de Laclos, Voltaire, Molière—none of it was for me. To the horror of every literary professor in Oxford." She spun around, waving a hand in dismissal. "I'm probably the only actress on the planet that couldn't stomach my way through Madame Bovary. Performing classics is one thing. Drudging through their obtuse prose is entirely another." She pressed her knuckles against her smile, her eyes shining. "Give me a good murder mystery series any day. Blood, gore, back-alley chop shop. No doubt it's the proletariat in me. At least that's what Cate's father liked to blame." Her laugh was dry.

Alex took the bait, despite knowing it for what it was. She couldn't help herself. She knew so little about Catharine and it was obvious Nathalie was willing to share. Too willing, probably.

"You knew Catharine's father?"

"Mais oui," the woman—she was prettier than Alex first realized—tilted her head in a cavalier gesture as if to say *but of course, why wouldn't I?* and swept back her long, dark hair. "I have known Cate a very long time. Probably longer than you have been alive." She laughed and Alex felt her jaw tighten. She was mocking her for no purpose other than to flex her superiority. She was almost worse than Victoria.

"You both went to school together, right?" Alex studied the sculpture in front of her, trying to appear indifferent—both to Nathalie's clandestine jibing and her level of interest in the question.

"Yes. I met Cate in the autumn of our first term. She was the youngest student in our year—just turned seventeen—and I was of course the oldest, having started two years late. I think she may have thought I was slow and taken pity on me.

"Ignore her, Alex." Catharine stepped into the room from the upper level staircase, carrying a tray of tea. "She's making up things. I showed her no pity at all—in fact, I found her rather insufferable at the start. Still do, sometimes, honestly." She arched her eyebrows at Nathalie in something that felt like a barbed warning, before setting the tray on the center table and upturning three porcelain cups. She had changed from her burgundy taffeta gown into jeans and a plain black t-shirt, her face freshly washed and hair pulled back loosely at the nape of her neck. She looked an entirely different woman without the formality of her attire and the subtlety of her makeup. Different, but neither one less beautiful than the other.

"Here," she said curtly to Nathalie as she crossed the room with two cups she'd poured, though there was a smile behind her terseness, "black, like your soul."

"They don't call me the Queen of Darkness for nothing."

"No one calls you the Queen of Darkness," Catharine rolled her eyes, handing Alex the second cup, doctored with milk and sugar. "Do you see now why I found her insufferable?"

Alex said nothing, but was relieved to see the nettling Frenchwoman was smiling with only good humor, unperturbed by Catharine's banter.

Retrieving her own cup, Catharine took a seat beside Alex while Nathalie dropped herself to the floor, spreading the black skirts of her dress out around her. She took a sip of her black tea, made a face at Catharine, and then leaned back on the knotted wool rug with her hands laced behind her head.

"Before I was so rudely interrupted, I was telling Alex how we attended Oxford together. Well, mostly attended together," she added with a laugh, her eyes flicking toward the settee. "*You* attended. I spent the majority of my time drinking and smoking behind the black-box theatre with the gaffers to avoid slogging my way through *The Importance of Being Earnest* and *All My Sons*." She rolled onto her side to face them. "If you can believe it, Miss Grey, there was once a time when the indomitable Mrs. Cleveland was actually a devil-may-care reprobate. I believe she even left class early once under the guise of being unwell in order to watch the end of my third year stage play. A real rogue, she was."

"Don't believe a word she says," Catharine brought her legs up underneath her, leaning back against the cushions, unfazed by the teasing. "All that smoking and drinking got to her memory. I was nowhere near as yawnsome as she'd have you believe. There was once an occasion I even missed curfew in my hall of residence."

At that Alex laughed, feeling some of the stiffness of the evening dissipating. Nathalie retorted in French, but it appeared affable, and then climbed to her feet in a languid stretch.

"I can't stand the thought of being wrapped like a sausage in these Godawful skirts for a single second longer. Come, Alex, you must be as miserable as me. Shall we change?"

"I—I don't really—"

"I'm sure I have something you can wear. We've got to be about the same size."

Alex hesitated. There was really nothing she wanted more than to get into something more comfortable. She didn't mind formal wear when it fit the occasion—but the thought of sitting around eating Chinese food and playing cards while stuck in heels and satin was almost tempting enough to take the woman up on her offer.

Almost.

"Thank you, but I'm all right—"

"Nonsense—I can think of only one activity where lying on the floor in a cocktail dress is ever remotely comfortable, and I assure you, I am not speaking of playing card games. Come, we'll find something more agreeable. Half my wardrobe has been left here over the years," she said with an air of flippant coquettishness before strolling out of the room.

Without much choice, Alex followed her down the hall.

Chapter Thirty-Eight

Catharine tossed the San Francisco Chronicle on the end table when Nathalie sauntered back into the room and fixed her friend with a scowl. "I know what you're about. You never could just leave well enough alone."

Nathalie feigned a blink of innocence but Catharine brushed it aside. The entire evening she'd been playing one of her games, showering Catharine with blatant affection in an imbecilic attempt to draw Alex to jealousy, and it was becoming acutely embarrassing. "Cut the act, Nat. All night you've been at this nonsense and you're helping nothing. You promised me."

Nathalie spread her hands with a dismissive tilt of her head before settling onto the floor. "La jalousie est une persienne derrière laquelle l'amour se cache souvent." It was a quote from the French playwright, Louis-Auguste Commerson. *Jealousy is a shutter behind which love often hides.* She wouldn't be Nathalie if she didn't have a quote up her sleeve when she'd been called out and found guilty of meddling in affairs that were not her own. Always some manner of justification. But two could play at that game.

"'Jealousy is no more than feeling alone against smiling enemies.' Elizabeth Bowen."

"You cannot quote an English novelist and pretend she would know anything about love."

"She was Irish."

"Whatever—the sentiment stands." Nathalie pursed her lips, annoyed. "Sometimes an extra push is needed."

"Sometimes you push too hard." Catharine tossed two packs of playing cards to her friend and went to the bar for a bottle of scotch. "Just be yourself, will you? There is no game that needs playing here."

"All of love is a game. If you do not recognize that, it is no wonder you've been living alone with your heart of stone for the past twenty years." She begrudgingly took the scotch offered her. "You won't take any risks."

"I beg to differ. It was a risk in itself just allowing the two of you to meet. Which I'm on the verge of regretting. Besides," Catharine knelt to the floor and retrieved one of the packs of cards, opening it to shuffle, "you're not exactly the first person from whom I would seek relationship advice."

Whatever snide rebuttal flew to Nathalie's lips was extinguished as Alex appeared on the landing dressed in yoga pants and Nathalie's favorite *La Femme* t-shirt—a sign in itself that Nathalie wasn't as unfavorable toward their guest as she made effort to appear.

"Ah, better," Nathalie rendered a brief nod of approval, returning her attention to the shuffling of the cards, but looked up again with piqued interest as Alex crossed barefoot into the room. "Oh là là! I wish I could say I looked like that in those pants. Tell me, are all footballers as fit as you?"

Catharine had to clear her throat to prevent the scotch from going down the wrong pipe. The damn woman had no filter.

Alex covered her embarrassment with a laugh, a hue of red sweeping up her cheeks.

"Nat—" Catharine's warning hissed between her teeth, but Nathalie paid her no mind. As always.

"What? I'm serious! I've never had much interest watching a ball get kicked around the grass—but I'm realizing now maybe it's not about the ball at all. I may have to rethink my stance on sports." Nathalie stacked the cards in front of her and motioned for Alex to join them while Catharine tipped back her tumbler, draining her glass, before pouring herself another.

"She tells me you are quite a swimmer, too—"

"Will you just deal the damn cards?!" Scotch flowed over the rim of the glass and Catharine cursed to herself, flicking whisky from her fingertips. "Do you care for a drink, Alex? I find a touch of scotch lessens the intolerability of present company." She was only half-teasing.

Alex seated herself cross-legged on the rug and shrugged nonchalantly, a hint of her self-assurance returning, despite—or perhaps with credit to—Nathalie's teasing. "It would give me an unfair advantage," she indicated the cards, "if I were the only one sober. And I like to beat my opponents fair and square."

A slow smile lifted the corners of Nathalie's lips, her eyes sparkling with the challenge. "Then no handicaps for you," she snagged the bottle and poured two fingers, passing it over. "Now—beauty always wins the shuffle." She set the cards in Alex's lap.

"In that case," said Alex, thumbing through the deck with agile fingers, "the honors belong to you, Catharine."

Caught off guard by the playful repartee, Catharine felt her own cheeks color, her face warm from more than the liquor. She couldn't remember the last time someone had made her blush. She looked down, cutting the cards, trying to avoid Nathalie's furtive smile.

Chapter Thirty-Nine

By midnight the three women had finished the greater portion of a fifth of whisky. Nathalie'd out-poured the other two with impressive stamina, but Alex could tell the night was catching up with her. She wasn't wasted, but her voice had grown low and her accent heavy, betraying her rising inebriation, and in turn, emboldening her mischievous manner.

They'd eaten take-out straight from the boxes while sprawled across the living room floor, blundering through a game of Quatorze that had to be restarted more than once due to their dwindling ability to count.

Somewhere between rounds four and six, Alex decided the Frenchwoman wasn't as awful as she'd initially imagined, and by round nine—and four shots of whisky deep—she came to the conclusion she might even like her. She was an odd combination of bluntness and doublespeak, spending half the time running her mouth with no filter, while the rest was dedicated to an equivoque wordplay she was certain was meant only for Catharine. But there was no malice to it, and eventually Alex ignored it all together.

As the spirits dwindled, the stiffness of Catharine's propriety went with them, bringing a smile more freely to her lips and a looseness to her demeanor. Alex found herself pursuing her laugh, seeking ways to draw it from her, delighting in each success. She loved the way her eyes brightened, and the fine lines that appeared at their corners. The way she fussed with her hair each time she set down a losing hand.

At the close of the game Alex was declared the winner. *Beginner's luck*, according to Nathalie, as she flicked her cards in an arch of red and black, scattering them across the rug.

"I don't think I've sat on the floor playing cards, drinking scotch and eating take-out since I was at university," Catharine laughed, balancing the half-finished tumbler of scotch on one knee.

Nathalie pushed herself into a sitting position, her smile askew. "There are a lot of things you haven't done since Université that you should try again."

Propped on her elbows, Alex had been separating the two decks, but from the corner of her eye caught the seething look Catharine shot her friend. The Frenchwoman blithely ignored the warning, either too drunk or too determined to get a rise out of Catharine. She continued with her one-sided riposte. "You know, joie de vivre, and all that rot," she imitated the French catchphrase in Catharine's English accent with perfect accuracy.

Alex kept her focus on the organization of the cards, biting her lip to hide her smile. Nathalie had been relentless in her teasing of Catharine throughout the evening—most of which had been brushed off with practiced indifference—but this last quip found its target, drawing a crimson flush from neck to brow.

"What time did you say your flight was?" Catharine asked, unamused.

"Oh, I've got another hour or so," Nathalie answered brightly, reaching over to take the tumbler from Catharine's hand, draining it with a flip of the wrist. "Shall we play another game?"

Alex knew she should head home. It was a forty-minute cab ride to her apartment and it was already after midnight. But she couldn't bring herself to leave. Not yet.

"A drinking game, perhaps?" Nathalie held up the glass in an imaginary toast when no one immediately answered.

"You are cut off." Catharine plucked the glass from her hand, shaking her head with a half a smile. "In fact, I don't know if you are even in any condition to fly. Maybe you should cancel the four a.m. and take something a little later?"

Alex counted the cards for a third time, fighting a sinking feeling of disappointment she found absurd. What did it matter if Nathalie stayed or went?

"Can't," Nathalie rubbed her temples, "I've got rehearsal at five. I'm cutting it close as it is."

"You'll be regretting those last two shots tomorrow."

"Probably. But it's been worth it." Her tone was devoid of all flippancy. "I haven't seen you this happy in a long time."

There was such an unexpected genuineness to her words that Alex glanced up, feeling as if she were sitting privy to a conversation that was only meant for two. The room grew quiet, the only sounds coming from the flicker of the fireplace and distant hum of cars passing on the boulevard. And then the silence was unexpectedly broken by the shrill buzzing of Alex's cell phone reverberating through the room. The noise was so sharp, so incongruous to the stillness that had surrounded them, it made her jump, bringing Nathalie to laughter in turn. Lunging to her feet, Alex was surprised to find the effects of the scotch much stronger than she'd anticipated, but still managed a mostly even gait to her handbag.

"Late to a midnight tête-à-tête?" Nathalie mused, regarding her with a scrutinizing query.

Alex glanced at her phone, scanning the brief text, before clicking it off and slipping it back into her bag. "My teammate checking in." She could feel Catharine's eyes following her as she returned to the pile of cards on the floor.

"Good teammate to check in so late." Nathalie's singsong voice was investigative. "No boyfriends?"

"Nat!" Catharine protested.

"I'm just making conversation!"

"*No.*" The answer came out more curtly than Alex meant it. She couldn't expect Nathalie to know the subject was a sore one. That her breakup with Caleb and the viral video that followed was one of the lowest points in her life. She forced herself to shake off her defensiveness, stuffing the cards back into their boxes. "No boyfriends."

"Ah." Nathalie paused a second. "Girlfriends?"

"You are unreal," Catharine snapped, genuine anger flaring for the first time of the night. "And entirely out of line—"

"It's a simple question! Only you rigid Brits and orthodox Americans take such offense to it, bon sang!" Nathalie challenged Catharine with annoyance of her own.

"No girlfriends," Alex cut in, almost drawn to laughter at the unexpectedness of the question and upset that had followed it. "My longest standing relationship has been with a sixteen ounce ball for the majority of my life. It's been consuming, to say the least."

"Career before love—how very *American*." Nathalie gave a disapproving tsk tsk. "In France we have a saying that goes '*Il n'y a qu'un bonheur dans la vie, c'est d'aimer et d'être aimé,*' which translates roughly to—there is only one happiness in life, to love and be loved."

"Don't mind her," Catharine rose, her composure recovered, "she has a quote for every situation in life. Brokenhearted? Quote. Angry? Another quote. Sad? Do not fear, she'll fix it with a quote!" She shook her head, turning her eyes to Nathalie. "I'm just surprised you went with Dupin instead of Molière. He is usually your go-to for quotes about love. What is it you tell me all the time? *Vivre sans aimer n'est pas proprement vivre?*"

"Is it not true?" Nathalie said and Alex thought she might actually be a little stung at Catharine's mocking. "Is living without love really living at all?"

"Such impractical talk of romance is for the artists and the poets—and apparently the *actors*," Catharine bent to retrieve a misplaced Joker from the floor, flipping the card toward Nathalie. "Jokes on you," she quipped with a surprising amount of petulance. "The rest of us know there is plenty to life that doesn't include a skewed idealist's philosophical outlook that no longer exists in modern times." She crossed to the threshold. "I'm going to make you tea to take to the airport."

"You didn't always believe that," Nathalie said to her back as she disappeared from view. "The years have made you cold."

Catharine gave no response.

With a palpable frustration, Nathalie stared at the card in her hand for some seconds before she folded it in half, creasing its wax exterior, and dropped it on the end table. She then rose and crossed to the wall of glass overlooking the bay, staring out at the blinking lighthouse on Alcatraz in silence.

Trying to skirt around the unexpected tension in the room, Alex quietly retrieved her phone and flipped open her texts to compose a message.

"You know she's fond of you, don't you?"

The question caught Alex off guard. She looked over to where Nathalie stood, still facing the balcony, uncertain if she'd heard her correctly. "I'm sorry?"

"Don't play coy, Miss Grey. That's my gig and you don't do it very well." There was a seriousness to her that had been lacking from the entirety of the evening. A sudden sobriety teetering on the cusp of hardness. "You seem genuine. Intelligent. Driven. I can see the allure." She found Alex's eyes in the reflection of the window, staring back at her with a scrutiny that forced Alex to look away. She wasn't sure if she feared she'd see something she shouldn't, or not see what she should. Or what it even was she was looking for.

Nathalie turned on her heel to face her. "I just hope you realize this is not a game to her. That you are here for the right reasons."

"I—" Alex started to defend herself but stopped short, uncertain of what she was defending. She forced herself to hold Nathalie's eye, refusing to be made guilty with no offense committed. "If I have given you the wrong impression," she said carefully, "I—"

"On the contrary," Nathalie interrupted, returning to the table where the remainder of the bottle of whisky sat, pouring herself another shot, "you've given nothing but the right impressions. I just don't want to see her hurt. She's not as indestructible as she seems."

Catharine's footsteps sounded on the hardwood floor and both women resumed their silence while Nathalie finished her drink. Alex glanced at the text she had composed, then hit cancel. It could wait.

Chapter Forty

When Catharine returned from seeing Nathalie off to the airport she found Alex gone and the sitting room empty. She must have slipped out while Catharine hunted for Nathalie's cell phone—left 'somewhere,' according to her inebriated friend—between the guest room and the front entry.

She stood for a minute in the threshold. The trio of glasses had been stacked on the table and the takeout dishes tied neatly in bags, ready to be carried down to the bin. It was all so very *Nathalie*—to come in like a whirlwind, stir things up, and then try to piece the disarray back together last minute before bolting off again.

Catharine drew in a long breath and let it out slowly, repressing an unwelcome twinge of disappointment. It was nothing more than the aftermath of the high of the evening. Of the cold reality of finding herself alone once more.

She crossed to the table and took up one of the glasses—Nathalie's, probably, from the claret hue of lipstick along its rim—and poured herself the remainder of the scotch. Maybe Nathalie was right. Maybe the years had made her cold.

Or maybe it had nothing to do with the years. Maybe it was ingrained in her, just part of who she was.

She sat on the arm of the settee and picked up the empty bottle of Macallan, tracing the label with her thumb. Maybe she was more like her father than she cared to acknowledge. Maybe she'd held onto more of him than she realized.

She laid the bottle sideways on the end table and considered pouring out her glass, but took a sip instead.

She drank because of him. Whisky, specifically. Because he hated it. Because he'd never touched a single drop.

His father—her grandfather—had been a dedicated alcoholic. Not the public variety who left his demons on display, but the subtle type. The kind who rose on time every morning, showed up at his office to put in his twelve-hour day, and returned home each night to a bottle of Famous Grouse to wash his torments away.

If he'd stayed behind the locked doors of his library, his wife and sons may never have cared. But with the draining of every bottle rose a malevolence with an insatiable appetite. He would sit at supper, his aggression simmering, until it boiled over in the blink of an eye, leaving the Brooks household on the qui vive, ever ready for an explosion. The result: a wife who scarcely breathed too deep around a husband she feared to displease, and children who strove for an impossible perfection to gain the affection and attention of a man who could hardly remember their names.

Benjamin Brooks found his brother, Samuel—four years his senior—hung from the open beam ceiling in his father's library on his thirteenth birthday. It wasn't something Benjamin ever told Catharine—he spoke nothing of his youth—but her mother had discreetly shared stories from her father's past, probably hoping to instill a sense of understanding in her daughter for the way her father behaved. To hope she could find forgiveness for a man who was as cold and impossible to please as his father was before him.

But she'd found no forgiveness. Found no understanding for the man who'd terrorized her life. Instead she'd only found ways to cope. To battle him in the few ways she knew how. Where Colonel Brooks had never touched a drop of alcohol—a devote teetotaler himself—Catharine spent her first year at Oxford learning how to drink. Not out of necessity. Not out of enjoyment. Only out of spite. Not heavily—she didn't have the stomach for it—though she would have liked to lead her father to believe she did.

The whisky unfinished, she abandoned the glass on the end table and set the bottle upright, unable to shake the train of her thoughts from him. There were so many things he would hate about her life. So many things he would hate about *her*. *Would*. And *did*. His disapprovals of her would always outweigh her achievements. They would always trump her successes. She had wanted once, more than anything, to gain his acceptance. No different than he had sought from his own father. But it would have been easier to catch light in a box.

She was startled out of her reverie by the sound of the sliding door to the balcony, and looked up to find Alex stepping out of the darkness into the dimmed lights of the room.

"I'm sorry," she apologized, realizing she had surprised Catharine. "I didn't hear you come back in."

"I thought you'd gone." Catharine didn't get up from where she sat. "I couldn't really blame you if you had. Nathalie can be a bit much sometimes."

Alex smiled. "She's a lot. But I like her." She closed the door and took a seat on the footstool in front of the settee. "I wouldn't have left without saying goodbye."

Catharine looked down at her, the two of them sitting so close their knees were almost touching. So much had happened since that first afternoon in Daufuskie. So much had changed. For both women.

But had they changed enough?

Nathalie was right. She hadn't always had such a skewed outlook on love. But for more than twenty years she'd set everything aside, closed everything away. Her past. Her dreams. The things she desired. She'd pushed all her energy into her work. All her focus. And it had paid off. WorldCargo—Brooks Corporation's largest entity—was the second largest shipping company in the world. A 15.3 percent market share. Over 50,000 employees across 103 countries. A fleet of 1001 vessels. And more than three hundred ports served. The revenue more than tripled from the day she assumed control from her father fourteen years prior.

But yes, it had made her cold.

And it left a void in her life no amount of success—no amount of mergers or acquisitions or trades or growth—could fill. It wasn't unhappiness. She wasn't—as a rule—unhappy. But she wasn't happy, either. Or fulfilled. She was just—existing.

And Alex Grey was the first person she'd met since Nathalie who made her think there was perhaps more to life than simply watching it pass her by.

"I can never tell what you are thinking when you look at me like that," Alex shifted on the seat with a self-conscious laugh, breaking Catharine's train of thought.

Embarrassed at her wandering abstraction, Catharine looked down at her hands, toying with her wedding ring, turning it around and around in circles on her finger.

She wished she had just taken the damn thing off.

Ah—but the media. They would have a frenzy. Trouble in the *Cleveland Kingdom*—as she and Carlton had been coined in the press years ago. *Brooks Kingdom*, if anyone really cared to take note. It annoyed her endlessly that the empire she'd built had ever been linked to the Cleveland name. One day she would take back her identity—but the time wasn't yet. And she could not risk the scrutiny, so for now the ring would stay.

"You do that when you're nervous." Alex surprised Catharine by reaching forward and taking her hands in hers, stopping them from their cadenced fidgeting.

"Do I?" Catharine half-laughed—a little diffident—as Alex examined her fingers as if they were artwork on display. When she was finished she turned her hand over and ran her thumb along the creases in her palm.

"Palmar flexion creases," Alex said quietly. "When I was a little girl my mom would read my palms to me. If my father had only known—oh, the *blasphemy*." She smiled as she touched her fingertip across the longest line, tracing it down to the heel of Catharine's hand. "Your life line," she said, then touched the line in the middle, "your head line," and lastly she drew an imaginary mark across the crease at the top of the hand from index finger to pinky, "and your heart line." On this last line she lingered.

"And what did your mother say about yours?" Catharine asked, looking at Alex's younger, smoother hands holding hers.

For a second Alex paused, lost in her own thoughts, before a smile crept to her lips. "Well, she must have misread a few things." She looked up at Catharine, her hazel eyes shining, before her smile turned rueful. "I have to go." Her eyes met Catharine's, unwavering. "But not because I don't want to stay." She stood, still holding her hands, their eyes level from where Catharine was sitting on the arm of the settee. "HEG arranged some kind of last minute photoshoot in Oracle Park tomorrow morning. That's what the text message was about."

Catharine nodded, trying to hide her disappointment. She'd thought to offer her her guest room. To invite her to stay. To have tea in the morning before she drove her home. She was glad she hadn't. To save herself the embarrassment.

She hid her sadness behind the wryness of her smile. "So much for Hargrove's rest on the Sabbath."

"Profit before principles, of course." Alex laughed, but the sound was strained.

"Do you want me to call you a cab?"

"Thank you, but I'll Uber."

Catharine nodded. Of course she would. She began to withdraw from Alex's hands, but Alex caught her wrist before she could turn away.

"I want you to invite me back, Catharine." There was no vacillation to her tone, no uncertainty in her gaze. "I want to come back."

It caught Catharine off guard. Her assertiveness. Her confidence. That was usually Catharine's proclivity, but now the tables were turned. It wasn't often she found herself without a reply.

She looked at her for a moment, aware of the pulse in Alex's fingertips beating against her wrist, before finally breaking the stare. "Then come back," she managed with a casualness she didn't feel, shrugging through the smile that flitted around her lips.

Alex hesitated, unblinking, gathering herself, before suddenly leaning forward and kissing Catharine quickly on her mouth—her lips barely brushing hers—and then turned and hurried from the room, never looking back.

Chapter Forty-One

Amelia pushed through the cafe door with her elbow, her cell phone tucked between shoulder and ear, a coffee in each hand.

Jogging across the street through traffic she trotted to where Alex was waiting, perched on the concrete pillar beside the steps leading to the ticket window of Oracle Park, her arms wrapped around her to keep out the morning chill.

"Yeah, well, it's some bullshit, really," she was saying as she handed one of the coffees to Alex and retrieved the phone with her free hand. "Charity or not, we showed up as we were asked with less than eight hours of warning, and they couldn't even have the decency to let us know they were running late? *Hours* late!" She listened for another moment and rolled her eyes at Alex, her lips drawn vanished into a thin line. "Look, it's Sunday, we both have better things to do than wait around for some junior photographer of *Christian Teen*—or whatever it's called. Grey and I are going home." She paused, listening. "Yeah, well, you can have Hargrove himself call me if he has a problem with it. We don't want to be late to church, you know?"

She hung up.

"Three hours of lost sleep," she hopped up on the pillar beside Alex.

"I can't believe you just hung up on Regina." Alex shook her head, smiling. Regina was the assistant manager for *Kickstar*—the one who signed their checks, established their contracts, and oversaw their schedule.

"Yeah, and?" Amelia was still steaming. "Hopefully she's over in her office telling some mid-level intern 'I can't believe we pulled Walker and Grey out on a Sunday morning for nothing! Heads are going to roll!' Because this is ridiculous." She sipped her coffee. "I mean, they could have at least given us a heads up a couple hours ago. If they had done this to Valencia or Clay they would have bent over backward in apologies and efforts to make it right."

"Valencia and Clay would not have shown up for a last minute charity shoot at six in the morning on a Sunday," Alex pointed out, referring to two of the star players on the LA Sharks pro men's team, also owned by HEG. "That's where we went wrong in the first place."

"Yeah, well, it'll be the first and last time."

"I doubt that," Alex teased, sliding to her feet. "Are you really going to church?"

"Grey, I swear," Amelia looked over, incredulous, unable even to smile. "Is your sarcasm meter broken or something? Do I really look like I am running late to church? Have you ever known me to go to church?" She cocked her head sideways, her angular jaw jutted out. "I'm not really the church going type, you know?"

"Is there a type, exactly? I mean, it takes all kinds, *you know*?" Alex mocked back, falling into step with Amelia's shorter stride but still struggling to keep up.

"Hellfire and brimstone is just not my thing. I've had enough unholy folks tell me I'm on a short bus to hell—I don't need to hear it from the holier-than-thou lot, too."

"Why? Because of—I mean, you being—?"

Amelia stopped at the corner of King and 3rd, waiting for the light to change. "Because I'm gay? What? No. Jesus, Grey. Sometimes I wonder if you're not the full quid."

From Amelia's disapproving grimace it didn't take much to decipher her meaning. "No, I just figured—I mean, that's pretty much the first-class ticket to hell where I come from. No need to pass go, no collecting two hundred dollars—just—straight to hell."

"Passing go? Two hundred dollars? I—" Amelia stared at Alex as if she were speaking another language. "What the hell, Grey?" She shook her head. "Whatever any of that means. No, I meant because I'm an arsehole. I speak my mind. Tell people things they don't want to hear, you know? So, off to hell it is for me, then."

The light changed, but neither of them noticed.

"How have you not played Monopoly?" Alex was just as dumbfounded. "You want to talk about full quid or squid or whatever—and you don't know what it means to pass go and collect two hundred dollars? I don't even know if I can associate with you anymore."

"Were you actually trying to make a joke, Grey?" Amelia looked her over and up and down, as if she'd just sprouted a second head. "Is there really a sense of humor buried deep within that obstinately thick skull of yours?" She noticed the light and took off at a trot to the other side before the red blinking pedestrian appeared on the sign.

"I think you'll find my sense of humor in good working order," Alex trailed her onto the curb. "Just maybe not so much on no sleep on a Sunday morning."

"Speaking of no sleep," Amelia slowed, no longer in a hurry toward the ferry terminal. "This morning has been such a cluster, I forgot to ask—how was your date?" She said this last bit with a smirk, knowing she would strike a chord.

"It wasn't a date," Alex shot back, knowing she'd lunged to the defense too quickly, but unable to stop herself. All morning she'd wanted to tell Amelia about her night. Just to be able to tell someone. It was all she could think about. But now that the door to the conversation was open, all she wanted to do was slam it shut again. To keep it private. This one little thing that was hers and hers alone.

"Ah, this again." Amelia rolled her eyes.

"It wasn't." Alex tried to shrug casually but instead spilled a scorching stream of black coffee down the side of the paper cup, burning her fingers. "Damn it," she swore, switching hands and shaking off her fingers.

"That good, eh?"

"It was an opening for a show at Symphony Hall. A cellist I met last summer."

"I see. I hadn't taken you for a string aficionado. You are full of surprises." She raised her full eyebrows in mock appreciation. "In that case, how was your *non*-date? Concert ran a bit late?" There was a knowingness in the Australian's cunning green eyes that made Alex bristle.

"Not really. We grabbed dinner and played some cards afterward. I hadn't anticipated an early morning, so figured I'd make the most of my Saturday night."

"With a few shots of—" Amelia sniffed the air, "whisky? Bourbon?" Her lips curled into a slanted smile. "Sounds like a fun night. I don't know how you do the whole 'no sleep' thing though. I need like ten hours or I'm worthless." She stopped abruptly in front of the ferry terminal. The trains were down on maintenance—another joy of Sunday mornings—and they'd hoped to catch one of the ferries back to Oakland. But the line was outrageously long.

"There's no way we're getting on the ten a.m." Alex checked her watch and looked back at the line. The next ferry wasn't until one p.m. since it was a Sunday.

"And thank you again, Regina Schaff," Amelia drawled out, checking her own watch before staring up at the posted schedule as if she could manifest another departure. "My one day off this week. I'm not spending it waiting in line. Uber?"

Alex started to nod, then changed her mind. Maybe she wouldn't head back to Oakland just yet.

"I think I'll run a few errands and catch the one o' clock."

"Errands? Like grocery shopping an entire city away from your flat? Or errands as in: my night got interrupted and now I have a full day to make up the time lost?"

"*Errands*—as in—Elite Sports in the Mission District has a sale today and I want to stop by. You want to come?" she added, knowing full well Amelia would have no desire to spend any time longer than necessary away from her apartment. On Sundays she watched all the recorded matches from the previous week, spoke to her family back home and slept for twelve to fourteen hours. It was the one day she wanted to do absolutely nothing.

"A *sale*? No." She wrinkled her nose in disgust. "I'll pass, but thanks." She swiped open her Uber app. "You sure you don't want a ride?"

Alex tossed the rest of her coffee in a garbage can and slung her cleats and gear bag over Amelia's arm. "Take these back with you, will you?"

"Yeah, they're not as sexy as the heels you left in last night," Amelia shot up a brow. "Not quite the same appeal."

Alex blushed, thinking about the dress she'd left behind. She hadn't thought about grabbing it until after she was on the curb of Catharine's driveway, waiting for her ride, still in Nathalie's borrowed clothing and barefoot in the cold March air. She knew she'd probably looked the poster child for a domestic fight gone wrong, but that didn't trump the embarrassment of going back in to change—not after leaving in such a hurry. Not after kissing Catharine Cleveland. On the mouth.

God.

"Just drop them in my hall, will you?" She crossed between the cars to get to the other side of the street, offering half a wave behind her. She hated that Amelia could read her so easily. She never had been good at hiding anything.

As soon as she was around the corner she stopped, dropping onto a bus stop bench, deciding what to do. She pulled out her phone, browsing through her texts.

Three new messages. All from Caleb. He'd been on a push the last few days to reach her. For a couple weeks the calls and messages had slowed—after her birthday he was calling her a dozen or more times a day, even showing up at her apartment unannounced a week after the whole thing boiled over—but she'd pretended to not be home, hiding in her bedroom, praying he would leave without incident. And eventually he had.

A couple days later she thought she saw him on the outskirts of their training field. She'd been doing a 1vs1 dribbling drill in the box at the opposite side of the pitch and had never gotten a good look at the lone spectator, but he was gone—to her relief—by the time the exercise was over. It had just *felt* like him. And that night she'd slept on the couch at Amelia's apartment.

Twice she'd given in and spoken with him. Hoping a conversation would help him understand. She needed some time to think—some time away from him. But it only made things worse. He begged and pleaded and cried and now Alex no longer took his calls. She couldn't. She knew the next time she did it would only be to say something he did not want to hear. But not yet. She didn't have the energy for the fight. For now, she just hoped he would quietly come to terms on his own. The same way she had.

She swept the text notifications away unread and opened a new message.

Her fingers hovered over the screen, second guessing herself.

She'd *kissed* her, for God's sake. What was she thinking?

If she was honest, she was thinking she wanted to do it again. But— *Jesus*. She needed to get a hold of herself!

She typed out a short message and hit send before she could overthink it any further.

—Photoshoot cancelled. Are you free today?

Her legs jittered with the inability to sit still. Phone still in hand, she leapt up and turned up the block, unaware of what direction she was going. She just needed to go somewhere—anywhere.

Before she got to the next crosswalk her phone chimed.

Catharine had responded.

—Lunch?

Alex leaned against the crosswalk sign, heedless to the people forced to walk around her. She started to respond, then panicked, realizing she was in a pair of *Kickstar* branded warmup pants and neon pink running shoes. She'd never considered grabbing a change of clothes when she left her apartment at zero-dark-thirty. There had been no need.

She should have gone home to change before texting Catharine. In the fog of her sleep deprived brain she'd never considered that.

Alex began to compose an *I'm sorry, there's been a change in plans* but before she could hit send the phone rang.

"Sorry," said the familiar voice, "I'm at my office. It's easier to call."

"I didn't mean to bother you at work," Alex apologized.

"No bother. Are you in the city?"

"I'm still down at Oracle Park."

"Perfect. You're not far from me. Do you know where Bridgeview Tower is?"

"Not exactly. I'm sure I can find it."

"I have a conference call in London in a half hour I can't put off any longer." She paused and Alex could hear her flipping through paperwork. Now was her chance to ask to reschedule, she wasn't dressed for lunch— she didn't want to interrupt her at work. But her brain didn't formulate the words quickly enough.

"How about eleven? I'll meet you in the lobby. Is that too far off?"

"Eleven is great."

What the hell, Alex?

The phone rang in the background. "The lobby, then," Catharine said, and Alex could hear her smile before hanging up.

She slouched against the crosswalk pole, the waves of pedestrians parting around her like the Red Sea.

Checking her watch, she saw it was a five minutes to nine.

Maps indicated there was a Gap a couple miles away, not far from Bridgeview Tower.

She could use the run anyhow.

Bridgeview Tower hadn't been hard to find. Alex only needed to look up. The spiraling skyscraper was one of San Francisco's newest additions to the skyline, soaring above the city at a staggering 1103 feet. The tallest building in California, sustainably designed with function in mind—at least that was what Alex read on Wikipedia while she waited at the coffee shop across the street for eleven a.m. to roll around.

When she walked through the revolving doors into the lobby she found herself surrounded by walls of glass, the high-beamed ceiling melding into a moving wave of color as the tone slowly shifted from cyan to violet to magenta to moss, seamlessly flowing through a palette of pastels and earth tones whose shapes evolved into clouds and water and swaying grass. It was a mesmerizing effect, like fading into another world, the sounds of the city instantly vanishing with the rotation of the doors.

Alex swept her eyes across the lobby, finding Catharine sitting in one of the eco-design twisted bamboo chairs, a newspaper spread open in her lap.

"Can I help you?" A security guard she hadn't noticed was at her side. "Do you have a delivery?"

Alex stared at him. "Sorry?"

"Food drop-off is at reception—"

"I—I'm not—" She realized she was still carrying the shopping bag from GAP, her workout clothes and sneakers folded inside.

"Alex."

Catharine had crossed the lobby, where she now stepped from behind her, resting her hand on her elbow. "Thank you, Ron." She acknowledged the security guard, who nodded, before drifting back to wherever he'd come from.

"A bit gaudy, don't you think?"

Alex took a passing glance at the ceiling. "It's impressive."

"Call me old-fashioned, but I prefer my walls not moving." Catharine dropped her newspaper in a recycling bin made of burnt cork and led Alex back through the revolving doors to the empty landing. The offices were quiet on Sundays, with only a trio of businessmen carrying on a conversation at the base of the towering building.

"What are you in the mood for?" Catharine leaned against the handrail leading to the sidewalk level, her fingers drumming against her thigh. "We're within walking distance of a little bit of everything."

"I saw there were a few food trucks across the street," Alex gestured over her shoulder with her thumb, trying to keep a straight face.

"A risk taker," Catharine said drolly, her cheekbones rising with a closed-lip smile. "And are you sure it is a risk worth taking?"

"Are we still talking about food trucks?" Alex could feel her cheeks redden even as she said it. She wasn't very good at this game.

"Seeing as you dressed for the occasion," Catharine reached a hand forward and gently pulled a price tag off the lower hem of the navy satin button-up she'd picked up on her way to the tower, "I think we should splurge on something more than a taco truck." She looked down at the tag between her fingers and Alex felt the crimson in her cheeks flare, mortified.

"I was in my workout clothes," She confessed, looking down to make sure she had not missed any other tags or stickers. "I stopped to grab something to wear. I guess I missed one."

"And here I thought you were just planning to return it later," Catharine teased, pressing the cardboard tag into Alex's hand. "You know you're charming when you blush?"

Alex crushed the offending tag in her palm. Part of her hoped a blackhole would open beneath her and extinguish her from existence. But Catharine was smiling and Alex thought the embarrassment might be worth it if it made her look at her the way she was right then.

"Do you like Moroccan?"

"I—" Alex realized she didn't know. "I'm not sure. I like just about everything."

"Mes'Lalla, then. It's new. My assistant, Nicole, swears they have the best lunches in the Financial District. I think she's gone there nearly every day since they opened."

An hour later Alex paid the tab while Catharine had apologetically taken a phone call on the patio. They'd made it through lunch without any of the awkwardness Alex had worried might be present after the events of the previous evening. But her concerns had been for nothing. Catharine was as nonchalant and natural as ever, focusing the conversation on Alex's upcoming preseason games and inquiring how she was coping with her newfound attention that came with the *Kickstar* ad campaign. When the call came in they'd been talking about the vast disparity between the budget spent on the men's and women's teams by US Soccer—her interest focused on the imbalance per capita—but when she looked at her phone she'd excused herself immediately. From the table Alex could see her pacing back and forth on the empty patio, her face set and hands articulating her anger in a heated conversation. When she hung up and headed back toward the door Alex looked away, not wanting her to know she'd been watching.

"I'm so sorry," she slipped into her seat and set her purse on her lap to pull out her wallet. "I swear some people just know when it is an inopportune time to call and wait for that exact moment..." Her voice trailed off as she picked up the bill, looking at Alex's signature on the copy of the receipt. "I invited you to lunch," she admonished.

Alex just shrugged.

"I'll make it up to you. After this charity event is over this weekend, you must let me take you out." She drummed her fingers on the table, still worked up from her phone call. "I wish you would reconsider coming on Saturday." She looked up, hopeful, her fingers stopping their nervous tattoo on the table's edge.

"I'm not very fond of big events."

"Neither am I."

Alex laughed. "I doubt that very much."

"I'm good at them because I have to be. But it does not mean I enjoy them."

"Then why put them on?" Alex was curious.

"Most of them? Because Carlton loves to entertain. He likes to flaunt things, remind people who he is—what he has—what he is capable of. But that will come to an end soon enough." Her mouth drew in a tight line, her thoughts distracted.

Alex wanted to ask what that meant. What any of it meant. She'd seen a post on Twitter about his bid for the White House. It seemed impossible to think that the pompous ass she'd met on Daufuskie—the crass drunk she'd been forced to sit with in DC—could even qualify to run for lower office, let alone the presidency. What would it mean for Catharine? For their divorce? But it wasn't the time or place to ask. It was none of her business, really.

Catharine resumed the conversation. "The charity events, however, are mine. I do them because they actually make a difference. It's something I can do to give back. And maybe a little because my father always despised them." A hint of a smile curled her lips.

"Is he still alive?"

"My father?" Catharine laughed, her eyebrows raised. "As far as I know." Then, more seriously, she said "yes, to my knowledge, alive and well, still anxiously waiting for me to make a muck of something, no doubt. I haven't spoken to him in many years."

It was ironic—and sad—Alex thought, that this woman—this beautiful, influential, sophisticated woman—could still be cowed by a man who was non-existent in her life, living thousands of miles across the Atlantic. She wondered what dominion he could possibly hold over her after all these years.

"I have to run up to my office to gather some paperwork," Catharine changed the subject. "Do you want to come with me? Sundays are quiet in the tower. It's no Burj Khalifa but the view is really remarkable."

Alex was in no hurry. She'd have gone to fold her clothes with her at the laundromat if that's what Catharine had asked of her. "If it won't bother you."

Catharine smiled. "It won't bother me."

Catharine's offices were on the sixty-first floor of the sixty-four story building, the inscription beneath the button in the elevator marked only as BC Exec. On the ride up Catharine explained that Bridgeview Tower housed her immediate team's supporting offices—a dozen or so West Coast-based employees and her attorney's legal group. A fraction, Alex gathered, of the administrative staff. The rest of the company was based in locations all over the globe, with the largest branches in London, Shanghai, Cape Town, New York, and Melbourne.

The floor was silent when they exited the elevator, the doors opening to reveal a spacious central lobby with offices encircling the parameter, the closed doors bearing etched names in fogged glass.

The secretary desk was empty, a few post-it notes scattered along the surface and a coffee mug with the faint sign of lipstick on the rim sitting beside the computer.

Catharine paused to straighten a few papers on the vacant desk—a nervous habit, Alex realized—before stopping at a set of glass double doors in the northeast corner of the floor, swiping a card against the wall and stepping aside for Alex to enter.

The room was large and bare, with a U-shaped desk placed in the very center. There were no chairs for visitors and the only additional furnishings were a bookshelf and filing cabinet along one of the far walls made entirely of glass. Beyond, through the transparency of the exterior architectural beams, the city unfolded below them, rolling out into a picturesque view of the bay.

"I take it you don't get many visitors in here." Alex said, looking around at the lack of seating.

"We have conference rooms for meetings. My assistant, Nicole, is really the only other person who comes in here. It lets me focus better on what I am doing. People stay too long if they are able to sit," she said, unapologetically. Alex tried to hide her smile. It was so very Catharine.

She took stock of the rest of the office. There were no plaques on the walls, no photos, no signage—only a single framed newspaper article from the Financial Times that hung above the filing cabinet.

WorldCargo Under New Leadership the headline read, and below it: *Sink or Swim: Future Uncertain for Corporate Giant with new Captain(ess) at the Helm*. Then there was a photo of Catharine standing beside what looked to be the hull of a very large ship with the letters WOR—undoubtedly the beginning of WorldCargo—painted in white behind her. She was very young in the photo, but had the same intense eyes and knowing half smile to which Alex had grown accustomed.

The date on the paper read *2001*.

Alex quit reading the article, aware that Catharine had come to stand beside her, looking over her shoulder.

"My first year as CEO," her voice was very near her ear. "I think everyone thought I would fail. At least most of them hoped I would. I keep it up to remember where I have come from. And who I am up against."

"I'm no expert but it would seem you surpassed the journalist's expectations." *Captain(ess),* she reread with disgust. No matter who you were, it was still a man's world. No different than women's professional soccer vs. the men.

In the reflection of the frame she could see the sparseness of the office behind her—austere in its simplicity—not an item out of place, no clutter or debris, the few desktop folders stacked with precision. To the west, in the distance, the Golden Gate rose out of the fog beginning to roll in from the ocean, and below her, to the east, the Bay Bridge disappeared across the water into Oakland. She could see the new soccer stadium, its construction near completion, just a mile from her apartment in Jack London Square.

Her eyes drifted back to the photo of the young woman on the wall. "Was this when you first came to the United States?"

"No, I'd been here five years at that point."

"You look so young." How she could have married that pompous ass any younger than that was unimaginable. It was unfathomable to imagine her married to him at all.

"I had just turned twenty-five." Catharine shook her head, suppressing a sigh. "You are twenty-six?"

"Twenty-seven."

"Ah, twenty-seven," Catharine mused. "What I'd give to be twenty-seven again. To have beauty and youth still on my side."

Alex couldn't help but laugh. "If you don't think you still have beauty on your side you've got to be entirely blind."

"Oh, please," Catharine started, turning away from the window toward her desk, but Alex caught her hand, staying her.

"You're the most beautiful woman I've ever met." It came out more candidly than she'd intended, but this time it was Catharine who uncharacteristically flushed, a smile lingering on her lips. Alex expected her to come back with a quip or witty remark to break the tension, but she remained silent, looking back at Alex through judicial blue eyes, maintaining her own private counsel.

Alex wanted her to kiss her. She hadn't been able to think of anything else since her abrupt departure the night before and all morning had worried she'd been out of line. What if she'd misread Catharine's affections—her attentiveness—for simple affinity? She was warm and affable to all her friends. What if that was all it had been? And now here she was, making a fool of herself all over again. She was hardly an expert on reading people's emotions. Even on the field it was one of her weaknesses—reading the other players' body language was not her most natural talent. Something she constantly overthought.

"I'm sorry." She started to apologize, releasing Catharine's hand. "I—"

"Alex, do shut up," Catharine shook her head, reaching to place her hands on either side of Alex's neck. Alex had to close her eyes, certain Catharine would hear her heart jackhammering its way out of her chest. She felt her thumb run along her lower lip and could feel Catharine's breath against her face, shallow and uncertain as her own.

"Mrs. Cleveland, are you in?" A remote voice broke the silence and Alex started so badly she nearly tripped backward over the filing cabinet against the wall.

Even Catharine was disoriented, jolted from the moment, before quickly regaining her composure and crossing to her desk to hit a button on a small black box beside her computer.

An intercom.

Just an intercom, Alex realized, releasing a shaky breath.

"Yes, Nicole," Catharine said, a touch rushed, but otherwise masterfully collected. "I'm just grabbing some paperwork for Senator Cleveland." She released the button, waiting for the woman to respond, and looked over at Alex, unable to quell a laugh. "Sod's law," she said, her voice trailing into a smile.

Alex could only stare at her, still thrown off by the interruption, before smiling herself, leaning against the window, feeling her pulse rate begin its slow decline to normal.

The voice sounded again. "Will you be here long? Gordon's on his way into the office. The deal is ready to launch tomorrow morning."

Catharine drummed her fingers on the desk, thinking, before returning her gaze to Alex.

"What time do you go in tomorrow?" she asked, matter-of-fact.

"I—I don't." Alex could hardly remember what day it was. "I'm off until Tuesday."

Catharine tapped the button. "Put it off until Tuesday. Four p.m. That'll make it eight a.m. Wednesday in Guangzhou."

"Tuesday at four." The voice on the intercom sounded surprised, but didn't question Catharine's authority.

"Patch any calls tomorrow through to my cell. I'll be out of the office."

"Yes, ma'am."

"Let me know what Gordon has to say about Lei Xin and Zhidong. If he says it is ready to finalize I assume they have reached an understanding."

"I'll keep you posted."

"I'll see you Tuesday, Nicole." Catharine pressed another button and then pushed herself up from the back of her desk chair she had been leaning over.

"Have you ever been to Half Moon Bay?" She glanced at Alex before logging into her computer and sorting through a few file folders.

"No."

"Will you go with me?" Catharine didn't look at her.

Alex pressed her palms flat against the window behind her, feeling the chill of the glass restore some sensation into her fingertips.

"Yes."

Catharine nodded, her eyes still focused on her computer. "Give me two minutes to wrap this up."

Chapter Forty-Two

Half Moon Bay was only thirty miles south of the city down Highway 1, but the sleepy coastal town felt worlds apart from the non-stop rush and push of San Francisco.

Catharine had discovered the small oasis by accident over a decade earlier when she had been sailing to Pescadero on a solo trip along the coast. The town had a charm that reminded her of the villages in the country along the River Thames where she'd spent the summers of her youth.

Over the years she'd made the town her private haven—somewhere she could go, just for a night or two, when she needed to get out of the city—a place where everything was slowed down and she could wake to nothing more than the crashing of waves against the rocky California shores and birds calling at the break of dawn. Where no one knew where she was, or who she was, or how to find her. Her asylum.

The entrance to the Ritz was easy to miss if you weren't looking for it. Over a mile off the highway, past a residential neighborhood and campground, it wasn't trafficked by many who were not guests staying at the resort, most of which were honeymooners or internationals on holiday.

The drive from downtown was quiet. Catharine had to make a few phone calls to handle business that could not wait until Tuesday and by the time she finished the last call she found Alex leaning against the passenger window, fast asleep.

She flipped her phone to silent and turned the radio low, then let her own thoughts drift as she drove the familiar coastline, past the state parks and beaches, and the oceanside towns with names all ending in Point or Cove or Harbor. She'd made the drive dozens of times over the years, always by herself, work or finances constantly on her mind, but this time she couldn't focus on numbers or Guangzhou or even Carlton, who'd called that morning while she was at lunch to inform her he was arriving on Wednesday with his entourage and intended to stay until the gala.

At her house.

"The press will notice if I don't," had been his primary argument—which, in his defense, was likely true—but Catharine wanted none of it. Whenever he barged into her life he brought a world of chaos with him—with his mood swings and temper and grandiose sense of superiority—he sucked all of the air out of a room just by being in it. He had not stayed at the Marina house in years. He hated it and she hated him there. He was doing this to get even with her, but she didn't know how to stop him without making things worse than they already were.

With the election had come the media en force—and the scrutiny into every part of his life, which therefore bled into hers.

Yet here she was, weeks away from Carlton kicking off his official campaign trail, playing with fire.

Her brain told her to focus on that. Consider that.

Stop. Think this through. It was her common sense's resounding echo stuck on repeat. *What you are starting here is just as dangerous for her,* it whispered.

But Catharine slammed that door shut. Pulled the plug and left the practicality of reason writhing on the floor at the top of Bridgeview Tower as soon as she'd asked Alex to come with her to the coast. But the truth was, her reason had been slipping long before that. It had been waning since the day she met Alex Grey, and she'd come to the conclusion she was okay with it. She'd lived under the lock and key of sensible judgment for twenty-three years and grown exhausted of its demands.

Pulling into the valet porte-cochère, Catharine brushed Alex's hand with her fingertips, stirring her from her sleep. The young woman woke with a start, sitting up against her seatbelt, darting a glance toward the waistcoated attendants who were standing at their doors. "I'm sorry," she blinked her daze away, a little sheepish, "I can't believe I fell asleep."

"Afternoon, ma'am," a black-haired valet opened Catharine's door with a smile. "Luggage?"

"None today." They had left straight from her office. Catharine had offered to stop in Oakland if Alex wished to run by her apartment, but Alex had declined. There were a few shops at the hotel and anything else they needed could be found locally.

A keen-eyed, spindly woman stood at the reservation desk, her shoulders drawn back with an austerity that matched the severity of her bun. She was familiar to Catharine, and nodded curtly as she approached, already holding a keycard and receipt in hand. Catharine had finalized the booking before leaving her office, pleased to find her favorite suite, The Ritz Carlton, available for the last minute reservation. It was a brilliant set of rooms—the most luxurious accommodation the hotel had to offer—but most importantly, it was a two bedroom. A detail that would matter in the unlikely situation either of them were recognized.

"Welcome back, Ms. Brooks," the woman greeted with formal politeness, using the maiden name Catharine often traveled under, "I was pleased to see your reservation. May I confirm your two-night stay?" Her eyes flitted over Catharine's shoulder, falling on Alex, who lingered a few steps behind.

"Yes." Catharine checked her watch. It was a few minutes after two p.m. She looked back at Alex. "Dinner at seven?"

Alex only nodded, uncomfortable under the gaze of the receptionist.

"A table for two at Navio—windowfront if available, please."

The woman handed Catharine the keycards. "I will see that it is. Is there anything else, Ms. Brooks?"

"Not at present, thank you."

When they stepped out of the lift on the top floor Catharine led Alex to the end of the hall where the suite encompassed the entire corner of the southwest wing.

"How often do you stay here?" Alex asked as Catharine opened the door and stepped aside, allowing her to pass into the foyer. It was the first she'd spoken since they'd left the car, her voice strung with nerves.

"A few times a year, depending on my schedule." She would have liked to have found a witty remark, something to put her at ease, but she was feeling tense in her own right and kept her focus on hanging her coat and purse in the hall, before crossing to the double doors between the living room and formal dining room that led out to the balcony. Pulling them open, she stood on the threshold, breathing in the crisp sea air that smelled of salt and sunshine. Below, the resort courtyard was scattered with fire pits and lounging areas, empty in the early afternoon, but come evening they would be teeming with guests taking their after-dinner cocktails and listening to the live music from the patio bar. A hundred feet across the grass, the coastline cliffs dropped into the ocean, where the sea stretched out as far as the eye could see.

"Is Brooks your maiden name?" Alex came to stand beside her in the doorway.

Catharine kept her eyes on the horizon. There was such a familiarity between them, she forgot sometimes how little they really knew each other. How little history they shared. Alex knew nothing of her family—nothing of the Brooks legacy—of where she came from. She had never asked and Catharine had never offered.

"It is. I use it often when I travel. But always here."

"I like it. It suits you."

"It's more me than Cleveland will ever be."

Which was true. Married for twenty-three years and when someone asked her name her first instinct was still Catharine Brooks. She had never felt like a Cleveland. She never would. It was a title she had never cared to don. And soon it would be one she could slip off, like an ill-fitting coat, and hang up for good. She would always feel the weight of the name—after all, she had worn it more than half her life—but soon enough it would not be her burden to carry.

Catharine exhaled, feeling some of her nerves dissipating with the sereneness of the setting. A couple hundred feet off the sandy shoreline, one of Half Moon Bay's landmarks, Three Rocks, jutted out from the ocean floor, the rising tide slapping against the jagged surface of the trio. Come sunset the rocks would be covered with shorebirds drying themselves for the evening.

"I question sometimes," Catharine considered, watching the white spray of waves as they crashed against the sea stacks, "what would have happened that day on Daufuskie if you had not been there." She turned to look at Alex out of the corner of her eye. "The turn of events it may have set into place— macabre thoughts, really. And I can't help but wonder… was it fate? Divine intervention? Happenstance?" She laughed at the ridiculousness of her own question. "I don't even know if I believe in the first two."

"I guess it doesn't really matter, does it?" Alex was thoughtful beside her. "They all led to the same result, regardless which of the three was responsible."

Catharine acquiesced. "Fair enough."

Alex reached over, slipping her hand into Catharine's, entwining their fingers. "But I'm going to go with fate," her voice was quiet, smiling. "That this was meant to be. Because I doubt God had much to do with it, and I don't like leaving anything to chance." She reached her free hand up and closed the doors, shutting them away from the outside world.

Catharine felt her breath slow measurably as they stared at each other in the afternoon light, neither certain how to proceed. She could feel Alex's pulse pounding in her wrist, her fingers woven through hers, her breathing shallow in return.

"I don't really know what I am doing," Alex whispered, her own hesitant confession. "Or what to do."

Catharine brought her hand to Alex's cheek, brushing back the stray hairs that fell into her face, running her fingers along the line of her jaw and down her neck, lingering where her skin was softest at the hollow of her throat. Alex's breath stopped all together.

She thought about telling her she was just as uncertain—this was just as new for her—it had been so long. But she said nothing—the words were irrelevant—and instead slipped her hand around to the nape of Alex's neck, drawing her forward, leaning down until their lips brushed, a shuddered breath passing between them.

For a second they were motionless, their breath sharing the same space, warm and shallow, neither inclined to infringe on the stillness of the moment. It was the cusp of a threshold they had not crossed—the verge of a boundary they had yet to break. To move forward from this point was to warrant an agreement that they were willing to do this. That it was a risk they were both willing to take.

In the end it was Alex who moved ahead, bringing her hands to Catharine's face, pulling her mouth to her with an urgency that matched her own, a need that had long been silenced.

Catharine allowed herself to be swept from the world around her, lured from the hesitations, the *wouldn'ts*, the *shouldn'ts*, and all the reasons in between. She forgot about Carlton, and Guangzhou, about her father, and

Alex's contract with HEG. She found herself aware of only the taste of Alex's mouth, the scent of her skin. Her eyes closed, she could feel the path of Alex's hands at the small of her back, pulling her forward, closing the space between them.

It was curious—the ability for something to feel so familiar and yet so unknown. So immorally unprincipled, yet maintain the sensation that denying it would be the greater sin. In her youth, with Nathalie, there hadn't been much room for thoughts of morality. She hadn't dwelt on the dereliction of her responsibilities as an ethical and proper representation of her family's name. There'd been no concern for earthly duties versus heavenly obligations. Religion was not part of her upbringing, though her father had been reared in a devote Christian household. They had attended church—her father, mother, and Catharine—but it was less of a calling and more out of habit—just one more thing that took too much time out of the work day, her father had always complained. But something they did all the same.

Colonel Brooks' outrage had never been about the sin of it all—though he had certainly hurled the words *sin, immorality, blasphemy, abomination,* and *transgression* over and over at Catharine until she could hear nothing else—but that was not where the furor originated. He had no considerations for her heavenly salvation. The Colonel's outrage revolved around the worry of his loss of control of Catharine—his inability to force her to acquiesce to the standards of society and the expectations he held for her. Her deviance with the unbridled French girl was the least of his concerns—though it was the pillar that upheld his greatest fear: that Catharine would not allow herself to be manipulated or managed the way he had been commanded by his own father. That she was not enough afraid of him to live her life as he saw fit. But her actual transgressions had merely been the tip of the iceberg.

And over the years, even living in the heart of the Carolina Bible Belt with a man who fancied himself the very definition of the disciples of Jesus Christ Himself, she had not much worried herself for the laws of men versus the laws of God. What mankind did—so long as it was not detrimental to any other—was their own business, their own agenda. And she had lived her life by those standards.

But it had not stopped her from joining the Court of Public Opinion in questioning the morality of it—the *righteousness,* for lack of better terms—

in passing thought, but in this moment she was finally certain those who would object—citing God's law as evidence—were entirely wrong. This wasn't immoral. This wasn't sinful. It was merely human. It was nothing more than love. Love of another.

Catharine drew away to look at Alex, to hold her gaze. Both trying to find their breath, they stared at one another, the world tipping on its axis around them. Catharine scrutinized Alex for any sign of hesitation, of regret, of doubt. This was territory she had once known, but a path Alex had never tread. She needed to be certain.

But all Catharine found staring back at her was a reflection of her own desire. There was no apprehension. No reservation. Just someone who needed her as much as she needed them. And it was true—Catharine needed Alex. More than she'd ever realized. Wanted her. To share that same intimacy, to know those same secrets in return. She wanted to commit to memory her touch, her taste, the feel of her body against her own. It was a sensation she hadn't known in decades. One she had slowly forgotten over the years, the memories washed away with time and self-preservation.

It was intoxicating—standing there, suspended just one step through the threshold of a barrier neither had known if they would have the courage to cross. Intoxicating—and terrifying. The unknowns were vast, but the bridge of certainties had been burnt long ago. And the only path remaining was forward.

Looking at her, Catharine could see that Alex knew that, too.

In answer, Alex reached for Catharine's hand and brought it to the top button of her blouse, holding it there, her eyes never leaving her own.

"Show me."

Chapter Forty-Three

In another time Alex may have found herself awed by the magnificence of the master suite—the hexagonal design with its wealth of bay windows displaying a majestic panorama of the Pacific coastline and the infinity of the ocean beyond. She would have found the four poster bed romantic, the fireplace extravagant, the mahogany furniture chic.

But she noticed none of it at the time.

Instead, her thoughts were limited to rudimentary observations. Like the fact that her hands had stopped shaking by the time they crossed the doorsill, or that her pulse had leveled to a peak steady state of which her athletic trainer would have approved.

Ahead of her, Catharine stopped in the center of the room, turning to face her, the two of them remaining an arm's length apart. She appeared temporarily immobilized, static in her hesitation, uncertain how to proceed. For all of her confidence, her self-assured certitude, Alex could tell she was slipping on self-doubt. She didn't know how to move forward. This woman who dealt with many of the most powerful business magnates around the world, who navigated the tumultuous tide of American politics, who found herself at leisure with heads of state and nobility—she was vagrantly waiting for Alex to make the next move.

During her junior year at Clemson, her coach had told Alex she was destined to go pro. They'd been sitting in the training room, reviewing film from the previous weekend's game, and he'd paused the footage a few seconds before both of Alex's goals.

"These are the moments that distinguish you from the girls whose careers will end their senior year." He'd stopped and rewound the clips, asking her if she could see what he saw. At the time, she couldn't. He'd had to point out to her the decisiveness of her actions—the certainty of her execution which gave her a unique ability to finish. As soon as she had the ball, she didn't question her next move. She saw the goal, she saw her play, and she unhesitatingly followed through. Once she knew what she wanted, she knew exactly what to do.

This wasn't the same. This wasn't soccer—it wasn't a game. But Alex knew what she wanted. Even if she had no plan, no rules to see her through, she at least knew the way forward. Where to pass the ball.

Without a word she stepped to Catharine, bringing her hands to her face, drawing her fingers through the golden flaxen of her hair, finding her mouth with hers. She'd worried, if she hesitated too long, one of them would lose their nerve—or an interruption would occur—and the moment would vanish before them. It was all the encouragement Catharine needed to lure her from her apprehension—to draw her back to the present, wherever her thoughts had been.

Alex reveled in the nearness of her—the feeling of her body against hers, the reaction to her touch as her hands explored the shape of Catharine's shoulders, the swell of her breasts, the plane of her waist, the curve of her hips. She smelled of citrus, clean and fresh, smooth and subtle—a scent distinctly her own. Alex found herself engrossed by the satin softness of her skin, the way her cheeks brushed against her as Catharine drew her lips along the line of her jaw, her neck, the delicate place below her ear.

There was an overpowering intensity to the sensation—an all-consuming rush—standing there, her arms around this woman—this enchanting, magnetic, magnificent woman—who had once felt so unattainable, so out of reach.

Alex had daydreamed what it would be like—to kiss another woman, to touch another woman. *This* woman. She'd thought it might be strange. Uncomfortable. Her upbringing had revolved around the taboo nature of the act being perceived as such a mystery; the forbidden fruit, central to the Garden of Eden—a filthy, unimaginable sin. She'd not doubted it would hold a consequential sensation of guilt and debasing shame crushed beneath the weight of the Tree of Knowledge. And if there was, how could they be blamed? Women had been burdened with the guilt of the Original Sin since the beginning of time—at least, according to the Bible.

But all those thoughts proved to be nonsense. There was no shame. No guilt. No awkward uncertainty. Instead, she found only a feeling of comfort, of acceptance, of a sensation that had been missing in her life. She found a mouth that fit with hers, a body that responded willingly to her touch. It was nothing of what she'd ever known with Caleb or the boys she'd dated in college. There was nothing strained or forced or guarded. Nothing artificial. It simply felt right. Whole. Complete.

Catharine's hands moved to the fasteners of Alex's shirt, fumbling with the small black clasps as Alex lifted the hem of Catharine's blouse free and slid her palms up to touch the cool, silk skin at the small of her back. She could feel her tense, her body responsive beneath her fingertips, drawing in a quick, staggered breath.

Fussing a moment longer, Catharine smiled against her mouth, leaning back to look at the clasps. "We should have left the tag on this one," she laughed, flustered. "I hate it."

Alex returned her smile, watching Catharine's face twist in frustration until she finally managed to free the offending fastener, still laughing at herself. She seemed so unburdened in the moment, so removed from the conventional, proper businesswoman of the morning. It was a side of her Alex had glimpsed over the months but one that remained elusive a majority of the time, hidden behind the practiced rigidity engrained within her. But this person before her was none of that. This was the person Alex wanted to better know, to unravel, to demystify. She wanted to learn everything about her, solve her riddles, understand her dreams. And the realization of it, the intensity of it, almost frightened her.

She knew, with utter certainty, what she told Catharine that night at the Buena Vista Cafe had been true—she had never been in love. Not even remotely, if it was meant to feel anything like this. With Caleb it had been a chore. A necessity. A function dictated by the requirements of a relationship. Nothing more. And he had never even noticed—never known something was missing—just taken and taken and never given back. It had never been consuming, overwhelming, paralyzing. It hadn't been this.

"They're my chastity buttons," Alex teased, forcing herself free of the sobriety of her thoughts. She would have plenty of time to think later.

"I'd not expected a mind-bender," Catharine's lips were lurking with a smile. Alex found herself transfixed, momentarily immobilized as she watched the beautiful hands—so elegant, so expressive—move down the row of fasteners, unhooking each one in turn, until she was free to slide the shirt off her shoulders. There was a leisure to her actions, an unhurried deliberation that left Alex both aching and impatient, unable to stifle the sharp intake of breath as Catharine dropped her head to brush her lips across the top of her breasts.

"Alex?" It was just the whisper of a question. The consideration so quintessential of Catharine. Seeking her consent. Making certain they were harmonious in agreement.

Alex didn't trust her voice. Didn't trust whatever sound would come out. So instead, she reached back and unclipped her bra, before reaching for Catharine and drawing her blouse up over her head. She felt clumsy, uncoordinated, with none of Catharine's grace, her poise and discipline, but she didn't care. She wanted only to taste her mouth again. To feel her skin —smooth, bare—against her own.

As their mouths met, as she fumbled to unbutton her jeans, distracted by the tug of Catharine's teeth along her lower lip, and the palms that brushed her nipples, the two of them stumbled backward toward the bed, Catharine's urgency suddenly elevated, rising to meet her own.

With the clumsy discarding of the remainder of her clothing, Alex found her fingers tangled through flaxen hair as she sank into the cushion of the thick duvet, Catharine kneeling beside her.

It was midday, the light of the afternoon harsh through the windows, but even in its unflattering light, she was certain—for the millionth time— Catharine was the most beautiful woman she'd ever known. Skin she'd only glimpsed before—soft, pale, smooth—she now trailed her fingers across, exploring every curve, every plane. She lingered in the places that made Catharine's breath still—the contour of her hip, the length of her thigh, the swell of her breasts where she could feel her heartbeat quicken as she rose to kneel beside her, tentatively tracing the sensitive skin with her tongue. For what felt an endless freeze-frame, she breathed her in, absorbing her scent, her warmth, her reaction to her touch. Subtle citrus. Staggered breaths. The flutter of closed eyes and trembling limbs.

When at last Alex faltered, when her tentative exploration slowed and the newness of the situation brought her pause, Catharine effortlessly assumed the lead. With no words between them, she bade Alex lay back, her hands— those hands Alex felt she would never grow tired of watching—shifting into control, stealing Alex's breath with their teasing, their slow, deliberate progression, until at last, when she was certain she could stand it no longer, they found their way inside her, Catharine's mouth back on hers.

And in that moment, in the desperate tensing of her body, in the feeling of their limbs wrapped together as Alex pulled Catharine against her, needing more of her than she'd ever known was possible—and in the shuddered release of all her inhibitions—Alex was at last certain this was where she belonged. This was what she wanted. This was what had been missing all along.

For the first time in her life, something fit. Something felt right.

Chapter Forty-Four

The sun edged toward the horizon, casting its amber golden hue across the bed cover, turning the walls orange in its descent. Usually Catharine watched the sunsets from the balcony—alone, whisky neat, with the corporation on her mind. This evening, however, she only watched Alex—asleep beside her, her cheek pressed against her chest, dark hair falling across her eyes.

If the younger woman dreamt, she couldn't tell. Her sleep was deep, the waking world far beyond her. It seemed almost wrong to watch someone so closely, watch them at their most vulnerable state, unaware of being observed. But Catharine couldn't look away. She felt like if she did it might all vanish—fade, roll out into another long night of being alone. The balcony, the whisky, her thoughts awaiting her.

So, she studied Alex. She studied the raven-wing darkness of her hair, the sweeping length of her lashes, the contour of her jaw, slack with sleep. Bringing a finger up to trace the line from ear to chin, she ran the pad of her thumb across her firm lips, parted in slumber. The peaceful woman stirred, not in wakefulness, but the subconscious acknowledgement of another's touch—another's presence.

How peculiar, yet how remarkably extraordinary it was to begin to learn another's body as intimately as one knew their own. She followed the long, lissome muscles of the arm draped across her own stomach, relaxed in sleep, to the flat, curved structure of Alex's back and shoulder, turned up to the ceiling, strong and lean from years of training and dedication, yet still possessing the softness belonging only to a woman. Her hips, half-covered by the tangle of white sheet, disappeared beneath the covers, the trace of a nickel-sized tattoo in the outline of a soccer ball peeking out behind the linen a couple inches above her left hip bone. There was the indent of a scar along her clavicle and a trio of sun-kissed freckles that ran a straight line across the back of her neck, disappearing into her hairline.

Catharine closed her eyes, absorbing the sensation of the warmth and weight of the body against hers and the slow, steady rise and fall of Alex's breath against her chest.

It had been so long since someone slept beside her. First, she'd had Nathalie. Stolen hours before the dawn laying in one another's arms, always knowing it was destined to end in agony. And then, Carlton. In the first five years of their marriage she'd shared a bedroom with him, much to her silent dread, but eventually she'd untwined herself from the day-to-day lifestyle of a married couple and taken her own private accommodations. He hadn't cared. He'd hardly noticed. It made it more convenient for him to bring his secretaries and interns and the daughters of his colleagues to his bed. On the occasions he sought her as a wife she always returned to her own rooms after he had fallen asleep, desperate to scrub him from her skin—to erase all thought of him.

The memories of Carlton brought a rush of anxiety to the surface, despite the sereneness of the evening. The knowledge that he would arrive in three days, bringing with him all the chaos and disorder in which he lived—to take over her home—was enough to send her into a panic. But it was worse than that—after the gala he intended to attend several meaningless rallies along the coast, extending the initial four day trip to two weeks.

California would not welcome him with open arms; his campaigning was pointless in the Golden State. They would never vote for a radical-right-wing conservative Republican from the South—one who had repeatedly belittled their state, picked fights with their governor, filibustered their senators and stood for everything the progressive left was against.

He knew that.

A single rally would have sufficed the few West Coast extremist support-ers, but Carlton would never follow a logical course when he had the opportunity to trample Catharine's peace and privacy as he so enjoyed—lording over her to make his presence known. It was the easiest way to get at her, coming here, forcing himself into her life. The tension between them over the last few months was at an all-time high, with him having difficulty coming to terms that he no longer held complete control over his wife. He held enough—enough to scare her into sticking to their deal. The trouble he could cause for Brooks Corp was significant. Many of his threats were idle, but he did have enough connections, enough clout and enough power to affect her American ports and shipping terms—along with enough inside knowledge of her business to know exactly how to hit her the hardest.

And then there was always her father. Carlton stayed friendly with him over the years, knowing it came at Catharine's disapproval. It was just one more way to needle under his wife's skin, to exert his control, to nettle her. There was no doubt he could still influence him with his forked tongue.

The Colonel had always liked Carlton. A bootstrapper. A high-flyer. Yet, if her father had ever taken the time to get to know his son-in-law, he would have found he was nothing more than an egotistical bullshitter. The type of person her father hated most—a fraud and a phony whose success was garnered by riding the coattails of others. Of all the things Benjamin Brooks was, a fraud was not one of them. Every success he had ever enjoyed came at the cost of his own hard work and dedication, just like his father before him, and Catharine after. It was the only thing they shared in common. They all knew success was only attained and sustained by being the hardest worker in the room. And they had all lived by those standards.

Carlton, on the other hand, had given nothing and taken everything. And he would continue to take and take and take. As long as he could.

The power she held over him would only remain effective so long as she maintained her part of their bargain—to appear by his side as a dutiful wife, the face of support and allegiance, without any trace of scandal or hint of separation on the horizon. No presidential candidate could run a successful campaign in the middle of an ugly divorce, and he knew it. They were at a stalemate.

To make things clear, Catharine had her legal team draw up extensive dissolution paperwork that spelled out the terms of their divorce—including a clause that stipulated the agreement between them for the duration of the campaign. If his presidential nomination was affected due to any fault of her own the agreement would become null and Carlton would have recourse to fight for stock in her company and drag on a heavily contested divorce bound to destroy them both. But if she upheld her end, until the culmination of the election, the contract dictated a fair split of assets that left Carlton more than comfortable for any number of lifetimes to come, but kept her corporation separate, uncontested. He'd signed the agreement willingly enough—he'd never had any interest in the actual business of Brooks Corp., only the revenue it generated. The contract favored him, was more than fair to him, and required nothing of him beyond walking away from her at the conclusion of his campaign.

It was all very simple. But she knew, deep down, he would never let her go without full-scale warfare. Even if she gave him everything, it wouldn't be enough. He owned her and she had unclipped her chain and now he would do everything in his power to remind her that no one walked away from Carlton Cleveland. Not alive, anyway. Not intact.

So, her only hope was the election held in the balance. It was the only thing he desired more than his power over her. She had to bank on that. But if she did anything to upset the scales, to tip his nomination in a downward spiral, she knew his vengeance would stop at nothing until he demolished her to ruin.

If it had only been her life that hung in the balance—her company and her successes—she may have considered risking it to fight him. She wasn't the type to lay down and take it—she had her own connections, her own form of influence. It was what she'd planned to do when first informing him she intended to divorce. She would fight him and let the chips fall where they may, hoping to come out as unscathed as possible on the other side. But that had been her frustration and desperation talking. She'd acted without fully considering the consequences that would fall, not on her, but more importantly on the lives of more than fifty thousand employees that Brooks Corp employed. The tens of thousands of families that depended on her to do the right thing for the corporation and its subsidiaries. If Carlton destroyed her, he would subsequently destroy them.

She couldn't let them down after all they had given to her.

Yet here she was, risking it all. For if Carlton ever caught wind of this, what had happened with Nathalie would seem insignificant in comparison.

She inhaled a long, grounding breath. Her thoughts had to stop. This was not the time. She knew exactly what she was getting into coming here—the consequences had been weighed. There was no going back now.

Alex stirred beside her, stretching the muscles of her arms and back, her breathing pattern changing from the rhythmic cadence of sleep to the varied measure of wakefulness. She opened her eyes, blinking to bring her surroundings into focus, and found Catharine's gaze resting on her.

"Hey." Her voice was low with sleep.

"Hey." Catharine found herself tentative, waiting with a degree of caution. She wasn't certain how she would respond when she woke—if she would be regretful or shy or distant or embarrassed—any number of emotions that had the habit of following decisions made in moments of passion.

But her concerns were quickly put to rest. Alex smiled, the dimples in her cheeks lengthening as she squinted, faint laugh lines presenting at the corner of her eyes. "Is it still Sunday?" She propped herself on an elbow to look out the window at the sun hanging low in the sky.

"For a while longer at least." Catharine sat up, bringing the duvet with her, surprised to find herself a touch timid in her undressed state. "Do you still want to get dinner?"

The smile lingered around Alex's eyes. "Could we change the reservation to tomorrow?" She reached to capture Catharine's hand, pulling it to her lips, allowing the cover to fall to her waist. "Stay in, order room service?"

Reflexively, Catharine tried to regain the comforter, but realizing her intent, Alex laughed and shifted over the top of her, pinning her arms to her side, their faces a breath apart. "Wait." She was still smiling as she relinquished her hold to slowly pull the cover lower. "Let me look at you."

Her fingertips brushed an agonizingly slow path down her shoulder, across her breast, trailing along her side before coming to rest a splayed hand on her belly, her smile spreading at Catharine's obvious involuntary reaction to her teasing. She leaned down to kiss her. "You're beautiful," Alex breathed into her mouth, her hands venturing beneath the covers— more certain, more exacting than before. There was a confidence in her that had been previously dormant as she drew Catharine into her arms, their bodies melding into each other, eliminating the void between them. She dropped her head and kissed a trail down the center of her chest and Catharine closed her eyes, all thoughts of the tribulations that would soon present themselves immediately disappearing.

Chapter Forty-Five

The next morning Alex woke to the sound of Catharine's voice muffled through the walls, incisive and terse, habitual, she'd come to learn, of her business conversations.

She pulled on a robe that had been laid across the foot of the bed and found a toothbrush on the marble sink beside a handful of other toiletries—all set out in perfect symmetry. The display made her smile—it was so very Catharine—and she replaced everything exactly as she'd found them after washing her face and brushing her teeth.

Heading out the double doors, she found Catharine sitting at the long dining table wrapped in a robe, her hair drawn into a loose bun, legs tucked underneath her on the chair, porcelain mug in one hand and cellphone in the other. Facing the balcony, her back to the room, she stared out into the foggy morning.

"I don't care what time it is in Guangzhou," she was saying as Alex paused in the living room, not wanting to disturb her. "You get Zhidong out of bed and on the phone in the next half hour with Gordon Liebermann or WorldCargo is going to walk. Shenzhen has an equally lucrative offer on the table and I won't hesitate a minute to pull the plug on this project this late in the game." She paused, listening to the voice on the other end of the line. "No," she said flatly, setting the cup down on the table behind her, "I won't wait until this afternoon. This deal was already finalized. If Mr. Zhidong has any intentions of saving it and working with us in the future, he'll call Mr. Liebermann." She glanced up at the large analog clock on the wall. It was a few minutes after seven. "He's got a half an hour, Mr. Xin. Not a minute longer. When that time has passed my next call will be to Shenzhen. So it's all up to Mr. Zhidong now." There was the muted sound of the other caller before Catharine abruptly responded in what Alex could only imagine was Mandarin. She slapped her knee with her empty palm, emphasizing the foreign words, then curtly disconnected the call and dropped her phone beside the coffee mug, wrapping her arms tightly across her body, still staring out the double glass doors that led to the balcony.

Alex's bare feet were silent across the hardwood floor as she came to stand behind Catharine, gently setting her hands on her shoulders, causing the woman to start with surprise before she relaxed, tilting her head back to look up at Alex.

"I hope I didn't wake you." She took hold of Alex's hands and pulled them down across her chest, hugging them against her.

Alex didn't ask if everything was okay—clearly it wasn't—and she didn't inquire about the call; it was none of her business. Instead, she leaned down and kissed Catharine's forehead, squeezing her hands in hers. "Is there anything I can do?"

How different Catharine looked—her hair pulled back in a messy bun, her face washed clean of makeup, the immaculate tailored clothing that spent the night in a trail across the bedroom floor now hung neatly in the master suite closet. This person in front of her was the core of Catharine Cleveland—all her layers peeled back like an onion, drawn away one by one until the very center was revealed, no longer protectively shrouded. This was the person no one else got to see. This was the nucleus of who she was. And at that moment Alex was certain she was the most beautiful woman she had ever known.

"You can bear with me through one more phone call," Catharine said through an apologetic smile, sitting up to swivel her chair toward Alex. "And then enough of business for the day."

Whatever that phone call had been about, Alex couldn't fathom Catharine's business would be completed for the day. Part of her felt like she should ask if she needed to return to the city. She didn't want anything to go wrong with whatever deal was falling apart on her account. But the other part of her didn't want to know if that was the better option because—selfishly—she wasn't ready to give this up. Here, in the privacy of the secluded oceanside resort, they had no one to answer to—no agendas or meetings or trainings or prying eyes. But as soon as they were back in the city she knew this—what they had here—would be lost.

Her selfish side won out. "Take all the time you need."

Catharine brought her hand to her lips, kissing her palm before picking up her cellphone with a sigh.

As Alex walked back toward the bedroom to shower, she heard Catharine say "Matthew, get Carlton on the line," and then she shut the door, the voice smothered through the walls.

That evening after dinner they wandered to the patios overlooking the golf course and ocean and settled down beside a fire pit furthest from the other guests, seeking solitude and privacy.

Alex found it strange—confining, even—to be out in public with this woman whom she had shared more of herself with over the last twenty-four hours than any other person in her lifetime, and yet to be unable to touch her—to hold her hand or sit too near or laugh too closely with. She had never wanted those things with Caleb. She'd hated it when he would kiss her in public, or reach for her hand when they were walking, or refer to her as his girlfriend to people they'd just met. It always felt wrong. Fake. Like she'd been playing a part in a movie that wasn't her own. But it wasn't like that with Catharine. While shopping in the boutique stores on Main Street that morning or walking along the cliffside that afternoon she had wanted to reach for her hand, to touch her arm, to walk hip-to-hip, sharing in all those intimacies that crossed the boundary from friendship to lovers.

But she didn't. They couldn't.

She could feel Catharine's tension the moment they stepped through the suite doors—by her rigidity while speaking to the receptionist that had checked them in the night before about making a new dinner reservation to the way she enunciated the word *friend* to the concierge that inquired about their stay. Even her awkwardness at dinner when the waiter asked if they were celebrating a special occasion. It wasn't like her at all—the uncomfortable stiffness that came across as cold and indifferent.

Now, away from monitoring ears and scrutinizing eyes, Alex reached a tentative hand to Catharine's chair, touching her knee.

"Is everything okay?" she asked, concerned to learn the answer but needing to know nevertheless.

Catharine almost flinched at the touch, startled from wherever her faraway thoughts had lingered, and haltingly set her hand on top of Alex's with some reservation.

"Yes," she rallied a smile that softened when she met Alex's eyes. "I've been dreadful, haven't I?" Her fingers pressed Alex's hand firmly against her knee. "I'm sorry."

Up the walkway, near the rear entrance to the hotel, the quiet night was broken by raucous laughter as a couple of men settled beside a fire pit with their dates.

Catharine glanced at them, pausing for a second, then sat forward in her chair. "Walk with me?"

They walked along the paved trail to the path that led down the cliffs to the beach below, the tide high along the sandy shore. The last rays of light had faded from the horizon and they had to carefully pick their way along the footpath to avoid the driftwood and stones that had been turned up over time.

Once at the water's edge Catharine stopped, stepping out of the sandals she had picked up in town, and walked barefoot into the damp, cool sand. Alex followed a few feet behind her.

The beach was deserted. There was no sign of anyone else in sight— neither on the shore or along the cliffs. Encouraged by their solitude, Alex reached to take Catharine's hand, staying her from her walk. "Talk to me, please," she whispered, unable to mask her concern. She lifted her hand to Catharine's cheek, stepping closer to her. "What's wrong?"

Gently, but deliberately, Catharine pulled Alex's hand from her cheek, but remained holding it at her side.

"We have to be so careful, Alex," she sighed, squeezing her hand in her own.

"No one is out here—"

"I have learned the hard way that the most trouble comes when you think no one is watching."

"Is that what happened? With you and Nathalie?"

Alex hadn't asked Catharine if it was Nathalie she spoke of that night on the pier in Fisherman's Wharf. But it seemed clear enough the two women shared far more of a past than Catharine did with any of her other friends and there was a familiarity between them that extended beyond the parameters of friendship.

Catharine seemed neither surprised nor perturbed by the inquiry.

"We were young and full of ourselves and felt invincible," she said at length, her voice filled with a degree of melancholy Alex had not heard in her before. "We made so many mistakes." She took in a deep breath of salt air, exhaling it slowly. "I don't want to risk that with you. We both have so much to lose."

Alex felt an icicle of fear sprouting up inside her, casting its tentacles up through her chest, making it difficult to breathe. She'd been under no illusion coming here that they shared a precarious situation. Catharine—with the constraints of her marriage and pending divorce and the added pressure of the election and public scrutiny. Along with her business, though Alex still didn't fully comprehend what that entailed. And for Alex, held to her own limitations between HEG and *Kickstar*—far less paramount, yet hazardous all the same.

At the time she'd not worried much about it. Maybe it was just a weekend fling, a couple days they would share together—unlikely to be lasting or sustainable in the position they were both in. But now, the thought of ending this—this thing that had just begun—this feeling of belongingness, togetherness, *happiness*... She could not bear the idea that it might be over. She did not care about HEG or *Kickstar*. She did not care about Carlton Cleveland and his presidential run.

"Will I see you again after we leave here?" Her voice was choked and she was afraid with the next breath she might actually cry. Turning away, she couldn't stop herself from shivering, the chill of the night settling deep inside her bones.

She was surprised, then, when Catharine laughed—and though the sound was neither harsh nor derisive, filled only with amusement, it grated on her nerves, sparking her to anger. How could Catharine not understand she was serious? How could she not tell how scared Alex was that she was telling her goodbye?

"Oh, Alex," Catharine said, and though her face was veiled in darkness Alex could tell she was smiling. "How do you think I could possibly leave here and not see you again? If I had ever thought that was the case I would never have asked you here in the first place!" She still had her hand in hers, fingers laced together, the cold water lapping at their feet.

Alex felt the grip of ice begin to recede, but not without leaving a dull ache behind. "Is it even possible? This...?" Her voice drifted, uncertain. She didn't know what to call it, whatever this was. It wasn't a relationship, but more than a friendship. She didn't even know if Catharine wanted it to be more than what it was. Or if it even could be.

But those weren't questions for now.

Catharine squeezed her hand, stepping closer so their faces were only a few inches apart. "It would feel more impossible to *not* have this." She was ardent, the laughter gone, her smile vanished, and Alex realized Catharine was just as worried as she was about losing what they'd started. "Which is why we *must* be cautious. Even when it seems pointless. Even when it seems safe. Do you understand? Someday there will be a time when it won't be so. When *we* can decide what others know, and not care about the consequences. But that time isn't yet. For either of us. Tell me you understand." The fervor of her voice died away, softening as she stroked Alex's palm with her thumb.

"Yes." She understood. She understood the real fears Catharine faced, and for good reason. But what she mostly heard was *someday*. Someday, meaning, the future—meaning Catharine was looking ahead. Planning ahead. This was no less temporary for her as it was for Alex.

Suppressing a sigh, Catharine looked down at their joined hands before looking over the blackness of the water. "You must promise me this: there are things that will get hard ahead of us—difficult things—things that will test us both… promise me you'll not hate me for them? And promise you'll forgive me if I ever seem cold or uncaring?"

"I could never hate you," was all Alex could find to say, her voice trembling with emotion.

Through the dark Alex could see Catharine begin to raise her hand, wanting to touch her face, but stopped herself midway, abiding by her own rules. "Let's go back inside," she whispered, and Alex could hear the same yearning in her voice she herself felt, standing there, wanting nothing more than to be able to kiss, to hold her.

Late that night they lay in bed, their limbs entwined and bodies pressed together, the windows open and the sound of waves filtering in with the refreshing sea air. Alex had her head on Catharine's chest, staring at the vaulted ceiling, thinking about the inevitable return to Oakland in the morning. In just two days the Sirens would play their first official match—a preseason exhibition game against the Stanford women's collegiate team, before Alex left the following week for a ten day training camp with the USWNT in Colorado. She'd gotten an official invite from Isabelle Atwood the previous week, and though she would be forced to miss the Sirens second preseason game, her coach, Rodney Collins, had given her leave without hesitation. It would be her first experience training with the national team—and it was her biggest chance to make an impact on her eligibility in the player pool. Unlike most camps, this one wasn't attached to any international matches, but it was well-known the ten-day training would be the deciding factor for the twenty-three player roster called to the SheBelieves Cup the following month. And although Isabelle Atwood would already have a good idea of who she was going to play, there was always the possibility she could change her mind—find herself impressed with what Alex could bring to the table—and give her a shot to earn her first cap with the National Team.

Alex had ten days to get that done. And for the first time in her life she felt ready. She knew she was national team caliber—mostly due to Amelia's relentless pushing to get her there, along with her insanely critical, yet surprisingly supportive, "encouragement"—as the Australian liked to call it. Her game was at its peak, even coming straight from off-season.

Soccer should have been the only thing on her mind—her only focus. She knew that. But knowing in less than twelve short hours she would be back in her apartment, not knowing when she might see Catharine again, her thoughts were drifting. She wondered if Catharine would even still be in California by the time she got back from Colorado. She'd mentioned business in London and a forced trip to DC—in which case, when the Sirens played the Capitol Tyrants...

Don't be an idiot.

Annoyed at herself, Alex tried to shut off that train of thought. Catharine couldn't just veer off the senator's campaign trail and show up at her games. She'd told Alex the basics of her agreement for the divorce; enough for Alex to understand she was still bound to her husband for at least another year, at minimum. But laying there in the dark, feeling the rise and fall of Catharine's breath against her cheek, she couldn't think of much else.

"Are you awake?" Catharine's voice, low with her own internal deliberations, drew her from her thoughts as she reached a hand to run her fingers through Alex's hair.

"Yes."

The room carried a weighted silence as Catharine's fingertips moved to drawing nonsensical designs along the curve of Alex's back. At length she sighed, battling an internal reasoning of her own. "Come to the Gala this weekend." Her fingers paused in their idle task.

"Isn't that a bad idea?"

"I won't be able to spend much time with you there."

Alex laughed at her honesty. "Then why should I come?"

"Because I want you to," Catharine said simply, as if that were reason enough.

Alex smiled. "Do you always get what you want?"

She could feel Catharine smile in the dark. "In most cases, yes." She lifted her hand to Alex's face, tracing its outline. "You will come?"

It was almost a question—but one that only left room for the desired answer. Alex caught her hand and kissed her palm.

"Yes."

Chapter Forty-Six

A historic landmark, the San Francisco City Hall was famous for its turn-of-the-century French Renaissance architecture, popular with tourists and locals alike. Proud and stately at the center of the treelined plaza, the Beaux-Arts monument lit the night with its four ornate floors of marble and magnificent rotunda—boasted to be the largest in the country.

On the night of the HOPE Charity Gala every detail of the extravagant structure was illuminated by white and blue rays flooding up from the lawns, creating an incandescent globe of light visible from across the city. Liveried valets parked cars and attendants directed guests up the limestone staircase through the three arched doorways leading to the rotunda. The press—sectioned off from the entry—clamored behind red velvet ropes, calling for the invitees to pause for photos or a quick interview. It was reminiscent of the clips Alex had seen on TV of the Met Gala and the red carpet walks in Hollywood.

"There is a private entrance" Amelia told her as they climbed the staircase, "for those who don't wish to be bothered by the media."

"Why didn't we take that option?" All week Alex had been regretting her agreement to come. She was so far out of her element she felt like she barely knew how to walk, let alone walk in heels, and temporarily forgot the spelling of her last name when the uniformed doorman checked her off the list to allow admittance into the hall.

Three days earlier, after she'd had the honor of scoring the first goal in the history of the Sirens FC in the match against Stanford (a header only made possible by a picture-perfect cross from Amelia) all she'd been able to think about as her teammates celebrated was whether she'd hit the ball hard enough to draw a bruise—and if so, would it be gone by Saturday?

"That entrance is reserved for mates a touch more prestigious than us," Amelia winked, soaking up the atmosphere and absorbing the grandiose aura of the evening. Not in the way Caleb had—to him it was about putting himself at the center of attention—using the environment to elevate and highlight himself. Amelia simply enjoyed the ambiance of the event—the electricity that sparked through the air at the grandeur of it all, the elite set of people, the excessive opulence, the majesty of the gala.

And all Alex felt was out of her league.

For as laid back and unexcitable as Amelia was, she'd been undeniably thrilled when Alex told her she'd changed her mind about attending. She'd immediately grown obsessive about what they would wear, who would be there, what entertainment would be provided. A fortunate shift of focus for Alex, because it meant the Australian's attention was channeled away from her unaccountable two-day absence from Oakland.

After coming home from Half Moon Bay to a less than stellar training, Amelia had relentlessly badgered her about her disappearance all through dinner that first evening.

"You can't vanish for two days with nothing more than a text that says you're taking some time—then show up and play piss poor ball the night before our first game, and expect me to just drop the subject and carry on as if nothing happened. I know you better than that, Grey. Something's up."

Alex wasn't good at lying. She'd been a painfully honest child—a trait established by her uncle's pick-your-own-switch guideline—and rarely varied from any form of the truth unless it came to keeping secrets or avoiding the need to unnecessarily hurt feelings. But in this case, she couldn't tell Amelia the truth—even when she really wanted to. To talk things over with a sympathetic ear. She just couldn't risk it. So in the end she'd told her that she needed a couple of days to herself—that the strain of the new team and call-up to camp and expectations from HEG and *Kickstar* and the blow out with Caleb had reached a boiling point and she'd decided to take a little time to figure herself out. Which, in many ways, *was* true. She had needed to figure things out—Amelia just didn't need the details.

Cynical, Amelia had backed off. She still suspected something—she was no fool—she just didn't hold Alex's feet as close to the fire. "Just don't crack on me, mate, we're counting on your left foot," she'd grudgingly dismissed her. Then Alex told her about her change in heart regarding the gala, asking if she'd still come with her, and Amelia's interest in her disappearance waned almost entirely.

They'd spent two days—and far more money than Alex cared to think about—shopping for the perfect attire. The invitation advised a Roaring Twenties dress code, which Amelia assured her was a lot easier to manage than many of the themes from previous years.

"People spend like fifty thousand quid on dresses to go to this thing," Amelia chastised when she balked at the three-hundred-dollar price tag on a pair of low black heels custom of the period.

"I wouldn't spend five hundred *pesos* on a dress to go to a party," Alex argued.

But now, coming through the front doors and being escorted like classy cattle into the main building of the rotunda, she was grateful Amelia had forced her to buy the shoes.

Loathe to wear a dress, Amelia had settled on vintage women's togs—the sporting apparel, mostly equestrian, of the time: knee-high brown leather tall boots that laced up the front, loose tan trousers, and a white dress blouse beneath a tweed waistcoat, complete with slack bow tie and vintage navy walker coat that hung below her knees. She'd found a tweed newsboy hat to complete the look, and despite her short hair and square, muscular physique, she managed to look just feminine enough to get away with the outfit. And look ridiculously chic sporting it.

Alex had gone for simplicity and comfort, finally swiping her credit card for an uncomplicated black Marta flapper dress with elbow-length loose sleeves and a hemline that fell just below her knees. To appease Amelia, she'd also bought black lace gloves and a cloche hat, and promised to adorn herself with faux pearls and allow Amelia to paint her in makeup relevant to the period.

"You know, it's more of a guideline than a rulebook," Amelia had teased while they were shopping. "It doesn't have to be perfectly period accurate. You can wear something above the knees and show off your shoulders— you've probably got the best body in all of the league—it wouldn't hurt to flaunt it a bit."

"Says the girl who looks like a cross between Jay Gatsby and Katharine Hepburn coming off a fox hunt."

"Touché."

But in the end, Amelia had convinced Alex to let her cut off the sleeves and turn the hemline into an asymmetrical waterfall that started mid-thigh and tapered just below her right knee—a look even Alex had to admit turned out rather striking.

"Next time you tell me *I'm* the one full of surprises, I'm just going to remind you that you morphed into Coco Chanel and hand-altered an entire dress and turned out movie-quality period makeup when I know for a fact you've never so much as owned a tube of lipstick."

Amelia had only shrugged. "We've all got our secrets, right? Like where you can disappear to for two entire days…"

Alex had dropped the subject after that.

It was less crowded inside the rotunda, despite the hundreds of dazzlingly dressed guests milling about the round tables, exquisitely draped in silk tablecloths with flower arrangements redolent of the twenties. Waiters in knee-high trousers and formfitting waistcoats scurried about, offering appetizers and endless trays of champagne in crystal flutes.

Alex was slow to recognize anyone. She'd never followed celebrity circles and the political realms and foreign dignitaries were far beyond her wheelhouse. She was able to pick out Roger Federer, the King of Tennis, and Amelia was remotely impressed with her recognition of Princess Anne's daughter, Zara—the eldest granddaughter of Queen Elizabeth the II—who she recognized from the equestrian team at the 2012 Olympics, but beyond that the people Amelia pointed out she wouldn't have known on TV or the news, let alone dressed in costume at the gala.

There were Hollywood elitists, heads of state, royalty whose names she couldn't pronounce, American politicians, Social Media Influencers and Fortune 500 business executives she, nor Amelia, had ever heard of before.

"Are you ever going to fess up how you got invited here?" Amelia nagged for the hundredth time since they'd walked through the doors. She no longer expected an answer. "My mum's never going to believe me when I tell her I dined in the same room as the Obamas and Nicole Kidman."

"My aunt and uncle wouldn't even know who Nicole Kidman was—and wouldn't have been willing to sit in the same room as the Obamas." She rolled her eyes, thinking about all the off-color, inappropriate, unashamedly bigoted comments her uncle had made over the years. Reeking with blatant racism. Misogyny. Homophobia. As a pastor. A devote Christian. A leader in his community.

She could only imagine what he'd think of her now.

Alex tried not to look for Catharine. There were so many people spread out between the rotunda and balconies she didn't know if they'd ever be close enough to speak—or if it would even be acceptable to try—but she still couldn't keep herself from scanning the faces in the crowd.

They'd spoken twice since Catharine dropped her off at her apartment Tuesday morning. Once after the game against Stanford—Catharine had called to congratulate her on the win—and then again after an unintentional butt-dial on Alex's part the following night. It had been late, after ten, and she'd spent an embarrassing amount of time staring at Catharine's phone number, trying to decide if it would be inappropriate to text her goodnight while Carlton was staying in her house. She'd decided against it, slipped her phone in her pocket, and then been mortified to hear Catharine's muffled voice a short time later while she sat on her kitchen counter eating peanut butter out of the jar. After a profuse apology, to which Catharine had only laughed, they'd had a short conversation, but Catharine had been uncharacteristically distracted, the stress of her week taking its toll. Between dealing with Carlton and navigating a large transaction gone sideways for her business in China, Alex hadn't known much of what to say, and Catharine hadn't been overly transparent. If it hadn't been for Amelia, she would have skipped the gala—made some excuse about training or having the flu or suddenly being abducted by aliens, for all she cared—anything to avoid any awkwardness between them.

Late last night, however, Catharine had texted her. Just a simple *I miss you*. But it was enough for Alex. Enough to know nothing had changed—it had just been a long, taxing week.

The cocktail hour was coming to a close and attendants were ushering guests to their assigned seating. To Amelia's delight, and Alex's utter dismay, they found themselves on the rotunda floor, despite both assuming they would be seated in the balconies, with the less showy names of the evening. The rotunda was reserved for the most prestigious guests—dignitaries, A-List celebrities, politicians, royalty—even Billie Jean King had been seated in the north light court and Tiger Woods on the Mayor's Balcony.

"This is unreal," Amelia sat eagle-eyed as the guests began to fill the seats. "I finally know what it must feel like to be Cristiano Ronaldo."

"Only with more international goals," Alex noted.

For once Amelia didn't take the opportunity to gloat, her focus spinning on the room around them. "You know, Grey—one day I will figure out who you had to root to get this invitation."

Alex shot her a disdainful look, but was saved from further comment by the candelabras dimming as the band came to the close of *Ain't Misbehavin'*. A young woman, not much older than Alex, stepped to the podium at the top of the marble staircase wearing a sequined dress and ornately beaded skullcap—a staple of the silent film stars of the time—and blinked out over the crowd. She looked nervous, her hands working at the material of the dress, and when she finally spoke into the microphone the din of the room did not subside and few heads turned her direction.

"Good evening, everyone," she spoke again, louder, but the guests mingled on and her pleas for silence went unheeded.

Alex felt for the girl. She couldn't imagine trying to politely hush such an eclectic group of individuals and still maintain her dignity.

She leaned over to tease Amelia that they needed her to use the ear-splitting finger whistle she utilized in training, but before she could make the quip another voice came over the microphone, this time without the hesitation or uncertainty of the previous speaker.

"Good evening and good welcome!" The voice was strong and commanding—no louder than the girl in the sequined dress—but unwavering in its tone and demanding of recognition. It carried an English lilt Alex had come to know well.

The hall silenced.

"It is time now to take your seats and turn your attention to the woman we all have to thank for putting this remarkable evening together. I ask that you please give her your full regard and respect as she begins our evening with an introduction to the development and growth of the HOPE Foundation and the mission we have all come together to support. Without further ado, I am pleased to introduce Nicole Garrick of WorldCargo."

Catharine stepped from the podium to allow Nicole to resume her speech, placing a reassuring hand on the younger woman's shoulder as she passed her to walk off the platform.

"Well," said Amelia close to Alex's ear, "I guess that answers that question."

Alex shushed her with a glare. "I'll explain it later." She'd been dreading the moment Amelia saw Catharine, knowing she would recognize her from her apartment—but now, after that comment... *fuck*.

The Australian lounged in her seat with a smug look, crossing her arms and turning her attention to the speaker with mild interest.

Alex's eyes followed Catharine as she walked to the railing of the balcony, stopping beside a large marble pillar, and looked down over the crowd. She looked timeless—radiant in a vintage floor length gown of white, adorned with silken fringe following a spiral pattern from hemline to waistline, before disappearing at an angle into silver sequins and small cut diamonds that decorated the intricate ornamentation sewn from hip to shoulder. Her long white opera gloves came up just above her elbows, laced with the same delicate fringe embellishing the dress. On her head was a flower beaded white headband that matched the detailed pattern of the dress, complimenting her blonde hair that had been pulled back and braided into a woven arrangement above her neckline, leaving her neck and shoulders bare save for a single string of pearls.

Magnificent, Amelia had described her when she'd shown up at Alex's apartment a few weeks prior, and magnificent she truly was—but here, amongst these people, in this place—this was her element. How this woman, who effortlessly rivaled the beauty and grace of all the other ostentatiously gorgeous women in attendance—supermodels, fashion designers, Hollywood megastars—could be the same woman Alex had dragged onto a dock near death in Daufuskie the summer before—the woman who'd shown up unannounced to watch her play ball in Portland—who she'd drank Irish coffees with in a tourist bar in Fisherman's Wharf—and the woman she'd spent the two best days of her life with just a week earlier... how they could all be the same person suddenly seemed unreal. Impossible, even.

She was just Alex, from Carlisle, South Carolina—a town boasting a population of less than five hundred people. Her successes in soccer seemed so pale, so minute to that of everything else around her. She felt glaringly out of place, sticking out as if she were a sore thumb. Surely everyone could see she didn't belong here. She wasn't like Amelia, who could make herself at home everywhere she went—making friends with anyone she chose to speak to. She was so easy and comfortable in her own skin, unconcerned

with what anyone else thought of her. It was a trait Alex was jealous of—
one she had never possessed. From early childhood she had always felt like
someone was telling her how to dress, how to act, who to be. It hadn't left
much room for Alex to find herself—to be herself—whoever that was.

Last weekend, she thought. Last weekend she was the closest to herself
as she had ever been. And this weekend—she couldn't have felt further
opposite.

There was a brief round of applause and Amelia said something she
couldn't hear just as a hand touched her shoulder, drawing her out of her
reverie and back to the table through the curtain of a fog.

"I'm sorry?" she said to Amelia, while simultaneously looking behind
her.

For a split second she didn't recognize the woman—her dark hair pulled
back beneath a white fedora, dressed in a black pinstriped suit, complete
with waistcoat, tie and blazer, a long, unlit cigarette dangling out of a
cigarette holder in her hand. She looked every bit a model for YSL—both in
dress and attitude—confident and provocative, if not a bit amused.

"Bonjour, Mademoiselle Grey," she said with a smile, her head tilted to
one side, looking Alex over with subtle scrutiny.

"Hi," Alex faltered, forgetting Nathalie's last name. "I—I barely recognized you."

"Ah, yes, I'm afraid I may have come out looking more Bugsy Siegel
than Marlene Dietrich," she laughed, gesturing with her cigarette.

"No," Alex disputed. "You look fabulous, really."

"Merci, mon chérie," she said, quite genuine, then leaned closer between
Alex and Amelia so the conversation remained between the three of them.
"I will let you in on a little secret. I was at Catharine's yesterday helping
with some final arrangements and overheard Mr. Cleveland make a remark
that no respectable woman would wear a suit—not today nor a hundred
years ago—so here I am, in all my trousered glory. I had to change my
entire wardrobe last minute." She winked and flicked her eyes to Amelia. "I
see we are kindred spirits, mam'zelle."

"I'm not sure I would go so far as to call myself respectable," Amelia
offered her crooked smile, the one that made her rakish in nature.

"Even better," said Nathalie, her coppery eyes shining. She held a hand
out to Amelia. "Nathalie Comtois."

"Amelia Walker."

"Ah, Eastern Australia," the Frenchwoman smiled. "Coastal?"

Amelia tipped her head, surprised.

Nathalie gave a nonchalant wave of her cigarette. "I have a bit of a fascination with dialects."

"Impressive." There was no hint of her initial sarcasm. "And how do you two know each other?" she looked between Alex and Nathalie.

Alex opened her mouth, but no words came out.

Nathalie smiled casually. "We have a few friends in common."

"I see," Amelia mused. "I am learning so many things about you tonight, Grey." She raised her brows, glancing in Alex's direction, before turning her attention back to Nathalie.

Dinner was being served. Waiters appeared from every corner of the hall carrying trays and glasses, laying out specialized dishes in front of patrons who had returned to their previous chatter during the dinner break. The other guests at their table paid them no mind, absorbed in conversation amongst themselves. Foreign diplomats—to Amelia's disappointment— neither she nor Alex recognized.

But with the arrival of Nathalie, Amelia no longer cared about the rest of the table. She was wholly engrossed by the French actress who had taken up the empty chair beside her, promising to move if the tardy patron arrived.

Relieved to have gotten off the subject of Catharine, Alex surveyed her surroundings while the two women exchanged a flirtatious conversation, thinly veiled as a battle of wits. If that was what it took to keep Amelia occupied, more power to Nathalie, Alex thought to herself, tuning out the talk of *raison d'être* and other philosophical nonsense.

Alex took another scan of the room.

Catharine stood beside a table near the bottom of the grand staircase, smiling at a group of men dressed in tailcoat suits, one of which had his hand on her hip, laughing louder than the rest of the table. Even from where Alex sat, halfway across the pavilion, it was obvious Carlton Cleveland was already drunk—and Catharine was doing her part in damage control, discreetly trying to quiet his raucous laughter and avoid his indecently wandering hands.

The Senator's Wife

Alex watched her collect the hand he tried to slide down her hip in her gloved fingers and give it a patronizing pat, all while nodding cordially toward the man seated beside Carlton, deep in conversation.

How ridiculous it was to feel a twinge of jealousy toward the senator. Alex forced herself to avert her eyes to the band that had resumed their jazz set on the staircase.

He was her husband, after all.

Yet knowing he could sit there, in front of all these people, and make his vulgar comments, disrespecting Catharine the way he did; that he could touch her, command her, treat her with the contemptuousness of his disregard, and she could do nothing about it—it brought a surge of anger she hadn't known before, and flared her jealousy anew.

"What crazy train are your thoughts off on this time?" Amelia flicked Alex's arm. "Earth to Alex."

Alex redirected her focus to their table, finding both women staring at her. "What?"

"You see the nonsense I have to deal with," Amelia quipped at Nathalie, shaking her head in indignation. "She's going to make me go off like a frog in a sock."

Alex didn't have a chance to ask her what the hell she was talking about before Nathalie lifted her eyes over Alex's shoulder, smiling broadly at someone behind her.

"If it's not the lady herself," she said with exaggerated deference that brought a laugh from the lips of the addressee. "Are you certain you can be seen with the lowly likes of us at the commoner table, Mrs. Cleveland?" She exchanged a knowing smile with her friend before turning to regard Amelia. "I know you know Miss Grey, but have you had the pleasure of meeting Miss Walker, who joins us from the Land of Oz?"

"Very briefly." Catharine extended her gloved hand to Amelia, who stood, too quickly, to shake it. "Miss Walker. So nice that you could join us."

Seeing Amelia at a loss for words was something Alex had never witnessed—and was an occurrence she thoroughly enjoyed. For all her friend's swagger and flaunting confidence, even she wasn't immune to Catharine's effusive charm.

"I'm honored to be here, Miss—"

"Mrs. Cleveland." Catharine nodded before turning her gaze to Alex. "Miss Grey." She smiled, her blue eyes veiled beneath long lashes, "I hope you have found the evening agreeable. I placed this rogue across the room so she would not bother anyone, but I see she took the seating chart as a suggestion," she gave Nathalie a deliberate smile and Alex found herself envying the easy way they had together, so comfortable and effortless, with so much unspoken said between them.

"You placed me with a bunch of dullards," she used the word with perfect imitation of Catharine's accent, earning a laugh from Amelia. "I can't be blamed to have sought better company."

"Catharine!" Carlton's inebriated voice cut through the din around them. "There you are." He swept his gaze across the table, taking attendance, before deciding none were worthy of his acknowledgement. "Saturday next —Mr. Vancouver has invited me to speak at the *Young Republicans for California* rally in Fresno. I will need you, of course, to be there. Get it in our schedule."

"I can't. It's Miss Comtois' opening night in New York. I have already committed to attend."

His eyes, red with bourbon, darted from his wife to Nathalie, still seated casually beside Amelia, her legs crossed and arms folded neatly across her chest, looking up at him with a certain amount of defiance Alex could feel crackling in the air.

"Well, then she'd best hope her show will run for more than one night," he drawled with no effort to hide his sneer, speaking as if Nathalie wasn't even there.

"I have already made my plans—"

"Cate," Nathalie cut in, not wanting Carlton to cause a scene. "Another night is fine."

"—and I intend to keep my schedule, as promised," she finished, ignoring the Frenchwoman.

Anger flashed across the senator's face, his dark eyes smoldering, but with a grunt he seemed to remember himself and where he was. "We will discuss it later—but as Ms. Comtois clearly understands—my election comes before her little exhibition." He looked at Nathalie, his eyes squinting beneath heavy lids, daring her to challenge him.

"Of course, *Mr.* Cleveland," Nathalie said tartly, ignoring his senatorial title, her French accent more pronounced than usual, lips clamped so tightly together they'd all but disappeared. She'd cast off her civility and thrown caution to the wind, ignited by his disparaging remark. "There couldn't possibly be anything more important than a rally in a state that will throw your fifty-five electoral votes to the wind come next November—if you are so lucky as to even make the docket." She rose to her feet, her eyes never leaving his.

The muscles in Carlton Cleveland's hands twitched and Alex realized it was all he could do to keep from striking her. She wondered if that was his go-to—punching women.

"Mrs. Cleveland," Nathalie turned from the senator and addressed Catharine with a curt nod, "if you'll excuse me. I think I'll step outside for a smoke. L'ego de ton mari étouffe." At this last comment one of the young men across the table looked up from his soup and laughed, shooting a smirk at Alex.

No clue as to what Nathalie had said, Alex smiled back reflexively, her mind whirring in other directions. But with Nathalie departed, the senator sought to turn his wrath elsewhere, and catching the tail end of the exchange between Alex and the Frenchman, he'd found a new scapegoat.

"You find something humorous, do you?" He spat the words at Alex, his cheeks crimsoning as a tick appeared below his right ear. Taken aback at finding herself the sudden butt of his fury, Alex looked up in surprise, shooting an uncertain glance at Catharine.

"Don't look at her. You look at me. I'm the one speaking to you."

"Carlton," Catharine laid a hand on his arm, her voice sharp as glass, but he brushed her off angrily.

"Who are you, even?" He continued, looking between her and Amelia with no recognition in his intoxicated stare. "Do you know who I am?"

Alex could feel Amelia bristle and wanted to tell her to leave it, she could handle herself, but she didn't dare turn her focus from Carlton. She had dealt with men like this her entire life. This was something she knew how to handle.

"I meant no offense, Senat—"

"Are you serious?" Amelia snapped and Alex felt her heart take up an internal warfare, battling itself between wanting to stop entirely and race toward an ungodly number of beats per minute. "I don't give a bloody fig who you are—"

"*Carlton*," Catharine grabbed his arm, this time unwilling to be disregarded, and stepped between him and Alex. "They're just girls," she hissed between clenched teeth, her back to the table, "and this is not worth the scene you are about to make." He started to speak again but she dug her nails into his arm, silencing him. "Listen—I will go with you to Fresno next weekend. Please, return to your seat with Senators Chisholm and O'Riley."

"Do not *manage* me, Catharine," he growled, and Alex saw the muscles tighten in her back, her free hand clenched into a fist at her side.

"I swear I will not hesitate to have you thrown out of here," she whispered so quietly Alex could barely make out her words, but Carlton clearly heard her, because his face went an ashen hue of rage before turning scarlet, the tick at his jaw quickening.

"Come, darling," she said, taking his elbow and steering him toward his table, her voice laced with acid. "I would hate for you to experience this dish served cold."

When they had gone, Amelia turned to Alex in disbelief. "Who the hell was that?"

"Senator Carlton Cleveland—South Carolina."

"He's a fucking wanker as far as I'm concerned—"

"Amelia!" Alex tried to quiet her, looking around cautiously, grateful no one else paid them any attention. She continued in a whisper. "Yes. He is an ass. There is no doubt about it, but he is her husband—and he's running for president, so please..." She spread her hands in a plea. "Just let it go."

"*He's* running for president?" Amelia's mouth twisted into an incredulous smile sans any humor. "That sod of a prick is running for president?" She laughed, sucking her cheeks in, hollowing her face. "You Americans really will put any old swine in leadership. And his wife—your friend, from the apartment? She lets him talk to her like that? To *you* like that?"

"What did you expect her to do? Look where we are! We're in the middle of a room with some of the most distinguished people in the world, for God's sake. The last thing she—or us, for that matter—needs is a scene!"

"A scene be damned. I'd never let anyone speak to me—or my mates—like that. No matter who they are." She pushed her soup bowl aside, annoyed. "You need to stand up for yourself, Grey. All you ever do is roll over. Y'know—you could really be someone if you weren't such a sook. That's your biggest problem—on and off the pitch." She stood. "I'm going to get some fresh air."

Chapter Forty-Seven

Dessert was over and the alcohol was being abundantly poured. Catharine contemplated a scotch—her part of the night was finished. She'd made her speech about the successes of HOPE—from its inception, ten years earlier, to its present-day presence throughout the globe—seventy-four countries and counting; over five hundred thousand children and young adults put through an education that otherwise would have been unattainable. She'd hit all the key points, emphasized the continued partnership the Foundation would maintain with WorldCargo, and then not-so-subtly instructed her peers to open their pocketbooks to guarantee the children of the new decade would be receiving the same benefits as those whose lives were changed over the previous ten years.

Those were the things Nicole could not do. One had to have a certain amount of clout to be able to encourage others of their station to deal out their money freehandedly. It was the most despicable part of the evening— but she reminded herself it was for a good cause—and now the rest of the night was up to Nicole. Which wouldn't be too much of a task. The foot-work was done. Keep the patrons soused, provide them with entertainment, and they generally kept from killing one another.

She took a rear staircase from the Mayor's Balcony into the hall separat-ing the north light court from the rotunda and stepped into the first of the arched entryways leading into the main pavilion. Beyoncé and John Legend were doing the 1920s duet—*Pack Up Your Sins and Go to the Devil*—not something Catharine would have chosen for the specific audience, but Nicole had been insistent it would be a hit, and from the look of the crowd she appeared to have been correct.

Catharine leaned against the cool surface of the marble archway, looking over the sea of heads to the seats she'd assigned to Alex and her friend. She'd been trying to get back to the table all night. Ever since Carlton had managed his impeccable timing to be a bastard—something he had perfected over the course of their marriage. It was the one thing she could always count on him for—to pick the most inopportune moment to be himself.

He'd since settled back at his table with his league of cronies and remained put all night, sloshed to the gills and only vaguely aware of the goings-on around him. Matthew would have his hands full getting him back to the Marina District without him picking a fight, pissing himself or providing the media with their much-craved footage of the presidential hopeful behaving like the drunken imbecile he was.

But that was Matthew's problem now. It had been her problem for twenty-three years—nearly a quarter of a century—and with the sudden realization it simply wasn't of concern for her anymore, the feeling was liberating. Unshackling. If he made himself a fool, so long as it was not directly involving her, that was on him. Let him ruin his candidacy. His career. Whatever meager reputation he had amongst those whose personal reputations were as questionable as his own. The one thing she'd been made certain of tonight—after his spat with Nathalie and his treatment of Alex—was the certainty that she positively hated him. Plain and simple. There was no other feeling to assign it. She'd felt indifferent toward him over the years. Annoyed. Frustrated. Disgusted. But she'd never felt the sheer loathing she found for him while standing at that table, listening to him berate the people she cared about. The absolute bitter detestation.

The song ended and a handful of guests from Alex's table—French dignitaries and an ambassador from Belgium—rose to mill about, destined for the bathroom or the bar, leaving Alex alone, save for a prince from Qatar and his wife, whose attention remained on the stage. The Australian hadn't returned since the debacle with Carlton, and Catharine had spent the last hour agonizing over Alex being left on her own—with her unable to do anything about it. This wasn't the evening she'd intended.

Nathalie was also missing, but that came as no surprise. She was no stranger to quarrels with Carlton, and it was common for her to disappear when she needed to cool off—lest her temper boil over and she truly tell him what was on her mind, muddling any possibility of sharing the same airspace with him again with any chance of civility. A feat she had achieved —for Catharine's benefit—all these many years. One she would not be asked to manage much longer. That was Catharine's mantra, her saving grace... none of this would last for much longer.

The next artist took the stage—Elvis Costello—and the lights dimmed once more. Against her better judgement, Catharine left the peace of the alcove and navigated her way through the dinner tables, nodding politely at the sea of faces but pausing for no one. Rarely did she stop to socialize in any one place at her own events—time and planning seldom permitted it—but tonight, with no further obligations on her plate, she would make an exception. A risk, she knew. But one worth taking.

She had to talk to Alex. To apologize. To make the evening right.

Without a word she slipped into the empty seat she'd deliberately left available beside Alex, who'd been facing the stage with little interest, but now sat up, stiff and silent, her eyes never wavering from the singer.

The charismatic London musician struck up the intro to a modern cover of *It Had to Be You* as the hall went dark and the patrons quieted, the clinking of ice against crystal glasses the only accompaniment to the music.

Closing her eyes, Catharine listened to the familiar lyrics, trying to center herself from the stress and tension of the evening. She and Alex had hardly spoken since leaving Half Moon Bay. Alex had played her first game with her new team less than fifteen miles from her house and Catharine had been unable to attend to support her. Unable to do anything more than make a ninety second phone call to congratulate her.

Fifteen miles.

And tonight had started off no better.

She drew a deep breath, listening as the singer crooned on.

> *It must have been that something lovers call fate*
> *Kept me saying "I had to wait"*
> *I saw them all*
> *Just couldn't fall 'til we met*

Catharine opened her eyes and leaned forward, propping her gloved arms onto the table, her chin atop her entwined fingers. "Come back to my hotel with me tonight." She spoke below the tone of the music, loud enough only for Alex to hear. They both stared straight ahead.

Alex said nothing.

It had to be you
It had to be you
I wandered around, and finally found
The somebody who
Could make me be true

"I'm sorry about earlier. I just wanted to get him away from here. From you." Catharine looked down at her hands in front of her.

And could make me be blue
And even be glad just to be sad
Thinking of you

"I can't just leave Amelia here," Alex finally said, never looking away from the stage. Her face was an indecipherable mask, her eyes hidden beneath the brim of her hat.

Some others I've seen
Might never been mean
Might never be cross, or try to be boss
But they wouldn't do

"I think you may find Amelia is getting along fine on her own." Catharine's voice maintained a neutral tone as she turned ever so slightly to look at Alex. She had a sneaking suspicion about where the Australian girl had gotten off to. "In any case, I will see that she gets home safely—by one manner or another."

For nobody else gave me a thrill
With all your faults, I love you still
It had to be you
Wonderful you
It had to be you

"What do you mean 'fine on her own?'" Alex frowned. "I won't just leave her. We came together."

"Trust me, will you? Please?" Still looking forward, Catharine sat upright, dropping her elbows from the table to reach beneath the tablecloth and find one of Alex's hands with her own.

For nobody else gave me a thrill
With all your faults, I love you still
It had to be you
Wonderful you
It had to be you

The song came to a close and Catharine was forced to withdraw her hand to clap with the rest of the audience. Alex sat beside her, neither clapping nor breathing, entirely emotionless.

"After this song set is over go through the first alcove on the right and straight down the hall past the entrance to the north light court. Security will let you pass." She looked over at her. "Please."

Alex met her eyes briefly as the first few chords to *California, Here I Come!* strummed over the sound system, before turning her attention back to the singer, again hiding beneath the shadow of her hat. For a moment Catharine thought she would not respond, which was in itself response enough. But as she rose to leave, Alex nodded. "All right," she whispered, her mouth hardly moving.

Catharine left the same way she'd come, making her way to the arched exit, grateful for the low light and cheerful stanza of the melody that kept the audience's attention drawn to the stage. As soon as she was obscured in the dim hall, she stopped to lean against the cool marble wall, breathing a sigh of relief. To be out of the limelight. Out from under the stress of the evening. Away from it all. But just as quickly as the burden of the gala faded, a new tension took its place, though this one carried very different sensations.

Alex. She'd agreed to come. To leave, in the middle of the gala. It was stupidity. Catharine was playing with fire once again, and still, she couldn't stop herself. She didn't know what the hell she thought she was doing.

With a decisive intake of breath, she straightened, collecting her composure. It was too late to change her mind now.

The Senator's Wife

She'd stop, speak with her head of security—and then there was one last task to handle before she went to meet Alex.

Two hundred fifty-six spiraling steps and more than one vertical ladder later, Catharine stepped through the *restricted access* door onto the rotunda rooftop. Another time she may have found it more amusing, but her bare feet were aching from the climb—her heels abandoned at the bottom of the first narrow *do-not-enter* stairwell—and her tolerance for nonsense was running at an all-time low. But she had promised Alex.

Before the door had even closed behind her, she was at least granted the satisfaction of knowing she had guessed right, and the trip was not for nothing. Between the hushed laughter and stench of cannabis wafting through the chilled air, it wasn't difficult to find the two women in the dark shadows of the rooftop, perched moronically on the wall at the base of the spire of the dome, looking over the edge into the lower courtyard three hundred feet below.

Nathalie was leaning back against the flat surface of the wall top, a joint in one hand and the other lazily hanging off the side of the building, her eyes turned up to the starless sky. Beside her the cocksure Australian sat with both legs dangling over the front, clicking the heels of her boots against the marble, cradling a bottle of champagne between her knees. They were laughing inanely at something Nathalie had said when Catharine stepped into view, her stockinged feet muted by the gravel flooring.

"Bloody Christ!" Amelia lurched, nearly losing hold on the champagne bottle. "That's a piss poor way to creep up!"

Nathalie shot upright, concealing her joint in the hand she dangled off the side of the wall, and swung her feet to the rooftop. "Pour l'amour de Dieu, Cate! Qu'est-ce que tu fais?!"

"I might ask you the same," Catharine said flatly, looking over the little scene before her. "What the devil do you think you are doing? I swear," she stepped past Amelia and bent over Nathalie, plucking the blunt out of her hand and grinding it against the guardrail.

"Did you lose your stilettos on the way up, mate?" Amelia offered a crooked smile, her voice thick with smoke and alcohol. "Barefoot on the ladder and all?"

Catharine glanced at the younger woman, a little incredulous at her familiarity, then turned back to Nathalie. "You've outdone yourself this time —up here getting stoned and boozed with—with—" she didn't know exactly what she wanted to say that wouldn't come out far more severely than she meant it, so she just shook her head instead.

"How'd you find us? Did that security guard say something?" Nathalie at least had the decency to look penitent.

"Nah," Amelia waved off the inquiry before Catharine could answer, "that bloke was a clown—if he fell into a barrel of tits he'd come out sucking his thumb. No way he saw us."

Catharine stared at her, opened her mouth to respond, and promptly shut it again, before turning her attention back to Nathalie. Even in the low light she could see that her makeup was smudged and her hair tousled, and the Australian's hat was missing with her bow tie loose and askew. They were a perfectly guilty mess.

"Just an intuition on your ridiculously predictable nature." Catharine took the extinguished joint and tucked it in Nathalie's vest pocket. "Sober up, both of you. Maybe—" she gestured toward her friend's face and neck, "—try to straighten up a bit before you go downstairs." She shook her head again, careful to hide her smile. "I'm leaving Malcolm to drive you to the hotel and Miss Walker to her apartment. Ou retour à l'hôtel avec vous," she added with a dismissive flip of her gloved hand. Nathalie could bring the girl with her to the hotel for all she cared—which, given the state of the two of them, seemed the more likely outcome.

Amelia cleared her throat, her voice still heavy with smoke and slurred with champagne. "I've got to find Alex."

"Tonight, Miss Walker, with all due respect—you will do well to simply look after yourself. Or after Mam'zelle Comtois," she nettled, unable to flush the sarcasm from her tone. "You may rest assured, Miss Grey is perfectly fine."

She took one last look at the pair. It was no surprise she'd found Nathalie here. It was where she'd always gone when she was upset—up. To the roofs. To the balconies. To the top of the catwalks in the university theatre when they'd been young. Anywhere to contemplate the world over a cigarette or a good cry, depending on the situation. And she'd anticipated finding the Aussie with her. The way the two of them had been eyeing one another at the table… It was just like Nathalie to find a kindred spirit to share in her tumultuous moods when she was feeling down.

"Cate—"

"Don't forget you have an early flight Monday morning." She turned to leave, feeling a touch of guilt at her intrusion. They'd clearly been having a splendid time—whether they were making fools of themselves or not. "I'll see you sometime tomorrow. Tu es au-delà de tout espoir." *You are beyond hope,* she chastised with the glimmer of a smile before turning toward the stairwell. For a moment the only sound was the gravel crunching beneath her feet, but as she pulled open the heavy steel door she heard the smother of stifled laughter behind her. Their evening was evidently far from being ruined.

Chapter Forty-Eight

Hotel Fairmont was little more than a mile from City Hall, but the Saturday night traffic was crawling through Nob Hill and every red light went against their favor.

Alex found herself growing anxious. The longer they waited at each signal the more she became aware of the forced conversation between them, the drive too short for anything meaningful, yet long enough to allow moments of silence to feel awkward.

"You're certain Amelia will get home okay?" She watched as pedestrians on Van Ness Ave. cruised by faster than they were driving. She'd felt guilty, leaving her there without a word—but Amelia had been the one to disappear. Besides, she was a big girl, more than capable of taking care of herself.

"I'm certain."

Alex didn't question Catharine further.

Waiting to turn right on Bush St., Catharine glanced at her phone for at least the tenth time since they'd left the venue, clearly waiting for something. She seemed abnormally uneasy.

"Are you sure that—"

"I'm sorry about—"

They started talking simultaneously and stopped, waiting for the other to continue.

"You were saying?" Catharine glanced at her, her blue eyes shielded.

"Oh." Alex regretted breaking her silence. "I just—are you sure you can leave? With the gala still going on?" It was a stupid question. Of course she could leave. She could do anything she wanted. Catharine was entirely adept at handling her own business.

Catharine gave a perfunctory shrug. "Nicole will be all right. It's good for her to get out from under my wing once in a while. And I have a feeling

318

my imbecile of a husband may manage to behave himself better if I'm not in attendance. At the very minimum, I won't have to bear witness to whatever foolishness he drums up next." She rubbed her temples with her fingertips before returning her hands to the wheel, pulling onto the one-way street. "I'm truly sorry, Alex—for him—what he said to you. How I handled that. I should have done that differently. It's just that sometimes, the only way to manage him without an even bigger scene, is by placating him."

"You don't have to apologize for him." Alex stared at the dashboard, embarrassed it had been brought up again.

"Then I apologize for me. Because of all the people in that room I should have allowed him to treat poorly, you are the very last person."

They drove on in silence, passing Huntington Park, Hotel Fairmont coming into view ahead of them. Alex considered asking about Nathalie—she'd not seen her return the rest of the evening—but decided against it. The further they could get from conversation leading back to Carlton Cleveland, the better.

"I'm glad you came tonight." Catharine looked over at her as they waited in line for valet parking. "Despite everything. I know it wasn't your idea of an enjoyable evening, so I really appreciate you being there. It meant a lot to me."

"I'm glad you invited me."

Catharine scoffed, disbelieving, and Alex shook her head.

"No, I mean it." Even with the run-in with Carlton, she'd been glad to be there. She'd loved watching Catharine work—she was extraordinary at what she did, the way she could command a room. But Alex didn't know how to tell her that, so instead shrugged, making light. "I mean, I could have skipped a few things—Beyonce, for example, isn't quite my scene." There was relief in seeing Catharine laugh, the both of them knowing Beyonce was the least of her concerns over the course of the evening.

But the night had also shown Alex a side of Catharine she'd barely glimpsed before—a glaring reminder of how little she actually knew her. It had been astonishing to witness the respect she commanded without ever saying a word. The dawning knowledge that she was viewed as an equal amongst an elite set of people encompassing some of the most powerful figures in the world.

Alex didn't know why she'd been surprised. She'd of course already known Catharine held a prominent position in the sphere of business—she'd read the article on the wall in her sky rise office—CEO of WorldCargo. She'd seen the beautiful homes on the water. The luxury in which she lived. But some part of her had still applied much of Catharine's success to Carlton. Assumed it was his name that garnered them significance. His wealth on which they thrived.

Tonight told a different story. Carlton was irrelevant when it came to the bigger picture. It was Catharine who held the influence. Catharine with the weight of authority. Amelia had laughed when Alex had been visibly stunned glancing through the program—reading the welcome note at the bottom that listed Catharine not only as CEO but owner of WorldCargo. And below that, a website for a corporation called Brooks Corp.

Welcome back, Ms. Brooks. She could still hear the way the woman at the front desk in Half Moon Bay had said her name.

"Wait 'til I tell my dad I've got a mate shagging the owner of the company he works for—he'll want to know if you can put in a good word for him on his next raise." Before Alex could respond Amelia had waved her off. "I know, I know, she's just your *friend*." She'd drawled out the word, making quotations in the air. "I still say hangin' and bangin'."

Alex had fixed her with a glare, but her mind had been too preoccupied with the reality of the situation to argue. It was something she'd never taken into consideration—that instead of some high-level executive, Catharine might actually *own* the company. That she might be part of some colossal parent corporation that bore her name.

And she hadn't had a clue. Because she knew next to nothing at all.

"In for the night, madam?" The valet that received Catharine's keys was unable to hide his sweeping double take beneath the brim of his bowler hat. And how could Alex blame him? She was simply stunning, even with her coat draped over her gown.

"Yes, thank you." She tipped him and turned away, oblivious to the attention of the attendant. She was good at that—carrying on as if she had no clue the world fawned at her every move.

Alex followed her through the extravagant arched entry, the dozens of United Nations flags fluttering above them in the evening breeze.

Like the San Francisco City Hall, the Fairmont Hotel was a masterful representation of early twentieth century architecture, with few artistic changes over the course of the last hundred years. Romantically old-fashioned, yet brilliantly restored, it offered all the modern convenience one would expect of a luxury hotel. Alex couldn't help but slow her steps to appreciate the ornate beauty of the Beaux-Arts design.

Catharine noted her admiration. "The architect that restored the Fairmont after the 1906 earthquake was a woman—one of the first famed female builders."

"Julia Morgan—the same architect who designed Hearst Castle."

Pausing at the top of the landing, Catharine's eyes flicked to Alex with a quaint smile. "You never cease to surprise me, Miss Grey."

"My father was an architect. He loved French neoclassicism. I can name all the greats." She swept her gaze across the entry, taking in the marble columns and grandiose ceiling with its highly decorative design. "The actual artistic composition of this hotel was designed by the Reid brothers. Ms. Morgan leant only her structural knowledge to the building."

"Did you want to be an architect?" Catharine asked, continuing through the doors.

"No. I never had the imagination for it."

"Then the world of soccer got lucky."

"Welcome back, Mrs. Cleveland," the doorman doffed his hat, stepping aside for them to pass.

It was different here, in the heart of the city, in Catharine's own town. The anonymity offered at Half Moon Bay with its quiet, non-speculating atmosphere was gone. At the Fairmont it seemed everyone knew Catharine's name, nodding and smiling as she passed. They followed their hellos with glances at Alex, brimming with vague interest. Who is this inconsequential girl, their looks seemed to say, and why would Catharine Cleveland keep such company?

Alex stared at the reflection of the two of them in the gold sheen of the elevator doors, Catharine—elegant, ever poised, enchanting in white satin, and Alex—an impostor in a costume, unsettled and uncertain, and she had to wonder herself: *Why does she keep such company?*

The doors slid open and without a word the attendant pressed the button for the twenty-third floor—the top of the tower.

Inside the suite Catharine hung her coat and turned to help Alex with her own, before stopping to listen to the messages on the phone blinking red on the desk in the foyer. She must have stayed more than just this night at the hotel, as there were signs of her inhabitance—a folder on the dining room table, a pair of gloves draped over the back of a chair, an electric kettle by the sink.

Alex stopped in front of one of the panoramic windows and looked out over Coit Tower, trying to force herself to shed the edginess of the evening. Of Carlton. And Amelia. And the simple depleting nature of socializing.

"You're quiet tonight."

Alex turned to find Catharine watching her from the entry, her steady gaze inquiring.

Crossing to her, she lifted the cloche hat from her head and dropped it on the couch beside them before placing a finger beneath her chin, tilting her face up so she could meet her eyes. "Will you tell me what you are thinking?"

Nothing—it was the evasion that sprang to mind for a question difficult to answer, but she knew Catharine would see straight through the lie. Alex had no ability to hide her feelings the way Catharine could.

"I—honestly, I'm a little overwhelmed." She would have liked to look away, but forced herself to meet the blue eyes steadfast. If she was going to be forthright, she may as well own it all the way. "I guess tonight has been a little intimidating. *You* are a little intimidating, to be honest."

"I am no different a person today than I was last weekend," Catharine said gently, her finger still at Alex's chin. "This is still me."

"Maybe not different, no… but I think who you are is different than who I imagined you to be—that I didn't really understand who that was to begin with… the person you were—to me." Alex stopped talking, realizing she was making no sense, speaking in riddles, for something she didn't know how to explain. How did she tell Catharine she was too insignificant, too inconsequential—that no matter what successes she ever found in her own life, she would never be the person Catharine needed her to be. Their lives were too different—too contrasting—for Alex to ever fit into the world in which Catharine lived. She would always pale in comparison.

"Obviously I was not so ignorant to think there was no disparity between us—I just had not realized to what degree. I mean—" she faltered, trying to find a better explanation, but came up empty-handed. "I'm just—*me*. I'm nobody, in the scheme of things."

"I know you are not so provincial to judge the worth of a person based off their affluence or social standing," Catharine cupped her chin between her thumb and forefinger, her voice laced with a coloring of vehemence she had not expected. "Look at me, Alex."

Alex shifted her eyes to meet Catharine's, her own frustrations giving her courage to ask the question that had been plaguing her all evening.

"But why me, Catharine? That's what I don't understand. With all of this —" she waved her arm around at the luxurious suite, trying to encompass the totality of Catharine's unfathomable life with any kind of simplicity, "— with everything... why me? It doesn't make any sense."

"Does life ever make sense?" Catharine asked genuinely, her face so close to Alex's she could smell the faded fragrance of her perfume, hear the quiver to the breath that brushed her cheeks. "If you try to make sense of everything that happens in this life, you will spend the majority of it seeking resolutions that will never exist." She sighed and dropped her hand from Alex's face, taking a step back. "Why did our paths ever cross on that island? Why were you in the right place at the right time? If you had been one minute later, or left thirty seconds sooner, this moment, this conversation, this time and place would never even be happening."

She shook her head, frustrated by the turn of the conversation. "There aren't answers for that, Alex. I can't give you reasons for the way things are. But what I can tell you is you are one of the only people I have ever met who has looked at me—really *looked* at me—and seen *me*. Not seen a business opportunity. Or a paycheck. Or a hand out. Or the means to an end. A deal to be made or a solution to be obtained. Do you understand? That is all my life has been made of. That's been all I've ever had." Her voice shook, the words nearly coming across in anger, but looking at her, it wasn't anger Alex saw—but concern. Concern she wouldn't understand.

But she did.

She did understand. The feeling of being found, seen, understood—when you didn't even know you were waiting for someone to come find you. When you didn't even know you had been lost. That was what she understood. And that was what Catharine had given her. The fact that she, in some small way, could have done the same in return had never crossed her mind. That Catharine ever could have needed finding seemed impossible. With all of her confidence and assuredness and endless conviction.

Catharine reached forward, taking her hands, seeking an answer, but Alex hesitated to respond. There were still things that scared her. She wanted to tell Catharine she was worried she would grow tired of her. That she might one day grow bored. That she was terrified of the heartache if Catharine proved impossible to hold. Losing her would be far worse than never having her at all.

But she said nothing. What would it matter if she voiced her own fears? It wouldn't change the course of things. What was going to happen was going to happen—and sometimes she just had to be willing to take a chance on it. Off the field, taking risks had never been Alex's forte. She didn't like anything with an indeterminate outcome. She preferred to know if she worked hard and put in the time, whatever her goal was would pan out. And this certainly wasn't that. A secret affair, with an enigmatic woman, who happened to be the wife of the man running for President of the United States had not been on her radar. And when she thought of it like that it seemed more outlandish than ever.

But that really wasn't what it was. Was it? It was so much more complicated than that.

"Will you just trust me, Alex?" Catharine spoke as if she'd been privy to follow the course her train of thought had strung her along. "There aren't many things concrete in life, I promise you that. But the one thing I can tell you is—in over twenty years there has never been a single soul I would risk everything for. I had resigned to living the cards I'd been dealt. But you came along, and honestly, from our first conversation forward, I have known that I wanted you in my life. And if you will just bear with me long enough to ride out this abhorrent situation with Carlton—as ludicrous and maddening as it will be—if you can be patient enough to wait that out—I think we could be truly happy together, Alex. I think we are good for each other."

Alex slowly released her breath, feeling the weight of the millstone around her neck disintegrate with the unburdening of her doubt. She didn't know what to say, but now it was for an entirely different reason. To hear Catharine ask her to wait—to be reassured this was not just a passing whim

—a couple days or a week or a month that meant nothing—that it was something as important to her as it had become to Alex...

They couldn't possibly know the outcome, or how it would work out, but just the knowledge that this woman wanted her—wanted to share her life with her, enough that she was willing to chance an unpredictable future—it was more than enough for Alex. It was all she could ever ask for.

"I wonder if you'll be saying the same thing," Alex said, slow to smile, "when you have to put up with me after a game where I've been red carded —or when I've been benched to give a rookie minutes—or we've lost a championship to a team we were leading three to nothing at the half?"

"I suppose you are expecting me to learn what the term 'red card' means?" Catharine teased in return, bringing her hands to Alex's face and running her fingers into her hair. Her voice lowered, shifting from its levity. "Do you know how distracting it was to stand on those stairs tonight and try to give a speech while all I could think about was how much I wanted to be alone with you?" She leaned forward, their lips brushing, her words spoken into Alex's mouth. "And being forced to sit through an entire dinner trying not to stare at you while the Prince of Denmark bemoaned to me about the decline of the Danish krone?"

Alex could feel Catharine smile against her lips and closed her eyes, allowing herself to shed the disorder of the evening. She could have told her she'd barely been able to find a single moment over the course of the week where she'd not had Catharine on her mind. That her coach had threatened to bench her for their first preseason game because the day she returned to training from Half Moon Bay she'd missed nine of ten penalty kicks against their third-string keeper.

She could have told her she'd composed at least a dozen text messages over the last five days—ranging from *I think we've made a terrible mistake* to *I don't know how I will get through this week without seeing you again* and everything in between—all of which had been deleted after staring at her screen for senseless amounts of time, realizing she sounded like a lovestruck teenager.

But she didn't tell her any of that. She didn't need to. Her breathing and her body betrayed her secrets, and she knew by the shifting insistence in Catharine's kiss she could feel it too.

With no more words spoken, Catharine bade Alex turn to face the window, her breath leaving a clouded stain against the glass. Twenty-three stories below the city unfolded into a maze of lights, disappearing at the water's edge, where the blackness of the bay swallowed all luminance of the night.

But the view was forgotten as warm lips kissed the nape of her neck, fingers finding the half dozen clasps sewn into the back of her dress. Alex had to close her eyes, to steady herself against the glass. To force herself to breathe as Catharine lifted her hem, her knuckles brushing the length of her body as she raised the lace and chiffon over her head.

There was something intensely intimate about the slow procession of being undressed by another person; allowing them to expose your body at their leisure, to reveal the secrets underneath, to explore those places withheld from all others.

Catharine lingered, the tips of her fingers tracing the slope of muscles from her shoulders to the crest of her hips, before turning Alex to face her— to press her against the chill of the windowpane, leaning in to run her lips from her cheek, to her jaw, to the hollow of her throat. She took her time, drawing her palms across the length of her ribcage, the contour of her breasts, the flat of her abdomen, before finding the small of her back, pulling her into her embrace, compelling her body to forget its previous hesitations and reservations.

Just as Catharine was in her day-to-day life, as a lover she was equally assertive—self-assured—unfaltering. With the sense of unfamiliarity and uncertainty that had been inevitable the weekend prior no longer prevalent, she had an easy confidence Alex found comfortable to fall into, forgetting any sense of shame or guilt that had inescapably worked its way into her head over the last five days.

It became impossible to think of anything beyond her touch, her lips, her hands. Alex let her mind insulate itself to all but the current moment— trying to memorize every detail about her—the way her hair hinted of citrus, the subtle taste of Hennessy on her tongue, the involuntary reaction to her body's responsiveness at the sensation of her exploring hands. At once becoming familiar, yet seductively unknown. She felt as if she drifted, suspended in a dream, swimming amongst the intoxication of its pleasures.

The time passed, the moon shifting in the sky, the dome of the City Hall illuminated in the distance, the gala going on without them.

Later, though Alex could not have guessed how much time had passed, she woke on the couch to find Catharine standing with her back to the room, her gaze turned out the picture window overlooking Treasure Island and the Bay Bridge. The clouds had rolled in, leaving a starless sky, while the abyss of the ocean had been turned into a canvas streaked with red and white from the taillights of the Saturday night traffic on the bridge.

She had dressed in her slip, the glimmer of the white silk iridescent in the glow of ambient light filtering from the foyer, standing so motionless she could have been cast of marble.

Alex rose, glancing at her dress that had been folded neatly on the coffee table, but left it untouched before crossing toward the window. She stopped behind Catharine, placing her hands lightly on her hips and resting her chin on her shoulder to look down at the courtyard. There was a bustle of activity in the plaza as people filed into the foyer, valets dashing to and fro. Top hats. Tuxedos with tails. Cocoon fur coats and fringe wraps, feathered headbands and beaded evening gowns. The gala had come to an end.

"Can they see us?" Alex asked, soaking in the warmth of their two bodies, peaceful in the silence of the suite so contrary to the commotion twenty-three stories below.

Catharine met her eyes in the reflection of the glass, her lips playing at a smile. "Isn't your concern a little tardy in that respect?" The insinuating eyebrow she raised brought heat to Alex's cheeks as her mind replayed the ardency of their evening. The chill of the window against her burning skin. Their shared breath, short and erratic. The palm prints left behind on the spotless glass. The weakness in her knees. The insatiable, intemperate desire.

Stepping to the side, Catharine continued, her eyes unabashedly sweeping the length of Alex's unclad body in the mirrored panels. "Not the way you wanted to make the evening news? Perhaps your next viral video? HEG might love that."

"There's no such thing as bad publicity, right?" Alex returned her puckishness, grazing her palm down Catharine's hip to capture her hand, entwining their fingers. "Go big or go home?"

"Hmm," Catharine amended with a smile, "there may be caveats to that notion."

They stood watching the scuttle of activity in the plaza.

"Are you sorry to have missed the end of the gala?" Alex asked after a moment, her mind unforgivably returning to the land of responsibilities and obligations that loomed over them.

Catharine turned to regard her, her expression quizzical, if not entertained. "You tell me—did I seem sorry?" She smiled at Alex's blush, lifting a finger to touch her lower lip, drawing it down, her fingertip trailing to her chin, her neck; lower. "Let's see—an evening with a mob of stuffy, impossible-to-please, drunken socialites or a night here, alone, with you. A tough call."

Alex laughed, catching her hand in its downward progression, and raising it to kiss her fingertip. "Aren't those your friends?"

"I think you will find I have very few friends, Miss Grey."

Alex started to tease her that she was by far the most social person she knew—always an event, a party, an outing—but before the words left her mouth there was a blistering pounding at the door that jarred both women out of tranquility, causing Catharine to spin toward the entry hall. The drubbing came again—not the tentative inquiry of a guest, but a loud, demanding hammering, as if one had been unreasonably shut out from their own home or separated from their own property.

"Open the door, Catharine!"

In the blink of an eye, Alex watched Catharine's face go through a multitude of changes: surprise, disbelief, anger, and fear. It was this last emotion she hated the most—so unnatural, so out of place on the beautiful, confident woman.

"Open the damn door!"

In a handful of steps Alex was back to the couch, shrugging on her dress while Catharine cussed under her breath, snatching up her phone from the dining table to look at her messages.

"Malcolm was supposed to..." Her voice faded as she turned to look around the room, her face ashen through the dim glow of the foyer light. She paused, gathering herself, and looked to where Alex knelt, pulling on her heels. "He won't go away until I see him." She was composed again, ever decisive, but Alex still thought she could detect a grip of fear hidden beneath her collected exterior. "I'm going to have to deal with him and it may not be terribly pleasant." She picked up Alex's hat and placed it in her arms, before gathering the dress she'd discarded earlier in the evening and slipping it over her head.

"Do you want me to—" Alex looked around, "hide? Go?" There weren't really places to hide, and even the suggestion of it seemed childish and futile.

"No. No." Catharine shook her head, still working through what to do. "It won't do any good. Just… sit, please. I will deal with him."

Her voice was strained, the color not yet returned to her cheeks. She leaned forward, kissing Alex's forehead, before flipping on the nearest light and turning for the door.

As Alex took a seat, trying to look occupied with her phone, she felt her heart jump as the door shook beneath a third and final pounding. And then Catharine unlocked the deadbolt and Carlton Cleveland stormed into the room.

Chapter Forty-Nine

"I swear to God, Catharine—"

Catharine tried to hold her ground in the doorway, disallowing him access to the room, but Carlton was plowing past her before her hand ever left the deadbolt. He stumbled into the foyer, his gait unsteady, and wheeled on his heels to face her.

"How *dare* you!" She hissed at the forced intrusion, incredulous at his audacity. That he would shoulder his way into her room was brazen, even for him.

She'd known there was a possibility he would come. It was why she'd instructed Malcolm to inform her when Carlton left the venue—to give her time to prepare. Just in case. But Malcolm had reported his departure over an hour earlier, and advised the caravan of his entourage had turned west, the direction of the Marina District. Even still, Catharine had stood at the window and watched the lobby entrance for almost an hour, far longer than it would take to make the short drive to the Fairmont. She'd finally felt it safe to assume he'd gone straight to the Marina house, where he could black out with his lackeys; maybe even convince some junior lobbyist to his—*her* —bed.

Clearly it had been wishful thinking.

"You cannot barge in here, uninvited. I won't have it, Carlton." Out of the corner of her eye she caught a glimpse of his two suits who tailed him everywhere standing a few paces down the hall. He followed her glance and reached to shut the door—he would not want them to see their row—but she managed to get her foot in the way, hoping witnesses might quell his rage.

"You left me looking like a fool tonight!" He shoved his face close to hers, his breath reeking of bourbon, still wrestling with the door.

"Carlton! I have company!"

Her words didn't register with him. He was too irate.

"You just fucking walked out—not a single thought of decency inside your idiotic head!" He spun, steadying himself against the wall, and stomped toward the living room. "You just pulled one of your God damn—" Startled to see Alex sitting on the couch, he stopped dead, his entire body frozen. "Who the hell—" His voice rose a half octave in pitch before he placed a temporary hold on his tantrum. "I—" He stammered, his mouth opening and closing, and shot a seething look at Catharine, who had followed in his wake. "You should have told me we were not alone." He smoothed his tie in a senseless action, the distended veins at his temple pulsing an erratic pattern.

"I'm sure you remember Miss Grey." Catharine defaulted to a genial manner, trying to assuage him from his inanity, to restore some sense of civility between them, but there was something about him tonight that was different. Tonight, for the first time in their marriage, there was something about him that scared her.

She didn't dare look at Alex. To draw any more attention to her than she already had. "She and several friends are joining me for drinks. I expect them any minute. What is it I can do for you, Carlton?" If she was diplomatic, indulgent, there was a possibility he would say what he came to say and then storm off. Disappear and sleep off his rage.

"I will speak with you alone." He stared at Alex without any sign of recognition. She doubted he even recalled her from his eruption earlier in the evening. If someone had nothing to offer—nothing to bring to the table —they were not worth his time.

"Carlton—"

"Excuse your friend," he said under his breath, turning to look at her, "or I will excuse her—whichever you prefer."

Catharine considered refusing him. Insisting he be the one to leave. She was so tired of his demands, his outbursts, his mood swings. But if she did, there was no telling what madness she might invoke. And she did not want Alex involved in it. He was barely on the brink of holding it together and there was no telling what he was capable of if incited further.

"Miss Grey," Catharine despised the sound of the words in her mouth. Despised the degradation of being forced to say them. How they made her feel. How they would make Alex feel. "Would you please give us a moment?" Her fingers tapped an agitated cadence over the material of her gown as she forced herself to meet Alex's eyes. "There's a bar downstairs—Laurel Court. I will meet you there shortly."

There was a hesitation in Alex's return gaze, the subtle rising of a protective demeanor, and Catharine gave an imperceptible shake of her head. There was nothing she could do. It was best if she left. And thankfully Alex seemed to understand.

She stood and started for the door.

"Wait!" Carlton jabbed a nicotine stained finger in Alex's direction as she crossed into the foyer. "I know you! You're the girl from the island."

"Good evening, Senator," was all Alex offered as she disappeared into the hall.

When the door closed, Catharine wheeled on Carlton, her own fuse igniting. There was no placating him tonight. He'd come for a fight, and this time she'd give him one.

Match them tit-for-tat.

She'd heard him say it often enough. Match their outrage. Meet their bullshit. It was his motto on the Senate floor. *When someone rises to punch you, you punch first.*

"You have no right—barging in here like this. I am not at your beck-and-call, Carlton. I am not playing anymore of your pathetic games."

"You will play the games I tell you to play," he snapped, closing the space between them in a few charging strides, "or have you so conveniently forgotten our agreement?"

Before she could argue none of this was part of their agreement, he was off on another tirade.

"You left! Without a word! What an ass you made me look when Bill Sherwood asked us to join him for a nightcap and I obliged, not even knowing you had gone! My own wife, damnit!"

"I was exhausted, Carlton. It has been a very long day—I needed to get off my feet. To take a breather from the evening. My part of the event was finished and you were busy with your colleagues. I didn't want to interrupt you."

"Oh, quit with the bullshit, Catharine! You love making me look like an idiot."

The words flew to her tongue to tell him he needed no help in that department—he was an expert at looking the fool, bar none, but the cautious sector of her brain demanded she reel it back—try diplomacy once more. She just wanted out of the conversation. Wanted him to leave. But there was something different about him tonight that made her uneasy—something behind the pulse at his temple, the unfocused glint of his eye.

"It had nothing to do with you." She took a breath, trying to manage her tone. "I was tired. I have friends who traveled a long way to be here tonight staying at the hotel—I wanted to meet them for a drink before they left in the morning."

"Who, the girl from the beach? How the hell are you even in contact with her? I paid that boyfriend of hers five grand to keep his mouth shut—but they just keep turning up! And now you're seeking her out, for Christ's sake?"

"I was meeting Ms. Comtois here," Catharine said, hoping to steer the conversation off of Alex, but as soon as the words were out of her mouth she regretted them. Carlton despised Nathalie. Had loathed her since the first day they met. Because she didn't cower to him. Acquiesce to him. Hang on his every word. She cared nothing for his political ambitions and wasn't afraid to tell him as much. The words they'd exchanged at the gala were mild compared to many of their encounters over the years.

"That stupid French bitch?! The toe of his dress shoe smashed into the leg of the coffee table, a splintering sound swallowed by the fury of his eruption. "You humiliated me in front of the man I've asked to be my running mate to spend the evening with that worthless, leeching whore?!" A switch had flipped, a rage exploding in him she'd never seen before—not in all their fights over the decades of years. The glasses he'd shattered. The walls he'd destroyed. The names he'd called her. She had never seen him like this. It was as if something had been set loose, broken free. There was no rhyme or reason for it.

"Carlton!" She needed him to see logic. She'd left a dinner without asking his permission—it was a lesser offense in their long history of confrontations when it really boiled down to it. It warranted nothing of this furor. "This is ridiculous! She is my best friend—I left the gala an hour early to—"

"Ridiculous?" The word was quiet, seething. "You think any of this is *ridiculous*?" He took a step forward and stopped, the muscles of his thick jaw ticking. "*Ridiculous* is that petty, despicable trull trying to embarrass me in front of the French Ambassador in the middle of dinner—or my wife threatening to have me thrown out on my ear. I'll tell you what, Catharine," he leaned forward, his voice a hoarse whisper, the pulse below his ear hammering, "you'd better get your little French dog on a leash—or I swear to you, I will find someone to teach her where her place is! Perhaps you'll both learn a lesson."

Catharine whirled, her rationale dissipating. It was the tipping point—his final affront. He could threaten her—he always had—but to threaten someone she loved... "Don't you dare—"

"Don't I dare *what*?" He caught her forearm in his fleshy hand, jerking her toward him with more strength than she'd ever given him credit for.

"Get your hands off of me." She hated that it came out choked—frightened—but he was as drunk as she'd ever seen him, and his threats were no longer feeling idle.

"I think you forget your place and who I am." The words were dark, repulsive at her ear, his bourbon breath damp against her cheek. He'd clamped her arm so forcefully she was beginning to lose feeling in her fingertips. "I should remind you I'm still your *husband*." His free hand caressed her cheek in a taunting display of affection, a derisive laugh escaping his full lips. "But I'd sooner fuck a dog."

"I'd have pity for the dog!" Catharine clawed at the back of his hand, desperate to pull away, but found herself overpowered as Carlton wrenched her arm behind her back and flung her to the window, pressing her face into the glass.

"On second thought," he forced himself against her, grappling for her hair, dragging her head back until her only view was off the ceiling. He buried his face in her neck. "Tonight I'll make an exception."

A wave of nausea rose, threatening, as her skin revolted at his touch. She did not doubt he meant to follow through—tonight there was no bluff. This went far beyond his posturing, his usual goading bluster.

"Carlton." She despised the tremble in her voice, but forced herself not to struggle, not to panic. It was exactly what he wanted. Her fear. Her fight. She could feel him wrenching at his cummerbund, groping at the buttons on his pants, crushing her with the weight of his body against the glass. She could feel the hardness of him. Smell his sweat. But he was inept in his inebriated state, and as soon as she felt him ease his hold to reach for the hem of her dress she threw herself against him, driving her elbow into his neck.

Caught off guard, he stumbled backward, losing his balance over the coffee table, before catching hold of the back of the couch to save his fall. But she didn't have enough room to run, and as soon as she took the first step he was staggering toward her, blocking her path. "Bitch! I'll fucking —"

"If you touch me again I swear to God I'll stop at nothing to see you exposed as the drunken, raging bastard that you are!"

The threat of being outed—of kissing his presidential dreams goodbye—momentarily checked him. He wavered, his eyes unfocused from the alcohol, and appeared to consider his options, rocking back a step—and then, before she realized what was happening, he lunged forward, striking her full force across the mouth.

"You insolent cunt," he roared, unhinged, snatching her hair into his fist and slamming her face against the window. A burst of light exploded, swirling her vision with a sea of stars. And then he struck her again. And again. And Again. Until there was nothing but the bitter taste of bile, nothing but his voice echoing through the deafening explosion in her head. "I will fucking destroy you!" He held her by her hair, her legs buckling beneath her, his face inches from hers. "If you so much as breathe a single word against me I'll—I'll see that you regret it for the rest of your life. You think you're better than me? You think your daddy's money makes you untouchable? You high and mighty bitch—think again. You don't know what I can do! To you. Your business. Your friends." He twisted his hand violently, rolling her head back, forcing her to look at him. "Do you hear me?"

She said nothing. Her head was swimming, her vision a spinning kaleidoscope of color, the roar of blood rushing between her ears muffling all sound. There was some ingrained piece of her—a stubbornness she could not control—that kept her from crying, silencing the sob that rose to her lips, denying him the satisfaction of knowing how much he had hurt her—how terrified she was. Somewhere, in her disordered consciousness, she thought he might actually kill her. And she was helpless—unable to fight back.

He'd struck her before—a few times in the past. At the beginning of their marriage, when he was drunk and heated over something that hadn't gone his way. But it hadn't been like this. It had never been like this. His ego and his arrogance were spiraling out of control. With the presidential race on the line his previously latent threats had suddenly turned very real. He was not exaggerating. He *could* destroy her. And in turn, she could likely do the same to him—fighting fire with fire until they both watched the world burn.

Or she could be patient. Wait. Maintain a controlled burn until he smoldered himself to ashes. Let him destroy himself from within.

And even dazed, half-conscious, she knew the latter was her better option. She still held the upper hand. His desire for the presidential nomination outweighed every self-serving dream he'd ever had—and she could take it from him. She knew it. And he knew it. It was the only thing keeping him from killing her tonight.

"We had a deal," he panted, a degree of de-escalation present, though he still had not released her from his hold. "You'd best remember it." He stepped away, shoving her backward, her legs giving out as she slid down the glass. She could hardly sit up, struggling to keep the room from spinning, fighting to find her breath.

"Tell me you understand." He smoothed his shirt and rebuttoned his dress pants, rubbing at a spattering of blood that stained his cuffs.

Catharine stared at the floor. Blood was flowing from somewhere, pooling at the corners of her mouth, metallic against her tongue, before rolling off her chin and dripping onto the beige carpet. She thought inanely of the cleaning fee—how the housekeepers would get it out. How would she ever explain it?

"Did you hear me?" His anger was simmering again.

"I heard you, Carlton." She was grateful her voice no longer shook.

"Monday morning we go to Los Angeles. I expect you to be with me." He strode toward the door, pausing to look back at her, his hand on the latch. "You brought this on yourself, Catharine. I've been reasonable. I suggest you follow suit if you want this to work out." He spoke as if they had come from a business meeting. A simple disagreement over the font on a letterhead. Or what flavor coffee to stock in the break room.

She didn't look at him. There was a heaviness enveloping her, a dark curtain fighting to be let down. It was all she could do to keep her eyes open until she heard him close the door. Until she was certain he had gone.

Chapter Fifty

The bartender made last call. Alex glanced at her phone—it was after one-thirty. She'd been nursing the same glass of gin and tonic for over an hour and a half sitting there waiting for Catharine.

For not the first time, she considered going back to the room, worried something had happened. She'd texted Catharine once—*is everything ok?*—but the message remained unread. It wasn't like her to not respond. To leave her waiting. But it was more than likely she was still dealing with Carlton. Whatever that entailed.

"Alex?" A shadow passed over the screen of her phone and she turned to find Nathalie Comtois standing behind her. Her makeup was smudged, her eyes red-rimmed, and she bore a seriousness Alex had not seen in her before. "Catharine asked me to find you."

"Oh." She tried to hide her surprise. She'd not even realized Nathalie was staying in the same hotel. Or how she'd come to be part of tonight's awkward situation.

"Listen, I'm not supposed—" She paused, deliberating something, and passed a frustrated hand over her eyes before looking back at Alex, her expression promptly changing. As if she'd made a different decision than the one she'd originally planned. Her face shifted—annoyance—anger—Alex wasn't sure which. She found her impossible to read.

"I'm sorry, but something's come up and Catharine's arranged for a driver to take you home."

Alex wasn't sure what she'd expected her to say, but it certainly wasn't that.

"What?"

"To your apartment. The driver is waiting out front."

"What's happened? Is everything okay?"

Nathalie's lips parted to speak, followed by another flash of indecisiveness, and then she waved her hand in a dismissive gesture, more at herself than Alex. "Please—just—it's been a long night for everyone—"

Alex slid from the barstool and grabbed her hat. Whatever this was wasn't right. "I'd like to see Catharine before I leave."

"You can't!" Nathalie snapped the words, stepping in front of her. "She doesn't want to see you."

Alex was taken back by the statement—by the directness of it. Why would Nathalie say that? "Then I'd like to hear that from her," she managed, beginning to step around the Frenchwoman to head for the elevators.

"They won't let you up," Nathalie called behind her. "You're going to embarrass yourself. It's a restricted floor."

Alex stopped mid-step, turning back sharply, feeling her own anger rising. "Why are you doing this?"

"I am only relaying a message—"

"Why would she send you instead of telling me herself? I mean, she could have texted me two hours ago. Not sent you to gloat over—"

"This isn't personal, Alex! Don't make it into something it's not."

"Not personal?" Alex laughed, incredulous to the turn of the evening. It wouldn't be personal if she hadn't just spent the night making love to Catharine Cleveland prior to being sent from the room when her husband showed up—and then been told to wait in the bar for two hours before being dismissed by her ex-lover like an unneeded call girl. *That* made it personal.

"Look," Nathalie's expression softened, "I promise you, you don't understand—"

"What could there possibly be to misunderstand?" Alex yanked her arm out of reach of the hand Nathalie tried to set on her, turning toward the lobby, afraid she was going to cry. Cry from the frustration of not knowing what to think. From the humiliation she was beginning to feel. She did not want Nathalie's sympathy—it was worse than her callousness.

"Catharine will call you tomorrow—"

"Tell her not to bother. I have to pack for Colorado. I shouldn't have gone out tonight, as it is. I have a few busy weeks coming up—as she no doubt will, too." She wiped the back of her hand across her eyes, mortified to find it came away wet with tears.

"Alex—"

"Please give Mrs. Cleveland my thanks for the offer of her driver, but I can get home on my own."

"Your friend Amelia is waiting for you in the car."

Alex couldn't help but turn at this last admission, staring blankly at Nathalie—who met her eyes with a chilled impassivity—before a slow dawning understanding came over her.

Amelia, disappearing from the gala—she nor Nathalie seen again. The way the two had been carrying on at the table. Catharine's vague reassurance that her friend would be just fine. It made sense now—ridiculous, infuriating sense.

"Good night, Nathalie."

A man in a suit was waiting for Alex beneath the awning, an umbrella in his hand. She'd never seen him before, but he greeted her as *Miss Grey*—the two words unveiling a heavy Scottish accent—before he opened the umbrella and ushered her to the idling car.

As he closed the door behind her, Alex found Amelia dozing against the opposite window, a coat not her own drawn to her chin.

"I can't believe you." Alex felt her frustration mounting, growing angry at the entire evening.

"Oh, hey, Grey," Amelia yawned, never opening her eyes. "Didn't expect to see you again tonight."

"You just left me."

"Figured the way ol' Greta Garbo was eyeing you at dinner, you'd fair the night without much concern."

Alex was too angry to be embarrassed. "So you just—upped and went home with Nathalie?"

The corners of Amelia's lips raised in a smile, her eyes still shut. "Is that her name?"

"What the hell, Amelia!" Alex slouched back against the headrest, disbelieving.

The Senator's Wife

"Bold of you to spit the dummy when I'm the one who should be mad. I was having a bonzer night until—Nathalie, did you say it was?—got a call from your—*friend*. Cut the fun short, that's for sure."

"Aren't you—don't you—?" Alex started again and stopped. "Don't you have a girlfriend?"

Amelia opened one eye, squinting against the lights as they pulled away from the hotel. "Say again?" She stretched in her seat, moving into a more comfortable position. "Oh, yeah, that."

"Well?"

"Well what? Call it a very understanding relationship, if you like."

"One that lets you just hook up with strangers?" Alex didn't even know why she cared. It wasn't her business. But she was angry, and she wanted to find someone to take it out on.

"Oh, bloody come off it, Grey! Are you my mother? It's just sex! Something you should try more often, apparently—it might help you unwind a bit. Step down off that high horse, even."

Alex twisted the felt of her hat in her hands. "I can't believe you. I can't believe any of this."

"Lighten up, Grey. No wonder she sent you home. You're wound tight as a top."

Alex ignored her. "Have you been smoking? Weed?"

"Goodnight, Mother," Amelia turned the collar of the coat up, disappearing behind it.

Alex shook her head. "You're incredible."

"That's what she said." There was a smile in Amelia's voice, and then she was asleep again.

Chapter Fifty-One

Catharine was sitting at the vanity in the oversized marble bathroom when Nathalie returned. She didn't look up when her friend set her hands on her shoulders, instead continuing to stare at her unrecognizable reflection in the mirror, her face already swollen and burning a coral red where the darkest bruises would soon develop. Her lower lip was split in more than one place, a souvenir from Carlton's Blue Hose class ring, and continued to bleed despite Nathalie holding ice to it for over twenty minutes when she first arrived. But she couldn't feel the lip. Or if she could, the pain was too insignificant to notice compared to the torrential throbbing behind her left eye where her brow and cheek had swollen to meet each other, sealing the eye shut between the rapidly coloring skin. Through her monocular vision she watched a droplet of blood fall to the white bodice of her dress, disappearing into the already saturated material and flowering down the lace fringe.

"Bon Dieu," Nathalie exhaled, reaching a careful hand to Catharine's cheek. "It's already turning color. This is going to be such a mess by morning." She set down the ice bucket she was carrying and filled a wash towel full of cubes.

Catharine finally lifted her eyes to meet Nathalie's in the mirror. "You found her?"

"Yes."

"And how did that go?"

"About the way you would expect. I probably could have handled it better, but..." She shrugged. "Under the circumstances."

"You're an actress."

Nathalie pressed the ice to Catharine's cheek, ignoring her wince. "Believe it or not, the profession doesn't really crossover when your head is spinning with images of the sanguineous aberration of your best friend's face. I did the best I could with what you gave me to work with—which was nothing."

"Was she upset?"

"Yes."

Catharine looked away from the mirror. "But you swear you did not tell her—"

"I did not tell her, but I should have. She has a right to know. It would have gone better if I had." She squeezed Catharine's shoulder with her free hand. "You know she should be the one up here with you, Catharine. Not me."

"You're the only one who can see me like this. The only one I can trust to…"

Nathalie shook her head in the reflection as Catharine's voice faded. "To what? Not say anything? The man belongs behind bars, Catharine. And you just want me to turn a blind eye while you turn the other cheek? To what purpose? So the next time he's in a rage he can beat the shit out of that one —"

"Nat, please." She didn't have the energy for the fight. She averted her gaze back to the mirror, staring at the disfigurement of her face. Her eye. Her cheek. Her lip. The back of her head. How many times had he hit her? She didn't even know. She looked like she'd been pummeled with a baseball bat. Felt like it, too. It was impossible to imagine what it would look like by morning.

She wasn't a stranger to blackened eyes and bloodied lips. Her father had frequently gotten his point across with the back of his hand, and on more than one occasion Nathalie had spent the early hours of the morning trying to conceal Catharine's bruises with makeup and smartly worn accessories, making her presentable enough to attend classes without turning heads.

"Can you fix this?" Catharine touched the eye that was swollen shut, flinching at the brush of her own fingertip.

"No." Nathalie shook her head. "This isn't dabbing on a bit of concealer to hide a black eye. This is really going to be a mess for a few weeks, Cate. There's no hiding this."

"There has to be something. I have to go to LA with him on Monday."

"You have to be joking!" Nathalie withdrew the ice pack and stared at her in disbelief. "You can't seriously be considering going on his little crusade with him—after this!"

"I don't have a choice."

"Of course you do! Bon sang, Cate! How can you be so stupid? After all these years—"

"How can you be so blind?! Do you think I enjoy this?" Catharine swiveled in the chair to look at her. "You think I like this?!"

"I think you are letting it happen!" Nathalie flung the towel onto the vanity. "I think you have gotten so accustomed to it you just let it happen and you use the excuse that there is nothing you can do so that you don't have to take any action!"

"You have no idea what you are talking about!" Catharine flared, defensive. "You have no idea what I am dealing with—"

"How could I when all you do is shut everyone out? Cate!" Nathalie knelt in front of her, taking her hands in hers. "All these years you have taught him how to treat you by allowing his tantrums—his threatening words and hostile demands. You have taught him what is acceptable. And look how it has escalated! This—*this*," she gestured at Catharine's face, "is inconceivable, even for him! Five years ago—*one* year ago, he never would have dared go so far." She squeezed her hands, imploring her to look at her. "This has to end."

"I am trying to end it!" Catharine found herself choked with tears and took a moment to look away, composing herself. The last time she had cried was the day she stood in her father's foyer and told Nathalie she was to be wed in America. Twenty-three years ago. She was not about to start crying now. She looked down at her lap, at the ruin of her dress. "I am trying, Nat. But he is as volatile as I have ever seen him, and I believe he would make good on his threats if I were to do anything drastic. The end is finally in sight—I just have to ride out this final stage."

"Ride it out to what? Until he gets angry enough and does this to you when there aren't half a dozen witnesses that saw him enter your hotel room? Sometime when he really could get away with killing you? You— *dead*—that would be convenient for him, wouldn't it? You said yourself tonight you thought he was deranged enough to do it!"

"And I meant it—he was! But I can't just go whistleblowing without suffering more repercussions than I think I could handle. He would go after everything I love, Nat. He's already threatened to come after you."

"Let him," Nathalie shoved herself to her feet, "I can take care of myself. But I won't bear it if something happens to you, Cate! Not when we could have stopped it. Turn him in! God, woman, look in the mirror and see what he's done to you! This is enough right there to—"

"Enough to what? Incite him further? He wouldn't spend a half an hour in jail. Not with his connections." A derided laugh escaped her lips, opening the split once again, bringing the taste of iron to her tongue. "As soon as he walked out the courtroom door he would wage a full-fledged war against me. It isn't worth it," she quieted, her voice beginning to sound distorted by the swelling around her mouth. She drew a tissue from the vanity and dabbed it at her bleeding lip. "I promise you that."

Nathalie shook her head, but didn't argue further. She knew her well enough to know Catharine wouldn't change her mind. She wasn't as brave as Nathalie. She never had been. Nathalie would set fire to the rain to topple an injustice. But that was not Catharine. In business she was indomitable— she would battle for her company. Her employees. Her friends. But she had never been good at fighting for herself.

"Did you tell her I would call tomorrow?" Catharine asked when they had both been silent long enough.

"I did." Nathalie busied herself with wringing out the wet washcloth. "She said she may not be able to take your call because she would be traveling to Colorado."

Catharine could tell from Nathalie's dallying there was more to it than that, but she didn't push the matter. She would call her anyhow. Alex wasn't supposed to leave until Monday morning.

And then would come the task of trying to explain the situation—to make her understand, without revealing anything. She could never know— she could never see her like this.

Catharine sat forward in the chair, dizzy with the movement. The ice and shock were wearing off and a blistering headache was creeping into place. "Help me out of this, will you?" She motioned toward the clasp at the neck of her dress. "I just want to shower and take a bottle of Advil."

Nathalie reached for the fastener, but then paused, fishing her phone out of her pocket and swiping open the camera.

"What are you—oh, bloody no, Nat! No!"

"I'm documenting this. Don't argue with me, you won't win. If something ever happens to you, I need proof." She held the phone up, waiting for Catharine to acquiesce. "They'll never be seen by another eye unless you're dead, I swear it."

Catharine began to issue her protest—she would be damned before there were photos of her in this state—but then reconsidered. Nathalie was right. If something happened to her, this might be the only evidence against him to see that he did not get away scot-free.

Flipping on the vanity light, Nathalie snapped her photos, but halted when she saw Catharine's forearm and elbow and the unmistakable bruising his fingers had left when he'd restrained her against the wall. "Cate, did he...?" She swallowed, staring at the marks. "Did he..." She looked up, meeting her eyes in the mirror, and Catharine understood.

"No. He threatened—but—no."

Nathalie said nothing, finishing her photos, and then returned to the clasps.

In the small hours of the morning, long after the ruin of her dress had been discarded and Nathalie had helped wash the blood from her skin and hair, Catharine lay awake in the king-size bed with the curtains drawn to block out the lights of the San Francisco skyline. Nathalie was asleep beside her, having stayed at Catharine's request, her rhythmic breathing comforting against her back.

It hurt too much to sleep. It nearly hurt too much to breathe. The long minutes ticked by as she stared into the void of darkness, trying to keep her bitter thoughts at bay. But the suffocating stillness became unbearable. For the first time in her life she felt entirely defeated. The tears that had threatened all evening fought their way back to the surface, unwilling to be denied—heedless to the barriers she'd constructed, the boundaries against vulnerability she'd put in place.

When she'd moved to America, Catharine promised herself she would never allow anyone to have the control over her that her father once had. That she would never let herself fear someone as she had once feared him.

The Senator's Wife

And for all these years she had managed to keep her promise. Even with Carlton's maniacal ego and irascible temper, she had never feared him— until tonight.

She felt the first tear trail down her cheek and tried to blink the rest away, but this time they were not to be held back. Her chest heaved against the pressure of her staggering breath, a sob escaping her lips, and she finally let go of her control and allowed herself to feel the heartache of her anguish— her tears coming unchecked, wracking her body through the painful release of her despair. It was cathartic, cleansing, the liberation of anger and frustration, hurt and sadness that had built up over the years. And somewhere amongst her sorrow she felt Nathalie reach for her, wrapping her in her arms, pulling her to her and holding her as she wept, carrying her through the darkest hours of her life.

Chapter Fifty-Two

It would have been convenient to blame her exhaustion on the elevation of the Colorado town. The senior camp was being hosted less than twenty-five miles from the base of the Rocky Mountains, but in reality, the town sat barely over six thousand feet and the altitude played only a small factor in the fatigue Alex found herself battling by the end of the fifth day of training. The truth—she'd never pushed so hard in her life.

Atwood had called twenty-seven women to camp—the best players the US had to offer—and though the camp wasn't officially attached to a tournament, everyone attending knew it would be the deciding factor for the twenty-three-woman SheBelieve's Cup roster. Four would be cut. And Alex didn't want to be one of them.

But the competition was brutal. Twenty-five of the players were National Team regulars, consistently called-up from the pool. Eighteen of which had been on the squad for the Olympic Games two years prior when the US had brought home the gold. There was only one other rookie, a forward, Beth Nunez, who joined them straight from Penn State, and the rest were a tight-knit group of veterans, many of which had been wearing the Stars-and-Stripes since they were teens—every one of which intended to earn a position on the World Cup roster the following year. A roster, like the SheBelieves Cup, with only room for twenty-three. So it was unlikely Izzy Atwood would take a chance on a player with no previous international experience—not when the majority of the current squad had been blossoming under her leadership for the past five years.

Still, there was always a chance. Nothing was ever set in stone. And she had invited Alex to play—she wanted to see what she could offer. That had to be a good sign.

So day in and day out, through every minute of training, Alex left everything she had on the field. She was first to breakfast, first to the bus, first to the pitch, first to afternoon workouts, lifting sessions and dreaded repetitive drills. At night she took a page out of Amelia's book and watched tape on each day's session, noting the other players' strengths and weaknesses so she could best compliment her value on the team. She didn't know if it would be enough, but she did know that she would leave the ten-day camp having given everything she had to give.

She knew most of the women from her five seasons in the NWSL, and several even from collegiate ball, but it was only Sawyer and Erin Halsey she knew beyond the surface. Having them there—both longtime staples on the squad—helped ground her and make her feel more at home.

The fifth day of camp stretched well into evening, running a three goal shooting drill as the sun dipped behind the Rockies, the stadium lights of the training center illuminating the drizzle falling from the cloudy night sky. Alex's hair was plastered to her face, her scrimmage vest damp from sweat, her calves screaming by the time the whistle blasted to call it quits for the day. The coaching staff brushed through a few short notes, administered feedback from the day, and cut the players loose for the evening. They'd resume training at seven the following morning.

On the way to the locker room, Monica Ashby—a defender from the Texas Bluebells who'd only earned her first National Team caps the previous season—fell into step with Alex and Sawyer. She'd held a relentless, unwarranted grudge against Alex that had started during a semi-final match between Texas and South Carolina three years earlier. Rage had narrowly defeated the Bluebells in a 2-1 78th minute upset after Ashby had been red carded and sent off the field on an irresponsible studs-up tackle inside the eighteen. She'd wiped Alex's legs out from under her and landed her on her face, forcing her out of the game under concussion protocol. But the play had drawn a penalty, which Abby Sawyer put in the back of the net, and the Bluebells had been unable to equalize being a man down with limited time on the clock. Alex had never blamed Ashby for nearly knocking her teeth out—regardless that the play had been reckless and juvenile—but the defender had never gotten over the red card and had antagonized Alex every game since.

Since arriving at camp, Alex had managed to avoid Monica—there wasn't much time for socialization if you didn't seek it—and the play on the field had been business-as-usual, to her great relief. But she knew something was brewing as the girl trotted alongside them.

"My high school coach had a sign in his office that said, 'How to succeed: Try hard enough. How to fail: Try too hard.'" She looked directly at Alex. "Pretty sure that was written for you, Grey. You look like an idiot out there. We all know the front line's locked in—I hardly know why they bothered to bring you and Nunez up here. Y'all don't stand a chance." Alex continued toward the tunnel. She wasn't interested in Ashby's game.

"You know what sign my coach had hung in her office in high school, Monica?" Sawyer slowed her steps, unwilling to let the dig go. "'Be careful of the toes you step on today because they might be connected to the ass you're kissing tomorrow.' Now shut the fuck up and move along."

Ashby stopped, glaring over at the pair. "Well, excuse me if I'm just trying to give a little friendly advice. Your girl's trying too hard, Abby. It's humorous, at best."

"The only thing humorous is you trying to pretend you could read in high school," Sawyer drawled out in her midwestern accent, never looking behind her. When they hit the tunnel she said, more quietly to Alex, "ignore that bitch. Only thing she's got going for her is a forehead the size of a small country—makes for an efficient header."

Alex couldn't help but laugh. "Three years is a long time to hold a vendetta. I'll give her points for commitment."

Inside the locker room Alex stripped out of her gear, listening to Sawyer and Halsey argue about what they were going to do for the night. It was the first time they'd found a few hours of downtime since arriving at camp and Sawyer wanted to get dinner in town while Erin grumbled the only thing she wanted to do was see the back of her eyelids from her hotel room for the next ten hours. Alex had to agree with the keeper—the last thing she wanted was to have to get dressed and drag herself to a restaurant. But she didn't get a chance to tip the vote before Jill Thompson—a veteran striker from the Texas Bluebells who had started her National team career on the U-15s in junior high—poked her head around the corner, breaking up the conversation.

"Hey, Grey, you've got a visitor."

Alex, one cleat on and one cleat off, half walked, half hopped around the partition to see what she was talking about.

The Senator's Wife

There was no one in the doorway that she could see. "I'm sorry?" She frowned. She didn't know anyone in Colorado and the camp had been closed to the public, with only the final day allowing admittance to some of the local club and school teams to come and watch the senior side play.

"Visitor. Outside. Looking for you." Jill spoke in her short, abrupt way, neither friendly nor disagreeable, just straightforward.

"Thanks." Alex nodded and walked back to her locker feeling a touch of panic. There was only one person who would come looking for her—only one person, outside of soccer, who even knew she was here.

Catharine had tried to call her a handful of times. First on Sunday, the day after the gala—but Alex had been packing for camp and didn't answer the phone. She'd watched it ring instead, counting how many times the phone buzzed before sending the call to voicemail.

Seven.

She couldn't answer it. She was angry. And she'd grown angrier over her sleepless night, the longer she dwelled on the situation. Amelia—who had woken up stoned and hungover late that morning—had offered no explanation as to why Catharine had abruptly ended their evening. The only thing she'd been able to tell Alex was that Nathalie had received a call in her hotel room and had gotten dressed in a hurry and left. A half hour later she'd returned, brusque and distracted, and told Amelia she had to go home and there would be a driver waiting for her in the courtyard.

"And that's all I know, Grey," Amelia'd shrugged, uninterested in the conversation. She'd been nursing too much of a headache to do much more than lay on Alex's couch and work her way through a gallon of water and handful of ibuprofen while Alex packed. "Shortly after that you showed up, bitched at me all the way across the Bay Bridge, and the next thing I remember is waking up on your couch."

Alex hadn't inquired any further.

Catharine had left a message. It was brief—she sounded tired and a little unclear and asked for Alex to please call her. But nothing more than that.

The following day when Alex had been at the gate to board her plane Catharine called again. And this time Alex sent it straight to voicemail. She couldn't answer her phone on the passenger boarding bridge, she told herself. But she knew she wouldn't have answered even if she could. Her feelings were hurt. There was no excuse she could imagine that would warrant sending Nathalie to retrieve her at the bar and send her home—in a waiting car, like a paid escort. After hours of waiting. That in itself was message enough. Catharine was the one who had asked her to the hotel, after all. Alex had not asked to come there. And no matter the reason, Catharine could have at least had the decency to tell Alex herself. She didn't need Nathalie to come and handle her. What had Carlton said at the table? *Don't manage me, Catharine.* Maybe there was more truth to that than she knew.

She boarded the plane and promised herself she would call her back when there was some free time.

But Alex had made certain from the moment she arrived at camp that there was no "free" time. If she wasn't training or doing team building exercises or eating with the squad, she was sitting in front of tape, rewatching matches from years past and focusing her entire attention on the game.

At least, that was what she told herself.

The truth was, as soon as she was off the pitch, she could barely get Catharine off her mind. While sitting in her hotel room watching the '99ers trounce Nigeria in Chicago or the 2011 team fall to Japan, Alex struggled to keep her attention on the game and had instead been replaying every minute of the night of the gala, trying to figure out what had gone wrong and where.

She'd thought about texting Catharine, but it seemed too impersonal. They needed to talk. But she didn't know how to start it. Or if it was even a good idea while she was still in Colorado. Part of her wanted to get it over with. If they could talk, maybe she could refocus her energy on the camp. Quit worrying about it and keep her attention on the game. While she was on the field her competitive drive and muscle memory took over and dictated her tunnel vision stay tuned to the task at hand. But off the pitch her focus faltered, which was becoming an undesirable pattern when she needed all her wits about her if she was going to make this team.

But her performance on the field was consistent. If something went wrong in the conversation, if it distracted her further…

She decided it was best to leave well enough alone. Her personal relationships had no business sneaking into her professional endeavors. She would deal with it when she got home. These ten days were about nothing more than the SheBelieves roster. It needed to stay that way, for her own sake.

So, the audacity of Catharine to show up here—in the middle of her training camp—unannounced, was really pretentious. And Alex had a half a mind to tell her so.

But there was part of her that fed off the adrenaline at the thought of seeing Catharine, despite the hurt and anger of the weekend past. Just knowing she was here, that she'd made the effort to see her... and down the intoxicating rabbit hole of Catharine Cleveland she went.

Alex pulled off her other cleat, tossed it in her locker, and dragged on some track pants over her shorts. The Colorado weather was chilly at night, dropping into the low thirties, and certainly wasn't a South Carolina or California spring. Tying her running shoes and bundling into a sweat shirt, she closed her locker and tuned out Sawyer and Erin's continued debate before walking out the backdoor, unnoticed.

"A." The familiar voice called to her from the tunnel, just a few steps from the locker room door.

"Caleb." She was certain she had been unable to mask her disappointment. "What are you doing here?"

Chapter Fifty-Three

A quarter after nine on Saturday night, Catharine phoned Nathalie from her room at the Radisson in Fresno. It was after midnight in New York.

"Bonne soirée, mon amour," Nathalie answered on the first ring, a tipsy lilt to her voice. Catharine could feel her smile, three thousand miles away, and it made her heart ache for her jovial friend. She should have been there this evening—Nathalie's opening night on Broadway—far away from this cramped little town and its throng of blinkered, Middle America, Republican WASPs who had come to support her husband's speech on "returning California to its Heritage" and "restoring" the state to its "former glory." Promising to "silence" the city dwelling majority and take the West Coast stronghold back to its Republican roots. A whole lot of verbiage with no actual agenda. Just drivel and smoke and mirrors to rally the less populated towns and farmlands to do their part: *vote, vote, vote.*

Vote for what, Carlton? Was all Catharine could think, standing on the stage, an oversized pair of Prada glasses covering the worst of her eye, her cheek and lip still swollen but relatively hidden beneath layer upon layer of carefully painted makeup. *A self-serving Neanderthal?*

"A bad fall in the shower," she'd heard him say to his campaign manager, Adam Buckley. "Lucky we don't sue Fairmont for it."

She hadn't gone with him on his Southern California tour. She hadn't even left the suite at the Fairmont until Thursday night to return to her home. There had been no way to conceal the appalling spectrum of color covering the catastrophe of the left side of her face. When Carlton came by on Sunday evening to demand she meet him at the private terminal Monday morning he immediately changed his mind. "You can't be seen like that!" It had been more accusation than anything else, as if she'd done it to herself. "People will talk. God damnit! We'll make a statement you've been ill. Taken a fall."

Never once did he apologize. Not a single hint of remorse for what he'd done. And she had to look at him—to meet his eye—and know he knew she had no recourse. Know he knew he'd gotten away with it, and she was still left to his every whim.

Catharine rearranged her planned meetings, sent Nicole to London on her behalf, and conducted her business by email, telling her staff she'd been feeling under the weather and to reach out to Nicole instead. But by the weekend Carlton had been back on the push to have her in Fresno. "They expect to see you, Catharine—it looks bad, you always off on your own agenda." But she knew the real drive behind it was simply to force her to be there—for no other reason than him knowing she didn't want to come. He got off on the control of it, the power. And he loved the show—his ideal marriage: an attractive immigrant wife with a prospering business—the American Dream—neglecting to ever mention Brooks Corp's long standing success prior to arriving in the States. It had thrived here, but it would have thrived anywhere under Catharine's guidance. "It wasn't the port that mattered—it was the captain at the helm." At least that was what had been written in the liberal editorial section of the Fresno Bee in response to the platform Cleveland was running on. But that was where the flattery for Catharine had concluded. "Don't be fooled by the Clevelands' US-based business claims: more than eighty percent of its employees and eighty-three percent of its revenue come from out of the country—the very opposite of the senator's policy for returning jobs to the American citizens. It appears if the South Carolina senator wants to walk his talk, he needs to start with his own company."

His company was all Catharine got out of the article. It would have been laughable if it hadn't been so insulting. To even insinuate that Carlton Cleveland had even the most infinitesimal role in Brooks Corp's success was positively infuriating.

Catharine turned her mind back to Nathalie on the other end of the line. In the background she could hear laughter and chatter of the opening night party and the celebration that ensued.

"I am sure you were superb," she said, trying to keep the wistfulness from her voice. "I am so sorry to not be there."

"There were so many technical failures you would have been driven crazy," Nathalie laughed, trying to make her feel better. "It will all be ironed out by the time you come. More importantly—how are *you*?"

"I'm really good, Nat," Catharine lied. She had not called to take away a single moment of her friend's triumphant evening.

Nathalie, not one to be put off, did not let it go so easily. "I don't believe you."

"I am. Truly. I feel better. Good, even. I'm back to work on Monday. Everything is okay."

"Have you talked to Alex?"

Catharine considered lying again—it would be so easy to say yes, all was well, they were both just busy.

"No, I'll try her again when she is back in Oakland. I don't want to bother her at her training." She hoped the nonchalance in her voice was enough to set Nathalie off the subject. "I was thinking of coming out to see your show next weekend."

"I would love that."

Someone was calling Nathalie's name in the distance.

"You go, Nat—I just wanted to call and congratulate you. I'm so sorry I wasn't there to support you."

"You'll call me tomorrow?" Nathalie hushed someone who was trying to talk to her. "In the afternoon?"

"Tomorrow, then."

"Je t'aime, Cate."

Catharine hung up and tossed the phone onto her bed, pressing her forehead against the Windex-streaked windowpane, looking down over the fiberglass pool and unadorned concrete slab that made up the courtyard.

Carlton would stop by soon. To gloat his successful rally and rub his presence in her face. Ever since the night at the Fairmont he'd taken a sick pleasure in forcing her to be near him—holding her hand at press conferences, putting his arm around her in campaign briefings, kissing her on stage. A repulsive show of dominance which Catharine simply felt too tired to fight.

She'd thought those days in London after losing Nathalie had been the worst days of her life—and for more than twenty years, they had been—but this week she'd discovered a new unprecedented low. One she wasn't even sure how to rise up from.

She took one last glance at her reflection in the light of the window—at the continuously changing colors of her face—and went back to her bed. For the first night in a week she didn't bother to check her phone to see if Alex had returned her calls.

Chapter Fifty-Four

"Two pints of the vanilla porter," Caleb said to the platinum-haired wisp of a bartender who strode up to them in a crop top and nose ring with the attitude of a local who'd dealt with far too many tourists over spring break. She barely acknowledged his order but grabbed two glasses anyhow.

"Just one," Alex adjusted herself on the hard wooden stool top.

"Oh, come, Grey, you love the sweet porters. It's a good one here."

"A water with lemon, please," she said to the bartender, ignoring him.

"Which is it?" The girl shoved out her hip, annoyed, holding the glasses in front of her.

"A water." Alex already regretted agreeing to get dinner with him. "Why are you here, Caleb?"

"I had a job in Grand Junction. Someone mentioned the US team was training here—so I thought I would say hi."

"That's like four hours away."

"It was worth the drive to see you, A. You haven't called me back in almost a month."

Alex thought about gently misguiding the truth, massaging it to come across as less harsh, less final. Something along the lines of *sorry, I have been so busy.* Or *I just had to have some time to myself.*

But she couldn't bring herself to say it. It wasn't true. And he had never taken a subtle hint in his life.

"I didn't want to call you back, Caleb. I wanted to try and salvage our friendship—we've been friends for so long and you've been such an important part of my life—but you can't be *just* friends. We can't go back to that now, after everything…" Her voice trailed off.

"You said you needed a break, A!" He was incredulous, as though the idea had never occurred to him. "A *break.* You didn't say you wanted to end it!"

"Because you only hear what you want to hear, Caleb! I have told you from the beginning I wasn't okay with—with *us*. I tried. I tried my best, I swear, and I just can't."

His beer arrived and they both were silent, waiting for the bartender to walk away, but the woman lingered, washing glasses, her ear pricked to their conversation, never bothering to bring Alex her water.

Caleb reached forward and brushed the collar of Alex's sweatshirt to one side, exposing the bare skin of her neck. "I've never seen you without your necklace," his voice was flat, devoid of emotion.

She'd removed the soccer charm in Half Moon Bay and hadn't been able to bring herself to put it back on. It felt too heavy, too full of the past. She leaned back, away from his touch.

"Is there someone else?" he finally asked once the bartender was out of earshot, taking an order from a couple across the bar.

Again, Alex wanted to lie. *No. No, there was no one else.*

Would that have even been a lie? Was Catharine someone else? Did whatever they have—didn't have—count?

If another person was on your mind most of your waking hours, it probably constituted as *someone else.*

She looked at him, no longer seeing the boy she'd once known. All she saw was the man who never once asked her what she wanted. Who capitalized on her successes as his own, pushed her to do things she never wanted to do, and—though she was sure it had never been his intention—made her feel smaller and more dependent than she had ever been in her life. The twelve-year-old boy who used to enthusiastically run up and down the sidelines cheering her on every time she had the ball was gone.

She drew a long breath before letting it out between pressed lips, anxious how he would respond. "Yes."

He set his beer down, untouched.

"Who?" For once he was listening to her. Finally listening.

"It doesn't matter. It's not someone you know." It wasn't a lie, really. He didn't actually know Catharine.

"Wow." He worked his jaw as if he had taken a blow, before looking away, trying to hide the hurt that washed over his face. "I wanted to marry you, Alex. I wanted to spend my life with you."

"I'm sorry, Caleb." She reached to touch his arm but withdrew it as he turned his back to her. She was afraid he might cry.

"Congratulations on the team, A. I have no doubt you'll make the roster." He pulled out a twenty dollar bill and dropped it on the counter, never looking back.

Alex sat at the bar for a while after he'd gone, watching the people filing in for dinner and drinks. The National Wildlife Refuge drew a lot of visitors throughout the year, and despite the threat of a late spring snow, the small city was teeming with tourists, now settling in for a nightcap.

She thought she should feel sad. She wanted to feel sad. Caleb had meant so much to her. He had been her constant, her certainty, her champion. But it was gone. Those days were gone. She cared about him. She always would. She just couldn't have him in her life the way he wanted to be there —so it was better for them both to cut the tie completely. It hurt; hurting him. It had never been her intention. Despite his ego, despite his desire for control, his intentions had been good. He was a good person. Just not the person for her.

She pulled out her phone, her mind already drifting.

Catharine hadn't tried to call her since the airport.

She opened her browser and typed in *Carlton Cleveland*, the most recent news links popping onto the screen. An article about Carlton Cleveland in Orange County at an *Every Heartbeat Counts* rally put on by the OC Women's Republican Club. Another article about a protest in Los Angeles outside the Beverly Hills Hilton where a caricature of the Republican candidate had been spray painted in a mockingly derisive fashion on the wall of a subway in front of the hotel where he and his campaign party had been staying. And today, from nine hours ago, a photo of Carlton and Catharine on the stage of the University of Fresno amphitheater, surrounded by signs that read *Cleveland for President - Save California* in red, white and blue.

Catharine was not smiling, her eyes hidden behind dark sunglasses with a silk scarf tied in an ornate knot that nearly covered her chin, her hair loose and straightened, hanging in her face. She had more makeup on than Alex had ever seen her wear. If she hadn't been standing next to Carlton, she would barely have recognized her.

The Senator's Wife

Alex scrolled the article. Just more editorial opinions on Cleveland and his campaign trail, which was due to head to Arizona and New Mexico over the following two weeks, according to the post.

At the end of the page there was a brief mention of Catharine. "Cleveland was joined today in Fresno by his wife of twenty-three years, the heiress and CEO of Brooks Corp., better known by its subsidiary corporation, WorldCargo. After an illness that kept her off the campaign trail, Mrs. Cleveland is expected to speak at the Arizona Women's Republican Convention February 28th."

Alex looked at the photo again.

Carlton, his arm around Catharine, smiling like a schmuck into the camera, waving at the crowd. How could no one see how miserable she was?

She slipped from the barstool and weaved her way through the pub. It had grown packed since she arrived. It was just after eleven. Only ten in California.

She stepped outside, welcoming the blast of cold air from the stuffy bar and walked briskly toward the hotel where the team was staying. Outside the lobby she stopped, rubbing her hands together, trying to warm her fingertips enough that her touchscreen would recognize them against the cold. The wind had picked up and her breath was showing up in short, cloudy puffs.

Was it too late to call? Would Carlton be there if she did?

She scrolled to C and hit Catharine's number before she could talk herself out of it, counting the rings until she heard the distinct English lilt say her name, surprised.

"Hey," she hesitated in response. "I hope I didn't wake you."

"No. I'm awake." Catharine paused. "Is everything all right?"

"Yes." Alex hadn't planned out her conversation or what she would say and now found herself lost for words.

Catharine continued carefully, concerned at the late night call. "Is everything going okay at your training?"

"Yes. It's been tough. These girls are really good." It wasn't what she wanted to talk about.

"Where are you?"

"Commerce City."

"Just outside of Denver. It must be cold there."

They were both quiet again. It was small talk; awkward, halting words that meant nothing. Alex stamped her feet. Her watch indicated the wind-chill had dropped the temperature to twenty-two degrees. The short walk from the pub to the hotel had been bearable, but now, standing stationary in the wind, she didn't know how she would stand it much longer. But she couldn't go inside, not to the lobby, where the girls hung about, nor to her room, where her bunkmate—a defender from the New York Wizards—would already be asleep.

"What happened the other night?" she finally asked, walking back and forth along the sidewalk to the hotel entrance, trying to keep her voice from shaking in the cold.

Catharine did not immediately respond, but Alex could hear her sigh on the other end of the line.

"I had a situation with Carlton. It's difficult to explain."

"You couldn't tell me yourself?"

"No," Catharine said, simply. "I couldn't."

"But you could tell Nathalie?" She hated the way the question made her sound, but she had to ask it. She needed to understand, to be able to let it go.

"Yes. I could." There was a hint of frustration to her voice. Or was it impatience? She couldn't tell. The bitter night air was raw, agitating against her nerves.

"I see." It came off more curtly than she would have liked.

"Nathalie is not your enemy, Alex. I promise you that. She was only acting on my behalf. If you're worried about me and Nat, you are mistaken and don't understand—"

"That's just the thing, Catharine. I don't understand. No, I'm not worried about you and Nathalie—I wouldn't even know what to be worried about. I don't have any rights or claims to you—we don't have anything, really."

"Don't say that." Catharine said, then added more gently, "I don't think you mean that."

"I don't even know what I mean," Alex let out a deep exhale, watching the steam dissipate into the brittle air. It was true, she didn't know what she meant. None of what she was saying was coming across right and she didn't know exactly what she wanted to hear. She just knew her feelings had been

The Senator's Wife

hurt and it was making her insecure. That was the heart of it. But she didn't know how to say that to Catharine.

"I'm sorry. I'm tired and cold. It's like twenty degrees out and I think it's going to snow." She wavered. "I guess I just wanted to hear your voice."

"Will you let me come see you?"

"Here?" said Alex, surprised. "In Colorado?"

"Yes."

"Camp isn't over until Thursday morning."

"Would you be free for dinner Wednesday night?"

Alex hesitated. Thursday they didn't have training—just a breakfast meeting before the players flew home to be with their club teams for the weekend. "It's a long way for dinner."

"I don't mind. Would that be okay?"

"For you to come?"

"Yes."

"Yes." *I would like that*, she wanted to say, but didn't.

"I'm glad you called me, Alex. I was getting worried."

"I'm sorry."

"I promise I'll try to answer your questions when I see you. What day do you have to be back in California?"

"Tuesday."

Catharine didn't respond.

Behind Alex the lobby doors opened and two of the girls came out, laughing. Alex couldn't tell who they were immediately with their coats zipped to their chins and beanies pulled down around their ears.

"Oh, hey, Grey," greeted one of the girls. It was a forward from the Portland Warriors—a consistent starter for the National Team—Ashley Rivers. She was friendly and genuine and very good at her game. Alex liked her.

"Hey," Alex nodded, trying to pull her mouth away from the receiver. The other girl glanced up over the team-issued parka, her narrowed eyes only slits in the lamplight. It was Monica Ashby.

"Your boyfriend head out already?" she said in something of a sneer. "That him on the phone?"

"No." Alex said shortly.

"Hey, Grey's boyfriend," Monica singsonged toward Alex, "you're pretty cute! Call me when you get bored with Miss Goody Two-Shoes!"

"Monica, quit," Ashley rolled apologetic eyes and lipped an apology, but Alex only turned away, pressing her phone more firmly against her ear. "Sorry," her steps cut a path through the frost covered grass as she moved away from the intrusion.

"New boyfriend already?" The teasing smile was warm in Catharine's voice.

"Caleb showed up unexpectedly tonight."

"To Commerce City? That's not exactly a hub."

"He was in Grand Junction on business. It was good, actually." Alex realized it was true. "I think he finally understands we're over. I told him —" she paused, not sure if she should continue, but the words were already out of her mouth, "I told him there was someone else."

On the other end of the line Catharine laughed. "Did you?"

It was no longer the windchill to blame for the flush in Alex's cheeks. She wished she hadn't said anything. It seemed suddenly presumptuous. "I mean—"

Catharine interrupted. "I hope I'm that someone else."

Now it was Alex who couldn't help but smile. It felt good to hear her say that. After the previous weekend and everything that had followed.

"I should be getting to bed," she said, breathing in the relief of the conversation. Filing away the comfort of her voice. "Wednesday?"

"Wednesday."

"Good night, Catharine."

"Good night."

Alex slipped the phone into her pocket, rubbing her numb hands briskly together, not really caring that she couldn't feel her fingertips.

"We're going to grab a drink, Grey," Ashley called across the courtyard, seeing that she was off the phone. "Join us?"

"Not tonight, thank you," she waved halfheartedly in their direction.

She felt like going on a midnight run.

Chapter Fifty-Five

Izzy Atwood wasn't known for her pomp and circumstance. She wrapped up the Wednesday afternoon team building session with a few brief notes on the upcoming SheBelieves Cup schedule, the travel itinerary, and told the players she would be in touch with those selected to the roster within the next couple of weeks. She thanked the women for their hard work and dedication, apologized that she would miss the following morning's final breakfast with the team, and then turned the evening over to her assistant coach, Trent McGuire, while she headed out to catch a plane to attend a coaching convention in Illinois.

Trent was a more flowery orator. He showered praise on each athlete, pointing out growth and development he'd noticed throughout the camp, gushed about the endless possibilities the future held with the remarkable depth of the US Team, and expressed his disappointment that the SheBelieves roster was limited to twenty-three. "If I had my way, all twenty-seven of you would be flying to Tennessee at the end of the month. Every woman in this room deserves to be on that pitch!" It was the gentle let-down reminder that four women weren't going to find their names on the roster for the opening tournament leading into the World Cup qualifying year. And then he reminded everyone they had an early breakfast before the final wrap, and cut the girls loose for the evening.

The women stretched and yawned and drifted into conversation as they dragged their tired bodies off the mats where they'd finished the last of a series of team building exercises. It was just after five p.m.

"I think Erin's finally relented to grabbing a beer," Sawyer nudged Alex with her toe as Alex climbed to her feet, ready to make a break for the door. She'd have to skip the bus from the training center—it took too long—and had decided to just run the mile back to the hotel. Catharine was supposed to pick her up in less than an hour. "What say you?"

"I can't." She glanced at her friend. Of all the nights Halsey finally decided she'd go out, of course she'd pick this one. "I—have plans."

"Plans?" Sawyer gingerly hopped to her feet, nursing her taxed muscles. "Like, I'm-staying-in-to-watch-more-twenty-year-old-game-tape plans, or *plans* plans?"

"Um, the latter, I guess." Alex shifted uncomfortably under Sawyer's gaze. She'd hoped to make a quiet disappearance without anyone noticing. It wasn't unusual for her to take solo-time at the close of the day.

"Tell me they're not with Caleb. I don't think I could deal with you ditching us for him. Not after all that boy's put you through." Her full lips turned down, disapproving, as she followed Alex to the hall. "I can't believe he showed up here like he did—all peacocking and high-and-mighty."

"No. Not Caleb. That's over and done."

"Doubt it." Sawyer rolled her shoulders, still shaking her body loose. "That boy won't take a hint."

"Well, done on my part, at least." Alex glanced down the hallway, making certain they were alone. "It's just—well, a friend is in town—"

"You and these friends I've never heard of that show up at the most random places. Like Miss Hot-Stuff last year whose face is plastered all over the news right now while her husband is running for president."

Alex bit the inside of her cheeks, shooting another look down the hall— she was terrible at secrets—and Sawyer was quickly onto her. "Oh my God," she tsk-tsk-tsked, unable to hide her grin. "It's that same damn woman, isn't it?"

"Abby—" Alex triple checked their perimeter. All the other girls were still in the multipurpose room. She sighed. There was no point hiding anything from Sawyer. She would turn into a sleuthhound if she felt like she wasn't being keyed in, and besides, she was loyal as an apostle when it came to her friends. "Yes. It's the same woman."

"And she just happens to be in town again on business? Just another fluke crossing of paths, I suppose?" Her eyebrows were arched in dubiety.

"No." Alex chewed on her lip. "She came to see me."

For a few seconds Sawyer studied her, assessing whatever between-the-lines message Alex was sending, and when she finally decided the missive was decoded loud and clear, said, "You don't think you might be playing with fire there?" Now she was the one to check their surroundings. "That husband of hers—"

"I know." Alex held her gaze, steadfast. "I know. Sawyer, you won't—"

"Don't insult me, Sugar." She reached forward and squeezed her hand. "I know you're a grown ass adult, Alex, and I won't tell you your business, but I'd be remiss in our friendship if I didn't urge you some caution. People like that—"

"She's not like that, Abby, she's—"

"I'm not talking about her, Plum. I liked her in Portland. I mean her husband. You seen any of his nonsense on TV? People like that don't like others playing with their toys. They don't share very well."

Alex didn't tell her Catharine was getting a divorce. It wouldn't have changed anything. "I know."

"Just be careful, will you?" She was still holding her hand.

"I am. We are." *We*, thought Alex. She'd never felt part of a *we* before. She glanced at her watch.

"Get on, then," said Sawyer, smiling. "I always knew you'd find your way to the team at some point. This one—" she motioned toward the room where a few of the women were starting to pile out into the hallway, "and the other, more exclusive one, so to speak." She winked. "You're just a late bloomer is all."

Alex waited for Catharine in front of the Macy's across the street from her hotel. She'd asked to meet her there, away from the sharp eyes of her teammates who never missed anything when it came to each other's personal lives, but as she loitered on the dark curb in front of the closed department store with bars on its windows—a handful of questionable teenagers strumming about the parking lot—she wished she'd found a more appropriate location. A feeling that was magnified when the black sedan pulled up to the corner, a hired driver at the wheel. She'd assumed Catharine would come herself, rent a car as she'd done in Portland, but as the driver came around to open her door she felt like she was stepping out of a scene from *Pretty Woman*—sans Richard Gere and thigh-high vinyl boots.

"Miss." He nodded.

"Thank you," Alex mumbled through the anonymity of her scarf and beanie, clamoring into the backseat with all the elegance of a polar bear.

The windchill was below freezing and her team-issued USWNT parka had seemed an appropriate choice before she found herself sitting in the back of a luxury sedan.

"Hello, Alex."

She wondered when, if ever, the sound of her name on Catharine's lips would cease to give her butterflies. She pulled the scarf down below her chin and dragged the beanie off her head, aware of the static electricity that suddenly decided to cling to her hair. The cab was dim and she could see little more than the shape of Catharine's shadow.

"Thank you for coming." Alex flinched at her own words. That was what you told someone who spent twenty minutes window shopping your tourist boutique before they walked out the door. It wasn't what you said to the person who had flown a thousand miles to see you. She glanced toward the driver in the front seat, uncertain what exactly she could say or do.

Her breath caught as Catharine leaned across the seat and kissed her cheek in greeting. Ever poised, perfectly casual—a discipline Alex envied immensely.

"I thought we might get dinner?" Catharine sat back, facing forward, her hand lingering on the seat between them. Alex wanted to take it but didn't.

"I think the nicest thing in Commerce City is TGIF, but Denver's close by, if Pizza Hut's off the menu."

"Tempting as you make it sound, I thought we might go to Vail?" Catharine looked over at her, the features of her face slowly growing discernible as Alex's eyes adjusted to the dark. "Away from—" she gestured at the hotel across the street where Alex's team was staying, "—all of this."

Alex hesitated. Vail was at least a hundred miles away, and even though the training was technically over, she was still expected at breakfast at six-thirty in the hotel. Getting dinner out wasn't breaking any rules but it went without saying she was meant to be responsible. "It's quite a drive, isn't it? I mean, I'd love to, but I have a meeting in the—"

"Twenty minutes, give or take. I will have you back at your hotel tonight before ten." She regarded Alex through her unreadable smile, a challenge for her to accept.

"All right. If teleporting is in your power, Mrs. Cleveland." She returned the smile and was about to look away when the light from a passing car illuminated the lower half of Catharine's face. In the flash Alex caught the glimpse of a line across her lower lip—an imperfection of freshly healing skin—and an unnatural asymmetry beneath her makeup. Catharine followed her gaze and only shook her head at Alex's silent inquiry.

"We can talk about it later." Her eyes were back on the hired driver. "Tell me about your week," she said, not giving Alex the chance to analyze her further.

Fifteen minutes later Alex found herself looking down over a rolling blanket of darkness, the Rocky Mountains ten thousand feet beneath her.

"We'll be touching down in eleven minutes, Mrs. Cleveland," the pilot's voice came through the headset, the only sound to break up the whir of the single-rotor engine of the helicopter and the rapidly increasing crescendo of her heart. Beside her Catharine looked out over the obscured wilderness, entirely unfazed by the flight.

"I wish it wasn't dark," she spoke into the microphone of the speaker, "the mountains are majestic in the daylight."

Alex was too shy to respond, realizing anything she said the pilot would hear, too, so instead she only smiled and tried to force herself to relax her grip on the armrest. She'd loved flying in small aircraft as a child, her father had been a fan of everything aviation—planes, gliders, even hot air balloons —but after her parents died in a seaplane in Alaska, Alex had never found herself comfortable on anything other than the largest commercial airplanes. And even then she had to coax herself through every takeoff and landing. So the unexpected drops and lifts of the rotary-winged machine was giving her cardiovascular system a run for its money.

An embarrassing reaction she was unsuccessful at hiding from Catharine, who reassuringly covered her hand with her own as the helicopter descended into Vail.

A young man, sharply dressed in contrast to the aviation jumpsuits and flight boots of the ground crew on the helipad, ran forward to offer his arm to Catharine as she stepped down from the skid in her heels, his fair hair tussled by the spin-down of the rotor. When he looked up through the blinking green light of the aircraft, Alex recognized him from the night of the gala. He was the man who had driven she and Amelia home.

"Welcome back, Mrs. Cleveland," he yelled, his thick Scottish accent cutting through the murmur of the engine, "I haven't seen you in at least an hour! I trust you pleasantly kept sufficient space between you and the ground on your return journey."

It took Alex a moment to realize he was teasing Catharine, a familiar playfulness to his tone, one of which she did not seem to mind.

"I thought you promised fair weather, Malcolm," Catharine rebuked him, fastening an extra button on her coat. "This is not what I had in mind."

"My sincere apologies, ma'am. I promise to do better for you next time." He turned toward Alex, beginning to offer her a hand, but she had already committed to jumping to the landing pad, an action that raised an amused smile from the Scot as she dropped down between them.

"Did you look into the flight plans for tomorrow?" Catharine regained his attention.

"Aye, ma'am. All's satisfactory. Nicole's emailed your itinerary."

He opened the waiting car door and doffed an invisible hat. "Mrs. Cleveland, Miss Grey." Alex was surprised he knew her name.

"Keep them on standby, Malcolm," Catharine motioned for Alex to take a seat ahead of her.

"Ma'am."

Alex watched out the window as he jogged in polished black Oxfords back to speak with the pilot before returning to the driver's seat.

"Are you flying back home tomorrow?" Alex tried to hide her disappointment. She'd hoped, with her limited morning engagement, Catharine might be willing to stay for the day—that they might get to spend some time together.

"No. To New York."

Alex watched the green and white lights of the helipad fade as they pulled onto the main road. "Oh."

"Nathalie's show opened last weekend," Catharine continued by way of explanation and Alex's thoughts returned to the scene at the table where Carlton's tantrum had initiated the downturn of the evening.

"I'm sure it will be wonderful." Internally she chastised herself for feeling jealous—an absolutely ridiculous sentiment toward Catharine flying to New York to see her best friend. It shouldn't have come as a surprise. Why wouldn't she? It was no different than her flying here to take her to dinner. But somehow knowing she was leaving for New York the following day irrationally cheapened the effort of the trip to Colorado. No matter that she knew the evaluation was entirely out of line.

She was just still hurt about the previous weekend and had hoped for more than a rushed dinner to resolve whatever had happened between them.

Catharine must have felt the sway in Alex's thoughts, because—despite Malcolm's presence in the front seat—she reached out and brushed her fingers against Alex's cheek, her touch warm against her chapped skin. "I was hoping you might want to come with me."

"To New York?" The train of Alex's thoughts derailed.

"Yes. I thought we could leave here whenever you were finished tomorrow and return to San Francisco Sunday evening?"

The car pulled beneath the main entrance for the Four Seasons Resort and Malcolm stepped out to open the door. Above the glass entrance to the hotel a thermometer read fourteen degrees, the cars and SUVs around them blanketed in a fresh dusting of snow. There were a handful of families checking in for the weekend, porters following behind them pushing wheeled carts laden with luggage, rushing to get out of the freezing breeze.

"Hey!" Passing into the main lobby a man coming from the opposite direction stopped to address Catharine, his family trailing behind. He wagged a finger at her, narrowing his eyes. "You're Cleveland's wife." It was clear from his tone the recognition was not of a positive nature.

Alex could see Catharine's step falter, deciding between ignoring the encounter or acknowledging the stranger, and in the end her courtesy prevailed. "I am."

"You tell your husband he can shove his 'Save America' campaign up his smug, self-righteous ass. You millionaires think you can throw your money around and tell the people what they're supposed to believe all while pissing on the working class from the comfort of your catbird seat. Your husband is nothing more than a shit-spreading baboon speaking out of both sides of his mouth. Tell him to stay in South Carolina where he belongs!" He took a step toward her, worked up from his soliloquy, but before Alex could even wrap her mind around the confrontation, Malcolm was suddenly there, between the two of them, the flat of his hand firmly against the man's chest.

"You keep walking, *sir*." He'd lost the boyishness of his easy demeanor and there was no question he would more than welcome the opportunity to hand this man his hat.

"Malcolm." Catharine touched his arm and the Scot withdrew a step before she turned to address her critic. "Your concerns are duly noted. Rest assured, your message will be relayed to the senator."

At his wife's embarrassed urging the man continued down the hall and Malcolm waited beside Catharine and Alex until he was through the front doors.

"Ma'am?"

"We're fine, Malcolm."

The sterling blue of his eyes flicked once more to the retreating figure of the man before he looked back, the puckishness of his smile returning. There was no question he did more for Catharine than drive her to-and-fro and arrange her travel schedule. "I'll be a whistle away if you need me."

"You know," said Catharine, unperturbed, when she and Alex were through the lobby. "I've heard Carlton called many things, but a shit-spreading baboon may take the cake."

When the concierge saw Catharine she came around her desk and greeted them warmly. "Mrs. Cleveland, we were able to make those reservations for you for seven-thirty."

Alex had to hide her smile. She doubted Catharine had ever considered they might not be able to accommodate her reservation, no matter how last minute.

"Thank you," Catharine nodded, but didn't slow her progress toward the elevators.

Inside Catharine's suite, the sound of the door clicking shut behind them brought a sigh of relief from the flurry of the last hour. Alex felt like she hadn't had time to catch her breath since her initial run from the training center, beginning with the apprehension that always seemed to lead up to seeing Catharine, to the surprise flight she hadn't mentally prepared for, and the awkward altercation with the man in the lobby.

Catharine's equilibrium, on the other hand, appeared undisturbed as she hung their coats in the entry hall. Her double-breasted cashmere and Alex's US Soccer parka side-by-side—the odd contrast a pinnacle of the disparity to their aberrant relationship.

"So will you come?" Catharine picked up the conversation from the car as she stopped in front of Alex to loosen the red, white and blue soccer scarf still knotted around her neck.

For the first time since they'd arrived, Alex had the opportunity to study Catharine's face in the bright light of the ceiling lighting. She could see the zigzag line of healing skin across her lower lip and the undeniable trace of ebbing swelling that formed from the bridge of her nose to her left brow. Meticulously covered in makeup—but visible under scrutiny all the same. Things that had been hidden in the photo of she and Carlton the previous weekend. Sunglasses. Scarf. Her hair styled to frame her cheeks.

"Are you sure that's a good idea?"

"Alex." The word was a sentence all on its own. Frustration. Rebuke. Discomfort under her stare of observation. Catharine started to turn, to walk away, but Alex caught her arm. She was unwilling to be put off this time. Unwilling to let the elephant in the room that reeked of a senator from South Carolina get swept under the table.

"Are we going to talk about this?" Alex brought her hand to Catharine's cheek, swiping the pad of her thumb across the uncharacteristic heaviness of her makeup and along the puffiness below her eye.

"There is nothing to say."

"This was the night of the gala. This is why you sent me home?"

Catharine drew herself away from Alex's touch, walking across the room, her agitation palpable. She dropped her purse on the sofa before stopping to stand in front of the sliding glass door of the balcony that looked over the mountain scenery, but the LED lighting bounced off the frost covered panes, blocking out the vistas and casting back nothing but her reflection. One she was clearly loathe to view. Her frustration mounting, she turned back to the room.

"What do you want me to tell you, Alex, that you can't already see?"

She was nothing of the composed woman of moments earlier, the woman who hadn't blinked an eye at the verbal assault from a stranger, the woman who was endlessly capable of hiding behind her practiced smile and the veiled expression of her eyes. She looked on the edge of falling apart, on the brink of breaking down.

"Why didn't you tell me?"

"I didn't want you to know!" She dropped onto the leather sofa, her voice quieting with the deflation of her anger, melding into something far worse —far more discomposing. Grief. Anguish. Sorrow. "I didn't want you to see me like that."

Alex went to her, to sit beside her, and brought an arm around her shoulders even when she tried to pull away. Catharine sat stiff, tense, gathering herself as she calmed her breathing, staring at the floor.

"Has this happened before?"

"No—not like this."

"Is there no recourse?"

A laugh, little more than a scoff, escaped her lips, but her body slowly loosened, relaxing against Alex's side. "Not recourse that would bring any desirable outcome. I just want him out of my life. I want a clean severance to our ties. I don't want to spend the next decade fighting him in court."

Alex still didn't understand. What could hold her so hostage to silence that she would allow him to get away with something like this—as violent, as personal as what he'd done? It was sickening to think he would just walk away, unscathed, and continue to smile for the press, to use Catharine as his pawn, to even dare to dream of holding the presidency. There was nothing worth that.

"So it's because of your business?"

Catharine turned to look at her, and as close as they were sitting, directly beneath the light, Alex could again see the discoloration beneath her eye, the swelling above her brow. She couldn't imagine how many times he must have hit her—what he must have done—for the injuries to her face to still be as visible as they were twelve days later.

"No." Catharine ran her fingers along the smooth mahogany of the sofa arm, carved into the shape of a bear claw, considering her response. "I am afraid I am well past fighting for the company now. In the beginning that was the case—I did not want to battle him for Brooks Corp, but now, if I had it all to do over..." Her fingers stopped their idle trail and she turned her attention to Alex in earnest. "Had I ever known—had I ever imagined that you and I would be together, like *this*," she gestured at the narrow distance between them, "I never would have agreed to holding off on filing. To stick with him through the election. I would have cut the cord straight from the start. I would have fought for Brooks Corp—against him and my father—in court, and dealt with whatever outcome came about. But now, as deep as I am into this—if I renege and he were to find out… about us… he would hold his failure over the election against me and go after—" She paused, reconsidering her words, starting again. "He is a vindictive man—with enough power to make him dangerous, and if he blames me for his loss he will stop at nothing to retaliate against me—and he knows the easiest way to do that is by hurting the people that I love. I will not risk that. Not for anything. It is no secret that Brooks Corp has been my life—I have fought for it all these years—but it is insignificant, compared to…" Her voice faded, her fingers resuming their tactile busywork against the wood.

Alex was silent, unable to focus on the inference that the man currently running for President of the United States might literally put a hit on her if she continued sleeping with his wife, and instead was focused on Catharine's latter implication that *she*—Alex—held more value to her than her company—her life's work—her world.

Catharine misread her. "I don't mean to scare you, Alex—I promise you —"

"You haven't scared me." Alex took her hands, swallowing away the unexpected emotion that caught her off guard. Less than two weeks ago she'd thought Catharine had an abrupt change of heart—that she'd sent her home after having second thoughts. But now—the people that I love, she'd said. *That I love.* That was not a change of heart.

She smiled, opting for humor to ease the heaviness of the sentiment. "I may not be a political junkie, but I've watched enough *House of Cards* to know what happens when you get caught sleeping with the politician's wife. I've known that from the start."

Catharine laughed, a mild rebuke of disapproval hidden in the shake of her head at the dismissal of the seriousness of the conversation, but Alex had achieved her goal all the same—alleviating the tension between them.

"So does that mean you'll come to New York with me tomorrow?"

"I think you know that I would fly with you to Mars if you asked me to."

The corner of Catharine's lips turned in a teasing smile. "Bold—coming from someone who left nail indents in my arm during a mild fifteen minute flight over the Rockies."

Alex would have razzed her with the irrefutable evidence that helicopters were thirty-five percent more likely to crash than planes, but the miniature grandfather clock on the mantel chimed, indicating the half hour. It was seven-thirty.

"I've made you late again, Mrs. Cleveland," Alex baited, willing Catharine to lean forward and kiss her—but as soon as she did, Alex caught her shoulders and held her at bay, laughing. "Oh no you don't. I will not let you kiss me here. Because if you do I'll end up asking you to call down and cancel dinner all together—and the next thing I know, I'll be trying to convince you to let me stay the night—to fly out in the morning—when I already know the morning fog is going to ground that chopper and I'll find myself in Vail while my teammates eat breakfast in Commerce City. And *that* is the slippery slope of what comes from kissing Catharine Cleveland. As tempting as it may be." She stood, still smiling, and offered Catharine her hand.

"Is that so?" Catharine arched, entwining their fingers.

"Entirely."

Catharine rose and Alex kept her hand in hers, though she did not lean forward to kiss her. She'd been half-teasing at the start, but the domino effect was real, and she decided it was best if she kept to her strategy. "In fact, I'd better bring my coat downstairs. But I will be finished by ten tomorrow morning and I have to admit—I hope your invitation to New York is a shameless attempt to seduce me."

Catharine raised her hand to her lips, regarding her beneath the length of her blonde lashes. "You're on to me, Miss Grey," she smiled, before turning for the entry closet.

Chapter Fifty-Six

The Tennessee stadium was packed, despite the frigidity of the early March evening dipping below freezing as the tournament kicked off with a mid-week game. Catharine settled in her aisle seat a dozen rows from the grass, grateful for the anonymity of the layers of winter clothing, bundled beneath scarf and hat and upturned collar.

It had been three weeks since she'd seen Alex. Three weeks since they'd navigated an awkward hug farewell on a Sunday morning in a crowded terminal at JFK—Alex on her way home to preseason in California and Catharine off to join Carlton on his whistle-stop tour through the southwest.

The night before, as they'd arrived at Catharine's pied-à-terre at The Carlyle after returning from Nathalie's show, Alex had received a call. She'd glanced at her screen, then paused, looking up at Catharine in front of the lobby lifts.

"It's—" She didn't finished her sentence, just returned her attention to the mobile before taking a shaky breath.

"This is Alex."

There was a moment of silence as she listened, nodding mechanically, staring at the image of the crystal chandelier reflecting off the polished marble floor. Catharine could see the fingers trembling on the hand hanging by her side and had to stop herself from reaching out, to take the hand in hers. The lobby was busy on a Saturday night with traffic coming and going from the bar. She couldn't risk it. Not after it had become clear someone was following her—first at the theatre, and then later on at dinner. Even Nathalie had noticed the man in the scarlet Braves cap staring across the tables, never even bothering to look away when Catharine met his stare head on. There was no question he was Carlton's man, meant to send a message—to let her know he was controlling her from three thousand miles away. And it was working, because even standing there, watching as Alex's

377

face shifted from its ashen hue of trepidation to the sheer shock of disbelief, and then the joy of jubilation, Catharine did not reach forward to take her in her arms. Even knowing there was no way the man in the hat had followed them past the doorman into the private lobby—even knowing Alex was receiving the most important phone call of her life.

"Over-steeped scalding Lipton or three-day-old reheated dark roast, your choice, ma'am?"

Catharine blinked from her reverie and raised her eyes from beneath the knit cap pulled low across her brow to find Malcolm standing in the aisle, two steaming paper cups in hand. He'd accompanied her to the stadium as he'd been accompanying her for weeks, ever since the night at the Fairmont Hotel. She would not allow Carlton anywhere near her without the Scot within calling distance, and now when she traveled, she elected to bring him along. Enough so that her husband had actually had the audacity to question the relationship—for once the lunacy of a rumor she wasn't inclined to dispel. She'd known Malcolm nearly all his life—his father had worked for her father in security, and when Malcolm had graduated university he had come straight to the States to work for her. Cheeky, impudent, full of rakish charm—he was infallible in his loyalty and one of the few people she could trust. Her *Yes-Man*, Carlton had labeled him in animosity years before, as if it were a fault.

She took the cup in his left hand—coffee, black—and moved over a seat to give him the aisle. The two teams had taken to the field to run through their warmups—England in red and the US team in white—weaving through a series of exercises to prepare for the match. Her eyes had followed Alex from the moment she stepped through the tunnel to the pitch, but with Malcolm's distraction, took a moment to regain sight of her again, the players all donned in long sleeve shirts and thick tights to fight off the cold.

It was Alex's first game rostered with the USWNT, and though she'd forewarned Catharine she might not even find minutes in the match, Catharine had flown from New Mexico to Nashville, unwilling to miss it— even if all she ever saw of her were these brief minutes of warmup on the field.

"I imagine certain interests make you a turncoat tonight, ma'am?" Malcolm said after God Save the Queen and the Star Spangled Banner were sung.

"I think living more than half my life in the States gives me the right to choose," Catharine said curtly, ignoring the boldness of his innuendo. She knew he knew. And he knew she knew he knew. But it wasn't up for discussion.

"Well, at least we'll be rooting for the same side, ma'am."

"I hadn't fixed you for a US fan." She picked up the coffee and took a sip, trying to hide her grimace at the staleness of the brew.

"Like any good Scot, I'm the number one fan of whatever team is playing against England. Now," he turned in his seat and shot her a wry smile, "do you need a briefing on the laws of the game?"

"Please remind me, Malcolm," Catharine battled through another sip of the coffee, "when was the last year Scotland qualified for the World Cup?"

His smile grew. "You can take the lass out of England, but you can't take England out of the lass. You've still got the sassenach saltiness in you." He turned toward the center circle where the teams prepared for kickoff. "Just let me know if you need me to point out what direction they should be running."

"If we were at a golf game I might be more interested in your opinion. It's about the only thing Scotland excels at across the globe."

"Suit yourself, ma'am. I'll be here when you need me." His smile lingered as the play got under way.

Catharine tried to force her attention onto the game—to watch the plays as they happened on the pitch—but her gaze kept finding its way back to the sidelines, directly across the field where she could see Alex sitting on the bench.

They'd talked almost every day since New York—early in the morning, before Alex left for training, or late at night, when Catharine returned to her hotel room after sitting through one of Carlton's nauseating rallies in another piffling town.

Alex had been nervous about the call-up—anxious about the tournament —a grueling schedule of three matches in three states over the course of a single week. She'd laughed when Catharine told her she would come watch the opening game in Tennessee.

"I'll probably warm the bench all ninety minutes," she'd warned, insisting she didn't want to waste Catharine's time. "I won't even be able to see you after it's over—we fly straight to New Jersey."

"I don't care. It's worth it to me." And it was, whether Alex ever set foot on the grass or not.

There was a roar from the crowd and Catharine turned her attention toward England's goal in just enough time to see a blonde-haired girl in the US uniform drive the ball past the diving goalkeeper into the back of the net. Following suit of the other fans, she jumped to her feet, cheering as the US took the lead. But as she settled back to her seat and glanced at the scoreboard she saw it still read 0-0 and a collective boo rose up from the crowd as the referee was jeered from the stands.

"You don't know why it was called back, do you?" Malcolm teased her through the folds of his upturned collar, winking as she rolled her eyes. "The lass was offside." He smiled even harder when he could see she had no idea what that meant. "I thought football ran through your English veins?"

"Do you want to wake up and still have a job tomorrow?" Catharine raised a lofty brow before turning back to the game.

At halftime—the US leading 1-0 off a goal from Alex's friend, Sawyer—Catharine left Malcolm behind to stretch her legs and work her way to the restroom. The concourse was overrun with teenage girls in Jerseys sporting the names of various players from the US team, and out-couples of women standing in the beer lines, holding hands, while the parents of young children tried to keep from losing their energetic offspring in the crowd.

As the second half of the match was getting ready to start, Catharine worked her way toward her section, turning down the stairs. A man paused to let her pass, a child in his arms, and offered her a smile. Catharine would have smiled in return, thinking nothing of it, and continued on her way, but the red of his hat caught her attention and an unwelcome tightness gripped her chest as she saw the scripted capital A on his cap, representing the Atlanta Braves.

It wasn't the man she'd seen in New York—he was nothing similar at all —but the hat was the same style and shade of red, and the sight of it caught her off guard. Perplexed by her reaction, the man stepped around her and carried on his way, while Catharine hesitated another moment by the handrail. It was galling to find herself so on edge, strung so tight at the most benign encounters. But ever since Fairmont—ever since Carlton had shown a side to him she hadn't been willing to acknowledge existed—she found herself ill at ease. She knew it was madness—the risk she was running, continuing on with Alex. Colorado. New York. Tennessee. No matter how careful she was, what precautions she took, it was still insanity to think they could come out of this unscathed. But she didn't know any other way. She couldn't fathom ending it. Couldn't imagine giving up on the promise of what they could have—if they could just hang on long enough.

The whistle blew to start the half and Catharine made her way back to her seat. Malcolm was sitting silent, his eyes turned toward the field, a smug expression on his face, offering no acknowledgement as she sat down. It took her a moment to figure out from where his source of entertainment arose.

Alex, she realized—Alex was no longer on the bench. She scanned the players on the field, quickly locating the familiar sight of the dark bun Alex wore high on her head to keep her hair under control and the number eleven on her back—a number, Catharine had learned, she'd worn since high school. At once the discomfiture of her thoughts faded as she sat forward in her seat, her full attention on the game, the knuckles of her hands white from where her fingers dug into her knees. This was Alex's dream in the process of being realized. The culmination of a lifetime of dedication, of endless labor, of the daily grind of maximum effort without any promise of a payoff. Yet there she was—wearing the uniform of her country—earning her place amongst the best in her field.

And Catharine was fortunate enough to see it—to be there—to watch her push through the glass-ceiling of her career.

Despite Malcolm's teasing, he wasn't wrong. She didn't know much of anything about football. Only what she'd picked up from Alex over the course of conversation. She didn't know what made a foul a penalty, or what made a free kick direct or indirect. Or how to even differentiate the two. Nor did she understand what Malcolm meant when he told Catharine Alex had a keen *first touch* or what rallied him to his feet to curse at the ref for being "bloody blind" when one of the English players took Alex down from behind and continued with the ball.

But what she did know, when the final whistle blew, and the US had won the match 1-0 with the late first-half goal, was that Alex worked as hard as every other player on her team and that she had found her place amongst her equals, and been accepted in return. She watched the women hug her, slap her back, ruffle up her hair. The goalkeeper, Halsey, pressed her cheeks between her hands and screamed something in her face before wrapping her in her arms and lifting her off the grass, swinging her around. She deserved to be there and deserved every ounce of joy her journey ahead would bring. The possibility of a World Cup. The Olympics. And everything in between.

And Catharine meant to be there for her. To support her. To cheer her on. Whatever it would take. Whatever must be done.

As the players came to the sidelines to sign autographs and take selfies with their clamoring, waving fans, Catharine stayed in her seat while Malcolm excused himself to give her a moment alone.

She knew Alex was looking for her, her eyes scanning the section she'd told her she'd be in, and when she found her she paused on the sideline, a slow, knowing smile spreading to her lips. Her white jersey was covered in grass stains, her hair disheveled, mud splattered across her cheeks, and Catharine was certain she was as beautiful as she had ever seen her—as perfect as she had ever been. Catharine returned her smile, the two of them finding a moment amongst the chaos—the acceptance of how things were, where their current lives had taken them, but with the promise of something more—a glimpse of a future they might hold.

"Thank you," Alex lipped the words after a second, holding her gaze just a moment more. It wasn't *I love you*. It wasn't the ability for Catharine to step across the space that divided them, to celebrate beside her. It wasn't the walls of their constraints and obligations tumbling down. But it was enough for Catharine. Enough to know this path they were on was the right way— the only way—forward. That whatever it would take, whatever lay ahead, neither of them would face it alone. Even if it meant, for right now, they remained a dozen rows apart.

ABOUT THE AUTHOR

Jen Lyon is an avid lover of sports, travel, theatre, and the ocean. When she isn't writing, Jen can be found sailing, browsing the shelves of her local bookstore, cheering ardently at an NWSL soccer match, or training horses at her Southern California horse ranch, where she lives with her wife, Donna, and their dogs and horses.

Follow Jen on IG @jenlyonauthor where she unapologetically spams her page with photos of her corgis, dachshund, horses and obscenely large Maine Coon cats.

OTHER BOOKS BY JEN LYON

Caught Sleeping: *The Senator's Wife Series Book II*
Whistleblower: *The Senator's Wife Series Book III*
The Unfinished Line

COMING SOON:

Duplicity: The Senator's Wife Series Book IV
Fade In, Fade Out: Sequel to *The Unfinished Line*
Curse of Queens — medieval sapphic trilogy
Let Them Burn — sapphic pirate adventure

ACKNOWLEDGMENTS

This book would never have been made possible without the unfaltering, unequivocal, indefatigable love and support of my brilliant wife, Donna. My most devoted cheerleader. My tea steeper. My dedicated First Draft Reader. My muse. My rock. My best friend. Thank you for everything you do for us. Thank you for always believing in me. I love you.

To my mom, Melodie, who has read every word I've written since I was four years old. My toughest critic. My champion. The one who read me bedtime stories every night, filled my head full of marvelous tales, and taught me the power of the written word. Thank you for always encouraging me to keep on writing. I love you to the moon and back.

To my furry best friends, Piper and Josey Wales—who snuggled with me through a dozen rewrites, snoozed beneath my desk while I stared day in, day out at my computer screen, and kept me company in my office without a single woof of protest.

And lastly, to the incredibly talented, brave, resilient women of the USWNT and NWSL. Thank you for everything you have done, not just for women's sports, but for women as a whole. For using your voices, your platforms, and the eloquence of the Beautiful Game to continue to lift women up and push through those glass ceilings. LFG ladies! LFG!

www.ingramcontent.com/pod-product-compliance
Ingram Content Group UK Ltd.
Pitfield, Milton Keynes, MK11 3LW, UK
UKHW041342270325
5191UKWH00036B/381